WITCHES' RINGS

Some other books from Norvik Press

Sigbjørn Obstfelder: *A Priest's Diary* (translated by James McFarlane)
Hjalmar Söderberg: *Short stories* (translated by Carl Lofmark)
Annegret Heitmann (ed.): *No Man's Land. An Anthology of Modern Danish Women's Literature*
P C Jersild: *A Living Soul* (translated by Rika Lesser)
Sara Lidman: *Naboth's Stone* (translated by Joan Tate)
Selma Lagerlöf: *The Löwensköld Ring* (translated by Linda Schenck)
Villy Sørensen: *Harmless Tales* (translated by Paula Hostrup-Jessen)
Camilla Collett: *The District Governor's Daughters* (translated by Kirsten Seaver)
Jens Bjørneboe: *The Sharks* (translated by Esther Greenleaf Mürer)
Jørgen-Frantz Jacobsen: *Barbara* (translated by George Johnston)
Janet Garton & Henning Sehmsdorf (eds. and trans.): *New Norwegian Plays* (by Peder W.Cappelen, Edvard Hoem, Cecilie Løveid and Bjørg Vik)
Gunilla Anderman (ed.): *New Swedish Plays* (by Ingmar Bergman, Stig Larsson, Lars Norén and Agneta Pleijel)
Kjell Askildsen: *A Sudden Liberating Thought* (translated by Sverre Lyngstad)
Svend Åge Madsen: *Days with Diam* (translated by W. Glyn Jones)
Christopher Moseley (ed.): *From Baltic Shores*
Janet Garton (ed.): *Contemporary Norwegian Women's Writing*
Fredrika Bremer: *The Colonel's Family* (translated by Sarah Death)
Hans Christian Andersen (ed.): *New Danish Plays* (by Sven Holm, Kaj Nissen, Astrid Saalbach and Jess Ørnsbo)
Suzanne Brøgger: *A Fighting Pig's Too Tough to Eat* (translated by Marina Allemano)
The logo of Norvik Press is based on a drawing by Egil Bakka (University of Bergen) of a Viking ornament in gold, paper thin, with impressed figures (size 16x21mm). It was found in 1897 at Hauge, Klepp, Rogaland, and is now in the collection of the Historisk museum, University of Bergen (inv.no. 5392). It depicts a love scene, possibly (according to Magnus Olsen) between the fertility god Freyr and the maiden Gerðr; the large penannular brooch of the man's cloak dates the work as being most likely 10th century.

Kerstin Ekman

WITCHES' RINGS

Translated by Linda Schenck

Norvik Press
Norwich
1997

Original title : *Häxringarna* (1974) © Kerstin Ekman
English language translation copyright © Linda Schenck 1997.

British Library Cataloguing in Publication Data
  Ekman, Kerstin
    Witches' Rings
    1. Ekman, Kerstin — Translations into English
    I. Title.
    839.7'374 [F]
    ISBN 1-870041-36-4

First published in 1997 by Norvik Press, University of East Anglia, Norwich, NR4 7TJ, England
Managing Editors: James McFarlane, Janet Garton and Michael Robinson

Norvik Press was established with financial support from the University of East Anglia, the Danish Ministry for Cultural Affairs, The Norwegian Cultural Department, and the Swedish Institute. Publication of this volume has been aided by a grant from the Swedish Institute.

Printed in Great Britain by Page Bros. (Norwich) Ltd., Norwich, UK.

Translator's Introduction

'Stories,' the narrator of *Witches' Rings* tells us, 'are wiser than we, and more mindful, and slowly they change us.' Kerstin Ekman's stories are deeply committed to this very kind of gradual but inevitable change. In *Witches' Rings* there are a number of occasions on which history almost, but not quite, repeats itself. Edla Lans, for example, who appears to be the novel's protagonist in the early pages, is literally and breathtakingly replaced by her own daughter, both in the story-line itself and in the life of Edla's mother, Sara Sabina. Just as the narrator underplays this change to the reader, it also takes several years and many stories for Edla's daughter to make the full connection: 'Carefully, the story added a piece of knowledge Tora needed: Edla had not been her sister as she had always thought ....' In the final chapter, when Sara Sabina lies dying, she says: 'I guess you'll have to let the others know. Afterwards.' The narrative continues: 'Tora was silent, trying to figure this out, and then she realized that her grandmother was speaking about her other children, who were much older than Tora and whom she seldom saw. They were really her aunts and uncles.' *Witches' Rings* is permeated by the inevitability of both change and continuity in society and in family history.

The novel opens with Sara Sabina Lans trudging from her country croft, Appleton, to the village to trade the wild cumin she has picked and cleaned for items like sugar and Brazil wood dye that she cannot cultivate or scavenge herself. In the penultimate chapter, Tora bakes quantities of the rye and potato loaves Sara Sabina had taught her the recipe for nearly a generation earlier, hoping to sell them at the market square and earn enough money to clothe and feed her sons. Everything has changed, and nothing. A woman's work is never done. There are 'magic' circles that mark both the enchantment of our individual and collective lives and their monotony. 'Magic Circles' was long the working title for this translation, which has ultimately become *Witches' Rings*, not least to mark the fact that females are the ones leading the way round the particular natural phenomenon to which the rings in the title refer, as the reader will discover.

In Kerstin Ekman's novels, form and content are inextricably intertwined. This is what makes these books both so rewarding and so challenging to read, and even more so to translate. *Witches' Rings* reflects life in its unpredictability, in the way time is sometimes compressed and at other times drawn out, in suddenly becoming incomprehensible, or enigmatic and dream-like. The first few chapters of *Witches' Rings* may require some benefit of the doubt, some extra attention and patience. There are questions not immediately answered. All is not instantly given. I have consciously resisted all temptation to make the novel less demanding for

6

the English language reader than for the reader of the original.

Witches' Rings begins in the mid-1870s and ends in 1904. It is set in a community that was a nondescript village before the coming of the railroad (nearly five years before the novel opens) and which is transformed into a bustling town over the thirty years that pass. One of the ways the changing society is portrayed is in the names people give to the places in their local surroundings and to one another. During the course of the novel, the village becomes urbanized, places that were countryside markers are incorporated into the town plan, and a new class of people arrives with the coming of commercialism, industrialization and mass transportation. Thus many of the characters in the novel have meaning-conferring nicknames and many of the places in and outside town have popular names reflecting origin and purpose. For instance, stationmaster Fredriksson buries his dear departed dog Mulle, after his death, at a spot just outside town, around which he later creates a little park, officially denoted Fredriksberg in his honour. The towns-people, however, call it by only one name, to his dismay: 'Mulle's End'. Although some of these names may ring slightly absurd to the English ear, it seemed to me important to convey their meanings, which often have ironic both social and physical connotations, wherever possible. Prepare to meet Tubby Kalle the tavern owner and Old Mothstead the farmer, and to visit the Pigpen and Louse Point. As the narrator points out: 'These are the place-names that go with derisive sniggering and garrulous gossip. These are the names you have to use day after day and year after year ....' Presumably these people and places, alien at first, will become as familiar to the reader as they were to their users.

7

Witches' Rings is the first volume in a tetralogy, published between 1974 and 1983, and narrating the lives of Sara Sabina and her successors until the present day. The tetralogy marked Kerstin Ekman's literary breakthrough and her development towards becoming one of the greatest voices in Swedish literature today. It is said that one of the indications of a classic is that it is no less spellbinding to read long after it was written than when it was new. Although twenty years is both long and short in the great scheme of things, the statement certainly characterizes *Witches' Rings*, which now appears in English for the first time and is still, unusually, available in print in paperback in Swedish, thus having earned the title of classic in its author's lifetime. English language readers may know Kerstin Ekman from her more recent novel *Blackwater*. Here is an opportunity to follow her stories back in time. Stories 'so much wiser ... than we' which, undoubtedly, change us.

LINDA SCHENCK

Witches' Rings

This was Sara Sabina Lans:

grey as a rat, poor as a louse, pouchy and lean as a vixen in summer. No one called her by her given name. He was hardly ever at home. He had his orders, his regiment at Malmahed and his drills with the officers on Fyrö island, strutting like a pheasant cock in his uniform. She had her children and the croft with its potato patch, a cottage nearly smothered in lilacs as the years passed, but where happiness had no place, at least not before 1884 when the train chopped the legs off soldier Lans.

She smoked hams for the farmers. That was her cleanest job. Otherwise, there was nothing so coarse, so filthy or so foul that she wouldn't do it. She scrubbed down cowsheds in spring. She took in laundry and helped with butchering. She laid out the dead. She toiled all her life for leftovers and favours. She was hardy as grass, prickly as nettles. Her gravestone is in Vallmsta churchyard. It reads:

Soldier no. 27 for Skebo district
Johannes Lans
b. 29 July 1833   d. 12 June 1902
and his wife
R.I.P.

11

It was a day in the early 70s when Sara Sabina Lans, the soldier's missus, made her way to Isaksson's general store and inn to sell cumin. It was a Sörmland September afternoon when she left. The sun was already so low that it reflected off the bits of broken mirror they kept in the cowshed window to ward off the evil eye. The lovage by the cottage door was past its prime and no longer smelt so foul. The trees had turned, except for the big birch under which the croft huddled. It seldom lost a leaf before All Hallow's Eve, because a white adder lived under its roots.

The soldier's wife was crossing the big marsh between Appleton and Goatwood, leaping from stone to stone with a pillow-slip of newly threshed cumin in her arms. Behind her was Frans, who died of a sore throat the winter after that uncommonly late, mild autumn. Edla came skipping along behind.

It was a clear sunny day, but there was a cold breeze under the alders in the marsh, and from the bright black holes rose a sour smell of stagnant water. It gave Frans goose-flesh to look about, but looking straight ahead was even worse, since his mother had hiked up her skirts and tucked them into her apron band. When she jumped, he could see all the way up her skinny, gnarled legs to her thighs. They were pale as death and covered all over with a twisted net of blue veins. Edla brought up the rear, her short legs making it hard work getting from stone to stone.

This was the short way to the train station, next to which Isaksson from Backe had moved with his wife, his shophand, and two housemaids just after the inauguration of the railway. He planned to move his entire business from the old courthouse square, and already had twelve coach horses in the stable. The iron rails had been in place for several years, all the way from Stockholm to Gothenburg, without getting stolen. The fifth anniversary of the inauguration was not far off. The inauguration had been an occasion of banners and blaring horns, of smiling, stiff-legged royalty stepping down from railway coaches. And it had not, after all, proven impossible to accustom slothful Swedish workers to the attentiveness required of those who serve the railway, or at least not completely impossible. At this very train station, which had been graced by eleven minutes of the royal presence for the inauguration, and which was 123 kilometres from Stockholm and 27 meters above sea level, stood Oskar Edvin Johansson, the pumpman, sometimes as much as a quarter of an hour before the train was due to arrive, with his cap pulled on and every button on his uniform jacket done up, with the water cistern full and the oil cans reflecting in the pale early autumn sun.

The station was built on the soft ground between two reedy lakes. The landscape was flat and the trees that did pull up out of the waterlogged soil strained for survival. Elks thrived here. There were three farms in the surrounding area: Mothstead, on ninety-year lease from the estate, Goatwood and Tramphut.

Three wagons stood outside Isaksson's inn and general store, a gig and two open carts, one of which was loaded with sacks of rye. Two farmers and one landowner's son were inside, conversing languidly. This young fellow had not left his whip in the sheath by the coachman's seat, but had brought it in with him. He was flicking the thong idly over the treacle barrel, where a couple of flies were buzzing. He was the first to notice Sara Sabina Lans come out of the brushwood at the edge of the marsh. He said, 'Well if it isn't that stingy disgusting old bat of a soldier's woman!' He would have spit had he not been too far from the spittoon to chance it. He stood there, legs astride but uncomfortable in this company, toying with his whip.

'I wouldn't say stingy,' said the farmer from Mothstead, who was nearest the window, staring at the woman as she emerged from the marsh and approached the store, a striped pillow-slip held tightly to her chest and two youngsters at her heels. 'She doesn't exactly have much to be stingy with.'

'No, but once she gets hold of something,' said Abraham Krona, 'she's like a vixen. Nothing can make her let go.'

They all laughed.

Outside, Edla was following her mother and Frans, sweat dripping down her back. Now their mother moved out of sight of the store. She wasn't withdrawing discreetly to change into clean shoes like ordinary folks did, since she only owned the one pair. She wiped her children's noses and changed her shawl.

At that very moment, the train approached, and Edla thought the end was nigh, that death was approaching, rolling down a mountain top. She had never been along to the station before. Now she screamed as loud as the whistle, and her mother had to hold onto her with one hand and slap her with the other. Frans, too, blanched slightly, but as soon as the first piercing din had passed, he started laughing. There were a lot more sounds before it all settled into short, regular puffing. The thought crossed Edla's mind that it sounded like a giant sitting straining in his privy, and she caught her breath, hiccoughing.

The train was in. A gate creaked open and a young man in a dark blue uniform with a gold-braided cap bearing the insignia of the winged wheel lifted two rucksacks down before he disembarked. He looked around at the flat, swampy landscape. The shiny rails vanished into a dull, low forest of pine and birch. He saluted hesitantly, and his greeting was answered from the far end of the platform by the stationmaster, who advanced towards him, realizing that it must be the new booking clerk who had just arrived.

Gustav Adolf Cederfalk, railway booking clerk by profession and Baron by birth, regarded the station. It was yellow, and one gable was covered in honeysuckle that had already gone brown. He glimpsed a head of shiny black hair, parted in the middle, in a window. This was the stationmaster's wife. In a few moments, when her husband had let the train go, she would let out the cat. The sky was September blue when Cederfalk looked up. Twenty-seven meters above sea level. 'Not much,' he thought, giving the hand of his new supervisor a firm shake.

While waiting for the stationmaster to raise the signal flag for the locomotive, he walked once around the station. That dark head of hair moved with him, from window to window, all the way round. Behind the building, the odour of coke and lubricant vanished. On that side was the pot-holed yard and farmer Goatwood's cows, who came all the way up to the gate to inspect him. There was the innkeeper's house with the three traps outside, and the horses with the reins around their front legs standing by the boom. The horse from Old Mothstead had a feed-bag. For a few minutes the cool September air was so silent that Cederfalk

15

could hear the oats crunching between the horse's teeth. Three big men came out on the stoop of the inn, to spit out their snuff and have a look. It was a tight squeeze, and the innkeeper hovered behind them in the doorway. In a lilac hedge near the inn, a drab old woman stood wiping a kid's nose with her sleeve. There was a second one holding her skirt-tails, staring at the departing train, snivelling loudly. Cederfalk turned around and walked back to the station. The men on the stoop were done spitting, and Sara Sabina Lans followed them inside. She opened her pillow-slip, displayed the cumin, and asked for salt, soda, coffee, and Brazil wood in exchange.

They say that contentment is a true treasure where poverty and want are constant guests, but soldier Lans' wife did not possess that virtue. On the contrary, she was infamous for her importunity and her greed. Isaksson gestured dismissively, explaining that she was being unreasonable. Still, the old woman persisted, and the three men began looking for seats amongst the barrels and kegs, sensing that they were in for a performance. Sara Sabina tended to spout off when someone annoyed her, and knew whole litanies of crude words.

This time, however, she kept her temper, asking him to weigh the cumin so they could agree on how much coffee, salt and soda he would give her in exchange. He owed her the Brazil wood, too, because he had cheated her last time. When she had opened it up to dye the warp for a rag rug, she thought it felt light, and had taken it to the steelyard to get it weighed. Quite right, too. It had been a pound and a half short.

Isaksson explained what happened to Brazil wood. When it had been removed from the keg, it dried out and weighed less. The only way to know how much it had weighed when sold was to soak it, mix it with fresh Brazil wood, squeeze out the water and weigh it again. He called in his shop boy to testify. The old woman appeared to concede, but demanded a pound of the cheapest pillow stuffing in return, and when the boy returned, looking tarred and feathered after having weighed out cotton grass in the storeroom, he was sure she'd wanted revenge.

Isaksson ran the cumin through his fingers, inspecting it with exaggerated care. He implied that there were both bugs and pebbles in it, but the old woman still didn't get riled.

'She won't give in,' said Old Mothstead with a smile, as Isaksson started weighing out the goods she requested.

'Won't give an inch,' added the landowner's son from Tramphut. Abraham Krona was standing further down by the door examining a tanned oxhide Isaksson had lifted down from the ceiling with his hook. He wanted it for shoe leather. Krona was a kind, dull fellow, Old Mothstead his opposite.

'Is it true you won't let go of something once you've got hold of it?' he asked.

The woman kept still and looked the other way.

'Krona said so a minute ago. That you were like a vixen: "Once she's got her teeth into something, she'll never let go," he claimed.'

Now soldier Lans' missus glared at Krona, who looked embarrassed.

'Let's see, then,' Old Mothstead egged them on. 'Have a tug of war with her over the shoe leather, Krona. You can let her keep it if she can make you let go.'

'I guess I can,' said Krona, proffering the piece of leather. The old woman was so fast to get her claws into it that all four men burst out laughing.

'Oh, no you don't,' said Old Mothstead. 'We said bite.'

She looked around the store at Isaksson and the grinning young man from Tramphut, at her children huddling by the treacle barrel and at Isaksson's wife standing in the doorway to the bar-room, watching. Then she turned towards Krona, who held the leather out in front of his huge belly, and she crouched down and sank her teeth into the hide.

He was the stronger, of course, and started right off by pulling her around the floor, to the vast amusement of the spectators. Even Isaksson's stern wife, who rarely cracked a smile, chortled with glee, and Old Mothstead slapped his thighs and flapped his apron and danced around the couple, who moved in ever larger rings amongst the kegs. The old woman let out noises. She sounded as if she was growling from fury and the exertion. Krona laughed and jerked the hide. More than once he pulled hard as they danced around, and the old woman rolled with the punches, but she didn't let go. She passed wind from running bent double, and with every fart the young fellow from Tramphut shouted: 'Hip hip hurrah!' Edla and Frans cowered by the treacle barrel, weeping for shame.

Now Krona truly began to see what was so funny about her not letting go. His huge hands held the oxhide firmly and he pulled her around in such wide turns that her heels clicked against the floor with each rapid step; all he had to do was stand there and tug.

'She'll never give in!' Old Mothstead shouted, and her teeth really did seem to be locked into the leather. Although she wouldn't be able to tear it away from him, the question

18

was whether Krona could make her let go. His neck was getting sweaty, and he was groaning from the strain of yanking her, time and again. Now the battle entered a new phase and the spectators fell silent as Krona attempted to rip the leather out of the woman's jaws. Each time he jerked, she just followed along, and not even when she slipped on her worn-down heels and slid right across the floor did she let go. Krona's downfall was that Old Mothstead had been so eager to follow the battle he happened to miss the spittoon. Krona lost his balance in the glob of wet snuff and tumbled backwards. He hit his head on a freshly-opened barrel of cleaning soap, dropped the hide, and blacked out.

'Wouldn't you know this would end in someone's coming to grief!' cried the innkeeper's wife, making a dash for the water scoop. Soldier Lans's old lady embraced the piece of soling leather and backed towards the door. But when she tried to open her mouth, her jaws had locked. Eventually she was able to extract the leather, but her jaws remained clamped. She vanished out the door without a trace, clutching the leather. Frans and Edla took the bags of salt, soda, and coffee and ran after her.

The 6:06 had departed, and the new booking clerk had taken his evening meal at stationmaster Hedberg's. The Hedbergs' daughter Malvina and the postmaster's Charlotte were walking, arms around each other's waists, westward along the tracks, towards the setting sun and the pine forest. However, they didn't go as far as usual, because Baron Cederfalk was expected to drop in at the postmaster's, too. Charlotte's mother had told her to be home early so she would have time to settle down and her cheeks wouldn't be too flushed.

That evening, Sara Sabina Lans also followed the tracks since it would have been difficult to carry the big piece of soling leather through the marsh. She walked with Frans and Edla, who carried her bags, and they saw the golden-eyes rise and fly off in formation as the sun hung swollen, hazy and red over Lake Vallmaren. Then the rails began to rumble with the 7:43 from Gothenburg, and they had to scurry down off the embankment.

There is a picture of Edla.

But how to describe a face? Is it thin or broad? Are the eyes deep set, and is the mouth unusually small or just tightly shut? The more familiar it seems, the more difficult it becomes to describe. You recall it as if in a dream and afterwards you couldn't possibly say what it looked like. Still, the expression on a face is the true message it reveals, and it remains.

Edla's face, the face of the thirteen-year-old with brushed-back tightly clasped hair, wears a solemn expression.

The picture was taken one market day in the new railway hamlet, in May 1876. It's hard to say what expectations Edla had when she got there that morning and changed her shoes behind the inn before crossing the tracks to the marketplace.

'There'll be an organ-grinder and things,' Lans had said.

'Sometimes dancin' bears and once I did see a fellow playin' the key fiddle!'

This market, however, was not one of the big ones, and couldn't compare with fair day at the grounds in Backe. Edla didn't want to go down to the livestock section, for fear of muddying her mother's shoes. She passed by the stands of the chair-caner and the copper-hammerer without a glance. When an old woman with filthy nails shouted after Lans that she had butter and honey for sale, Edla was the one to answer with dignity:

'We churns our own.'

The Jewish clock peddler had spread out his silk shawls, and had dowry chests with painted flowers too, but Edla wasn't very interested. She did spend a long time gazing at the few toys the tinsmith was selling from his stand.

A photographer from Stockholm had posted a sign offering people's photographic portraits for only half what it cost in the capital. Lans took his daughter Edla there to have her picture taken. Her mother, who didn't have the clothes to wear to market, had stayed at home and so she couldn't stop him.

The photograph of Edla has faded and yellowed now and her face is blurred. What shows most clearly is the plaid pattern of her dress. But her solemn expression remains.

H ow can you imagine I'd want your daughter in my kitchen, you filthbag!' was the answer Sara Sabina Lans got from Isaksson's wife when she came to ask her to take Edla into service. So soldier Lans wrote a letter to Isaksson.

To shopkeeper and innkeeper Isaksson I humbly request that my daughter Edla be accepted in service as you have announced you are looking for a housemaid at your Inn and I therefore in all humility enclose her certificate of birth.

Appleton 10 June 1876
Johannes Lans
District soldier
No. 27 Skebo

The innkeeper took Edla into service, not officially as a proper housemaid, of course, since she was only thirteen and a half years old and hadn't yet been confirmed. He hired her as a nursemaid for nothing but room and board.

Spotted brown as an old rural survey map, soldier Lans' letter made the rounds in the bar-room. The Innkeeper displayed Edla with: 'Here's the little housemaid who has been taken into service on the basis of a written application just like a stationmaster or vicar.' Edla was ushered out again with tears of shame and rage in her eyes, and through the kitchen door she heard the farmers guffawing as Isaksson read the letter aloud.

They'd wanted her to start right after midsummer, and she had arrived on an evening so dark and overcast that there was hardly enough daylight to see by at the kitchen table where the innkeeper and his drivers were at supper.

When she walked in, the innkeeper's wife was rending pork rinds. Hanna and Ida, the two fully-grown housemaids, were standing up eating. Hanna had hoisted her big bottom onto the woodbox to give her feet a rest. When Edla arrived, she shifted her plate to her left hand and extended her right. Ida, the tall girl, did the same, and her hand was big and rough like a man's. Edla was too timid to greet the men at the table. Out of the corner of her eye, she glimpsed a young lad somewhere near the pantry door, but she didn't let on that she'd seen him. An old woman was sitting by the hearth, but just as Edla extended her hand, the innkeeper's wife instructed her to get to work cutting the crusts off some bread. Edla realized that Scrub-Ärna, whom she knew by sight, was the kind of person you weren't supposed to notice. She was so old she couldn't get down on her knees any more, but just the year before she had still scrubbed the floors of the clubroom and bar-room after market days. She still came round the inn every morning, looking for something to do. She cut kindling without being asked, made sure the cat stayed outside on baking days, and stirred the roasting cumin so it didn't catch fire. She thought she earned herself a meal this way, and the right to sit near the hearth, at least in winter.

'Why, you're not dry behind the ears yet. How will you ever manage?' she moaned in Edla's direction, while also glaring sharply at Isaksson's wife who interrupted with:

'Isaksson's done now, so you can bring Aron in from the hallway.'

This confused Edla until Hanna nodded discreetly, her mouth full of food, indicating that there were two doors to the kitchen, and she went out into the draughty hallway, where she found the little boy whose nursemaid she was to be. He was squatting on a chamber pot, straining. Not a word did he say, and she wasn't sure he was old enough to know how to talk. She couldn't lift him; he was a fat little boy. He stared rudely at her out from under his very blond eyebrows, but when he felt the heat from the kitchen hearth reach him, he stood up and went in on his own. He had a red ring from the chamber pot on the pale goose-bumped skin of his bottom.

'Come on and get those crusts off, and drop the bread in here,' said the innkeeper's wife, shaking the pan with the fat from the pork rinds in it. This job was completely alien to Edla, and made her realize that the food was likely to be the best part of being in service. She was supposed to cut away the mouldy edges of the bread and throw them in with the pig swill. After that, the cubes of bread were fried in lard. When they'd soaked it all up, the innkeeper's wife poured in some milk and let it all putter. Then she served it straight out of the frying pan, without fishing out the pork rinds first.

After the meal Hanna did the washing up and the child, who had still not said a peep, sat on his potty as if he were glued to it. Edla dried the tin utensils on a dishrag and the innkeeper's china on a worn linen tea towel. She was in constant fear of doing something wrong, of taking the tea towel to a grimy frying pan or of cutting the linen with a sharp knife. Scrub-Ärna kept warning her about everything that might go awry, while the innkeeper's wife said nothing at all to her. She just kept rushing back and forth with the orders of fried eggs and sausage the innkeeper kept calling out.

The inn was a huge place, unlike a soldier's croft in every way. Even here, in the dark kitchen, she could see and hear its vastness all around her. When the four drivers and the other young man walked out the door Edla could smell the smoke from the coal-fired locomotives, and their piercing shouts flew straight into the warmth of the kitchen and frightened her. Gradually, the depot quieted down, and the innkeeper stopped calling orders. Finally, Hanna hung the washing-up tub on its hook and said, yawning loudly:

'Time to turn in, at last. And thank goodness.'

Oddly, Ida had left with the drivers, but Scrub-Ärna, who was still sitting by the hearth, whispered to Edla, standing so close that she could smell her sour breath, that that girl was filthy and had to be kept off kitchen work. Still, she was strong as an ox, worked harder than anyone. She was more like a farmhand, which explained why she had the privilege of turning in when the men did. Though the real reason was that she was so dirty.

'And the other one,' Scrub-Ärna whispered as Hanna's blue-striped skirt vanished up the attic steps. 'She thieves. Sure as my name's Ärna.'

Now the innkeeper's wife sent the old woman packing, and told Edla to sit and wait on a kitchen chair while she put her little boy to bed in the room off the kitchen, making it perfectly clear that that room was off limits to Edla. Later, she showed Edla the way to the clubroom, which was upstairs from the bar-room.

'Hanna and Ida sleep in the attic,' she explained, 'and the baker-woman needs the kitchen to herself. There's no room between Ida and Hanna, so you'll have to sleep here.'

It was a big room. Edla had heard of it. The wealthier farmers held their meetings up here, the curtains held the traces of their odours. The innkeeper's wife had brought a little oil lamp for Edla, and lit the wick so Edla could get ready for bed when she left. But it didn't illuminate the whole room. She had caught sight of a portrait staring at her.

She was to sleep on the table, which was almost as big as the whole main room at the croft. She'd been given two horsehair blankets to sleep on, and a carriage fur to wrap herself in, but her feet stuck out. She didn't dare blow out the light. The wick, with a circle of paper holding it up, swam in the oil. For a long time, she lay staring at the hesitant little flame. She remembered Scrub-Ärna's voice and the smell of her breath when she whispered of the innkeeper's wife:

'She's nasty, more dangerous than lye.'

Then the wick seemed to be shrinking and the level of the oil to have fallen, and she was afraid to let it burn any longer. She blew straight down into the glass to extinguish it, and crept, pulling the fur with her, all the way up to the other end of the table so as not to tip the lamp over if she tossed and turned. She lay there, listening to the sounds of the trains, and the guests slamming the doors of their rooms.

There were peals of thunder, after which the sky turned white. Not until almost four, when the rain began to pour down, did Edla fall into a fitful sleep. She didn't hear Hanna and Ida go down the attic stairs in the bitter light of dawn. No one woke her, she was simply forgotten that first morning. But it never happened again. That day, she woke up to the smell of bread baking and the sound of cursing voices.

She wriggled down from the table and looked out of the window. The yard between the inn and the station was flooded after the rain, and the mud sprayed off the wheels of the coach driving across the yard. It got stuck in the mud, and the coachman shouted and swore. It was hitched to a team of three, but was still unable to move forward without the assistance of two of the innkeeper's drivers, one on either side of the harness. A train pulled in, but the people down there didn't so much as give it a glance. The odour of coke mixed with the aroma of fresh bread. The hamlet had almost become a town, with fresh bread for sale every morning. Edla saw everyone's maids crossing the yard with their baskets : the postmaster's, the stationmaster's, the yard master's and the restaurant owner's. They stepped carefully through the mud to the door of the general store, and the drivers shouted at them. Edla began to whimper when she realized how late it was and how much she had overslept.

Down in the kitchen, the baker-woman was folding up her apron and preparing to go home. Edla saw her yawn unabashedly right in the face of the innkeeper's wife.

The baker-woman arrived every night after the others had gone to bed. The last thing the innkeeper's wife did was to measure out the flour. She mixed her first batch of dough at midnight. When the others came in from the milking to set the breakfast table, she was done, put one loaf in her basket and laid her folded, striped apron on top.

Within the week Edla had learned that everything that appeared so astonishingly arbitrary that first day — the yellow coach, the big chunks of pork, and the baker's yawn

— repeated themselves and were regular occurrences. It didn't take her long to work out the adults' routines. But she couldn't figure out the young lad she had glimpsed in the kitchen that first evening.

She often made up reasons for going around behind the storeroom or the stables, because they had no privy at home and at first she couldn't figure out where she was supposed to do her business. Wherever she went, that fellow's face seemed to turn up. She would crouch among the nettles, quick as a flash. In between, her stomach often ached from holding back. She thought he was mocking her with his grin. She knew the elbows of her dress were worn out, and the uppers of her boots were cracked. The second evening they told her to bring home the cows that were grazing behind the postmaster's. The lad turned up with a switch in his hand and helped her. He told her his name was Valfrid and he was Iskasson's errand boy. She didn't know what that was.

'You move up to shop boy if you're good and then maybe manager.'

Edla was silent.

'If you don't take to the railroad, of course.'

His face was square and his mouth large. His teeth tended to stick out even when he wasn't laughing. His cheeks were covered with big brown freckles. Now she realized he hadn't been mocking her by grinning, he was trying to get her to smile back. The real shop boy was hard on Valfrid, bawling him out so the walls of the storeroom echoed. Well, Edla knew we all have our crosses to bear, and that she, too, could expect no better than to be ordered about. She was youngest, after all, or so she thought. It was a long time before she found out that Valfrid had just turned twelve.

29

He ate with the second shift, the drivers who filled the kitchen with their deep voices and the smell of horses. The innkeeper usually had his dinner with the shop manager and the shophand. Their meals were a source of distress to Edla who was supposed to keep Aron quiet and serve the meal. Isaksson was the only one who spoke. He gave instructions about cracking open barrels, about which items sold by weight were to be put in bags, about which of the better customers were expecting home delivery that afternoon. The only person who put in a word was his wife, who tossed off comments over her shoulder.

That woman didn't seem to know before from after. She was entrenched in the present. She worked at a raging speed and never dwelt on anything. Edla saw chubby Aron playing with the wax orange blossoms that had been her bridal garland. Soon he had kneaded them to putty, and they ran between his fingers like fatty sausages. His mother caught him at it, slammed the dresser drawer and yelled at him. All this without interrupting for more than a moment her dull, dogged, days of endless cooking.

With one girl so filthy you couldn't have her in the kitchen and the other a thief you couldn't let out of your sight, it was only natural for the innkeeper's wife to use her nursemaid for some indoor chores. At first these were sporadic occurrences.

'You might as well wash those things up while I go to the chicken coop. It won't take a minute.'

Aron would play behind Edla's back. He almost never spoke. She stood at the washing-up tub, her head buzzing with all the noises around her: the horse's hooves and the iron wagon wheels, the train whistles, the voices and laughter from the bar-room. She remembered that at home in Appleton at midday you could distinctly hear the tapping of the woodpecker out in the forest when you did the washing up in the kitchen.

After a week the unpredictable had become the habitual and she knew exactly what she had to do. She was eager to please and wanted to prove that she was big enough to do even the heavier chores.

'You couldn't manage to bring in some water ...?'

She wanted to show that she could. When she felt an ache in the small of her back, she knew it was just the serpent of idleness turning her into a lazybones.

One Friday evening the farmers had a meeting in the upstairs room, and the next morning the innkeeper's wife was desperate to have the floor scrubbed. There wasn't a soul free to do it.

'Maybe you could start,' she said to Edla. 'I'll send Hanna up when she's finished down here.'

She gave Edla a bucket of scrubbing sand, and another of cooled washing lye.

'It bleaches really well,' the innkeeper's wife said.

She had to start by sweeping up all the loose dirt and manure the farmers had brought in on their boots after the cattle sale. The fine dust from the station yard was dry and rose around Edla's broom like smoke.

She felt important and grown up, surveying the soiled floor. She had lined up her buckets and brooms inside the door. There was a tiled stove at either end of the room, and the vents stared at each other like solemn, white cyclopses. Soon Edla was right between them on her knees scrubbing at the wooden floor with a tightly-bound root brush. She couldn't run it with her foot like a real washerwoman. The first time one of the sharp root ends pushed up under her thumbnail, her eyes smarted and she felt unequal to her task, wishing she was a fully-grown, solid working person.

Plank by plank she scrubbed the floor with the brush and the sand, poured the lye over, scrubbed again and then rinsed with a rag and a bucket of clean water. She was careful to mop it all up, as the innkeeper's wife had instructed, and not to let the lye-water run down into the cracks and stink. When she had done two long planks, she began to realize what a job she had undertaken.

Evening fell before she finished. Daylight was gone, and she scrubbed the very last plank without seeing it. When she came down, the innkeeper's wife said:

'My, that did take you some time. Didn't Hanna ever come up?'

When Edla didn't answer, she continued into the pantry with her basket of eggs. When she came out, she gave Edla one more look, sharp and fleeting, and said:

'Well, who could've known! You eat now.'

But Edla couldn't eat anything. All she wanted was to lie down.

'All right, tomorrow you can clean coffee with Valfrid in the storeroom. Tell them I said so. You can sit there all day.'

She had never been so talkative, but Edla barely heard her. She made her way back upstairs although the steps felt endless. Every muscle in her body was stiff, and she had a headache for the first time in her life, but she fell instantly into a heavy sleep. The room still smelled from the scrubbing. She hadn't thought to open the windows.

Downstairs in the inn, they had moved the tables aside for dancing. The noise woke Edla now and then. Hanna's voice rose above all the others.

'Just feel how sweaty I am!' she shouted, drowning out the fiddle and the stamping feet.

Still, Edla fell back to sleep, and in her sleep the floor she had scrubbed returned and she dreamed she was examining it inch by inch with its knots and its bumps and its long cracks, greasy with dirt. Terrified, she tried to free herself from the floor in her sleep but then it was as if she were standing staring at the wallpaper machine in the workshop of the addled cabinet-maker at Vallmsta. Instead of a roll of paper with a pretty flowered pattern, the floor she had scrubbed rolled out: the knots stared her in the eye, the cracks squirmed. She could see where the wood was worn down around a knothole, the spots where the wood was rough and grey, where the sand made it shine, where it smelt of spilt beer.

She tried to describe her dream to Valfrid the next day as they sat in the storeroom cleaning Brazilian coffee. This was the first time she had confided in him, and it upset him not a little. He wanted to hear every detail about the wallpaper machine and asked if she could take him to see it some time.

She had realized that Valfrid tended to blow things up. He had just told her he had inherited a pair of shoes from Franz Antonsson, who used to be shop manager but had gone home to his mother's and died of consumption. Franz had known the hymn 'Alone in the valley of death', and Valfrid had meant to learn it. But he couldn't get the shoes on, and without them he couldn't bring himself to memorize the song. He was nearly in tears, and complained to Edla in a most unmanly way: all his life he had dreamt of a pair of real shoes and now that he had them his feet were too big! Aside from his chilblains and the corn on his big toe, his feet were just too long, and he was prepared to take the axe to them. He tried to catch Edla's eye, but she persisted in staring down into the bag of uncleaned coffee. It was as if she was ashamed of him for getting carried away.

A couple of days later she passed the open door of the woodshed and heard a soft moan from inside. It was Valfrid. She meant to hurry on by.

'Edla,' he groaned.

He actually had one foot on the block and both hands around the axe. Edla saw, though, that he had long since decided not to let it fall. Still, his naked foot on the chopping block looked awful, his strangely long white toes with yellowing nails, and the filthy, damp cracks between them. Although she knew he was play acting, she was taken aback. Valfrid howled and swung the axe, then wavered and dropped it amongst the birch logs. In tears, he sat down on the chopping block. But he was crying mostly because Edla had not intervened, because she had seen through his show and stood there watching, arms across her chest, like a very old woman.

'I only meant to wait till you got here,' he wept. 'So you could take me to the barber surgeon's wife.'

Edla saw that he had readied a cart to serve as a stretcher outside the woodshed.

This was his only attempt to shorten his feet, after which he sullenly decided to take the shoes home to his family's croft, Nazareth, and give them to his brother Ebon. He was a bit dim and, in Valfrid's opinion, not worthy of the shoes.

'That miserable Ebon,' he muttered.

One Sunday in September Valfrid took the shoes to Nazareth. He asked Edla to come along, and she got the time off without having to explain, which she surely would

34

never have dared to do. It was the day after a market Saturday when they'd worked very hard. The inn had been full and the innkeeper's wife had forgotten all about her age, so she gave her part of the next day off.

First Valfrid bade farewell to the shoes. Every morning his first chore was always to polish the footwear of the innkeeper and the shop manager. In the winter he also had to light the fire in the bar-room and open the door to the shop to let the heat in. Then he would go out to the storeroom and light the little lamp under the cistern to warm the thick olive oil.

Ages ago, he had polished Franz Antonsson's shoes, too, early one morning when the others were done. The utterly flawless leather shone warmly. Before wrapping them in brown paper, he stood them on a sugar crate in the storeroom and looked them over very carefully. They were boot-type shoes that went part way up the calf. The uppers were creased, and Franz had been ill for so long that dust had accumulated in the creases. Valfrid wiped it away with his shirt-tail.

The more he saw of the world and of how people were shod, the more convinced he became that there was a link between a person's footwear and his character. At six each morning Petrus Wilhelmsson passed by on the way to his carpentry shop. He wore a black coat and checked trousers because he worked in an office. Wilhelmsson was never to be found in the bar-room at the inn, never in the company of loudmouths and drunkards. Valfrid thought you could see this in his very shoes, his box-calf boots which appeared to be leading him inexorably forward onto the path of justice and duty. They were stable as little tugboats, shiny, thick-skinned, with sturdy soles, and always pointing forward.

On the other side of the railroad, a farmer named Magnusson built himself a citified house, and called himself a contractor. But his high, greased leather boots revealed that he was still a farmer. He walked straight across the tracks without looking to either side, as if, all by themselves, his sturdy black boots, not polished but greased with fat, could make the switch engines stop rushing forward. So far they had done their job, he hadn't even had any close calls, while Valfrid, in his worn-down, outgrown work boots always had to rush across the tracks with his wheelbarrow, his heart pounding, to keep the locomotive from crushing him like a louse on the wallpaper.

When the Railway Hotel was full, better folks sometimes took rooms at the inn. Single rooms were available at one krona per night, so they didn't have to share with the drunken farmers. The only amenities, however, were a cot and a chair to lay one's coat across. The kind of guests who should actually have been at the hotel would put their shoes out to be shined, which provided Valfrid with sights that made him ecstatic and dangerously excited. In the world out there, there were kid leather shoes so soft and supple that they fit the foot like a glove (that didn't have chilblains, of course). Such shoes seemed to be made for an even, attractive gait. He hardly dared to think about what paths such shoes led down, or what their wearers' names might be.

Now, however, Valfrid was to be parted from Franz Antonsson's shoes, and thus also say farewell to a dream which he could only express by quoting the hymn: 'Alone in the vale of shadows, close by a sparkling stream ...' If there was one thing he knew, it was that Ebon's grossly black crofter's feet were not meant for those shoes.

Hanna lent Edla her shawl when they left, because her dress was worn out and not fit to be seen in public. Hanna crossed the ends of the shawl over Edla's chest and tied them behind her back. Then she gave her a gentle push from behind. They walked side by side, Edla and Valfrid, not knowing what to talk about at first. Being out walking brought them closer. It felt different from sitting in the storeroom cleaning Brazilian coffee together.

In front of the station, the yard was soggy after the first autumn rains and Mamsell Winlöf stepped across, in her velvet coat and her black skirt gathered at the knees. This skirt was the talk of the town. She had her little dog on a lead. It wasn't the kind of dog ordinary people would have, but the kind you might glimpse in a carriage bringing guests from the manor house to catch their train.

'Her name's Turlur and she's a bitch,' said Valfrid. 'But she'll die if she has puppies.'

The little dog was black and white with ears like butterfly wings, in a constant state of tremulous anxiety. Mamsell Winlöf urged her up onto the piles of earth that were shovelled up around the newly-planted, staked-up linden saplings. Back hunched and ears trembling, Turlur forced out little yellow sausages of excrement. Valfrid and Edla stood still, watching.

'You can see she gets nothing but cream to drink,' said Valfrid, 'poor little thing.' Alma Winlöf was in a rush to get back to her restaurant before the twelve o'clock train arrived. She lifted her little dog and carried her inside. When she was in a hurry she took determined, masculine strides despite her short steps, her skirt hovering an inch or two over the muddy mess.

'Let's watch the twelve o'clock first,' Valfrid proposed.

37

They made it just in time to see the food trolleys rolled out onto the platform by the two waitresses. Edla found the food more interesting to look at than the train. After a few minutes, Mamsell Winlöf came out. She had changed her clothes, and was now transformed into a serving woman, as always on this side of the station. She wore a starched white apron with the bib pinned to her black dress. The bottom halves of her arms were concealed in white sleeve covers.

Valfrid and Edla pressed up against the wall of the station when the train from Gothenburg stopped. The passengers were moving as fast as they reasonably could, walking or half-running towards the food trolleys. All those pounding feet and creaking boots above the locomotive's bursts of steam made Edla's heart skip a beat. She saw elegant hands reaching for glasses and sandwiches. Did everyone who travelled by train have such elegant hands and such moist red lips? And where were they headed? How could there be so many errands in the world that couldn't be accomplished on foot?

When nearly all the first-class passengers had descended, a man in a huge, sleeveless cape appeared. Both his cape and his trousers were made of lovely new cloth, black as pitch and reminiscent of coffin lining. His tall top hat shone, gleaming like the smokestack on the locomotive. Extending from the opening on the left side of his cape was a black leather case with shiny clasps, and he didn't put it down a single time during the meal break. With his beautiful rosy complexion, his smooth skin, his curly locks and his bushy eyebrows, he looked like many of the eminent travellers Edla had seen standing on the platform, eating and drinking. She couldn't possibly imagine what he was or what he did when he was not travelling by train. Valfrid, however, was full of words he tried out on people he saw when the train stopped.

'Sure to be a conjurer,' he said, 'or the chief court saddle-maker' .

'Shush,' said Edla, close to tears, 'you read so much rubbish. Shut your trap.'

When she saw the man in the coffin-cloth black cape, she wished Valfrid hadn't been with her. She wanted to contemplate him undisturbed. Suddenly he extended his arm, and the whole cape opened up, exposing the inside with its lining of shiny satin like a streak of crimson lightning against the grey station wall, sooty and spotted with oil.

Every time Edla was around when the train stopped for meal service she had seen someone as memorable as this personage. She was afraid that if she kept coming she wouldn't be able to remember every single one of them separately. For the first time, she felt a streak of anxiety mingled with her delight.

They walked on, side by side, between the stationmaster's house and the station, crossing the rutted, worn road for the loggers who came to the station hamlet from the north. There wasn't exactly a road all the way to Nazareth, but there was the path the railway officials used. It went up to Fredriksberg, a little hillock in the leafy forest that had been converted into an unpretentious little park by the efforts of stationmaster Fredriksson. He had had his English dog buried there, and so people always called it Mulle's End. Valfrid and Edla inspected Mulle's gravestone, on which the yellow birch leaves had fallen in a pretty pattern, glued into place by the night's rain. It bore his name and his dates of birth and death, and they figured out he had lived to be thirteen. He had been buried in a little box, with a fine blanket of plaid English wool for a shroud. Valfrid knew all this from his brother Edvin Oskar, who had worked for the railway long before the lines had been linked up. Edla asked for a detailed description of the blanket, and Valfrid provided it with no hesitation. He found it easy to fill in the gaps in both his own memory and others'.

'A dog,' said Edla thoughtfully, when she heard the blanket was plaid. 'There's something odd about it.'

Valfrid wanted them to stop and rest on the bench on the hilltop at Fredriksberg, but Edla didn't dare. A few minutes later it proved to have been a wise decision, when they heard the soft thumping of horse hooves, and Cederfalk, the booking clerk, came riding past on his brown mare. He was dressed in a plaid woollen riding costume rather than his uniform, and wore a little green hat with a plume. As Edla curtsied, she caught sight of Valfrid out of the corner of her eye, removing his hat and doffing it almost provocatively.

They walked through what used to be the big, black marsh without even getting their feet damp. The path to Nazareth was also Edla's way home to Appleton, except Appleton was much further away. The crofters' and day-workers' cottages hadn't changed much since she had walked here as a little girl, but there were more people living all along the path now, men who worked on the railway or at Wilhelmsson's carpentry shop.

The closer they came to his home, the quieter Valfrid grew. In the end he threatened to dump the package containing the shoes in the bushes rather than see Ebon's shit-kicking feet in them. Edla didn't answer, nor did she need to. The package stayed under his arm.

Nazareth was already full of Sunday visitors. The church was twenty kilometres away, and the only one who grieved over not going was Valfrid's grandma. Inside, the residents of the croft were sitting and standing on the stove side of the room, the Sunday visitors on the sofa side. The people who lived there were as grey as the cottage walls. But Edvin Oskar Johansson, who had been the pumpman to begin with, was now the night yard master and wore a double-breasted uniform, a striped cap and a white collar. His wife had on a blouse made of store-bought cloth, and their children were wearing clothes that were obviously not hand-me-downs. Valfrid had another brother who was also much older, Wilhelm, who worked at the carpentry shop. He was wearing a black blazer and a round-brimmed hat. The two had very little left to say to one another. The Edvin Oskars had brought a basket full of sweet rolls bought at the market, but no one had done anything about putting on the coffee pot. When Valfrid arrived with the package containing the shoes and a little bag of coffee bean rejects he had secreted away, it immediately became clear that there had been no coffee in the house until then, although no one had wanted to admit it. His mother was quick to bring out her coffee roaster, and Ebon and his younger brothers and sisters gathered kindling to light the stove. Soon the wonderful aroma of deeply roasted coffee beans spread throughout the kitchen, overwhelming the odour of poverty Edla found so difficult to bear now that she worked at the inn that smelled of fresh bread and fried meat every day.

Eventually the shoes, too, came out of their package and made the rounds so everyone could touch the faultless, glossy leather. Valfrid said they were made by the cobbler whose workshop was in the same building as the bowling alley. It took a few minutes for everyone to agree, because there were two cobblers in the village, but one was religious

41

and would never have lived in the same building where
Tubby Kalle sold beer. Valfrid appeared to have forgotten his
disappointment over his own feet being too big, and grew
lively and talkative from the hit he made with the bag of
coffee and the package containing the shoes. Ebon removed
what passed for his shoes, and he was sent outside with a
dab of cleaning soap and a bucket of water and told to make
his feet presentable. He retorted to the gathering that they
were probably all lucky they didn't have to take their shoes
off, which provoked both a reflex reaction in Edvin Oskar,
who quickly pulled his boots under his chair, and a slap
across Ebon's cheek that turned it bluish-red.

When he came back in with the shoes on, Valfrid's belief
in a deep connection between a person's footwear and his
character had suffered a serious setback. Ebon looked neither
more upright nor more refined; he was precisely the same as
before.

'They're a mite tight,' he said.

'It's your feet as are too big, you idiot!'

Valfrid could have wept when he saw the leather pulled
across Ebon's chilblains. He got them off with some effort,
and dropped them unceremoniously by Valfrid's chair.

'Couldn't you try them just once more?' his mother
begged.

'I'll be damned if I will.'

'I'm wondering what was wrong with that Antonsson
fellow who had such pathetic little feet,' crofter Johansson
proffered.

Strangely, Valfrid and Edla ended up carrying the shoes
back again. When they parted that evening and Valfrid
headed towards the room he shared alongside the stables

with the drivers, he shoved the package swiftly into her arms.

'You take them,' he said. 'You'll never get a diviner pair.'

He was right about that. Late that evening she tried them on in the club room. She had never had shoes where the right and left were different before, so at first she put them on the wrong feet and couldn't figure out what the matter was. When she got them on right, they felt just about perfect. She wished fervently that she wouldn't grow much more so they would always fit.

Dark autumn evenings arrived. Ida and Hanna sat near the stove, one at the swift, the other at the spinning wheel. They must have assumed that the noise of the winder and the wheel drowned out their whispering, but Scrub-Ärna was right there in the corner, straining to catch every word.

They had trouble getting the old woman to go home at night. She and her sister lived in a rickety hut next to the postmaster's home. The estate gave them a roof over their heads and a free supply of cordwood, because her sister had worked there all her life. The postmaster had put up a fence between his house and theirs, and let creepers grow up it, but the old women's cats were still a nuisance to him.

Scrub-Ärna listened, and then she gossiped. She made it known to one and all that the innkeeper's housemaids weren't God-fearing. Soon even Edla knew that Hanna, the cheerful, thieving one, had a bun in the oven. Edla asked the baker-woman what the problem might be and was told that it was the kind of problem that came of Hanna's letting drunken stage-drivers lie on top of her.

Hanna grew pale and wan and no longer wanted to join in on Saturday evenings when they cleared out the bar-room for dancing. When she and Ida went out to do the morning milking she first had to run behind the barn. Edla's face kept appearing, watchful.

Just before Christmas, in great secrecy she thought, Hanna slipped away to Ox Spring to see the old man who had a way with pigs and helped girls who were in trouble. When she was halfway out of town she heard footsteps, and turned around to find Edla running to catch up in the big checked shawl Hanna often lent her.

Hanna couldn't see what good Edla's curiosity would do her, but she let her come along to have someone to whom she could pour out her woes. What was more, she was intimidated by the old man at Ox Spring. Edla sat right up close to her throughout his reading, trembling just as hard as Hanna. They walked home without saying a word. The autumn air was heavy and the birds were silent. All they heard was the cracking of the thin layers of ice on the puddles.

'Wonder how long it takes to work,' Edla burst out. Hanna had to laugh, and give the little bundle walking beside her a pat.

'Don't you worry your heart about it,' she replied.

Hanna's belly just kept on growing after she'd been to Ox Spring. She was more cheerful though, and swore she'd demand her money back if it hadn't worked. Once Scrub-Ärna had spread her secret all over town, Hanna reversed her tactics and spoke openly about her shame.

After their walk to Ox Spring, Edla and big, jovial Hanna grew increasingly close. Edla worried about what would happen to the baby, where the baby clothes would come from and where Hanna would give birth.

Winter came, and the cold morning stars blazed. One morning, Edla was awakened before four and told to try to do what she could to make herself useful in the cowshed, since Hanna was ill and couldn't get up. It was after seven when Edla finally finished and was able to run up to Hanna's room.

45

She and Ida shared a bed, and Ida had put both their blankets over her, with an old coachman's coat on top. The barber surgeon's wife, who had been there all morning, was gathering her tubes and glasses.

'You sit with her,' she said to Edla. 'And come right down and get me if there's any change. I have to have my coffee.'

Hanna was lying on her back, her face ashen. She complained that her heart was pounding and she was dizzy, and she let Edla feel her heart galloping in her chest. When she tried to sit up, she fell right back and blacked out for a moment. She had been vomiting.

There was nothing Edla could do. She sat listening to the dry timber walls squeaking in the cold, and watching Hanna's face grow grey and damp.

'Have they sent for the doctor?' she whispered. Her lips were so stiff Edla could hardly make out her words. She nodded.

'But it'll be some time.'

He lived twenty kilometres outside of town.

'Take this.'

Hanna was holding something tightly. Now she fumbled it across to Edla. It was a small, folded paper.

'Get rid of this. Right now. You do as I say.'

Edla hid the packet in her dress pocket and stayed with Hanna until the doctor arrived.

'Do it right now,' Hanna whispered, the words almost indistinguishable through her stiff lips.

The doctor departed, and Hanna still lay there. They didn't talk about her, and there were long periods of total silence in the kitchen. But the following afternoon they heard heavy steps on the attic stairs. Edla rushed to open the vestibule door, and there stood Hanna. She had to hold on to stay upright, and her face was still ashen. The innkeeper's wife dropped what she was doing and stared. Hanna took the tin scoop from the water barrel and drank deeply. When she got Edla to herself, she began by asking:

'Did you throw that rubbish away?'

The girl nodded solemnly.

'And don't you dare say a word.'

She hadn't thrown it away, though. The paper was blue and patterned with stars, just like the fortunes you could buy at the market square. She had found some granular powder inside, and poured it into a broken-spouted jug she'd once found and kept amongst the childish treasures she saved in a worn-out shawl. She kept her bundle behind a pile of debris in the attic of the inn.

Edla followed Hanna's every move for a week, but could see no change once her heart stopped pounding and the colour came back to her face. Her waistline was just as big as before. So Edla poured the powder out of her creamer, letting it run down into a knot-hole in the attic floorboards.

When the bloom returned to Hanna's cheeks, Fru Isaksson threw her out, although until that point she had pretended not to hear the gossip in the kitchen.

'As long as I was pulling my load, she didn't notice, the stingy old hag,' Hanna said. 'But when I took sick, she went religious.'

She placed her packed case and her bundle on the kitchen table, as the innkeeper's wife had insisted on examining its contents before Hanna left.

'I won't spill any tears about leaving, and it was fun while it lasted.'

Hanna's voice was as loud as usual, and she patted her stomach. Scrub-Ärna said that evil were the deeds of darkness, and we would all pay for our sins, some of us in full measure.

Edla, however, stood to one side in the kitchen corner and watched Hanna gravely as she went on her way, listening to her laughter, which was louder and more shrill than in the days when she danced with the drivers in the bar-room.

Mamsell Alma Winlöf, the restaurant owner, used to be called Alma Eriksson and had brothers who went by that surname. It was said that she had started out as a pastry cook. Her mother made boiled sweets, her father was a coffin-maker.

Alma Eriksson left the railway hamlet for five years, returning as Mamsell Winlöf, and paying cash to purchase the railway restaurant. Where did her money come from?

Inside the restaurant there was a plush burgundy sofa. It was circular, with a velvet-covered cone in the middle, rising high above the backs of anyone who sat on it. This plush tower was flat at the top, and crowned with a vase of gracefully swaying wax camellias.

One day Magnusson, the self-made builder, entered the restaurant with a timber salesman he had just picked up at the train. Magnusson had never seen the sofa before.

'What the dickens?' he burst out, stopping short before the velvet altar, his jaw dropping. He wore shiny boots and a chequered suit, his pudding-bowl hair shiny with water and combed forward over his ears, his beard trimmed. He had dressed up and fixed his hair out of respect for his first visit to the restaurant, which was a far cry from the beer-reeking inn. He immediately appeared to lose all respect for the facilities.

Afterwards, he explained that in Stockholm he had once visited a place where you could buy a woman's services by the hour. He'd been left alone with a dark young lady in provocative clothing in a huge room smelling of high-class cigars. In the middle of the room there had been a circular red plush sofa. Magnusson had made every effort to contort himself and the young woman into its shape. She had been breathless with laughter, writhing like a snake around the velvet tower. He had tried to crawl up to her and do his errand, but in vain. In the end he'd realized that depravity and perversion weren't for him, and he'd left.

'Didn't you know that was only the foyer?' people asked him, but Magnusson declared it made no difference. The point was he knew where that sofa, and Alma Winlöf's fortune, came from.

It aggravated many people that coffin-maker Eriksson's daughter expected to be called Mamsell, but Magnusson's explanation of where her money came from lent the word an ironic undertone. In other words, it became easy to sound ironic when her name came up. Face to face, however, her brown eyes were unruffled and coldly calculating. On the village side of the station she was never seen in anything but a coat and hat and skirts so tight she could only take short little steps. She wore nothing but black and white on either side of the station. Her hair was jet, her skin ivory. She looked like and smelled of gentry.

When she moved back to the village, she no longer lived with her parents, but had a little three-room apartment in the restaurant building. She finished one of the rooms as a parlour. Her old parents didn't move in with her, either. Eriksson went on making coffins at one end of their house, while his wife made sweets at the other.

It was impossible to catch her out, not even when it came to her only apparent weakness, her tremendous interest in the details of other people's lives. She listened to gossip, but never passed it on.

Despite the fact that Fru Isaksson was one of her worst slanderers, Mamsell Winlöf was a regular customer at the innkeeper's store. Valfrid pushed the delivery wheelbarrow across the station yard several times a day. He would stay for a long time, and when he returned his breath smelled of lozenges. Mamsell milked him about everything that went on at the inn. Thus she knew that thieving Hanna had been sent away and why, although Fru Isaksson couldn't imagine why she was interested in the miserable fate her foolish housemaid had brought upon herself.

One day in late February she brought Edla back across the yard, against the wishes of Fru Iskasson, on the pretext of needing someone to carry her butter when Valfrid was unavailable. Edla looked down as she walked through the snow behind Mamsell and her little dog. In the restaurant kitchen, full of busy serving girls, Edla set down the tub and was told to wait. Mamsell went into her apartment and returned after a few minutes, still dressed in black and white, but now in a wide skirt she could take big steps in, and was transformed to something in between a working woman and a woman who's waited on. She began to interrogate Edla. Who was doing Hanna's chores now? Edla mumbled that she didn't know. Mamsell asked her to describe her own tasks: how much was she paid? Her board? Cloth for a dress?

The girl's answers were inaudible. She felt as if she couldn't escape those brown eyes, felt they were examining her the way the innkeeper's wife inspected a plucked hen before quartering it.

Edla was a nobody. She was worth no more than the work her hands could do, and that was a pittance. This was how she was accustomed to being seen, and all else frightened her.

However, although Edla's life was short and worth very little, she still had eyes to see and skin to get gooseflesh. Cruelty turned her stomach and she fled from folly, or ducked if she couldn't escape. She had ideas about almost everything she saw and enough sense to keep them to herself. Now Mamsell's sober gaze was picking at her poor protective cover, apparently demanding answers. Edla found a dishonourable retreat by bursting into tears when Mamsell said:

'Well, I can see you have your board, anyway. You've put on weight, haven't you? Let's see.'

She reached out for the girl to hold her by the waist, but Edla escaped.

She didn't reveal to Fru Isaksson what kind of questions Mamsell had asked. Tight-lipped, she stared stubbornly at the floor.

'You're impossible,' said the innkeeper's wife. And to her husband she added: 'She must be a little slow after all.'

But Mamsell Winlöf came to the inn asking how old Edla was.

'She's turned fourteen,' said the innkeeper's wife.

Mamsell had frightened them all.

The last wolf was shot in Vingåker in 1858, and that was a good thing. But when will someone crush the last wood-louse under his heel?

Endless drabness, toothless tedium. A banner flies from the fortress, but in fact it's all that's left. The grandstands were torn down, the commemorative plaques removed, all more than fifteen years ago. Flags and trumpets were put away, along with shields and emblems. Just the banner flies from the fortress, twenty-seven meters above sea level, and slightly less above Pig Field.

The next time Cleo makes her mark on a slate, a train grinds to a halt, screeching and hissing, and a royal head protrudes from the window of the Pullman car asking:

'What's the price of potatoes here, then?'

Well, that's a good question. The crowd cheers enthusiastically, the king withdraws his curly head, and the train departs. Left on the platform is stationmaster Fredriksson, the man who'd created the park. Or at least who'd seen to it that a grove of trees was thinned out, a stony hilltop made accessible. He wanted the townspeople to refer to it as Fredriksberg when they were out walking, but what did they insist on saying? 'Mulle's grave.'

Thus droops a banner over the fort.

The town square is a farmer's field, a crooked, boggy path leads through the village, just about good enough for the night soil wagon to roll down. During the early years there could be no market day until Old Mothstead had harvested his oats, and so the best years were when he let his field lie fallow.

The body of water that runs through the village is known as Trash Moat. Along its banks lie Pig Field, Low Meadow, Cats' End, the Boneyard, Old Man's Alley, Louse Point, Barefoot Bluff and Bald Man's Bastion. These are the place-names that go with derisive sniggering and garrulous gossip. These are the names you have to use day after day and year after year, even if you live in the area above which the banner flies.

Booking clerk Cederfalk gave new names to virtually every single grove and puddle in his world. He was the first Adam in the Garden of Eden, and he hoped that people's ears would open and they would realize that their language was filthy. He could converse with Malvina Lagerlöf and Charlotte Hedberg and Baron Fogel about Aurora's Shore and Echo Cavern, but he still had to translate when talking with anyone else.

One year on May Day he managed to assemble a decent coach and four, and he invited Malvina out for a tour. He had borrowed the coach from Heavenside, where Baron Fogel's uncle lived, and the horses belonged to Magnusson the builder. Strong, lovely horses were his pride. Malvina was allowed to go, but only with her elderly aunt as a chaperone. The wheels creaked, and Cederfalk and Malvina bounced up and down, with tolerant smiles. On the coach-box sat an inexperienced driver. Cederfalk had selected him according to the principle of the handsomest moustache and the cleanest uniform. They intended to be out and about for a while, which meant riding all the way up Tavern Road and back again. They couldn't possibly go to Mulle's grave, since the path wasn't wide enough for a coach. Next they would

54

take a spin in front of the station, where Cederfalk had cleared the terrain before leaving. He could only hope that no drunks had passed out in the lilacs in the meanwhile. They were to continue past the inn and Cats' End, crossing the railway tracks after the postmaster's house, by the Boneyard.

So far so good. But when they got to the tracks the coach had to stop for the driver to listen for approaching trains. And one of the horses farted.

Beside himself in embarrassment and distress, Cederfalk quickly stuttered: 'Pardon!' Malvina bowed her head and did not look up once as they drove back down the drive to Heavenside. The driver who had made such an indelible impression of incurable idiocy turned out to have it in him to spread the story that Malvina had replied:

'Oh, I thought it was the horse!' — which was a pure lie, a lie pure and simple. Beyond the one single word 'pardon' not another syllable was uttered until they were safely back at the postmaster's.

In '76 the Railway Hotel was expanded and now even a man of means could bear to spend the night in the village, since Mamsell Winlöf had had the second storey remodelled into comfortable guest rooms. It was a major refurbishing job, and while it was going on there were times when her serving girls had to roll out food trolleys again.

She also had a royal dining room fitted out. One must forgive and forget if one is to survive, not to mention that the price of potatoes had risen to nearly two kronor a barrel.

I n '76, Mamsell Winlöf acquired a friend. He was
Alexander Lindh. A shorter man than most, he grew
square and squat as the years passed. He had blue eyes,
a ruddy complexion, and dark hair cut so short that his scalp
shone through. His neck already had folds. His hair was
parted down the middle, his moustache thick. All his life he
wore his hair in the same style and walked with the same
short, dynamic strides. He was authoritative in spite of his
stature and had a tendency to take control. He was a quick
thinker, and a fast figurer while he talked with his dry
rasping voice that went staccato when he was eager. He
could sell just about anything at a profit and there was not
a situation in the world in which he felt ill at ease. Alien to
him were embarrassment, long-winded harangues and
emotional cause-and-effect relationships.

The first time, he arrived with a little rucksack, the next
with a suitcase. His father was a Värmland foundry owner,
and his own job was to travel around purchasing timber
from farmers. Probably he became Mamsell Winlöf's friend
because he questioned her about her business, thoroughly
and admiringly. He could see she was an enterprising
woman. He walked brusquely through her premises nodding,
without removing his stubby cigar from his mouth. When he
reached the circular red plush sofa he stopped, striking it
with his hand.

'This, however,' he said, 'is the property of the state.'
Mamsell nodded.

56

'Its mate is in the first-class waiting room at the Stockholm Central Railway Station,' he said.

'Yes,' said Mamsell, 'that's true.'

And so he became her friend. She saw to it personally that he had birch firewood for his tiled stove so he could safely open the stove doors in the mornings if he liked, although he set very little store by such favours. The station restaurant had three classes now. Sometimes, however, Alexander Lindh spent the evening in Mamsell Winlöf's own parlour. He had an inexhaustible supply of stories for her about his timber transactions, speculations and aspirations. She answered him sensibly, and her questions were discriminating. Alma Winlöf did not sit bent over an embroidery frame, she did not make silk tassels or lace doilies. Her hands were folded in her lap.

Through Mamsell he got to know more and more about the village. He knew that the postmaster's income from capital was over two thousand. He knew that the great Stockholm wood and coal empire from which the yard master's wife was descended had long ago gone into liquidation and that the stone mansions on Narvavägen in Stockholm the little woman sometimes daydreamed about had long ago been heavily mortgaged and then sold. He learned quickly who counted, from Mamsell Winlöf. Farmer Magnusson, who was not particularly welcome in the townspeople's sitting rooms, who did not trust banks and whose entire fortune was in a thick cowhide wallet in his inside pocket, was the man in the village who was responsible for all the new buildings that were going up. Petrus Wilhelmsson socialized with no-one and was at his carpentry shop day and night. He had begun by borrowing. Now he had money to invest. He had bought land and was expanding his shop. Mamsell lowered her voice when she spoke of him. Alexander Lindh had seen him at night in his house across the street. He lived in two rooms on the second floor. Late at night, he could be seen in there, a solitary man in a night cap, pouring over his accounts by the light of a little candle. It got dark and he was no longer visible, but the little candle kept flickering like a glow-worm inching along the columns of figures.

Mamsell Winlöf's excuse for entertaining Alexander Lindh in her own rooms was the long, raw chilly autumn in '76. His throat hurt and all his mucous membranes were swollen. Mamsell made him hot toddys and let him move into her parlour, for the heat. One of the serving girls would move his chair closer to the fire, while another obeyed the command to bring a little end table up next to it. By covering the end table with a big white linen restaurant napkin with the insignia of the railway woven into the pattern on the linen, the pretext could be maintained that Mamsell Winlöf was merely extending her restaurant service to where it was warmer.

Throughout the Christmas and New Year's holidays, Lindh was nowhere to be seen. He celebrated Christmas in Värmland and did not show up until after Twelfth Night, when he brought a hare for Mamsell with him. He had not shot it himself.

'My brother Adolf,' he said curtly in explanation; this was the first time he mentioned his circumstances in Värmland which included, as Mamsell had heard elsewhere, a wife and a brother.

She prepared the hare in the spirit of *la haute cuisine* as best she could with the assistance of cold-eyed, angry serving girls who suddenly seemed to have trouble understanding instructions. She had to say everything twice. They crossed the back of the hare with thin white strips of lard, and roasted him until he smelled like the juniper-covered hills of his youth. They laid him out with jelly and tiny pickles, braised mushrooms and capers.

Alexander Lindh did not appear for the dinner as he had implied that he would. Not until the Saturday after Twelfth Night did he say that now that all the Christmas partying was over he had time to have dinner with her. The hare fillets were ground in a mortar and pressed through a sieve with chicken liver, butter and cream, and the hare was reincarnated in the shape of a pyramid, decorated with star-shaped pieces of jellied consommé.

Oddly, the long hiatus seemed to make Lindh more at home than ever in Mamsell Winlöf's chambers. When he was comfortably installed in an armchair, equipped with his coffee and a little glass of arrack, his feet automatically sought the ottoman.

'Well, all I can say is thank heavens the holidays are over! Nothing gets done and altogether too much gets eaten. Incidentally, Mamsell Winlöf, I envy you.'

'In what respect?'

'In that your business need not grind to a halt. On the contrary, as I see it. You appear to have been fully booked, from first-class right down to third.'

'Ah, what I wouldn't give to be able to close down the third-class for good!' Mamsell replied.

'With your turnover?'

He knew very well, however, that what disturbed Mamsell was the visits she received from the wives and even the children of her third-class restaurant guests, who entreated and deplored her not to serve liquor to breadwinners.

'There is money here that never leaves the station area,' she sighed. 'Yard hands or brakemen who pick up their salary at the office and head straight for the third class bar with it.'

'You forget, Mamsell, that they do so of their own free will. Not to mention that you make it up to their families with your hampers.'

His tone of voice was slightly sardonic, as it tended to be when Mamsell touched on such topics. She did not like him to mention her deeds of charity. He had met her on the road, walking towards the most pitiful dwellings in the village, dressed in black and white, with no dog, and followed by two serving girls carrying hampers. She had just barely deigned to return his greeting.

'There are ever so many taverns,' said Lindh. 'And there's always the inn, in the end. I can hardly imagine old Isaksson closing down out of compassion for more unfortunate members of society.'

'Things are dreadful at the inn! One housemaid is doing virtually all the work. The other was forced to leave owing to an embarrassing condition that had begun to show. Children are exploited as if they were grown labourers and left alone at night.'

One of the difficulties associated with Mamsell Winlöf and her confidences was that she refused to devote herself solely to subjects of interest to Lindh. She often described the poorest, most vulnerable members of the community, and sometimes she sounded to him like the moralistic flyers the anti-obscenity groups distributed. Despite her good business sense, the woman, naturally enough, had no overview of society as a whole. She had no idea that a wider perspective was needed to solve these problems, nor did she possess the ability to think in abstractions.

'Isaksson has in his employ a girl who is barely fourteen, the daughter of a district soldier. Her name is Edla Lans. To start with she was to look after the little boy, or so they said. Now they have her doing full service, but they haven't changed her terms of employment. She's been told to sleep upstairs from the bar-room, in what they call the club room. It's easy to imagine what she's exposed to.'

'Thou art a true woman, Mamsell Winlöf,' said Lindh with a smile. 'You think of the little things, and have the kindest of hearts!'

He was happy. Alma Winlöf was still a real woman, in spite of being single and making money. Although she did not possess an embroidery frame, she stitched a lovely picture and didn't miss a single detail. He smiled sleepily in his chair, listening to the even rise and fall of Alma's voice. Suddenly she became vulgar. He was taken completely aback, because her well-modulated tone of voice did not change. God only knew how long she had been at it.

'People say this village has blossomed in the last ten years, that the railway is a blessing and, granted, things look pretty nice around here. The snow is merciful. But just you wait until summer. The rubbish heaps and sewage ditches give off a disgusting stink.'

Alexander Lindh was now sitting straight as an arrow in his chair, staring at Alma Winlöf.

'...The farmhand who could get no croft of his own since all the land was taken is now a yard hand. Soon he'll have a garret of his own and a wife and kids. I've been in those garret rooms with food hampers — once I saw a rat-bitten child.'

By now she appeared completely oblivious to Lindh's presence. She was leaning back in her chair in the most unfeminine way, her eyes half-open, speaking without pausing for breath.

'You'll say we do have the doctor and the barber surgeon, and of course they can come. You only have to go twenty kilometres to fetch the doctor, and he has assured us he makes no distinction between high and low. But what can the doctor do for a rat bite? I know mothers who live in the backwoods, far from all progress, and ignorant as the day is long. When their children get spots, they believe the evil fairies have slapped them. They pin bags of herbs to their chests, or pull them through hollow fir trees. And yet I think those mothers are better able to help their children than the ones in this village. What chance do they have to protect them? They are more helpless than superstitious, ignorant country fools. Their children hang around the platforms and learn to steal. A traveller drops a coin outside the restaurant — that's the start. And their fathers! They don't even have to trudge miles and miles for a jug of drink. No, all they have to do is walk into the nearest dank beer cellar, where there isn't even clean sawdust put out every day.'

The colour rose in Alma Winlöf's face that was usually so smooth and white. The thin skin of her neck and chin were pulsating, and her body was not itself, it was exuding an odour. Alexander grew impatient. He no longer heard what she said, and he thought with distaste and recognition: this is what happens when women, with their fragile nervous systems, drink wine or spirits. Soon she'll be rambling, her vocabulary is already betraying her background, she's forgetting herself. Her hair is coming undone and there is a pungent scent to her skin. Tell-tale signs. At the same time, he felt all his own blood descend to his sexual organ, his legs went weak and he felt dizzy from the loss of blood to the rest of his body. Still, he stood up on his short unsteady legs and emptied his glass. Instead of warning and reproaching this nearly undone and fragrant woman, he smiled at her and she was silenced, dumbfounded, in mid-sentence.

A thought struck him that would never have entered his mind with his wife Caroline. When he saw the fold in Mamsell Winlöf's neck, the soft recess that separated chin from neck, and which would probably separate one chin from the next in just a few years, he thought he would like to lay his sexual organ there. This was the way he would like to make love to her. It must have had something to do with her in particular that he was not overcome by an immediate sense of shame the moment he thought this. He had never taken a stand on all the gossip about her background and about the origins of her money. His statement about the red plush sofa was made out of sheer common sense. Moreover, he had only been telling the truth. Now his excited thoughts suddenly took a stand of their own.

When he embraced her it all happened so fast that he more or less came crashing down on her. She had leaned too far back in her chair, no longer sitting like a decent woman. As he came down upon her, she bucked from the pelvis, a rough jolt that threw him off her and landed him on the rug in front of her chair. It was instantaneously perfectly clear to him that no virtuous woman would have built-in reflexes enabling her to buck so sharply and so effectively with her pelvis as to keep herself from being mounted when she did

63

not wish to be. No, that had been an instinctive, depraved movement. His next manoeuvre came to him quickly, and he knew exactly what he would say when he had crawled back up. He could hardly be too bold.

But he never got up off the carpet. Mamsell Winlöf placed one hand, strong as a man's, on his chest and pushed him down. She burst into words that could have been a serving girl's, but her voice was that of a cultivated woman.

It did not become clear until several weeks later that Alexander Lindh was the man Alma Winlöf had been waiting for. He suffered defeat on the carpet in the sitting room, but was victorious on the chaise longue. He wore down her resistance with a strategy consisting of continual vacillations between attack and retreat. They wrestled in the easy chair, and he pleaded on bended knee at the fireplace, under a cross-stitched Aeneas dragging Anchises out of a Troy in flames. Behind the screen, Mamsell Winlöf struggled desperately to fit hook back into eye. She was tall and stately, Alexander Lindh was short but heavy. They tussled in the neo-rococo, ripping fringes in their silent battles. For nearly thirty seconds an étagier on thin curved legs stood poised to fall, ornaments trembling and glass clinking against glass while Alexander and Alma, who had caused the tremor, stood by watching until it decided to maintain its equilibrium. Turlur rushed back and forth across the shag rug in front of the chaise longue, yapping.

Every wrestling match brought him a little closer to her. Soon there was only one section of her body his hands had not yet reached — the part enclosed and ensconced by her corset. And then one night, or rather early one morning, it was undone. Alexander had fought until five o'clock. He was tired. His sexual organ lay soft and curved, slumbering against his thigh. He was utterly unable to enter the beleaguered Troy and to set it on fire. Alma Winlöf and he fell asleep side by side in her bed, naked and silent.

She was often happy during the time that followed. They shared a bed. Not until the early hours would he go up to his room in the hotel. At night, Alma would light the birchwood fire meant for morning, and let it burn with the doors on the tiled stove open. Warm lights and soft shadows played across their faces. They had been drinking Malaga and she was resting softly on her pillow. Strange pictures and disconnected words came and went through her mind in waves. Alexander, Alexander she repeated, thinking that his name was a long, softly curving bough extending over her head. Alexander loosens Alma's leaves, and lofty wine and linden boughs ... and windy vows and Alma's features in the mist between wet berry branches and under Alexander ... never had she known anything like this and it did not frighten her. In the morning it was gone.

The wrestling matches were a thing of the past, as was Alexander's astonishment that the woman who owned the burgundy sofa was a virgin. He took her seldom, as his organ was usually too soft. But Alma merely considered herself relieved of the ultimate bother, the unpleasant side of love.

He couldn't continue to stay at the hotel. It was too expensive now that he was spending such long periods of time in the village. He therefore rented a one-bedroom flat in one of Magnusson's buildings. It was on the south side of the tracks, the wrong side, but Lindh was already a welcome guest in the sitting rooms that counted, as well as in Mamsell Winlöf's, the one that did not count. It was an expensive flat, and set him back seventy to seventy-five kronor a

65

month. Still, he took it as a sign of the times that the prices of milk and wood were constantly on the rise in the village, and that a landlord could rent out just about any old shanty, cramped and with no facilities, and get two hundred kronor for it.

He still took his dinner at the railway hotel, and returned late, after supper at the postmaster's or a game of cards with the telegraph commissioner. Now, however, he just had a toddy in Alma's parlour. It would not look good at all if he were seen crossing the tracks in the wee hours to the building on the south side where his flat was. And Alma had to make do with embraces on the chaise longue.

Yet all embraces bring trouble and complications in their wake. Hooks have to be enticed out of eyes, layer after layer of cloth lifted aside, laces loosened. All the little tightly embroidered puffs have to be piled alongside the chaise longue, a towel spread on the satin. Afterwards, Alma had to run into her bedroom with her hand cupped like a bowl between her legs, to rinse at the commode. To this end, she had an enema bag with a hose and a bone spout and the water had a sour scent of vinegar, from the spoonful she'd added. Alexander kept his eyes closed throughout, and when she returned in her night-dress, having gathered up and put aside the piles of taffeta, shiny silk and white linen that were her clothes, he would open his eyes and say, with unfailing tact, 'I do believe I dozed off.'

What remained was for him to dress. Alma mixed him a night-cap in the hotel kitchen while he did. He was tired and wished he could fall right into bed. The underwear he'd had on all day felt grimy and foul at this time of night.

These troubles culminated one evening as Alma searched high and low for a hook to lace his boots with. Alexander's irritation grew, the folds of his neck went redder and redder, while Alma crouched at his feet desperately teasing the lace in each boot from hole number one to hole twenty-three.

After that night, he never again removed his boots under the hotel roof. But in all other ways, their relationship remained the same.

B aron Cederfalk, chief railway clerk, rode out every morning on a chestnut mare. Alexander Lindh moved out of his path, unfamiliar with horses and not especially keen to make their acquaintance. Cederfalk, however, made his mare dance right behind.

'Good morning, engineer Lindh. How are you keeping?'

'Just fine, thank you. And yourself, Baron?'

'Couldn't be better!'

Yellow linden leaves danced about horse and rider. The mare circled Alexander Lindh, who marked time in the same spot, irritated.

'I've had my Zulamite shod in the early morning hour,' Cederfalk said. 'Did you know that I had a blacksmith brought here just for her sake? That was three years ago. And now he's doing a booming business in horse shoes. All thanks to my glorious Zulamite!'

'That's what you think,' thought Alexander Lindh. Words spun like garlands out of Cederfalk's mouth. He was court poet in the salon of the postmistress.

Lindh had gained access to the sitting room of postmistress Lagerlöf, which was more than one could say for Cederfalk's blacksmith. Still, he may have more of a future than I do, thought Lindh. He had his dark moments, brief but extremely dark. He was the third son of an autocratic foundry owner. His grandfather had lived, unbroken, to be ninety-four.

Lindh's short legs had propelled him all the way up to Fredriksberg and Mulle's grave. He sat down on the bench and re-lit the cigarette that had gone out while he was walking.

Until six months ago he had thought his life would be one long wait for the moment when the blustering autocrat, who by all accounts might live to be at least ninety-four, passed on. Then his father shot himself, one evening in '76 where people were hunting woodcock, which was why no one reacted at first when they heard the shot.

His foundry was rotten to the core. The old man had concealed this state of affairs with his sound and fury for as long as he could. August, the eldest son, was a scrupulously honest man. He sold the house in which they had grown up. When the auction was over not so much as a salad bowl was left, after which August paid the debts he considered most pressing. Then the foundry declared bankruptcy and August emigrated, leaving Alexander with a fragile young wife and a brother who could barely look after himself, a tall, aristocratic man fit only to follow orders — the elegant Adolf.

So now Alexander was no longer a travelling timber buyer for the foundry. He bought timber and then sold it. He exported railway ties. He interested Magnusson the builder in a grain deal and encouraged him to invest in a grain storehouse where they could keep it. They became exporters, and after some time they had made so much money that Lindh could buy Magnusson's share of the storehouse back.

However, '77 was not off to an auspicious start. Basically, Lindh had nothing to store in the enormous warehouse but a batch of spade handles and snow shovels he had undertaken to sell on behalf of Petrus Wilhelmsson. He had to spend more and more time in the railway hamlet. The storehouse tied him down, it had to be used. He rode in wagons on rutted roads, and sometimes travelled short stretches by train. It did not take long for him to feel that he knew this region better than the one he came from.

Back in Värmland were his wife and Adolf. They were living with an aunt on the Lindh side, a widow with a small estate, but living on her charity wore on his wife's nerves. Adolf said nothing.

Alexander had long been negotiating to purchase a farmhouse on a piece of property north of the village. The innkeeper had a lease on the farmland, and if Lindh took the house that arrangement could continue. Magnusson had sketched a plan for making some relatively modest improvements that would transform the unpretentious farmhouse to something that might resemble a manor. Two small new wings, a little turret with a bell tower.

Now he had to make a decision. He was a man for whom decisions usually came easily. They were as natural to him as swallowing, or inhaling and exhaling. Now he was sitting on the bench staring blindly at Mulle's grave while his mind wandered in a way he wasn't used to. In his thoughts, he was formulating a letter to his wife describing the little manor by the lake. But he was nothing if not an honest man. He knew the lake was shallow and full of reeds, the land around the farm flat and dull. The air was thick with the smell of the swamp. A farm house with a turret and a bell tower was a far cry from a manor in Värmland. And yet he described it in his precise fashion so that her dreams would easily do most of the lying for him.

When he returned home, he committed the letter to paper. Never before had he sat writing a personal letter in

70

broad daylight. But he said to himself he was only doing it to see what such a letter would look like. He had still not made up his mind.

In the end, he never did. When he posted the letter it was with the reservation that the purchase deed had not yet changed hands. He could easily extract himself from the whole business, tell his wife that it had come to nothing. By the time he had received her reply, Magnusson was impatient for his answer, and Lindh had realized he couldn't possibly let his wife down. He had her letter in his breast pocket. She wrote that he had never made her so happy. 'This daily degradation and humiliation,' she wrote, 'is all the more difficult to bear without you at my side. You know, as well, what sacrifices I have had to make over the last year. Now that the end of this humiliation is in sight, I hardly know how I will endure another year's wait. My nerves are under a terrible strain and Adolf, as you well know, is of little or no help.'

While he was waiting for the farmhouse to be transformed, he rented two more rooms from Magnusson, hired a housemaid and purchased furnishings. One late winter's day his wife Caroline and his brother Adolf arrived by train. Mamsell Winlöf stood in a window on the second floor, nearly concealed by the cream-coloured silk curtain, watching. She saw a woman who was taller than Alexander Lindh. Her movements were slow, her eyes red-brimmed from chronic inflammation or melancholy. She wore a wrinkled silk gown that had required yards and yards of fabric. It was cut according to the fashion of ten years earlier, and with such a wide skirt, so many ruffled pleats and so much draped silk, she looked like an old woman as

71

she left the station slightly bent and leaning on the arm of her much shorter spouse.

T he snow melted, exposing the dead body of a man on a hillside just behind Tubby Kalle's tavern. There was a narrow alley between Tubby Kalle's long privy and the next building, where a yard hand lived. People called it Old Man's Alley. At the bottom of the alley was a little slope used by the three or four nearest houses as a rubbish dump. That's where he lay. The sockets of his eyes were sticky, his black coat was spotted with snow mould. The frightening thing was that no one knew who he was.

It had come to that. A man could get off the train for some unknown reason, stop in at the bar-room at the inn, go from there to the nearest tavern, and end up at the last outpost, Tubby Kalle's. Get himself drunk and shown the door. Perhaps take a few reeling steps and, finally, slide down the slope and not be able to get up again. There he lay still, with his feet in a set of bed springs Kalle had tossed out last autumn. He might have frozen to death. Perhaps something else had happened. Doctor Didriksson would settle the question.

The Doctor and Pastor Borgström from Backe shared a trap to the village. It was Annunciation Day, the trap shook and rattled along the rutted track, and the mud stuck to the wheels. The two officials sat leaning in opposite directions, in dull resignation. Inertia and Acedia were in harness.

'I detest spring,' the doctor was thinking. 'That's when the corpses show up. Excrement flows like rivers. I hate spring, early spring. The time of death and denigration. It's ages before things start to grow again. They say that autumn is when things decompose, but that's wrong. Autumn brings frost, before which the earthworms have skilfully pulled the leaves into the ground. There's nothing but the rough earth, with its thin matted blanket of hibernating flora and fauna. The smell of spices.' The doctor tried to recollect this to brace himself for the task at hand.

The body had been borne across the station yard on a door, across the tracks and the market square, up the hill to the Agricultural Guild barn, where the cattle were kept on market days until they were sold or awarded prizes. Farmer Magnusson had built the barn for the Guild. He still owned it. It was the only truly public facility in the village that was not in the station yard. The pastor was going to hold a service in the barn loft, where a table had been covered with a white linen cloth with lace insets, a gift to the community from the wife of the former stationmaster. Borgström had some church candlesticks and a couple of candles with him in a black bag. Women dressed in black were already at hand and ready to arrange the silver.

They had swept the floor and straightened the chairs into rows. A chartreuse painting of a gently smiling Saviour hung between the two windows. Still, nothing could disguise the scents of tobacco and sweet powder that permeated the air. The windows wouldn't open — they were rotten and jammed shut. The parson, plagued, moved into the back room, where whist players, lecturers and rustic comedians drank beer and changed clothes before performing. Normally he sent his assistant to hold services in this godforsaken place, but unfortunate extenuating circumstances had compelled him to come along personally, and he was now so

74

distressed that he was perspiring in the damp heavy wool of his cassock.

It was ten o'clock. At the inn, Ozman Cantor and his assistants, who had held a magic show here the night before, were still asleep. Cantor, whose accent was a combination of German and an equally foreign Swedish dialect, had been very close to taking a beating during the performance, which was too miserable to satisfy even the low expectations of this community. In order to wring a little extra money out of his audience, he had brought with him a pig to raffle off. Most travelling entertainers had a raffle, but Cantor never dared to show his audience the pig, and that was probably wise. Magnusson himself, concerned that people might be smoking in the loft despite his prohibition, had gone up personally to have a look. He had watched the magician sweat for a while, watched his heavy, bruised assistants move suggestively so the powder flew hot and sweet off their bare arms.

'Those folks can't do no magic, except possibly with their bums,' he let slip, and this was enough to trigger some sniggers in the mounting atmosphere of dissatisfaction. Thus Magnusson saved Ozman Cantor from the violence that was brewing.

His assistants had spent the entire night performing the only magic tricks they knew for members of the audience, after which they had slept like the dead, still smelling of powder, and now one of them awoke, tormented by an incredible thirst. When she went out to find some water, she bumped into Edla, carrying a heavy basket. As usual when she went out, she was wearing the shawl Hanna had given her, with the ends crossed over her stomach and tied behind her back. They stared at one another for a moment before Edla walked out the door to cross the station yard in her leaking boots. She wouldn't wear her new ones in the spring mud.

Doctor Didriksson had poked unenthusiastically about in the corpse of the man in the Agricultural Guild barn and then, beside himself with disgust and nausea, turned it over to the barber surgeon and the vaccinator to continue if they pleased. Didriksson's predecessor as provincial physician had mostly served the estate, the manors, the captain's lodgings and the parsonages. His specialities had been gastric disturbances and migraine attacks. Didriksson had despised the old doctor for his dinner invitations and card-playing evenings, and had taken up his post two years earlier, with entirely different ambitions.

Soon enough, however, the railway hamlet took the sting out of his desire to serve a wider circle of humanity than hysterical parsons' wives. It seemed to him that the railway carried around all the claptrap and refuse that sifted down to the bottom of a society. They fell ill in the waiting rooms and then, with any luck, died in the overnight rooms of the inn. His mission of saving lives seemed to him more and more questionable. There was nowhere to put lives that could no longer be carted around by the national railway company. At the provincial hospital half of the patients were already people suffering from venereal disease.

He did not know, and never would, who the man found on the slope behind Tubby Kalle's had been. He was indifferent to the cause of death, but his guess was intoxication and exposure. He walked up the already extremely well-worn staircase in Magnusson's sloppily-built structure, found the parson and sat down with him in the little room where magicians put on their costumes and where the clerical alb and stole were now lying across two chairs.

76

'This village needs a policeman,' Didriksson said.

'True, true,' said the parson, feeling tired at the very thought of all the social issues this corpse raised. One of them was the question of where to bury him. It would not do to bury an unidentified person in the Backe graveyard, the farmers wouldn't have it. This one could be shipped to Nyköping on the pretext that the provincial physician would have the resources to carry out a more informative autopsy, and hopefully they wouldn't return it.

Someone knocked on the door, as softly as if a bird had tapped it with its claw, and the pastor called 'Come in.' Edla opened the door and stood there, with a runny nose and carrying a hamper.

'I've brought the parson's meal,' she said, and both dignitaries stared at her. The pastor had no idea that his assistant had an arrangement with the inn. When he arrived cold and stiff on Sunday mornings in a far less pretentious cart than the one the pastor had hired, he began by having a little breakfast sent from the inn. Either Edla or Valfrid brought it up to the Guild loft in a hamper. He would have a flask of oatmeal gruel, stuffed into a stocking to keep it warm. The prunes floating in the gruel tended to get stuck in the neck of the flask. Fru Isaksson had put cold pork, sausage, eggs and cubes of smoked ham between slices of dark bread. The doctor and the pastor poked around in the hamper, laughing at the idea of the pastor's assistant sitting here every week, freezing in front of the little stove, eating all by himself. It was about as simple and coarse a breakfast as one could imagine, and they had no intention of eating any of it. But somehow the pastor broke off a piece of rye bread, and then began to eat the smoked ham, one cube at a time. The doctor lit his pipe, and the pastor sneezed loudly from the dust and the grains of powder floating in a ray of sun from the window of the loft.

That sneeze was a release. The pastor perked up more than he had in years. He felt as if he had been transported back to his student garret in Uppsala, and the doctor with his puffing pipe full of tobacco served to reinforce the illusion. The two gentlemen began to discuss religion, a subject the pastor hadn't debated in thirty years. The doctor found himself getting caught up in the spirit. He grew sarcastic and ironic, and was excessively and youthfully blasphemous as he tried to put theology in its place. In fact, he was suddenly more youthful than he had ever been in Uppsala. They spoke of the text for Annunciation Day, the most sensitive theological issue of them all.

'Tell me now, brother, what you intend to say to the wives of the stationmaster and the postmaster today — not to mention the wife of the yard master — on the subject of the Jewish girl of thirteen or fourteen in Nazareth, and of her fate.'

'Don't call it fate! We must recall that she had a choice,' said the parson, enlivened by the acrid tone of voice of the physician. 'She embraced the angel's message. We must recall that the Holy Spirit gave Mary a choice, he wasn't commanding her. My sermon will be based on the idea that God gives mankind a choice, and it is up to man to decide whether to respond in the affirmative. That's the Gospel. That's the miracle. Compulsion and commandments were the attributes of Judaism.'

'A nice thought,' said the doctor. 'But I'm sure, brother, you know just as well as I do that when Mary says yes, her answer is merely pro forma. Our lives are regulated by laws. If nature doesn't get her way, she resorts to coercion.'

Edla sat by the door waiting for the hamper which the gentlemen absent-mindedly emptied of everything but the gruel. She had no idea what they were talking about. They called the virgin Mary a Jewish girl of thirteen or fourteen. Was Jesus' mother the daughter of a Jew-peddler who sold clocks and old clothing at market? She didn't understand, didn't want to understand.

The doctor's eyes met Edla's. His gaze happened to fall on the girl by the door and for a few seconds they looked one another in the eye. He was startled and disturbed by what he saw, but he quickly put it out of his mind. At that age, children change so fast. He was caught in a hiatus between the theological discussion, with its tobacco smoke and its intoxicating freedom, and this Sunday in early spring with its mess of slushy snow. Out of sheer politeness he would have to sit through Borgström's sermon in the loft of the cattle barn of the Agricultural Guild.

He suddenly knew he would never make it through the sermon. He no longer cared what the parson thought, but rose and made his apologies. On his way down the rickety staircase he met the barber surgeon and the vaccinator, who were extremely upset. While examining the corpse they had pried open the man's jaws and had a look inside. The deceased had a communion wafer in his mouth.

That was the Sunday Edla got home to Appleton frozen through and with soaked feet after a dreary pilgrimage through the melting snow. Her eyes were black and glistened with fever, and Sara Sabina looked at her over her shoulder several times as she was making the fire. Nothing was said, however, mostly because the soldier was sitting in his seat by the window, holding forth. He went on about how his ability to formulate a letter had led to that wonderful domestic position for Edla. 'I wish you'd shut up,' the old woman thought, but she didn't say that, either. When it came right down to it, she did not think it was good for a daughter to hear a mother shout at the king of creation.

One of the ewes was in labour, and Edla went out to the sheep shed to see if her time had come. When she didn't return, they thought she had left for the inn without further ado. Edla never made a fuss. But the young girl had, in fact, climbed into the ewe's pen and laid two burlap bags over the straw. The ewe was all the way over in the other corner, head down, staring at her. Edla had decided to stay and see how it happened.

When Edla decided to do something, she took it seriously. She had long ago learned to ward off fear by making one little decision after another, and by implementing them promptly and uncompromisingly. She often impressed Valfrid, who tended to be frazzled and to run around mindlessly, fretting about what might go wrong. When he was worried, he could easily set the storehouse on fire, or cut off his thumb, or drop the key to the innkeeper's desk into the treacle barrel.

Still, the lengthiness of the ewe's labour was wearing away at Edla's grave concentration. The abdomen was distended and the udder was tense and hard. Edla was sure she had been sitting there for at least an hour, but nothing was happening. Against her will, and against her every intention, fear began to prickle her skin.

The ewe was in pain. Something was wrong. It was as if Valfrid were sitting beside her, whispering and egging her on. 'Can't you see something's gone wrong?' She must have seen animals give birth before, but she hadn't paid attention to the details. There was one thing she knew: it didn't usually take so long.

Hours must have passed, and the ewe was still standing there patiently bearing her pain. Edla could hear the cows silently chewing their cud on the other side of the wall. If she looked up at the opening, the daylight coming through the crack blinded her. The spring sun was baking the outside walls of the sheep shed, waking the nettles and insects to life.

Did the ewe know or not? Could she remember? And if this was her first time, how could she be so patient? As if she already understood: this was the pain I was born for. It's no use fighting. She rolled with the waves of pain, pulling her head back, shutting her eyes. She let the pain rule her, without asking what good it would do.

The hours passed. The udder was shiny and ready to burst, the teats were swollen and their colour shifted from rose to purple. She stamped, scraped her front hooves, walked round and round in the bed of straw, and lay down heavily. Now her belly was part of her again. Earlier, it had hung far below her, looking as if it didn't belong to the same body as her sharp backbone. She pulled back her upper lip as the ram had done when he mounted her, except that hers was drawn back in pain. Edla did not expect her to stand up again. She was so heavy and the contractions were so strong that she would not be able to stand again until it was over.

Yet there she was, on her legs again. She stood still for a long time scraping one hoof, holding her head stiffly to one side. Her back arched in pain. A violent contraction hit, and she bowed her head submissively, her big, dark eyes no longer seeing Edla or anything in the world around her. Her gaze was rigid, shadowed by her white eyelashes.

Her haunches seemed to grow heavier and heavier. Time and again she drew back her lip. Once, a ball of cud came up, but she swallowed it down without chewing. Then she dropped. Sounds began to come out of her, she moaned softly and regularly, her ears pulled back. Her gaze was dull and much lighter now, her pupils contracted to slits.

Edla leaned her head against the timbered wall. She was extremely drowsy, at the same time as she was inexplicably frightened. The next time she looked, the ewe was standing again, standing perfectly still with her head extended. 'This is going to go on forever,' Edla thought, dimly fearful. Time and again she fell, her belly heavy, and each time it was increasingly difficult for her to stand up again. 'Dear, sweet Lord, why does it have to be this way? Poor creature.' The ewe gasped in pain, silently opening her jaws wide. There was stretching and creaking, but she did not voice her agony.

The country mice were having a heyday around the drowsy Edla. They ran close past her feet and played in the straw she had spread out. The tail of the ewe stood straight out. Edla stared, only half awake, at the opening of her genitals. It was pale red and runny, and its folds and creases were in motion. She felt as if she had been staring at the hole for hours. The ewe gasped in pain, opened her jaws painfully wide and moaned. She was lying on her side, working, her legs stretched out straight. Her stomach rumbled, vibrating with air between the contractions. But why in the name of God was it taking so long?

Suddenly she saw a bright red bubble protruding from the hole. The ewe rose and bore down. Inside a tough membrane sac the colour of deep saffron, lay the lamb, legs curled, apparently lifeless. At that moment, Edla, sick with dread, realized what a still birth was.

She had barely begun to take it in when the ewe turned around and poked at the sac with her muzzle, uttering a three-syllable sound Edla had never heard before, a soft, safe sound. The new-born lamb kicked. It was alive. Edla wept with queasiness and joy and exhaustion. A second kick — but it looked as if the lamb would suffocate. No, the ewe began to lick the thick yellow membrane off its baby's head, constantly uttering those soft three-syllable sounds, chuckling. The lamb responded the moment its head was free, with a soft little scream, and then it wobbled blindly towards the udder, still half covered with the thick yellow foetal sac.

'No that was not what I thought it would be like,' thought Edla, as she climbed out of the stall, her stiff legs all pins and needles. 'Not a bit. Very, very different.' She had learned something. Out in the sunshine, she tried to sneak past the house and make her way down to the road without being seen from the window. She had learned. A woman who was giving birth must not rebel. She must work patiently, for pain is a strict taskmaster. See, I am the servant of the Lord. His will be done.

In mid-May Edla saw another birth. She came home to Appleton right in the middle of a working week, asked for her mother and was told she was at farmer Old Mothstead's, scrubbing down the cowshed.

Edla walked all the way there hearing neither the lark nor the cuckoo. She was white around the lips. When she walked into the darkness of the cowshed from the bright spring day outside, she was blinded. She heard her mother's voice:

'Have you taken sick?'

She nodded. Now she could discern the shape of her mother over there, as grey as if she had been broken out of a block of stone.

'Mother! Can you come home?'

Her girlish voice rung sharply in the stinking darkness. She sank to the floor — Edla, who was always so careful not to soil her dress or her shawl. Now she could see that the farmer himself was there too, standing behind the rear of one cow who had been kept back when the others were let out to graze. She had just calved, but was shut inside the stall, unable to reach her baby to lick it clean. Old Mothstead swished a bundle of straw around the muck under her back legs and threw it to her to chew. He tossed the limp calf onto an empty sack and pulled it away. The chained cow strained to get loose.

'What is it?' her mother asked, pulling Edla to her feet. 'Are you sick? Go on home, I'll be along as soon as I can.'

Edla grasped at the stalls for support. The new-born calf was lying at the far end. Old Mothstead had wiped him down with the sack, but he was still damp. He was trembling fiercely and his muzzle sought blindly in the straw, time and again, for a warmth he would not find.

'Mother, you'll have to come,' said Edla. 'There's no two ways about it. I can't manage on my own.'

She leaned on her mother all the way home. She gave birth that evening. All night she slept deeply, exhausted from her difficult labour. The next morning when Sara Sabina tried to show Edla her new-born daughter she was feverish and didn't seem to understand what had happened. She died on the third day.

H e's coming home. Get down his plate. Save all the pork just for him. Go up to the loft and get to bed, he's coming.'

She never called him Grandpa. Tora didn't know he was. Father, no that was out of the question. Perhaps one of the older boys might have called him that.

'He's off to Malmköping.' Tora listened. 'He's leaving.' Didn't she hear a brighter tone then, a tremor of pleasure? Just a hint. Once a year he went off to a party when Löfgren, the saddlemaker, had his birthday celebration. Tora was allowed to brush his uniform jacket and polish his buttons, just as if he were going to Malmköping. He took off his worsted trousers and the blue cap of the uniform he'd worn as a district soldier, and put on his dress uniform in its place, waxing his moustache. A full day of eating awaited him, and a permissible, almost sanctioned, drunken bash. With the only cell for solitary confinement being a shady lilac arbour.

At home they were always famished. The old woman put hen feathers in the bread tin to keep the children from snitching. Oddly, her kids had always been put off by feathers. Even her first batch. They had left home now, and two had died. Edla's daughter Tora called Sara Sabina Mother. Perhaps she knew no better.

Just a little over a year after Edla's death, Sara Sabina had given birth to a boy she named Rickard. It may not have been as great a miracle as the one her namesake in the Bible experienced, but it was a miracle nonetheless, and provoked many a knowing smile. If one counted backwards it was clear that this miracle had taken place on Midsummer when the ferns bloom and lots of other things happen that could not possibly take place any other night of the year. And Midsummer's Eve was the date of the saddlemaker's party, too.

In later years, Sara Sabina had begun to go along, taking Rickard and Tora. She had huge skirt pockets. Besides what she could take home, she counted on her youngsters to have the good sense to eat whatever they got their hands on. Lans couldn't object to her going, since it was not he who was related to the saddlemaker. Sara Sabina was his cousin, while the soldier's own roots disappeared quickly into murky anonymity. At the party, he tended to get drunker than most, but also to be more amusing. Although he wasn't even part of the family, he still told the story of his life to anyone who was willing to listen. He came from nowhere and had no idea who his mother was, he would say. It was probably just the usual old story of some poor young girl who left him on the doorstep, but he made it sound marvellous and strange. He had grown up in a distant parish and his first memory was of the big barn at the farm at Kedevi. He had lived there with the farmhand in a little room next to the milking shed until he was twelve. He would also describe the long pilgrimage from Kedevi to Vallmsta and how he fell down from a fir tree when August Wilhelm Johansson, the murderer, was executed.

That was a story Tora had already heard many times. But whether he was her father or her grandfather she did not yet know. Stories, however, are wiser than we, and more mindful, and slowly they change us. Much of what she needed to know in life, she had already heard. When they went to the party, she and Rickard slept on a bolster on the floor in the saddlemaker's workshop. Sara Sabina had wanted to bed her kids down in the straw, but Löfgren's wife felt sorry for them and led them into the workshop, where she laid a rustling straw-filled bolster on the floor. There was a smell of tar, and the window was open, onto the garden and the night. Birds were screeching in the distance. They could hear soldier Lans carrying on, and Tora listened sleepily. She always liked the beginning of his stories best.

It was on the morning of Easter Sunday when the sun was dancing, he would say. Or this happened two days before Midsummer's night when the ferns bloom. This was better than lying in the loft at home listening, because here he never got angry. He forgot they were there. Tora and Rickard lay on the bolster in the workshop, drawn as tightly together as the yarn in a skein.

At home, Lans would say that Rickard was just one big misfortune. The old woman's wrinkled body had produced him for no other reason than to give people a good laugh. Could be. But why Tora had come into the world he never said. He seldom noticed her. Only once in a while.

'Oh, Edla, she died, did our Edla,' he would say. 'Yes indeed.'

His eyes blinked, red and runny. There was so much you couldn't figure out. Truly. Boil a white snake and drink the broth, and you'll know everything. But you still won't understand.

It wasn't yet much of a Midsummer's morning. The sun had risen in a clear sky, now shadowed with rapid little clouds rushing incessantly from east to west. A housemaid with two pails slung over her shoulder came out onto the steps of the stationmaster's house and shivered. The grey wooden steps were spotted with raindrops, but she couldn't feel any rain in the air when she turned her face towards the wind.

On the other side of the tracks only the milkman's dog was up and about. He walked stiffly between the buildings, peeing against the hitching post in front of the warehouse. There wasn't much to be heard beyond the sound of the slowly running water in Trash Moat. The housemaid whose blood ran equally slowly at this early hour was just standing there staring vacantly ahead. The sound of clogs clattering against the wooden ties between the rails roused her, and she headed for the pump. On the other side, an old woman came out of a house and emptied a chamber pot over the fence right into her neighbour's chives. She practically had to vault over to reach, and slammed the door angrily when she went back in. The banging of tin milk pails from the dairy was followed by neighing and soft monotonous creaking as the blind horse began his rounds.

The workers came down paths and roads and muddy cart tracks across the field towards Wilhelmsson's carpentry shop. Ebon Johansson walked alongside his elder brother, but the closer they came, the further behind he lagged. In the end, he stopped in front of the gate, amongst the crowd of boys who waited each morning to see if there was work. Ebon was fourteen, however, and actually too old to stand with the boys. He was embarrassed, and stood to one side when the foreman came out to inspect the crowd.

'Five of you!' he said, and they all stood tall. You couldn't smell of drink or have tobacco juice running down your chin. The foreman himself couldn't care less, but sometimes Wilhelmsson, who was one of the founders of the Society for Workers' Enlightenment and Decency, would come out personally and check them over very carefully before they were taken on. The boys who had learned not to gape like fools in public were often the ones who were hired, since Wilhelmsson couldn't get a look in their mouths.

Since Ebon was not hired, he headed for the station. He could hear the saw blades beginning to cut the wood. He made wild faces to scare a couple of little kids who came running across the tracks, but they just made faces back at him. He recognized them, they were soldier Lans' kids, and they flew over Trash Moat so fast their feet didn't seem to touch the planks. He went and stood by a coal dock where the brakemen usually waited to see who would get work in the mornings. In this group, though, he was too young and didn't stand much of a chance. He stood poking the toe of his shoe in the ground. The sole had come loose and the soft coal dust slid in between his toes. A train came in from the south. He moved closer to watch.

When the crowd, with its bundles and baskets, had dispersed, a little man in a black coat remained. He had a stubbly beard and carried a walking stick. Three rucksacks lay at his feet. Ebon thought it was worth keeping an eye on him, since he would have to go somewhere sooner or later.

90

One of his boot heels was built up, so he must have a limp, and Ebon looked forward to seeing how he walked.

'Young fella,' the man suddenly shouted, without moving along. There was no doubt, however, that he was pointing his walking stick at Ebon, who just stared back.

'Come over here, fella,' the man said, and despite his strange way of speaking he sounded like a stationmaster at the very least.

' 'Scuse me?' asked Ebon.

'Are you idle, fella?'

Ebon gurgled indecisively in response, since he didn't know where the question was leading.

'Are you nimble?'

'Yea ....no,' answered Ebon, wondering if that was the same thing Baron Cederfalk means when he asked if you were a quick young man and could run and get some oil for the oilcans. Otherwise maybe he meant quick, like quick in the head.

'Would you like to sell papers?' the man asked.

He gave Ebon two of the rucksacks and they went off to the waiting room so fast that he never got to see what the man's limp was like. The bags were opened on a wooden bench. They contained newspapers and more newspapers, almost nothing else. Ebon glimpsed a night-shirt, shaving things and a few books. But now things were happening fast. A sizeable bundle of newspapers called *The People's Voice* was stuck under one of his arms. He was told an address to report to, and what his commission would be. In all the rush, not much penetrated.

'Try selling them to the workers during their dinner break. What else does this town have besides the carpentry shop? The workshop? Run now, as furious as you can!'

One of the station booking clerks had seen them through the ticket window and put on his uniform cap. He approached, hands behind his back. Ebon ran as fast as his flapping sole would allow.

Now the morning was far enough advanced for Baron Gustaf Adolf Cederfalk of the railway to get up out of his bed and have his hot water and razor brought in on a towel. Before the housemaid could get out with the chamber pot, Cederfalk had removed his India cotton night-shirt displaying, as if by coincidence, his large red sexual organ rising up at an angle between his little pale round belly and his scrawny thighs. He enjoyed exhibiting himself to the housemaid whenever he was fast enough. But if he gave her too much trouble she would refuse to come upstairs, and then old Botilda from down below would stamp painfully and angrily back up with his chamber pot. If Cederfalk hadn't noticed and was expecting the girl, he would be standing there with his shirt over his head, and Botilda would splash water and mutter 'Oh Lordy me, Oh me, oh my' as loudly as she dared. Cederfalk pulled the shirt down fast to cover his private parts, shouting:

'Out, you old hag, until I'm decent. Have you no shame?'

Sometimes you could hear him outside. His open window was on the gable side, and covered with honeysuckle.

A train rushed in and the two children from Appleton, now on their way home again, ran across the tracks in front of the locomotive, racing against the thick coke smoke. They were each carrying one handle of a basket with a piece of white paper spread across the top to protect the contents.

Working lads with tin pails boarded the train for Norrköping, to get the aquavit for the holiday weekend.

Out in the station yard, Mamsell Winlöf and merchant Lindh met. Mamsell was walking her little Parisina in the bushes, and the children stopped at a distance to stare, since from far off the dog looked as if she were shorn down to her skin. Mamsell inspected Tora with her sharp brown eyes, and then called to her. But the girl did not approach until Lindh, who was known for his kindness to children, had removed his coin purse from his pocket. Mamsell looked attentively at Tora's face, at her fair, pulled-back hair with curls dangling at her temples, and at her checked dress of homespun cloth in dark colours that wouldn't show the dirt. She looked straight into the young girl's serious blue eyes and asked her her name and age. Tora answered in monosyllables.

'Well then,' said Mamsell, brushing them off as if waving away a troublesome insect from her face. But Lindh had opened the purse his wife Caroline had crocheted for him, and the children stood still like dogs waiting for a treat.

'Where are you going?' he asked kindly.

'Home.'

'And where have you been?' he asked, smiling at Mamsell over their heads.

'To the ironing-woman to pick up some starch for the parson's at Vallmsta.'

'That's a long walk for such short legs.'

'Mother's going to do the parson's laundry, and she'll bring his collars home,' said Tora.

'She's not going to do laundry on Midsummer's Eve, surely?' Mamsell asked suspiciously.

'No, but she's going to soak it,' the girl replied promptly.

'All right then,' said Lindh, placing a five öre coin in the hand Rickard extended in the wink of an eye. They lifted their basket and flew off.

'Stop, you two! You've forgotten the most important thing of all.'

They stopped and stared at him.

'Say thank you,' said Mamsell impatiently.

Tora curtsied, her mouth tightly closed, while Rickard still couldn't get a word out.

'Right, off you go,' said Lindh. Perhaps Mamsell was angry, she just nodded curtly at him and went inside with Parisina. He continued on to the stationmaster's house where the local council was to meet at nine o'clock. He was in an excellent humour. He had walked into town from Goatwood, which had been re-named Gertrudsborg seven years earlier. Out there his wife lived far enough away from town to be out of sight and out of mind. Mamsell Winlöf had long ago accepted these altered circumstances or, rather, that circumstances had remained unchanged. A remarkable woman.

Eight o'clock came and went, and the lame agitator whom Ebon had mistaken for a preacher was putting up a poster on the side of the Agricultural Guild barn. Down at the carpentry shop, Ebon was crouching huddled up against the fence, his pile of newspapers close at hand, waiting for the workers to come out for their dinner break. Just then, Petrus Wilhelmsson came by. Ebon had been dozing and when he woke groggily, there was Wilhelmsson, standing in front of him reading *The People's Voice*. Ebon saw him from a frog's eye view, which made his straight legs in their tight checked trousers appear extraordinarily long.

'Come into my office,' said Wilhelmsson

'Well, I was only just... I'd thought... on the dinner break...' Ebon stammered. The man said nothing. His shoulders hunched, he led the way across the yard with long strides. Workers staggering under heavy loads of planks couldn't possibly step aside, so Wilhelmsson and Ebon had to zigzag over to the office building.

Once inside, Ebon had a long wait. He didn't dare put down his pile of papers. His arm fell asleep and he couldn't remove his cap.

Wilhelmsson sat there writing. Behind him on the wall were invoices and freight bills spiked on wire hooks. He used a simple tin pen, a glass inkwell and a sand blotter. He wrote on the cheapest sort of yellow straw paper, and at regular intervals he would get little bits of straw in the point of his pen and have to stop and clean it. He used a piece of felt that looked like a three-cornered pouch.

'How many papers do you have in your bundle?' he barked.

'A hundred,' Ebon nearly shouted. His mouth was dry. He was afraid he might wet himself.

'I'll give you five kronor for the lot.'

Ebon was gaping. Wilhelmsson went on wiping the point of his pen on the little triangle of felt, spotted with blue ink.

'Leave 'em over there.'

He pointed with the pen handle.

'Can you get me more?'

'Yessir.'

Fright made him eager, and he almost went off without being paid. Somehow he took the five kronor note and

95

crumpled it into his trouser pocket, realizing at that very moment that he should also tip his cap.

'Thank you!'

He recalled that his brother Valfrid, who was Isaksson's shop boy, said that in the business world people said 'my most sincerest thanks', but he couldn't get the words out. He rushed off to the house where blacksmith Eriksson's widow rented out rooms, and accounted for his sales to the agitator.

'Well done, m'lad,' the little man burst out in surprise. 'They must've ripped 'em out of your hands.'

Ebon scurried off with another hundred copies of *The People's Voice*. He ran back and forth until all the papers were gone. Wilhelmsson had told him not to bring more than a hundred at a time. That was the only condition. And Ebon was shocked to be paid five kronor every single time by this man who was said to be so miserly that he ate his gruel with an awl.

Not entirely without good cause did Valfrid Johansson consider his brother Ebon an idiot. So he could hardly believe his eyes when he saw his brother enter Isaksson's general store, moving with studied lethargy, waving a fistful of bills, the commission for his morning's newspaper sales. His gaping shoe sole pointed in the air as he walked. For a moment the coffee beans went on rattling into the bag of their own momentum, while Valfrid stood staring.

'Where'd all that money come from?'

Ebon told him. At that moment the innkeeper stuck his head through the door, asking routinely what was going on. He didn't expect an answer.

Valfrid liked to read. He read pamphlets on propellers and Morse code, electricity, apes, combustion engines and the life of Jesus. He knew what had gone on at the deathbed of Tsar Nicholas I and when Siemens made his first experiments with the electric railway in Berlin. It was only in the last couple of years he had developed this taste for great events and world progress. At Ebon's age he had still been lying with one hand under the quilt reading *The Spectre, The Pounding Heart, Tales from the Abyss, Memoirs of a Streetwalker* and other such tracts. All the while, his jaws had been masticating an intensely sweet mixture of sugar rock, raisins and broken biscuits from the shop. All that was long ago now, though. The previous evening he had read until the very last light was gone from his garret window, and the booklet he stuck under his pillow was called *How an Individual May Turn the Tide of History*.

'Idiot!' he said to Ebon, struck by how grotesquely reality could distort the truths contained in his pamphlets. 'Haven't you ever heard of socialism?'

'Yeah, that's when they take away everything you own,' Ebon promptly relied. 'Don't let you keep so much as a soup spoon.'

'You moron!' Valfrid moaned, one hand across his forehead to indicate the vertigo he experienced when leaning over the abyss of ignorance his brother represented. At that very moment, he also became aware of just how warmly he sympathized with socialism.

'Right! And now you've seen to it that not a soul in this community will ever know what socialism is. Aren't you pleased with yourself?'

'What's going on here?' the innkeeper shouted again through the doorway, and this time it was clear that he wanted an answer, so Ebon flapped out of the shop.

Actually, he was a young man of fairly good sense, so good that not even the terror he had felt in Wilhelmsson's office could restrain it for long. He recalled that a couple of years ago Wilhelmsson had paid two hundred kronor to the village for a license to serve beer. Yet he served no beer, he just wanted to be sure that the other three applications for licenses would be turned down. As Ebon had run back and forth between the agitator's and the carpentry workshop with the newspapers, he had gradually begun to understand. His conscience began to feel as porous and slushy as old snow in March. That was why he had pulled out the most reactionary definition of socialism he knew of when Valfrid asked. He'd heard it from Scrub-Ärna, who barely had a soup spoon to her name. Now Ebon went to Levander's shop in great haste and spent his entire commission before his conscience could get so muddy that he would step into it and get stuck. He sat on a coal dock with his provisions, thinking.

No, Valfrid was wrong. Pale blue semi-starvation had clouded Ebon's senses for thirteen years. Now that he needed to think, he discovered he was able to. He decided to find his brother Wilhelm, who worked at the carpentry shop.

On Alexander Lindh's desk, there was a bronze eagle holding a vanquished hare in its mighty claws. The eagle was poised upright, the image of bold, decisive action. The hare, however, was stretched out on a bronze plaque almost lasciviously, staring intently, his limbs hanging limply from his torn abdomen. Lindh often placed his hand on the eagle's head when he was being emphatic, and after seven years its bald head glistened. Right now Lindh was grasping his eagle nervously.

The local council and Doctor Didriksson were on their way into his office. He had moved the meeting from the stationmaster's to his own office, but would not believe his plans had worked until Cederfalk was actually seated. Stationmaster Cederfalk was the village champion of law and order, and chairman of the local council. Right now he was still standing, under the portrait of the most enlightened monarch in Europe, his hands behind his back. He was extremely displeased.

Lindh now rented a full floor office suite from Magnusson the contractor. When Mamsell Winlöf's serving girls entered with their hampers, the contents of which clinked under linen serviettes, the sound of their approaching steps could be heard from three rooms away. The staff stood writing at pulpits and desks. Lindh had enticed the council across the tracks with the promise of breakfast.

Baron Fogel, the railway clerk, rubbed his hands together over the hampers. He and Didriksson were gluttons, and had been easiest to tempt across the tracks. Magnusson had not come, and Lindh had intentionally told Petrus Wilhelmsson the wrong time. He was a teetotaller and would not be enticed by a breakfast. This had been Lindh's boldest move, and might easily be exposed. The vaccinator and the barber surgeon had also been told to arrive one hour later, as Lindh could not expect Cederfalk and Fogel to breakfast in their company. They, the local council and the doctor were to make an inspection tour of the hamlet to see that the regulations of the board for health and hygiene were being complied with. Power, glory and railway uniforms all had to be brandished to coerce the villagers to use garbage bins and latrine pails instead of pits and hillsides.

The serving girls from the railway hotel, dressed in black, spread a tablecloth across the desk, and Fogel clapped his hands in delight. The scents of clean linen and warm female flesh arose, along with the aroma of aquavit spiced with cumin and fish boiled with bay leaves. The girls loosened hake in aspic from its form, and lifted cut radishes out of a bowl of ice water. They opened like roses at room temperature. There were sliced ham and two kinds of herring, fresh bread and mature cheese. The butter was in a double-walled clay crock and was cold and bright yellow. The serving girls collected the empty hampers and curtsied as they departed, received a tip from Lindh and curtsied once again. This woke Cederfalk from his reverie, and he dug out his leather wallet and gave the girls each a coin. That was the moment at which Alexander Lindh was able to breathe a sigh of relief and invite the gentlemen to sit down.

'Cheers,' said Fogel. 'Have a spicy *eau de vie*. It will blunt your sense of smell for what we have ahead.'

Fogel and Cederfalk inclined their heads towards each other, two tall, upright men in uniform. Cederfalk's belly was small and round, ornamented with a gold chain. His uniform jacket and dark-blue vest were form-fitted across the arch of his belly. Didriksson was just as tall as the other two, but heavy set, and breathing heavily. Alexander Lindh was the shortest, but his powerful body conveyed considerable force.

A door in the outer office suddenly flew open, panes of glass rattled, and they heard Magnusson's deep voice and the pounding of his square-toed boots as he marched straight through the office, causing the terrified staff to rise halfway to their feet. He was waving a rolled-up paper, and he swore as he tossed it onto Lindh's desk, taking no notice of the meal. It stuck forcefully in the fish aspic.

'Read this!'

'All those who despise royalty, the insanity of warfare and the power of the clergy are invited to a meeting on Midsummer's Eve at seven o'clock. Should there be rain, the meeting will be held in the loft of the Agricultural Guild barn,' Fogel read, his voice dripping with sarcasm. 'Ah well, the least we can do is to rescue the aspic, for heaven's sake.'

He carefully dislodged the poster and folded it around the consommé cubes that had stuck to the back. He held it towards the door where the office personnel were glowering, and the crowd parted, making way for Fröken Tyra Hedberg, the only female member of the office staff. She pushed up her dress sleeves before accepting the roll.

'Lundbom, that idiot! Whoever allowed the Guild to hire him? Still, that barn belongs to me!' Magnusson shouted.

'No one said it didn't.'

'We will naturally see to it that this meeting does not take place, but there is no cause for such alarm,' said Cederfalk, returning to his post under the portrait of the monarch, scrutinizing Magnusson critically.

'I've already seen to it! That barn belongs to me and no revolutionary meetings will be held in it.'

'Well then,' said Cederfalk. 'The matter appears to have been dealt with. Personally, I might add that I believe our workers are too wise to be caught up in all this social democratic madness. It's bait only very hungry fish would take.'

Alexander Lindh agreed, but said nothing. He had walked over and positioned himself under the other portrait in his office, an oil painting of his father, recently made from a photograph. His father had now been dead for ten years. The artist had made foundry owner Lindh's legs far too long and his head much too large, but this was, after all, his first human being. He was a painter of elks. Lindh was listening without listening. The details passed him by. Magnusson carried on and was reprimanded. He demolished the radishes. Beer glasses clinked, Fogel helped himself to herring titbits with a long pointed fork and said that whoever this Lundbom was he appeared to be a supporter of the workers. 'An idiot! Just an ordinary idiot,' Magnusson reassured him with his mouth full, and passed the beer to Cederfalk, advising him to cool off. The stationmaster smiled tolerantly. Lindh stood under his father, who had been depicted with legs far too long, like the king of the forest, and silently thanked his lucky stars that an agitator had come to Magnusson's Agricultural Guild barn. For now the local council had met in his office for the first time and no one had even raised the question of whether it was a suitable venue.

T heir portraits have long since been painted and hung. Cederfalk with his hand inserted in his blue vest, his moustache wings waxed into a V pointing in the opposite direction from the one on his uniform cap. His eyes are white and blue enamel, like the sign on the door: peddlers prohibited. But the portrait was a lie even as it was being painted, since little blood vessels had burst and become visible; the enamel was spotted with rust and yellow streaks, and his robust, healthy complexion with its good circulation was already the same shade as pale butter in winter.

So few people around him. Just housemaids, filthy, scrofulous, thick-lipped children and sour-smelling workers. In the mornings he often descended to these circles of Hades, pulling up his night-shirt. But as the sun rose so did his vigilance.

Under the fly-tent on the dining room table, seven or eight flies buzzed dully, intoxicated by the smell and the vapours of arrack. They drowned in the amber liqueur, their movements heavy and increasingly slow.

Alexander Lindh had his portrait painted standing behind his Bachara carpet, so that its red radiance would be reflected in his visage. But it was impossible to depict his vigour, his sober, dry scent of healthy skin and clean nails, his abstention.

His community was a circular flower bed set in polished, white quartz. At the outer edge were little green plants. Row upon row continued towards the centre; the low, brown

African marigolds, the unpretentious sprays of baby's breath, candytuft and straw flowers. No row intruded on the space of the adjacent one; the purple sprite bowed down, its tall fans shading the Enchantment lily when it was most vulnerable. This tiered arrangement extended inwards with deep blue aconite and globe thistle. At the very middle stood the hardy, fruitful green stalks of maize.

The postmaster's wife had a circle of her own. In the thick winter's dusk, before the snow fell, her maize stalks went on rustling.

Embankment Brita's eldest son Valentin sometimes worked in Lindh's storehouse, running errands with a wheelbarrow, his wooden clogs clattering. He had been born hare-lipped, but Didriksson had stitched it up. Valentin was just pulling a cart to the carpentry shop, accompanied by Ebon. When they got to the gates, Ebon stopped. He wasn't allowed inside. His brother Wilhelm had a job in there, carrying planks. Wilhelm had been hanging around for an hour already, and had been reprimanded twice. When Valentin arrived with the cart, Wilhelm changed directions with his heavy load and approached them.

'It's over there,' he said, nodding in the direction of the stairs up to the office. 'Hurry up.'

The foreman had already noticed him, so Wilhelm bent to his burden again and vanished among the piles of boards.

The factory owner was leaving as Valentin arrived. The foreman was on his way up the stairs to grab Valentin by the shirttails to prevent this unfortunate encounter. But it was too late.

'I've come for the paper for the plaster ceiling ornaments,' Valentin stammered, breathless and hare-lipped.

'Pardon?'

'Merchant Lindh needs some paper. He's in a tight corner. He'd forgotten they were to be shipped on the twelve o'clock train.'

'Did you say the merchant had forgotten?' Wilhelmsson asked suspiciously.

'Not him. Fredriksson at the warehouse. But the merchant's in a tight corner because he doesn't have anything to pack the plaster ceiling ornaments in. They're supposed to be shipped on the twelve o'clock train.'

'Is it wood fibre he needs? Sawdust? What exactly?'

'Paper, said Valentin. 'Ordinary newsprint will be fine, sir, if you've got some. Easier to pack.'

'We've got no paper here.'

'He's willing to pay ...'

'Newsprint?'

'Yes, please, newspaper's quite all right,' said Valentin, staring Wilhelmsson straight in the eye until the older man finally turned around and looked at the piles of newspapers on the floor.

Outside the gates, Ebon had not expected the factory owner to be on his way out. When Valentin returned, his cart loaded with copies of *The People's Voice* and Wilhelmsson walking alongside him, Ebon almost rushed straight into his arms in his excitement. He caught himself in time to drop back amongst the nettles along the fence until he was so low that not even the brim of his cap could be seen. The nettles stank and stung but he held out.

A rain shower sprayed the roofs and the market place, which had been harrowed and sown with grass in the spring but was unprotected because there were no trees. One of merchant Lindh's messenger boys caught up with Wilhelmsson before he crossed the tracks to say that the meeting was being held at Lindh's office instead. Wilhelmsson thought nothing of it, wanting only to get in out of the rain as fast as possible. He had no sooner entered the vestibule when he met Alexander Lindh, carrying the agitator's poster, which Fröken Tyra had cleaned.

'Oh, that fellow's been causing me some trouble, too,' said Wilhelmsson. 'Did you get the newsprint?'

'What newsprint?'

'Hasn't it arrived yet?'

Then he was silent, staring hard at Lindh.

'Aren't you shipping plaster ceiling roses on the twelve o'clock train?'

'Pardon me?'

Wilhelmsson's face went taut. His mouth was a tight line and his protruding bushy eyebrows made it impossible to see his eyes.

'My mistake,' he said abruptly. 'Forget it.'

The other gentlemen now stepped out of the inner office, bringing with them the odours of food and aquavit out to Wilhelmsson, who stood deep in thought. Baron Fogel was so wound up that he had to sit down for a moment on the boot shelf and pull himself together. The assistant bookkeeper came in from the balcony and reported that the rain had stopped, but just to be on the safe side Alexander Lindh took a huge black cotton umbrella with him when they left. Wilhelmsson remained behind, grabbing the assistant bookkeeper by his lapels.

'Does a hare-lipped boy work in your warehouse?'

'I'm not sure, but I'll be happy to find out.'

'You do that.'

The bookkeeper ordered the office boy to run across and find out from Fredriksson, who managed the warehouse. The health inspection committee of the local council had made its way across the tracks and onto the property of the

Railway Hotel by the time he caught up. The barber surgeon and vaccinator were bringing up the rear, and their jackets were wringing wet from waiting out in the rain.

'A hare-lipped fellow called Valentin sometimes helps with the loading. Fredriksson didn't think he'd used him since May.'

'Surname?'

'He didn't know.'

'What's the matter?' Lindh asked. 'Something about one of my employees?'

'No,' said Wilhelmsson curtly. 'Just a mix-up.'

A train from Stockholm pulled into the station. The roofs of the cars were shiny after the rain. Eight formally-attired gentlemen standing in a semicircle around a manure pile watched the passengers descend and one of the gentlemen, stationmaster Cederfalk, took a few steps away from the manure on his long, regal, muscular legs. Aristocratic weekend guests descended from the first-class cars and walked towards the carriages from the estate that were waiting in the station yard. The horses were chestnut and long-legged, with crocheted cosies over their nervously twitching ears. The driver found it difficult to make them stand still for the length of time it took for the women to gather their skirts and ascend. A trap was loaded with the baggage, and a couple of crates of wine brought from Stockholm by one of the servants. The carriage wheels began to roll, and Cederfalk followed their departure, his eyes staring, cold and distant.

There was a better life. There was a world not criss-crossed by foul-smelling ditches and refuse trenches, a world not consisting of endless winter afternoons and rainy shifts on the grey wooden platform.

When the train had departed, the health committee and the local council were still standing in a gloomy semicircle, their hands behind their backs, around the enormous manure heap next to the yardmen's pigsty.

They were watched from inside the railway restaurant by a man who would otherwise never have deigned to set foot in a restaurant where liquor was sold, but who had now taken up his position behind a potted palm and was peeking out from behind a curtain to get a better view. This was the viper in their bosom, the fly in their ointment and the salt in their wound, Edvin G. Norrelius, the schoolmaster. Seven men and three women had applied for the position of village school teacher. Norrelius, who came from the south-east, had impressed them all with his qualifications and was voted in by an overwhelming majority. The Count had sent his estate manager with a proxy, and a request to vote last, but everyone knew very well that he wanted one of his own school teachers appointed. He had so many votes that he could easily reverse the decision even if there was a consensus among the rest of the inhabitants of the village. This time, however, he had abstained from voting, declaring that he had no desire to violate the express will of the village. So Norrelius it was.

Now this southerner's guttural r's could be heard at every single meeting at which he could conceivably justify his presence or otherwise worm his way in. He had led a contingent which attempted to get Isaksson, the innkeeper, voted onto the local council, but had failed. He supported Petrus Wilhelmsson's action to restrict liquor licensing. There were eleven establishments with liquor licenses in a village of eight hundred, not to mention the places that sold moonshine. Wilhelmsson, at least, acted out of religious conviction, while people tended to grumble that Norrelius was rather too weak when it came to religion for an educator of and model for the young. His great interest, instead, was social issues. This explained why he was now hiding behind the curtain. He had filed an application to have all manure piles removed from station property. He was an enemy of all swine, and was demanding a ban on pig-keeping within the village limits.

He was in the right. But he was in the right far too often and he spoke out on the issues that were dear to his heart, with his guttural r's and with much more zeal than situations demanded. Although one might agree with him in principle that there should no longer be pigsties within the village limits, such a ban would throw a spanner in the works of an establishment that had been a driving force in community development — the railway restaurant. Mamsell Winlöf ran her business according to the principle of natural cycles, and her pigs were now so refined that they turned up their noses at garbage that had begun to rot. Moreover, transportation cost money.

Under Norrelius' gaze, the chairman of the health committee, Doctor Didriksson, made a huge sweep of his arm in the direction of the manure pile, alluding to its removal. Cederfalk responded with a placid wave of the hand to indicate agreement, after which he semaphored a command in the direction of the station hands over by the wall. No one who observed this pantomime could misinterpret its meaning. It was so convincing that it would hardly have been surprising if the manure pile had mystically levitated itself off the station property and majestically vanished towards the horizon.

When this performance for the benefit of Norrelius in his hiding place was done, the group turned its backs on Mamsell Winlöf's gigantic pigsties and gazed instead at Cats' End, the black pool from which the railway's water reservoir was filled. It had been a dry, windy spring and the water level in Cats' End was so low that two decades' worth of rubble could be seen protruding from the sludge at the bottom, and nearer the banks there were decomposing sacks which at best contained nothing more than stones and drowned kittens.

'Clear it up,' Lindh ordered, and the vaccinator put it on the record.

'Railway property,' said Doctor Didriksson, and Cederfalk nodded slowly, his puffy eyelids closed.

Thus they continued, still on the north side of the hamlet, and the postmaster's wife waved to them from within her dark, trellised veranda. Scrub-Ärna's sister, with her cats and her filth, was still her next-door neighbour. Many of the wells, including Ärna's, had been covered over. Drawing water from them was prohibited ever since Doctor Didriksson had taken samples and declared one after the other to be unhealthy and full of germs. This meant that every serving girl in the village now had to cross the tracks to Dahlgren's property by the square and draw water from his well. He worked for the railway and had the only laundry shed for miles around. Trash Moat ran across his property, and he rented out his laundry shed for a fee. He was a wilful, self-important man, and said no to whomever he pleased.

The board and the council crossed over to the south side, and found no objections to what they saw at Dahlgren's. His well was clean, covered and locked, his refuse bins had been emptied. They moved along, cautiously crossing the ditches on narrow boards. They bumped into Abraham Krona the younger, who was carting away night soil barrels at the last minute before the inspection. The vaccinator noted a suggestion on the record, that soil barrels should only be removed by night, and Krona waved the thong of his whip. He sat high and still on his load, looking very much like his father, who had been granted the first community contract for soil barrel removal. His split beard, however, was still a youthful red.

The inspection tour was now being trailed by a group of children, who came closer and closer as the men moved amongst the pigsties, rubbish bins and privies. The children shouted with pleasure when red-footed rats shot terrified out of their holes. They sat watching from an outhouse roof when Baron Fogel poked his walking stick at something sticking out of a manure pile, certain that he would expose a batch of fermenting moonshine, only to discover a dead pig. Covering their mouths with their handkerchiefs, the troop continued.

Many workers had been given the day off or told to knock off early. The thin layers of gravel in the courtyards had been raked, and the grey wooden stoops were decorated for midsummer. The sweet smell of decomposition mingled with the bitter scent of birch leaves, and wilting lilac blossoms. Melodeons had begun to play, and anyone who inspected as closely as Alexander Lindh did took in the aroma of aquavit and newly-scrubbed necks. He never tired of asking the most remarkable questions about one rubbish pile after the next. Cederfalk was half-dead of boredom, and dragged himself from courtyard to courtyard out of sheer willpower, with the growing crowd of kids trailing behind.

Young workmen had begun to join the crowd, an accordion whined sarcastic comments. When the inspection tour had left Svensson the brewer's yard with its horrible rubbish pile on the incline leading to the dairy, soldier Lans came up from the brewer's cellar steps, which had been his observation point. He was tipsy, and in a high good humour, since he was on his way to the party at Löfgren the saddlemaker's at Ridgeview and had already begun to celebrate. He began to imitate Cederfalk's walk, and it was amazing how he made his tiny body resemble the stationmaster's. He walked on tip-toe, making his legs look longer than they were, added a distinguished swivel to his back, and blinked his heavy eyelids. Behind him was the crowd of children, young workers and the accordionist, shouting encouragement. Lans put his hands behind his back and bent down over the rubbish heap Svensson the brewer had tried to cover with boards that morning.

'And what have we here?' he said, prying up a board. 'Oh me, oh my. "Things are looking black," said a man looking up his wife's arse.'

Cederfalk saw this performance from a distance and realized that the inspection tour was turning into a farce. He sent the barber surgeon to tell Constable Roos to keep the crowd at bay. And so most people missed seeing what happened when the inspection tour stepped up to the house where the widow of tailor Short Legs lived. She didn't use the night soil emptying service, but was renowned, instead, for the abundance of her kitchen garden. Her house and outbuildings formed a rectangle, the entrance to which was cut off by open ditches. Early that morning, the widow had pulled in the boards, and now she stood on her side, curtsying. Baron Fogel was wandering around the perimeter

113

looking for a way in, and he tested the edge of a putrid ditch with the toe of his kid leather shoe. The widow appeared opposite him, curtsying politely, but the crowd, restrained by Constable Roos, couldn't hear what was said.

Between the privy and the wood shed a rubbish heap rose, making it impossible to get in that way. Tall Cederfalk was seen stretching his neck to look over the top. The children, spying from the tarred roof of an outbuilding, reported that all he could see was widow Short Legs curtsying on her side of the rubbish heap, addressing him in all humility.

When the inspectors had tired of peeking at the widow's bountiful garden and slipping into her ditches, they moved along, and the crowd rushed in to find out what had happened.

'What did they say?' they asked the widow. 'What did they say, ma'am?'

'They asked: how can we get in here, please?'

'And what was your answer, ma'am?'

'You just have to go round and about, I'm afraid' says I.

And widow Short Legs curtsied again as she repeated what she had said to the gentlemen.

'Good answer, ma'am!' the crowd shouted. 'What did they say then?'

'I can't recall, I was just too upsetted.'

Soon everyone knew how she had told them off, and in less than an hour boards had been pulled back everywhere and piles of rubble were blocking the entryways between privies. Alexander Lindh's neck was scarlet, and Cederfalk bellowed in the way he usually reserved for the train yard. And everywhere, submissive inhabitants approached the inspectors from inside their enclaves and told them they just had to go round and about.

Sara Sabina Lans had to wait half the day for her kids to bring her the starch for the parson's. If they'd had any sense in their heads, she would have gone ahead to Vallmsta and counted on their bringing the basket to her there. She had wanted to get the laundry soaking before evening so she and the children could get over to Ridgeview and have a share in the party meal. She did the washing for the parson's at a half krona a day. The housekeeper tended to disregard the time it took to get the laundry soaking the night before, although Sara Sabina wasn't inclined to let her forget.

When Tora and Rickard arrived she was angry, and they tried to placate her by telling her what they had seen in the village. They described how Widow Short Legs had talked back to the authorities, and all the garbage piles that had suddenly grown up between the buildings, blocking the way.

'So they just circled round and about the shame, did they?' asked Sara Sabina.

Tora was silent for a moment.

'The funny part's there to keep us from seeing the Shame,' her grandmother said, but Tora didn't know what she meant.

'What kind of Shame are they keeping in there?' she finally asked.

Her grandmother turned her back.

'All poor people have their Shame.'

'But why?'

' 'Cause Shame hides Want.'

'Well, that's good, then,' answered Tora, acting wise beyond her years, although she hadn't understood.

Her grandma had put a pot on her tripod and was making them some porridge before leaving.

'But want,' she added, 'conceals nothing. Want tells the truth.'

These words, too, were beyond Tora. She had to think. Perhaps this Shame was the same one she'd heard of before. You found Shame everywhere. Shame was like horse dung on the roads. Sometimes they would say 'Old Shame.' She imagined a stooped would-be gentleman in a bowler hat, sneaking around a corner.

But the funny part came first, and everybody knew what Fun was. Fun was the soldier who wanted Mother to sing and keep time by clicking her tongue against her palate while he and his mates danced. But if she didn't want to make her noises he'd strike her across the mouth until she sat down and did as she was told, and the men danced, bending their knees and clapping their hands. 'The fun is about to begin', said the old man, hitting his wife!

Want had to be the child in the wooden box she had once seen with her grandma, a child with closed eyes. The box was on trestles, and inside the baby lay nestled in wood shavings, covered with a piece of tulle with silver stars. One of the neighbour women standing over by the door explained:

'That's Want,' she said.

Yes, Want was the lard-white corpse of a child with blue shadows around its mouth. She would tell Rickard about it when they went to bed. But when it was time for her to go to sleep, the words had become a dance. First the dusty, grey, stooped would-be gentleman came strutting and turned the corner. Then came the white child with closed eyes.

Then came the Fun, the dancing soldier who hit his old woman until she sang.

The weather had cleared up around midday, the scuttling clouds drifting off over the marshes, and it looked as though Midsummer's Eve would be pleasant but cool. Valentin and Ebon had sold every single copy of *The People's Voice* in their cart for the second time, and were now sitting behind the lilacs by Tubby Kalle's tavern, drinking the beer they had spent their profit on. They could hardly report their double income to the agitator. Valentin had no principles, and upon due consideration Ebon found that keeping the money didn't violate his. He knew there was a hitch somewhere, but his head was light from the tepid beer, and he couldn't figure it out.

They had sold one copy to Schoolmaster Norrelius, who had surprised them by walking out of the Railway Hotel. He said he knew of this famed publication from *Our Fatherland*, had heard it was put out by a tailor and a couple of cobblers in rural Sweden, and was curious to read it. Later that afternoon, when they passed the schoolhouse with the sack of beer they were carrying carefully to keep the bottles from clinking, he was having his dinner on the schoolhouse veranda with his *People's Voice* open in front of him. He called them over, and Valentin cautiously slid the sack down into the ditch.

'Where is the agitator's meeting going to be held?' Norrelius asked.

'It were s'posed to be at the Guild Barn, but Magnusson himself turned him out when he saw the poster,' Ebon spoke cockily despite the fact he was talking to the teacher. 'Then he was gonna be at the Kvistertorp leasehold, except the Count was having company who drove past Kvistertorp on their way from the station and caught sight of the poster. So he were turned out of there, too.'

Norrelius sat silent for a long time, staring down at his plate, which Ebon could see was covered with potato skins and herring bones. He found it strange that the schoolmaster didn't eat any better food than he himself would be served when he got home, and dared to lift his gaze from the herring bones and examine Norrelius' face for the first time. The schoolmaster was a pale man with regular features and a soft, dark brown moustache.

'Do you know where the agitator can be found?'

'At the widow of blacksmith Eriksson's, having his dinner!'

He ordered them to fetch him.

'I am a friend of the working man,' the schoolmaster said by way of a greeting, shaking the agitator's hand heartily. 'But I want it said from the outset that I do not share your opinions. Offensive behaviour and unrealistic demands do not benefit the workers' cause! I would say that the riots you call strikes — ' he continued, but was hastily interrupted by the agitator, who was a head shorter than he.

'You may have whatever opinions you care to, Sir. But the lads told me that you had a place for our meeting. Is it true?'

'Yes and no,' replied Norrelius vehemently.

It took some time for the little agitator to realize that the price of holding his meeting in the schoolyard was a debate with Norrelius himself. Ebon and Valentin sank down behind Fru Norrelius' flower bed, behind beggarblooms and southernwood, listening to the exchange. They knew what Norrelius was like from the local council meetings, sharp and logical, with gutteral r's. But the little man was bull-headed, he didn't give up. Time and again he contradicted Norrelius, sticking his prickly goatee right into his face, and banging the foot of his walking stick hard on the veranda floor. Ebon did not understand their words, not until the agitator started to tell how that morning, when looking for a place to hold his meeting, he had taken a walk and gone all the way to Lake Vallmaren. There he had found forty-five men in a long row along the shore, busily making railway cross-ties. They were to be exported to England. The agitator had been told that it was such a rush order that they would probably have to work the whole of Midsummer's Eve to get it finished.

'A merchant by the name of Lindh had dredged up every crofter and day-worker he could find around here,' said the agitator, 'and his foreman was standing there encouraging the men to compete. Is that what you call free competition, Schoolmaster Norrelius?'

'I will not budge on that point,' Norrelius replied. 'Free competition between men strengthens the character and benefits both the individual and the collective, in the long run. Remove the drive to compete that spurs man to accomplishment, and you remove the very basis of our social structure!'

'Then tell me this: who wins the competition when Andersson the day-worker and Johansson the crofter have been cutting cross-ties for twelve hours, each trying to prove that he's the better man? Anderson still gets one krona and fifty öre for the day, while the foreman judges Johansson to have worked harder and gives him one seventy-five. But who is the real winner in this noble competition between free men?'

Now Norrelius was silent for a moment, during which something remarkable happened to Ebon. He felt a strong impulse to reply to the agitator's question, so potent and forceful that he completely forgot his fear and half-rose to his feet behind the beggarblooms. He was certain he knew the answer, it was on the tip of his tongue. But he couldn't get the word out.

His father was making sleepers at Lake Vallmaren that Midsummer's Eve. He remembered now that the same thing had happened at Whitsuntide. On that holiday, too, there was a ship in port at Gothenburg waiting for the last of the cargo to arrive by rail. That time Lindh the merchant had come out in person to explain to the men what the rush was. The agitator knew nothing about this. And yet he said:

'Why do you think there's such a rush on a holiday eve?' Now Ebon felt the same strong urge to answer, which was really very odd since he was within range of a schoolmaster. He rose to his knees, and his thick-lipped mouth began silently to shape words. The agitator caught sight of him and signalled him to speak. Ebon said:

'Because the next day's a holiday.'

'Which means?' asked the activist, pointing at him with a thin finger. Norrelius stared at Ebon who had risen from the flower bed like an ugly, fleshy stand of rhubarb amongst the flowers.

'That they get a day of rest,' he said. 'Without any work being lost.'

He fell back to the grass beside Valentin, who was in a fit of giggles over Ebon's daring to take part in the dispute, and with such seriousness. But Ebon could no longer hear him. He didn't give a hoot about what Valentin thought.

At Whitsun they had waited until almost nine for their father. He and Lina had stood at the window and watched him walking down the road at dusk. His gait was strange.

'Run and see what's wrong!' his mother said.

He found his father on the little stone ledge where catfoot grew in the summer. He had sunk down on the flat stone and was leaning on his elbow. Ebon trembled with fear as he ran towards him in the twilight, but when he came up close he could see his father laughing, although his face was grey in the dusky evening.

'I just can't walk another step,' he said. 'I'll be damned if it didn't catch up with me after all.'

But he had been the winner.

'Oh yes, you can count on me,' his old man had said, laughing and spitting a long, light-brown stream towards Nazareth, their cottage that he was dying to get inside, but which he couldn't reach until his legs would carry him there.

'I do not share your opinions,' the schoolmaster said, rising and extending his hand to indicate that the debate was over. 'But in the name of free speech I invite you to hold your meeting in the schoolyard.'

'Edvard!' said Fru Norrelius, who had been circling them uneasily throughout. He appeared not to have heard her.

'Edvard! Edvard!'

But the agitator and the schoolmaster had now been shaking hands so heartily and so long that she could see her

122

husband's decision was irreversible, and she went inside, pulling the door shut with a grunt.

'Now, however, we must develop a strategy,' said Norrelius, wagging his forefinger at the agitator, and it struck Ebon, despite his great gravity, that a lot of index finger wagging had been going on that afternoon.

'Not a word about the meeting until after four o'clock! Then put the posters up again, and spread the news with the aid of these sharp young men. At four o'clock a dinner party's being held by Lindh at Gertrudsborg for the local council and some members of the health and hygiene committee, I happen to know. After four, it will be plain sailing!'

Ebon walked slowly towards Nazareth to see if there was any dinner left at this late hour. In fact, though, he wasn't really hungry. For the first time in his life, he thought he could see who he was. He saw a rather ragged untidy figure in a black striped jacket with short sleeves, shiny with wear. He saw his disgusting cap so clearly that he had to put his hand on his head and touch it. It was amazing. He had had an altogether unusual morning. He didn't usually give much thought to the past, but now he could see himself tramping in the chilly morning darkness far, far back in time. He could see himself. It was amazing: he had been seen and named. Once again he put his hand to his cap, and then to his face, as if he were touching it for the first time.

When he got home, his mother had put branches of mountain ash in a jug on the kitchen table. The broken branches smelled acrid. His youngest sister had brought them home. She was too small to know the difference between mountain ash and birch, his mother laughed. He wondered whether he had ever seen her laugh before. She was so careful to pull her lip down over her cracked front teeth. Neither could he recall ever having smelt an odour so distinct as this bitter smell of mountain ash.

She asked what he had been doing. He couldn't think how to reply. It was overwhelming, it could not be shared. Suddenly he took the wood basket and rushed outside with it. Then he sat on the chopping block, touching his face cautiously. His cheeks were damp from tears, although he had not noticed them before. It was like injuring yourself in your sleep without knowing how, and waking up covered with blood.

The cook at Gertrudsborg came out into the yard in front of the kitchen, walking so swiftly towards the gate that the gravel flew up from her black dress shoes. Behind her walked a kitchen maid, her face swollen from weeping, carrying two knapsacks.

'Put those back!' the cook shouted, flailing her arms towards the girl. 'Have them sent to me with my chest. Let her go through them! I know what I can be accused of!'

She left the gate open and started walking the birch-lined lane towards town. When she had gone nearly half way she was given a ride by a tenant farmer, and thus did not meet up with Alexander Lindh on his walk home. When he entered his house the kitchen maid sat wailing at the foot of the stairs in the hall, and from upstairs he could hear the familiar short, breathless cries that led into his wife's attacks of hysteria. The housemaid ran past him, on her way up with a glass and a bottle on a tray.

'Where is Lilibeth?' he asked.

'In the garden with Miss Preston,' the housekeeper answered breathlessly, vanishing around the curve in the stairs. The tray clattered, and the cries from upstairs escalated. After some time they quieted down, smothered in sniffles and moans. Then, suddenly, there was silence. Alexander Lindh stood waiting, immobile. In the silence, the canary started to sing in the upstairs hall.

He refrained from going upstairs, sitting instead in the dining room reading his newspaper. Not until everything seemed to have settled down again did he call the housemaid to him and was told that the cook had walked out with the oxtail soup unsieved, leaving a scaled pike-perch on the kitchen counter that not a soul knew what to do with.

Lindh was not unaccustomed to household disasters, but his dinner guests would be arriving in two hours. He sent a message to the village, to Mamsell Winlöf, the restaurant proprietress. He still refrained from going up the stairs. Lilibeth, who was nine now, came back in with her English nanny, and Lindh explained to her that mother had been taken ill. She heard him, and her long, thin face betrayed no emotion whatsoever.

He waited until Mamsell Winlöf had arrived in a buggy with her girls and her hampers. Then he went upstairs and into his wife's bedroom where the shade was down and a bluish twilight reigned. He couldn't see her, only a shapeless disarray of textiles and pillows at the head of the great empire bed.

'Alexander,' she whispered, and he could hear that her voice was already slurred. 'I am distraught! It is all my fault!'

He was quiet.

'Are you angry? Of course you're angry! Now I've spoilt your dinner party. Have you cancelled? '

'No.'

'But the kitchen maid cannot cope with the meal, Alexander!'

'The restaurant proprietress is coming out.'

There was silence. Then he could feel, although he was at the door and standing at least three meters from her, how her invisible body stiffened in the twilight, could sense how her back arched until she was like a bow, her breathing growing shorter and more laboured.

'Quiet!'

'The restaurant proprietress! You mean — that woman. You cannot! Not here, in our house.'

He took one step aside and took hold of the window shade's drawstring. When the tightly pulled shade flew up with a snap like the sound of a face being slapped she hushed abruptly. She sat there staring at him, her face grey and dull, trying to hide her stringy black hair under her night-cap. He knew the scream that was coiled in her throat, ready to spring. On the night table stood the bottle of port and the glass, along with the bottle of medicine from Doctor Didriksson, which she had not taken.

'Another bottle of port will be brought up. And you will be silent. All evening. I do not want to hear a peep from up here.'

She crawled down under her cover and the shawls that had been laid over it. He went over and tried to locate her, seeking her fragile hand amongst the comforter and woollen shawls. When he found it it was limp and cold. He tried to rub a little warmth into it. Then he folded back the sheet until he found her ear, lifted away the stiff, shiny curls, and said softly, straight in:

'You know that you'll have to be quiet. I'll send you away, Caroline. You be quiet and it will be all right.'

He replaced the sheet and covered her cold hand. She had made a fist so tight that her knuckles were white, with protruding veins.

Mamsell Winlöf had the soup strained, after which she personally thickened up the broth. She had placed the pike-perch in the oven, sprinkled with breadcrumbs and dotted with butter, surrounded with cream, and she had got the kitchen maid started sautéing some plump mushrooms to decorate it with. She had brought out from her restaurant sliced cold turkey in consommé, and the requisite condiments. All she needed was a suitable green vegetable. The housemaid was setting the table, after one of the serving girls from the restaurant had helped her spread out the tablecloths. The nanny was writing placecards, with the most dreadful spelling. Another girl from the restaurant was out on the kitchen veranda turning the ice cream maker, and there was the sound of salt and crushed ice.

When the pike-perch was a lovely golden brown and its top fin crispy, Alma Winlöf removed her apron and her sleeve covers and left the serving to the housemaid and one of the restaurant girls. She found a mirror in the pantry where she could comb her dark hair and gently dust her bright red cheeks with rice powder. Throughout the meal she stood at the sideboard in the dining room, supervising the service. When Barons Cederfalk and Fogel passed, they shook her hand. Doctor Didriksson followed suit, but Magnusson the builder only grunted. She was apparently indifferent, greeting them all with the same subdued gentility, and without allowing her attention to falter for even a second from her girls, as they carried in the soup. None of the men's wives acknowledged Mamsell Winlöf's presence in the least, except that they wore that condescending look women put on when there are children or pets in the room.

Lindh held his first speech over the soup, welcoming his guests. He reminded them of the duty they had carried out that morning, but in a way that made it seem both odourless and elevated in retrospect. He went on to express his hopes that the town would prosper, in consensus and peace. He hoped that they would make a joint effort to spare their community from the terrible battle between the classes into which itinerant subversives wished to see them thrown, at which point master builder Magnusson uttered a hoarse bark, like that of a roe buck, in indication of his support for the speaker. Lindh highlighted the injustice and fruitlessness of struggles between the classes, and concluded with his vision of the society of the future: one in which each man worked according to his ability and in his chosen field, for the general good. The gentlemen lifted their glasses towards the middle of the table, where Mamsell Winlöf had placed the croquembouche, decorated with little flags, that was to accompany the ice cream.

She arranged a tray with a little helping of every dish, even a coupe of ice cream set in a container of crushed ice. The housemaid was sent up the stairs with it, and came down saying that the lady of the house had accepted it.

The women asked about Caroline. One by one, they tilted their heads and asked Alexander Lindh, in soft, confidential voices, how his poor wife was feeling. Her illness was publicly termed a terrible migraine, but the fact that she tippled was equally public knowledge.

The dinner had to be fairly short because, no later than seven o'clock, the stationmaster had to open the midsummer dance in the station yard, and they were all to go along. So Cederfalk was in a great rush by the time it was time for his speech of thanks, when all that was left was melting ice cream and the ruins of the croquembouche.

'Although the ancient oaks of tradition may not line our streets and squares,' he began, 'the young lindens of zeal and social progress have been planted in the soil of our fathers, and are now in the flush of their first leafy shade!' Postmistress Lagerlöf, who was ageing, but had not lost her touch for irony, managed to imply to Magnusson simply by rolling her eyes in the direction of short, stubby, but powerful Lindh that Cederfalk was playing on words. Magnusson chortled and shouted 'Bravo!'

Mamsell Winlöf stood immobile and listening by the side board, only her brown eyes shifting from one face to the next. When they arose she remained in position for some time, examining the wrinkled table napkins and the soiled cloth. The housemaid brought down the tray, but Caroline Lindh had not touched it. She had just kept it in her room for nearly two hours, sitting upright in her bed staring at the soup as it slowly grew a shiny skin. She watched the ice cream melt to sauce and the cream dry up on the morsels of fish. Now and again she sipped at her port wine. Finally she called for the housemaid.

'Take my meal down to Mamsell Winlöf,' she said, pushing away the tray. At first the housekeeper thought her mistress had done something to the food, and glanced down at the plates, prepared to see something nauseating. Caroline had pulled her top lip back exposing her front teeth, pointed and protruding slightly, like a rodent's.

I nnkeeper Isaksson sat drinking despondently. He was no longer a member of either local order and to be perfectly honest he didn't give a good God damn what the goodtemplars were up to. 'The Spring of Joy' was holding its midsummer meeting somewhere, probably at Petrus Wilhelmsson's. He was no longer a member. 'The Pure Spring' would also be celebrating midsummer. Once, long before the split, Isaksson had been made a member of the Spring, as the original order had been called, and had intended to be moderate both in his consumption and in his temperance, all for the sake of damnable politics. He had taken his lead from Schoolmaster Norrelius who had promised to launch him as a candidate for chairman of the municipal council. But it had all gone to hell, the whole Isakssonian contingent had lost the election, and if you asked the Innkeeper it was Norrelius' accent that was to blame — no self-respecting man from this part of the country would have such awful guttural r's.

He remembered Schoolmaster Malm from Backe. An honest man who taught them that the earth had been flooded three times. Why had they not had the good sense to take him for the job, as the Count had proposed? And to add insult to injury the humiliation when the Count abstained from voting, deigning to allow them to have their way! They might just as well have let loose a sack of vipers in the schoolhouse.

131

Another thing that had worked to Isaksson's disadvantage was that he consorted with farmers. They traipsed in and out of the inn and never patronized the railway restaurant. But there was now a generation in the village who didn't want to see their lives run by the parish farmers and their representative. Isaksson was out on his arse, as Magnusson had so aptly put it.

Everything was so refined nowadays. Locomotive engineers' wives wore hats and patronized the stokers' wives who lived across the hall but with whom they felt they had nothing in common. Men spent their time sipping sweet drinks at the railway restaurant. Interest had been indicated in a music parlour and a smoking room. The inn, however, still reeked of farmers, as it had for two decades. The customers at his general store started shopping at Levander's shop, and at Plantin's. Isaksson had not been put out of business, but his heyday was past. He would spend his Midsummer's eve drinking with the peasants.

In his attic room, Valfrid was ready, and preening in front of the fragment of mirror he had stuck under Czar Nicholas. He took his watch down from its nail and fastened the chain in one of his waistcoat buttonholes. His shirt front kept creasing, and he had to adopt a very dignified posture, bending forward to keep it flat. Whistling, he clattered down the attic stair, but passed the kitchen door on tiptoe so as not to arouse the instincts of Isaksson's wife to send him on an errand.

It was raining outside. The Maypole in the station yard had yet to be raised, and the flag was flapping wetly. He had made no plans, and was considering crossing the tracks to see what was happening on the other side. As he approached the yard, he ran into his brother Ebon along with hare-lipped Valentin.

'Now the swindlers who control this place are gonna get what they deserve up by the schoolhouse,' said Valentin. 'Come along and listen.'

'I was thinking of going to the dance,' said Valfrid.

'There'll be none but womenfolk there. Come along to the school.'

As they walked up the long hill to the schoolhouse, Valentin's sister Frida caught up with them. She was about the same age as Valfrid, and was wearing a hat. It was shiny with black lacquer, and stuck through with two big pins. As she was the sister of that incurably snivelling Valentin he preferred not to be seen in her company, not to mention that he found the fact that she was also the daughter of Embankment Brita somewhat intimidating. Her skin was as pale and translucent as her mother's, and she also had the same quick, hungry eyes.

'What a crowd there looks to be,' he said to no one in particular.

Of course neither Ebon nor Valentin responded to this attempt at making conversation.

'There must be at least three hundred,' said Frida.

'I had no idea socialism was such a major event,' said Valfrid with a weary sigh.

It would have been easy to arrange an accordionist for the festivities at the station yard, but Cederfalk wanted a fiddler. He had sent a request to Lasse from Vanstorp, but he refused.

'If you're going to have anyone, it should be Fiddlin' Ulla,' he said. 'Whatever I know, I learned from her.'

When the time came, Fiddlin' Ulla arrived, but Cederfalk was not pleased with this arrangement. She was a fat woman in her fifties, with broad, fleshy legs, who raised an inscrutable, dull face towards the arrangers.

'Good grief, woman,' said Cederfalk, 'we appear to have no choice. But can you play?'

' 'Spose I can give it my best shot,' said Ulla.

She didn't sound too bad to begin with, but her appearance was awful. The women who had helped to arrange the festivities looked at her skirt, which was of a piece with her bodice. The whole thing rode up, what with her hunched back and her huge breasts, exposing her calves almost up to the knees. She had a great big fiddle she held between her knees like a cello.

Unfortunately the rain wasn't letting up. At first they tried to be outside anyway, but after a while the whole event was moved into the waiting room, which had been decorated just in case. Hampers of refreshments had been sent down from the estate, as usual, and were officially presented by the housekeeper to Cederfalk, who led the crowd in a 'hip hip hurrah' for the Count and Countess. After this, Fiddlin' Ulla accompanied the folk dancers, playing simply and pleasantly, as the wife of the telegraph operator put it. Mamsell Winlöf had lent them two potted palms, which were placed in front of Ulla's seat so as to more or less conceal her.

The local folk dance group was made up of young people in folk costume. Baron Fogel's nephews from Heavenside wore soft woollen Lappish garb and had pipes in their mouths, unlit of course. One of them was the partner of Lilibeth Lindh, who wore a folk dress from Dalacarlia. The 'chamois' jacket was of yellow velvet, and it was edged in swan's down to resemble sheepskin. Her tall cap had silk tassels.

The folk dance group was followed by two young men from Ängeby, dancing the Ox Dance. The postmistress felt the fiddle now sounded harsher, nor did she approve of all the stamping, or how the two rivals boxed each others' ears almost too realistically.

'They get carried away so easily,' Cederfalk explained, 'but they're good lads.'

There was no doubt, however, that a coarse tone had crept in, not least into the fiddling.

When the public dancing began, Cederfalk had expected an introductory waltz, but it was a polska. The woman he invited to dance refused, put off by the unfamiliar bouncy rhythm. He went over and asked the housekeeper from the estate instead.

Fiddlin' Ulla, was playing with her mouth ajar, leaning forward with her fiddle between her knees. Fewer and fewer people took the floor, as the beat grew wilder. One after the other the couples went and sat down or stood by the refreshment table, drinking lemonade. The middle of the waiting room floor, however, was occupied by the stationmaster, circling the little housekeeper round and round. Her lips were ashen. She begged his pardon — but she was very tired! Couldn't they sit this one out?

They were alone. He swung out towards the edges of the room, almost having to lift his partner with every turn. They bumped into an enamelled spittoon, and it slammed along the floor, nearly drowning out the fiddle. This appeared to encourage Fiddlin' Ulla to play with even greater gusto.

'Do have a seat here, my dears!' cried the postmistress. 'Take a rest! Let me pour you some lemonade, Fröken Nebelius.'

But Cederfalk paid no attention. He spun awkwardly around with the housekeeper, who glared, her eyes wide and fearful.

'Stop!' she cried in the direction of Fiddlin' Ulla. 'I'm exhausted!'

Fiddlin' Ulla, however, was sitting with her head down, and only glanced up from under her eyebrows, bushy as a man's. She played wildly and hideously. Her sharp up-bows stung like the thong of a whip. Cederfalk would not look at her. His lips were white, and he circled on, his legs straighter and straighter. Time and again he kicked the spittoon. In the end it was as if they were dancing with that noisy receptacle into every single sour-smelling corner of the waiting room.

Suddenly, as if she had tired of a dull task her hands had performed without her heart being in it, Fiddlin' Ulla lowered her bow and stood up. Cederfalk stopped dancing just as suddenly, and the housekeeper, finding herself unsupported, reeled backwards straight into the arms of the postmistress.

Cederfalk took out his handkerchief and pressed it to his mouth. Then, without speaking to anyone, he walked out the door towards the railway tracks. Fiddlin' Ulla took her fiddle and exited through the door on the station yard side. She walked through the rain in no particular hurry.

It was pouring, and the party-makers in the waiting room looked out to see a thin little tattered soul with no umbrella leading the way across the rain-soaked yard at the head of a group of people all of whom held newspapers or shawls over their heads to fend off the rain. Two to three hundred people had heard the agitator speak up at the school, and many of them were now going along to the station to dance in the waiting room. The activist was going to take the last train. Alexander Lindh had sent for an accordionist, and the party was picking up speed again, although the spirit had changed, and the dignitaries were preparing to leave. Cederfalk had rested in his office for a while and returned at the very moment the agitator and his company tried to come into the waiting room.

'This is a private celebration for the inhabitants of this village,' said Lindh, who approached them at the door. 'You'll have to wait outside.'

'I've never heard of the waiting room of a railway station being a private facility,' said the agitator, who was precisely the same height as Lindh.

'Well, you're hearing it now!'

Cederfalk was standing there, apparently fully recovered.

'In that case, my friends,' said the agitator, opening his arms wide to indicate that his words embraced not only his

137

own followers but all those who were standing along the walls of the decorated waiting room. 'Let us then allow all those who regard a government railway station to be an appropriate place for the parlour games and charity of the upper classes to remain inside, while the rest of us anticipate the arrival of the train under the open sky.'

Things got lively as the troop crossed through the waiting room, and for one moment Alexander Lindh thought it would empty out, leaving only himself and his dinner guests. But it wasn't quite that bad. The lame agitator only managed to take about ten of the dancers with him, and Cederfalk signalled to the accordionist to continue. Still, whenever the music stopped the rain could be heard smattering against the roof, and from the platforms, the singing led by the little activist in the pouring rain.

'What's that they're singing?' asked the postmistress.

'I certainly wouldn't know,' Cederfalk replied.

'But I certainly do!' beamed Baron Fogel. 'It's *Sons of Labour,* a song by a cork-cutter named Menander.'

Frozen through and drenched, his leaflet soaking, Valfrid was singing on the platform. He held Frida's hand tightly and sang so loudly that now and then he was able to distinguish his own voice above all the others. He saw Valentin elbow Ebon, laughing at him, but what did he care? Wasn't he in the company of a man who'd been subjected to the slings and arrows of outrage throughout his career as an activist? And hadn't this increased his dignity and human worth? Valfrid had never seen, never heard, anything as splendid as this great agitator. And it seemed to him that the man's slight build and his limp were the very prerequisites for bringing out the grandeur of his soul. Oh, to be lame, cried Valfrid's heart, as he sang at the top of his lungs.

138

After the agitator had spoken, Valfrid had rushed forward to press his hand, and without a word about his brother Ebon's dark crime against *The People's Voice*, declared that he wished to devote his life to the labour movement, and no less to Social Democracy. Valfrid had no idea that Ebon had sold the newspapers a second time, and the agitator had no idea that they were brothers. So he offered Valfrid the opportunity to sell newspapers. Valfrid agreed before he had time to think, and there was no turning back. He who had been prepared to follow the activist anywhere, to get on the first train out of town and speak to the people and be spit on and denigrated as the agitator's equal.

Now the activist was leaving on the train and Valfrid and Ebon were left on the platform with a packet of newspapers apiece. They had agreed to take on the next issue as well. It would arrive by train, hot off the presses. So it was too late to pull out.

So what? What difference did it make that he was freezing cold and soaking wet — the activist must be every bit as wet! 'He was here,' Valfrid thought, 'and we had not so much as an umbrella to offer him.'

'Well, there's no denying the fact that we met a great man today,' he said, gripping Frida's hand. He would, indeed, gladly sacrifice his long, strong legs and his lanky body for greatness! For it was surely only right that a defective and vulnerable body should give proper expression to greatness that came from within. Oh, to be lame, to be lame!

It was still drizzling on the morning of Midsummer night when the fern was to bloom, but Johannes Lans was drunk

139

and thought he was marching off to war, his footsteps resounding.

When a servant of the King, a soldier from Sweden, was on the march, the sun stood full and round as if she were blasting a trumpet! The dust of the road smoked like gunpowder around his boots. It wasn't, damnation, raining!

Lans was not marching alone, however. Unfortunately he was trailed by his disaster of a missus, in leaking boots. She hadn't made it to the saddlemaker's party. Now she was walking faster and faster on her scarecrow legs, and when Lans noticed her catching up, he lengthened his strides.

The very grey demeanour of her, her disgusting face, made him painfully aware of his dream world. The next time his regiment gathered he would once again be standing alongside the mess trench in a stiff, grease-spotted leather coat instead of his uniform jacket. He would soon be too old, he was never going to make corporal. He could no longer recall how many times he had been disciplined for being drunk on duty. At home, Shame and Mockery lay side by side in the trundle bed in the kitchen, holding one another's sticky hands. Everyone knew that one of his kids was Edla's and the other the product of his own old age.

Sara Sabina had come to bring him home to Appleton and she was angry and tired. Lans made a detour to pass by the inn, where they saw the young people on their way home from the dance waiting by the edge of the meadow for some fresh milk. The dairymaids were already there with their pails.

Lans waved and hooted at them, and then ran across the station yard. Just to confuse Sara Sabina he jumped onto the tallest pile of coal over by the tracks. As he began to climb, the coal came loose under his hands and feet and he fell to his knees, sliding one step back for every two steps forward. He finally reached the top, looking down on Sara Sabina, who had sat down to rest on the coal-dock in the grey morning air.

'Oh, the magpie she sat on the stone cellar roof,' he sang jubilantly from above, only to slip right down the other side in a landslide of coal and dust. Then one of the station hands caught sight of him and ran towards him, swearing. By that time Lans was agile as a lad, and ran in circles around on the tracks to tease him. An early train came in, and although the soldier meant to beat it, he tripped over his own two feet. He was still laughing when the train ran him over.

A man's a man for a' that', said Soldier Lans to his missus, as there was seldom anyone else there to listen since the train cut his legs off and he was stuck sitting at home. 'A man's a man and I'm a man was born in Stegsjö parish on the big farm at Great Kedevi to parents unknown.'

'We know that,' said Sara Sabina, 'so read now.'

'Lemme see! A sinner lying in a stupor of sin.'

She wanted to learn to read, whatever good that would do her.

'A voice from heaven spake unto him: *Awake, awake, the word comes from within. The light of heav'n illuminates thy sin!*'

He had an elegant reading voice, and preferred passages he knew by heart. But his old woman was impatient and shoved the book under his nose, her lips mimicking his.

The fun was certainly over now, and here he sat with his old lady and his hymnal! Things were worst in the winter when there was hardly anything to look at. He could describe every knot in the cabin floor where he'd once danced with the other fellows, with Goatwood, Old Mothstead and Big Smith, with Wolftrack and the old man from Tramphut. Those had surely been the days, when he'd had two strong legs.

In the summer they could at least prop open the door and move his chair closer so he could sit watching for ermines and squirrels. He couldn't sit on the chopping block by the door because he needed to be able to lean on something. He was like a barrel of salt pork now, a body without legs. And the fun was definitely over! Goatwood and Big Smith were both dead, and the old man from Tramphut was in the poorhouse. Nobody could handle Wolftrack, who lived all alone, shut up in his cabin and getting worse by the day. The only one who came by every now and again was Old Mothstead, but he wasn't any fun anyway, an ageing toothless fellow who sat there complaining about how his legs hurt. His legs hurt!

'Oh, to have such problems,' said Lans, and then he tried to sing his old soldier's ditty for Old Mothstead, to jog his memory:

Oh I've deceived the farmers
And I've deceived the priest
Not to mention fair maids
Three hundred sixty-six
In my younger days!

It didn't help, though. Old Mothstead's eyes were bleary and his chin quivered.

Still, in a way, they'd been lucky. After the accident he'd received a pension of twenty-four kronor, been allowed to keep the cabin and a small adjacent plot. In all the reports, Appleton was described as a defective, inadequate soldier's croft, and Lans had always received an extra sum in compensation, which suited him perfectly, for he had never been much of a farmer. And now they let him stay on there, although it was really only because this was the cheapest solution for the parish, at whose expense Lans and his wife and children would have to be looked after, in any case.

When Sara Sabina had been out doing laundry or cleaning, she was always given something to take home, but Lans never saw that, never wanted to see. Although he still bragged that he would never accept handouts and charity, behind his back people laughed at him, knowing full well that, in secret, Sara Sabina all but begged. No one had ever seen her refuse an offer.

And so they lived from hand to mouth, until something big happened. Even foreseeable events threw them into chaos. When it was time for Rickard to start school, his trousers were so worn that his behind shone through, a pink sheen where the trousers were threadbare. This just emphasized the risks involved in having children when you were old and poor.

'This one's not gonna be able to go to school,' said Lans when he had seen about as much of that naked behind as he could bear.

'I suppose we'll get a pair of trousers from the parish, then,' Sara Sabina thought aloud.

'Over my dead body,' Lans said proudly.

There was, however, trouser fabric in the house. That summer, Sara Sabina could barely keep her eyes off it. Finally, she had to bring the matter up with him.

'We could use what's left of your trousers.'

'What?'

She had to repeat herself time and again. He was silent, dumbfounded. After a long time he glared at her, saying:

'Don't you touch 'em.'

To make her see that he was deadly serious, he waited a full day to bring it up again. Then, just as they were going to bed, when she had lifted his body into the bed in the main room:

144

'Don't you dare touch my trousers. Not as long as I'm alive.'

Really, she had intended to let them be, and she realized he meant business, that the empty trouser legs she had turned up and tucked in meant something to him. Yet the oftener she saw that flawless fabric, more than enough for a pair of trousers for the boy, the less convinced she became that it would make any difference whether or not he had his empty trouser legs. There was no question of his ever using them again.

Rickard was keen to start school, and she felt sorry for him. Late one August evening she made up her mind. She could hardly sleep all night for fear she wouldn't wake up early enough. She had to have the dawn light to work by, and it had to be done before he awoke.

She crept in silently and grabbed his trousers from the chair, shutting the door to the room behind her. She had greased the hinges with lard beforehand. It was so early that the dawn light was translucent and outside the window the leafy crown of the apple tree had a grey shimmer. She spread the trousers across the table and cut them swiftly.

There was plenty for a pair of boy's trousers, and before the soldier and the kids were up she had them half done. She had also turned in the cut edge of Lans' trousers and hemmed them down with small, close stitches. When she handed them to him his face fell, and his chin began to quiver like Old Mothstead's. She had been prepared for an explosion, and had thought out her responses to just about anything he might say. But he simply refused to be put into the legless trousers. He said not a word. He just rolled over on his side in bed, turning his back to the room, refusing to be lifted up and put in his chair.

It was a worse ordeal than she could ever have imagined. Rickard was frightened when his father wouldn't get up, and at first he refused to put on his new trousers. She really had to light into him before she finally got him off to school. He moved off stiffly, his legs so straight it was as if his tiny body was frightened of contact with the stiff cloth. And Lans lay in the main room moaning softly. He was far past human dignity of any kind, but oh, in the name of the Lord, how could she ever have suspected his dignity was housed in a pair of empty trouser legs?

She spoke with him and coerced him to be dressed and put into his chair. A couple of days had passed and he was suspiciously easy to convince. He had lost all his sting, which made her realize she'd better do something about it.

All that autumn, she scrimped and saved. She held on to every coin she made at washing, until she had enough to go to the clothing stand at the village market and buy him a pair of second-hand trousers.

'And they're not just any old trousers,' she said, spreading them out on his cover.

'So whose were they?'

'You guess.'

They were big in the waist, almost spherical down to the point where the legs began. They must have covered a huge stomach.

'I'd guess Tubby Kalle, the old tavern owner. Didn't he die?'

'The owner isn't dead,' she said. 'What's more, he's one of the finer folks.'

He guessed Levander the shopkeeper, and even the dairy owner, but he couldn't come up with anyone who had such a round well-filled belly. Finally he figured it out.

146

'Honestly?' he asked.

She nodded.

'The merchant?'

'Yes,' said Sara Sabina. 'Merchant Lindh himself. Of course, he'd given them away, but to somebody who sold them for cash for aquavit. And now they're yours.'

Without further ado she turned up the trouser legs and stitched them down with a threaded needle she'd made ready. He didn't want her to take them in at the waist, however. He had fun pulling them in and out over his belly, demonstrating the girth of the merchant who had paid good money for them, and what short legs he'd had, besides.

Yes, he was himself again. After a while she began to think he'd forgotten all about it. But she never did. Poverty was humiliating, as she knew better than most. She had been trying to teach him something along those lines when he lay helplessly whining over his missing trouser legs. But it seemed that for everyone there was a limit beyond which you couldn't humiliate yourself, no matter how poor you were, without losing yourself completely. She wouldn't forget it, and she wondered what her own limit was and when she would reach it.

At least they had one worry less when saddlemaker Löfgren took Rickard in, and promised to apprentice him as soon as he'd finished school. Löfgren was now certain he'd never have a son of his own. He had two fat, dark-haired daughters, each the apple of his eye. Still, he wanted to teach someone his trade.

They missed the lad, though. Lans had spent a lot of time talking with him the last few years. At least he'd been male. Now Lans sat at the open door listening for the sounds of the forest.

147

'Oh me, oh my,' he would say to himself, 'those were the days. At least people had a sense of humour. Nowadays the world's a crueller, harsher place.'

Sara Sabina would give him a nasty look, but he was just talking to himself. He was always hearing all kinds of noises from the woods, too: voices, hunting horns. But when she came to listen there was nothing, nothing but the trilling of the blackbird and the eternal cooing of the wood pigeons.

Tora often played on the stone slabs in front of the door, seldom listening to his talk, since he certainly wasn't talking to her. But sometimes the old couple talked with one another. She would wake up early in the morning to their voices, although she couldn't hear what they were saying. They were talking softly and eagerly, not the way they usually did. Once she didn't fall right back to sleep, but watched her grandmother carry the legless man's body to the window and put him on a chair. He was impatient.

'Will he be here soon?' he asked. 'Can you see 'im?'

Tora sat up so she could look out the window, too. It was dawn and everything seemed strange with the light coming from an odd angle. The south wall of the barn was still deep in shadow; she'd never seen it that way before.

But she couldn't see anybody coming. In the deceptive morning light nothing looked familiar. There were lots of things that frightened her out there. There were voices and cries from the marsh. She put her fingers in her ears, staring out with sleepy, burning eyes. Grey shadows vanished, rustling by the stone foundation of the barn. But nobody came. Down on the meadow clouds of haze rose and evaporated. Now the witches' rings were visible in the grass, down where she never dared to play.

She grew bigger and less frightened, and was not allowed to play all the time any more, either. Nor, of course, to sit with idle hands. She knitted black stockings for herself and for Rickard, hating them before she ever put them on, because they scratched so unbearably. Soon she had worn big holes in the heels and had to darn them. 'Morels,' her grandmother called her darns, and Rickard complained that her lumps made it impossible to walk.

The only real fun was cutting the discarded dresses of the parson's wife and daughter into strips for the rag rugs Sara Sabina wove. Tora would sit under the shadow of the morello cherry tree and it would almost be like playing a game, but she was careful not to say she was enjoying herself. The strips of thin linen and other fine fabrics lay at her bare feet. She wondered what they'd been doing when they wore these clothes. Some of the cloth had to be thrown away although it was quite whole. It was too fine and flimsy to make strong rugs.

Her job was to hold the loose ends of the warp while her grandmother set up the loom. With time she became quicker than Sara Sabina at threading the heddle, because her eyes were better. But it took a long time for her arms to be strong enough to weave the heavy rag rugs or to be able to mix the dough for potato bread.

'Put your arm into it, girl,' her grandmother said, and Tora gave her all. It was heavy work. The stiff dough wouldn't roll in the bowl.

The first time Tora scrubbed the kitchen floor, Lans was sitting by the door and Sara Sabina lifted him outside in his chair. He sat turned towards the kitchen, talking to Tora while she scrubbed.

'Well, the fun's certainly over,' he said. 'Things are getting serious now.'

Except for the occasional reprimand, he had hardly ever addressed her. Since he lost his legs, she didn't know what to think about him. In a way he was the same, just as frightening to her. But what had impressed her most about him had always been his legs in his big boots. In the old days, they would walk all the way to Ridgeview to visit the saddlemaker. He would thunder along the dusty road, never turning around to see whether she and Rickard were keeping up. And he wouldn't say a word to them all the way. Children should heed. That was all. But she had admired his long strides in his square-toed boots — at least he was a soldier and not just an ordinary dumb crofter. And he was her grandfather. Every time they got to a milestone he would take a break and light his pipe. But when they stopped he would turn his back on them, and of course he never talked with them.

Now he was old and had no legs and sat there on the chopping block by the door. Rickard had made a back for it, so he could sit up. Without support he would tumble, like an overfilled keg.

'Yes, things have changed. Truly they have.'

It was becoming clear that he was talking to her, not just rambling. Sara Sabina was off working, Rickard had left home.

'Yes, m'girl, the fun's over,' he said.

'Then Shame and Want will be along,' slipped out of her before she could think. She had no idea where it came from, but she knew they went together.

150

They held one another by the hand and danced in her mind, the stooped would-be gentleman, the bluish-white baby and the old man with his walking stick.

'What's that you said?'

It was the first time she had dared to speak up to him and what came out was so foolish. She was silent with terror and did not dare explain.

'I think she's a mite backward,' said Lans to Sara Sabina. 'That's all I can make of it.'

After that, he didn't speak to her any more. But he did make some show of vanity about her, asking Sara Sabina from time to time how the girl was making out at school.

'Her mother was no fool.'

Sara Sabina said nothing to that. But when he went on about how astonishingly fast Edla had learned the alphabet and to spell she interrupted him, sharp as the clip of a pair of scissors:

'And what good did that do anyone? She just went out into service two years earlier than she had to.'

'Yes, so at least she had her room and board,' said Lans.

Sara Sabina turned around then, so he could see her face. She had never before said a word about Edla's fate.

'She hadn't even been confirmed,' she said.

The soldier took in the look in her eyes and appeared to want to answer, but for once he couldn't get a word out.

There was only a single story about Edla. Tora had heard it for the first time when she was very small, and then it was really the story of the wise man over at Ox Spring, who rubbed wounds with sugar and cobwebs and cured girls who were in trouble by reading over them. Lans said the man had a little genie under the ring finger of his left hand whom he brought to life every night with a drop of blood. But Sara

151

Sabina took the story away from Lans, and soon Tora knew that Edla, too, had been to see the wise man read over a girl called Hanna. Stories are so much wiser and gentler than we that Tora came to realize over the years that both girls had actually crouched down and been read over by the wise man. Sara Sabina explained that he put a pair of scissors on the table when he was reading over girls, with one end pointing north and the other at the tummy of the girl. That was what made it work.

Carefully, the story added a piece of knowledge Tora needed: Edla had not been her sister as she had always thought, and one end of the scissors had been pointing at Hanna's belly, the other at Edla's.

'Did it help?'

At that, Sara Sabina's mouth, so thin and drawn that it looked as if it were stitched together, pinched up and she muttered softly. Slowly, Tora came to understand this story without fear.

But there had been no need for Sara Sabina to worry about Tora's finishing school early and having to go into service before her time. Although she was not backward, she was not especially clever. When she was studying her catechism, Lans asked anxiously:

'She's not one of the slow ones, is she?'

No, she had not been put in the slow group, nor at the end of the line. She was taller and bigger than Edla had been. Strangely, they had had more food for their younger children. Sara Sabina bought Tora a confirmation dress from the director of the poor house. It had belonged to a woman who had died, and Sara Sabina dyed it with Brazil wood. With fishbone stays at the waist, Tora looked both thin and stately. According to Lans, she was round in the right places.

But he couldn't make his peace with her borrowed hat. At first he had intended to forbid her to wear it, believing that, except for the gentry, of course, only a certain kind of woman wore a hat. He'd had to reconsider. All the girls who were being confirmed wore hats nowadays, hats that hovered high on their heads, fastened to their hair-buns with hatpins. Still, he didn't like it.

'Besides which,' he said, 'scarves made the girls' faces seem rounder and more kissable. In my day.'

Tora, though, couldn't imagine that any girls would ever have wanted to kiss him, even in his day. His white beard was getting greener and greener around his mouth.

Sara Sabina hadn't really wanted their youngest girl to have to toil for farmers, but of course it was out of the question for Tora to have her way and move into town. Mamsell Winlöf, the restaurant proprietress herself, had stopped Tora several times on her way to school and talked with her as if they were old acquaintances. Tora found this strange.

'You look like Edla,' Sara Sabina said curtly.

When she was studying her catechism she came home and said Mamsell Winlöf had offered her work in her kitchen. But Sara Sabina had said no. Said no in no uncertain terms and without an explanation. Tears of helplessness rose in Tora's eyes. She remembered once having been dressed up in a dress and black boots at the annual charity Christmas party. She had sat there in a fancy dress and watched four parlour pieces, in all of which the handsome Baron Fogel, stationmaster, played the male lead. There were two one-act comedies, 'An Uneasy Night' and 'The Rose of Kungsholmen', as well as the unforgettable 'Two Directors' in which the telegraphist's moustache had accidentally caught

153

fire when, in an unscripted move, he had stumbled into the footlights and overturned a kerosene lantern. Tora and three other children had declaimed the prologue stationmaster Cederfalk had written for the party. Her verses had been:

'Though no street lights we have to go home by
To the lights in our hearts we pay heed.
There are tots who in unheated rooms lie
And who suffer the harshest of need.

So when Bethlemen's star casts its light
From the heavenly vault of deep blue
Surely one tiny ray through the night
To the poorest of hovels shines through.'

She never forgot them. But when she got back to Appleton with the dress and the boots and her grandfather realized that she was meant to keep them after the party, he boiled over. He didn't accept charity. And so, feeling hateful and rebellious, she returned the best dress she had ever worn.

And now her grandmother refused even to listen to Mamsell Winlöf. Instead, she went grovelling to the farmers and when Tora was finally confirmed there was a place for her in service with one of Sara Sabina's relatives. The farm was called Meadowlands, and the farmer was well off. The first time Sara Sabina went there to ask about a place for her granddaughter was a Sunday, and there had been a boiled chicken with white gravy on the table. Sara Sabina had found this reassuring. Even the flies seemed fat and complacent in the big kitchen. Not until much later did she realize she had no idea how many mouths that chicken was meant to feed, and that she had certainly not been invited to stay to dinner.

Tora Lans was fifteen years old when she went to Meadowlands. She was strong and built for work, as her grandmother had said. She was blond and sturdy. Maybe there *was* something a little backward about her, Sara Sabina wondered anxiously to herself. Still, the main thing was that she was strong and capable. She had at least fifty working years ahead of her. It would only be natural if she eventually got together with a farmhand of her own age. She hoped they would be able to get a croft, and not have to be estate workers. Really, though, Sara Sabina would have liked Tora to find work at a manor, and learn a skill rather than manual labour. She had a dream after all her own years of heavy drudgery. She dreamt that Tora would become a dairymaid. But that dream remained her private secret.

She went to Meadowlands frequently to see how Tora was getting on. The woman of the house accused her of hanging around hoping to get something to take home, but Sara Sabina denied this vehemently and didn't let it keep her from going, because she had been feeling suspicious since the day she left Tora there. That day, they had stopped to rest their legs by a barn at the edge of the farm and caught sight of the words that had been etched deeply into the wall with a nail, and apparently kept fresh by many passers-by:

This is the road to Meadowlands
Where no servants stay, neither maids nor hands.

But Tora stayed.

She came home in the autumn of 1894. She had turned seventeen. She brought her bundle of things and said she wouldn't be returning to Meadowlands after the weekend. She told Sara Sabina the farmer's wife had thrown her out.

Sara Sabina should have hurried to get her a new position but quickly realized there was no point. Tora started to talk, hesitantly at first. Her story took all winter to tell, and was a lot like the song about the poor farmhand who wept inconsolably until the serving maid let him sleep in her arms. However, it had not been a farmhand but the farmer's own son, heir to Meadowlands. What had the poor girl imagined?

When she had finally allowed him to sleep in her arms he had been equally inconsolable until she had allowed him between her legs. And just like in the song, he felt that he would perish if she didn't let him put it in and jiggle it around. Eventually, she had let him have his way with everything, because she had never before seen love afflict a grown man so terribly that he cried like a baby. She had felt like the bestower of bounty, in addition to believing that every little jiggle brought her a little closer to a future as farmer's wife, with her miserly, loathsome mother-in-law relegated to a little cottage behind the main house. It had made semi-starvation bearable, knowing what the future held just around the corner.

Was she really a bit backward, as Sara Sabina had feared? No, not any longer.

When her belly grew round, she was shown the door, and of course the farmer's son had been inconsolable. That boy could really turn on the tears. But he obeyed his mother, and when it all finally came out, he just looked down and said he wasn't sure what to think. That was his reaction when Tora shouted at him that his mother was claiming he hadn't been the only one to have her.

The betrayal was the part of the story she found most difficult to tell. After that would have been the time for reproaches, for being bawled out. But the story had taken so long to tell that Sara Sabina never got out what she should have said. She was also too concerned about Tora's health. And Lans thought that was laughable, considering what a healthy, strong girl Tora was.

The very first month after she returned home, Tora was also more beautiful than she would ever be again. After this, her features grew coarser and the blotchy mask of pregnancy appeared on her face. As her compassion for the farmer's son had peaked during the haying, she was due in April. Sara Sabina spent the early part of the spring running errands to a childless couple in Stegsjö, trying to convince them to take Tora's child.

In addition to having a farm of their own, he was a tiled stove maker. They lived well, if sparingly. Their childlessness was a great sorrow to them. They were both nearly fifty and had abandoned hope. They had been talking about taking a foster child born to a good, healthy girl for years, but now that they had the perfect opportunity, they couldn't actually make up their minds. Sara Sabina was upset because she was wearing out the soles of her shoes running back and forth to Stegsjö all spring. Every time she got there they were sitting in the same position at the kitchen table, shaking their heads in unison, still uncertain. In the end she had to invent a shoemaker and his wife in the village who also wanted the child, and they finally made up their minds, although with great difficulty. She accepted fifty kronor from them to feed Tora well at the end of her pregnancy. She must really see to it that nothing went wrong now, the tiled stove maker and his wife insisted. Sara Sabina welcomed this fifty kronor note for more than one reason. It was now a barrier between the couple in Stegsjö and their vacillation. They could hardly ask for it back.

Tora had her baby in Easter week. Sara Sabina delivered her alone. She had put Lans to bed in the kitchen. Sara Sabina was the more anxious of the two. But Tora was healthy and laboured like an animal for more than twenty hours. She gave birth to a big, strong boy, and the old woman had never seen a newly-delivered mother so quick to sit up and reach out for the child.

'We'll have none of that,' said Sara Sabina.

The tiled stove maker and his wife were waiting out in the kitchen with Lans. They had demanded in no uncertain terms that the baby was not to be held by its mother. They were afraid she would want it back.

'Give him to me,' said Tora. 'I just want to hold him for an hour. Then they'll have him for life.'

She sounded furious despite her fatigue, and tried to get out of bed and walk over to her grandmother, who was bathing and swaddling him.

'He won't live without milk!'

'They've got a wet nurse.'

'Give him to me.'

She started to haemorrhage and stared down at her legs in fright. Slowly she got herself back into bed and lay very still. She was groggy and tired and fell asleep with tears running down her cheeks. Then they came in from the kitchen and touched her shoulder cautiously. She thought they were holding the baby and reached out for it, only to find the dry hand of the stovemaker's wife's in hers. She demanded that they shake hands solemnly and made Tora promise never again to have anything to do with the child.

'I swear. You swine,' said Tora.

The woman began to weep.

'She's exhausted,' said Sara Sabina. 'Don't you mind what she said.'

'Well, isn't this a nice start?' commented the stovemaker's wife.

'You get on home now,' said Sara Sabina. 'It'll be best that way.'

She was afraid they would begin having second thoughts. Out in the kitchen lay Lans, and for once in his life he was utterly silent and merely glared.

She only stayed another month at Appleton. Thinking she hadn't done enough, her grandmother wanted to get her another place on a farm. But Tora said she was going to town, to see Mamsell Winlöf who had once promised her a job.

'Life can be different,' she said.

'You don't know what you're talking about.'

'I've done all the farm service I ever mean to do.'

When she had left, Sara Sabina lived on the hope that Mamsell Winlöf would have forgotten her promise long ago. Because although it was clear enough that a young girl could have just as much trouble with the farmers as she might have in town, Sara Sabina hadn't changed her views. Farmers were at least predictable.

Tora came home, however, in a new black dress, and emptied a hamper from the railway restaurant in the kitchen. One container held a wobbly mass she said had been a star-shaped pyramid of fish aspic.

'Now life's going to be different,' she said. 'I'll show you.'

The hamper also contained day-old bread and sausage ends, but Sara Sabina couldn't take her eyes off the trembling pile of fish.

'There's nothing wrong with it,' said Tora. 'Except someone put their elbow in it. It's cold boiled hake.'

'That's not food for the likes of us,' whined Lans.

He grew increasingly lonely. Old Mothstead died. No one but Tora and occasionally Rickard came to Appleton and talked with him. He would sit and listen through the door, but he could never get Sara Sabina to hear what he heard: hunting horns and voices in the distance.

'I think you're getting hard of hearing,' he said. But he had no one else to talk to, so he would say to her as he so often had:

'A man's a man for a' that', and I'm a man as has lived his life. It began in Stegsjö parish on the farm at Great Kedevi.'

'Yes, yes,' answered Sara Sabina, 'but since you seem to have nothing better to do, you can copy out this curlicue for me.'

'Which one? *Whose is that voice ....*'

She wanted to learn to write now. It wasn't enough that he'd taught her to read in his first few years of being stuck in one place.

'Whose is that voice that makes my heart to tremble? An angel's voice it is, from heavenly choirs. Oh, sleep no more...' he thundered, relinquishing no opportunity to read aloud. But his old woman was as impatient as ever and pushed the pen in his direction. She watched attentively as he copied the difficult, spiralling W from the hymnal. The script writing he had learned decades ago at the regiment no longer came so

160

easily to him. But he never revealed his uncertainty to Sara Sabina.

'What good does it do women to write?' he asked. 'You tell me that.'

'None of your business,' she said.

As they were about to serve the soup, Ebba whispered something to Tora. Because her hands were full, she nudged Tora with her elbow. Tora's ear went bright red, probably just from the heat of Ebba's mouth, but it looked as if a blush had begun there. She took a deep breath to stifle her giggles, and the two girls entered the banquet room, eyes wide, not daring to look at one another for fear they would burst out laughing. When Tora set stationmaster Cederfalk's soup in front of him, he leaned forward, his bulging eyelids heavy, his eyes glassy. His large, impressive nose sought the aromatic vapours above the bowl. The man had an aquiline smeller, highly responsive, with coarse, porous skin. It was easy to imagine that his taste buds were on the outside, increasing his receptivity. Tora felt her blush mounting, her eyes filling. With stricken control, she put down two bowls of soup and walked stiffly out of the room and through the pantry door without looking at anyone, especially Ebba. Once out of sight, she bent double, over a table with baskets of cutlery. She tried to laugh silently, but little high-pitched giggles kept escaping. She felt the others poking and warning her, and then suddenly there was Ebba, hot, with tears of laughter running down her cheeks, throwing her arms around her. They laughed aloud, stifling their noise against one another's chests and necks. The embroidered edge of Tora's starched apron bib was damp, and the hair at Ebba's temples, which had been in such orderly curls, lay wet and straggling along her cheeks.

'Watch out, watch out,' Tora gasped. 'My apron!'

Then they separated. They had to. Ebba rushed downstairs to the kitchen and, a moment later, was serving in Mamsell Winlöf's private dining room.

'What was so funny?' Tekla whispered as she and Tora passed each other with their trays. Tora just hushed her. She couldn't explain. All Ebba had said was: 'Check Cederfalk's nose.'

Well, there was nothing funny about that unless you knew that two years earlier, when she was new at the railway restaurant, Tora had told Ebba in deadly earnest that all you had to do was look at a man's nose if you wanted to know how he was built somewhere else. She had heard it from somebody who worked at the inn. Ebba had corrected her, telling her that it was just an old wives' tale every girl heard at some point. Actually, the situation was precisely the other way around, and better she learned this now than suffer some terrible disappointment. If you saw a curved, aquiline, noble, boldly protruding, possibly even regally-veined nose, you could be ever so sure that all that man had in his trousers was a handful of loose skin around something that looked like a thumb.

'And that's the simple truth,' said Ebba.

Since that moment, they had had to hold their breath to keep from bursting into laughter every time they passed the elegant, unknowing daughters of the postmaster out walking with the handsome young station attendants, young men with bold noses. Still, Cederfalk's took the cake, Tora had to agree, although there was an impressive selection of noses around the long banquet table. There were also pursed lips that sought the edges of wine glasses and were related to those trembling noses. There were tongues, certainly not virginal, but not yet sandpapered or spoilt by cigar smoke and pick-me-ups, which gently rotated the sweetbreads in their mouths. Blunt but not insensitive fingertips palpated the first asparagus of the season, boyishly fresh and fragile. There was even Norrelius, the schoolmaster, who ate without paying the slightest attention to what he was shovelling in with his fork, and who was constantly looking around as he chewed for someone with whom to pick a quarrel.

The new schoolhouse had now been inaugurated. It had cost nearly thirty thousand kronor. Lindh the merchant now took his morning constitutional past the railway hotel, and turned to look back at the new post office, modelled on the Stockholm House of Nobility. Of course it was scaled down and foreshortened, and of course it was costly. However, it had been put in place to remove every trace of the pigsties, to transform the flat fields. When he got to the post office cum House of Nobility he turned around without crossing the street. From there he could see all the way to the new house he was having built for himself. It was modelled on the manor house. The manor, however, had been built when Sweden was a great power. His new home had to be reduced, cut back; it was a distortion of the original idea. But there it stood. Every morning, this view on his walk gave him the same thrill, the same pleasure. He was surprised that it did not diminish.

After this, being careful to avoid the cart tracks and potholes, he would cross the road to the railway park and continue his walk to Mulle's grave. He just wanted to give himself that extra pleasure of the view from the post office. Opposite the station there was now the new courthouse. Although it was only a wooden building and not much larger than the private homes lining King's Way, it gave them a more worthy place to hold Sunday services than the smelly loft above the Agricultural Guild's barn. He continued along the road to Ridgeview which, although it was rough and potted, bore some resemblance to a city street, for the first stretch. There was the new Savings Bank, a brick building with crow-step gables. He inhaled a strong scent of medicines as he passed. It sometimes annoyed him that nothing was just allowed to be what it was. There were church services and teetotaller's lectures in the courthouse. The pharmacy rented part of the savings bank. The entire ground floor of his own stately home was now office space, some of which was rented out to the telephone exchange. When he passed the open windows he heard Morse code being tapped, and from his own office he heard the light, eager noise of the ringing telephone, unlike any other sound in the world.

At the time the schoolhouse was being built, with its Romanesque windows and its stunted tower, Alexander Lindh altered his morning walk so it ended before Mulle's grave (which, incidentally, was hardly visible any longer, the gravestone having sunk into the grass). He would turn around at the bank, and walk back along King's Way and up to the school.

This morning, too, he had walked to the school and inspected the inauguration arrangements — the platform from which the railway band would play, the podium, decorated with the flag, branches and flowers. Cederfalk would later read his inaugural poem from there, and just now Lindh was sitting worrying that the former stationmaster would want to declaim it again over dessert. He intended to hold a little speech himself. He toasted the schoolteachers distractedly, staring at the waitress by the door.

Mamsell Winlöf preferred to hire tall, healthy girls with strong legs, cheerful girls. They ran up and down the stairs with loaded trays, leaving the doors ajar. The yellow cigar smoke and the heat hovered in the draught, and the voices wafted from one floor to the next. For the first few months Tora had felt as if the voices and the heat lifted her up the stairs, a hand beneath her buttocks. That was until she had worn down her boots — the uppers were now creased, the leather was too weak and loose, they gave her ankles no support. Now the heels were slanted, and she felt the uneven strain right in the small of her back.

She carried a tray in the palm of her right hand. Her left hand grasped the necks of three bottles of wine firmly and with accustomed skill between her fingers. She could carry four beer bottles like that.

'Send me waitresses, not barmaids,' merchant Lindh had once said to Mamsell Winlöf. Grim and furious, she had repeated his words to them. Now, however, she was elsewhere. She wasn't supervising as she usually did, statuesque in black silk at the sideboard. Tora shifted her weight to her right foot, and her hip shot out.

Lindh noticed that this was the same girl who had been to his office that morning. Alma had a telephone, but she preferred not to use it. On this occasion, he assumed she had been trying to avoid a confrontation.

'Mamsell Winlöf sent me to tell you that she cannot provide the catering for your dinner this evening unless you have it at the restaurant.'

The girl had been shown all the way in to his private office. His brother Adolf had stood beside her, blinking hard.

'Why ever not?'

'She hasn't the staff. She has a second dinner to serve as well.'

'Well, then she has nowhere to have us,' he said, 'if the banquet room is already booked.'

'No, the other dinner is in her private quarters.'

The girl hadn't looked him in the eye as she spoke. Her gaze sought the details of his office furnishings. Afterwards she would tell the other serving girls what Alexander Lindh's office looked like. He controlled his temper with difficulty, grasping the head of his brass eagle, and sent her away.

At home, he had no hostess. Caroline chose to remain out at Gertrudsborg. She wore nothing but wrinkled, loose-fitting housedresses. He preferred to order her cases of sweet wine through his business. Other than that, he asked nothing of Caroline, nothing at all. However, he was unable to entertain unless Alma Winlöf took care of the practical arrangements, and it embittered him. You don't build a new home and fill it with antiques purchased at auctions to have your business dinners at a restaurant!

He was dissatisfied with the service. It wasn't as quick as he was accustomed to, and a couple of the girls lacked demeanour and were flirting with Finck and Mandelstam, as if they were out in the public dining room. When Alma Winlöf's speciality, turkey chaud-froix came in, his suspicions grew. The platter looked all right when it was served at the host's end of the table, but further down he was afraid he glimpsed some greasy waxed paper among the croutons that ornamented the filled truffle. The jellied consommé cubes around the edge looked dull and disorderly as well. He tried to focus on it down there, but Mandelstam was helping himself and he just messed it all up even more, without noticing a thing. His eyes were glued to the waitress.

'You seem cheery today, Tora,' he whispered.

Her only reply was a deepening blush, and she looked away. Finck whispered something intended to make her laugh, but it failed. She moved along with the platter. The long, starched apron strings that were supposed to touch her hemline had begun to curl, and the ends looked as if they were playing with one another.

However, Alexander Lindh, who had been scrutinizing the service at the far end of the table, was now quite certain that his guests were being served from platters that had already been served elsewhere. He had begun to wonder whether the rushed service and the lack of attention were attributable to the other dinner party Alma was catering to in her own rooms. He missed Alma at the sideboard, keeping an eye on the girls. He was suddenly seized with icy fury at the thought that his guests were getting the second round, after someone else had messed up the platters.

'Who's Mamsell Winlöf serving in her rooms?' he asked the girl at his elbow.

'A private dinner party,' she answered, and it was perfectly clear that the line had been rehearsed. Lindh beckoned to his brother Adolf across the table.

'Go downstairs and find out what kind of private dinner party Alma is having in her rooms. And be discreet about it.'

Adolf blinked. He was handsome, he looked like royalty. His eyes bulged as much as Cederfalk's, his nose was aquiline. He lived, however, in a state of barely-contained simple-mindedness. His whiny voice and blank, pale blue

168

eyes often revealed helplessness and confusion. Still, he had proven to have a bent for bookkeeping and was manic in his attention to detail. He now ran the outer office. His neat lines of figures and his minutely perfectionistic appearance were a model to all. Each week he cut out merchant Lindh's sales barometer from the local newspaper and pinned it up on the office wall. Lindh now sold almost exclusively farming equipment, and the backbone of his product line came from Wärnström's.

Adolf had had a banner posted behind his brother's desk with the words:

MAY SWEDISH EQUIPMENT
TILL OUR SWEDISH SOIL

There was a circular picture of a huge harvester from the Alexander Lindh Sales Company reaping a field. It had been the cover picture of his calendar, because Alexander Lindh knew the value of advertising and saw no shame in it. Inside Lindh's head, next year's slogan was already taking shape:

MAY THE SOIL OF ALL THE WORLD
BE TILLED WITH SWEDISH MACHINES

He already exported a great deal, and would soon have sole rights to most of the equipment made in Sweden. The world was a big place, and he meant to have it. That is, all but Russia, a country that frightened him.

He was participating only distractedly in the conversation, his eyes glued to the door. He was expecting Adolf to return, but what he was really hoping was that Alma would come and take her place at the sideboard. He knew she was

169

annoyed with him for not having invited the schoolmistresses to his dinner after the schoolhouse inauguration. His sister-in-law Malvina was annoyed as well. He had pointed out to her that it was inconceivable for decent, unmarried women to accept an invitation to spend an evening out in a public place.

'You never know, they just might do it!' his sister-in-law had replied.

'That's the problem,' Alexander answered tartly. 'That's precisely why I have decided to spare them the embarrassment by not inviting them.'

'Your paternalistic beneficence knows no bounds,' said Malvina. Both at home and in company Adolf was totally inept. Malvina said and did as she pleased. She was one of the very first women to become a competition-walking enthusiast.

Tucker, the engineer who had been called in from England to plan the English dairy, had introduced lawn tennis the previous spring. Alexander found it a reasonable enough pastime, and financed the building of a court. He even enjoyed the sight of ladies lethargically swatting the ball to one another. However, now Mrs. Tucker, a pale redhead with a sharp voice, had invented this new recreation for the ladies of the very highest echelons of society (an echelon so thin that it could not bear even a hint of ridicule, as Lindh was the first to realize).

It was spring. The dirt road leading north towards Ridgeview was pitted with potholes from the rain. The ladies marched along through this cratered landscape with their skirts pinned up, carved walking sticks in hand. At first, one could hear high-pitched screams when they were splashed with the muddy, brown water. They took huge, masculine strides, standing tall. They were competition-walking. This was a sport.

They no longer sat demurely on their chaise longues and their curved couches. They no longer smiled silently over their embroidery frames. They returned from their race-walking to eat every last crumb from the platters of sandwiches set out for tea, to make jokes with Alexander, and to inquire about his exports.

Adolf returned. Alexander thought he looked disturbed. He slid past his brother, just brushing his ear with:

'I really can't say. You'll have to go down yourself, Alex, I honestly do not know.'

The dinner party was now at the point where people's senses were dulled. Soon they would no longer be receptive to anything at all. This numbness, this flagging vitality, could very well have been served a far less fine wine than the wine being poured. It didn't bother Alexander. He mumbled his apologies and left the table. Let them think what they damn well pleased. It was his party.

'I'm going down to see that the musicians are provided for,' he muttered in the direction of Adolf's blank expression, framed between two candle flames.

He had arranged for the railway band and some of the junior railway staff to dine in the public dining room. One of the barmaids followed him anxiously all the way down, and he signalled for a glass and proposed a toast to the red, sweaty faces. They shouted 'Three cheers for Lindh.' It was noisy down there. The snow-white tablecloths on the big serving table were now stained with beetroot. Passengers waiting for their trains were crowded into the other half of the dining room. For their sake, there was soured milk on the table, as usual, but now it was accompanied by roast veal, roast beef, and enormous towers of fish aspic. Alexander Lindh waved through the haze of smoke and said a few loud words no one could hear to the musicians. They cheered him again.

He left them, and his feet found their way readily down the long hall and the flight of stairs leading to Alma's apartment. He encountered two waitresses on the way, but he did not ask them to get Alma. He did not want to see her here. All he wanted was a peek at the party she was catering to in her private dining room, and for the sake of whom she had allowed the town dignitaries to be served from awkwardly repaired platters of food from which others had already been served. The thought of royalty and nobility had crossed his mind, but the royal dining room was shut and dark.

A third waitress came rushing out with a full tray as he stood in Alma's drawing room, and they nearly collided in the plush drapery. When she had passed, he moved the pleated red velvet slightly to one side. The odour that struck him from inside was hot from sooty candles, breathing skin, eau de cologne and the aroma of food. There were only women in there.

They sat close together, crowded around the oval table. Furniture had been rearranged, pushed up against the walls, but it was still so crowded that many of them had palm leaves tickling the backs of their necks, and the bookshelf looked as if it were about to fall over. Alma sat at the head of the table, and could not see him. All seven of the schoolmistresses were seated around her table, along with five or six sympathizers, spearheaded by Malvina Lindh, at the other end. Almost every one of them was a competition-walking convert.

Alexander Lindh was not one of those men who thought it unsuitable for women to eat, or even to be seen eating. Still, this was too much. He had never seen the likes of it; it was grotesque. Actually, he only saw one of them, his gaze locked into her and could not move on. It was one of the schoolmistresses. Her name was Magnhild Lundberg and she was no spring chicken. To his knowledge, she had no family, no relations in the community. It went without saying that she was a spinster. This single woman, no doubt a pathetic creature, occupied the seat next to Malvina's. She had a large linen napkin in her lap, stained with a wine spill that had dried violet brown. On the plate in front of her there was a half breast of a small woodcock, gleaming with gravy. Magnhild Lundberg was laughing with the others, but her laughter was distracted, her mind completely preoccupied with the fowl on her plate and the curly little morels she was stabbing one at a time with her fork and putting in her mouth. Her cheeks were red. She chewed hard on big mouthfuls. Then she inserted both knife and fork into the little hen and applied firm pressure, cracking the breastbone. She carved a huge bite of meat and put it straight into her mouth. Before she could swallow it she added a bite of stuffing, too. When Malvina Lindh made a comment, she was unable to reply at first. She chewed, shook her head, her eyes filling with tears of laughter.

He was utterly mystified, but there was one thing he realized clearly. After dinner she would not sit like the other women of her age he knew. When the card tables were set up, they would stay on the couches sipping mineral water, pale with the pain of suppressed wind.

Alma saw him. She was pale, her brown eyes meant business. He quickly let the velvet drapery fall, heard her excusing herself — she was going to see how things were in the banquet room.

She was dressed in black satin and wearing her garnets. The skin at her throat was so soft that her pendant appeared to be resting on cotton, and it gleamed brightly. It struck him suddenly that she must have bought her jewels herself. He had never given her anything. She had declined his gifts with an unusual intensity he pretended not to notice.

He straightened up. Alma's waistline must have doubled since he stood here in her drawing room for the first time, but she was also taller, or so it seemed. There was something upright about her; she grew straight out of herself.

'I see you're entertaining,' he said.

'Yes.'

He stepped backwards and felt himself almost stumble against the fire screen. He knew the room well and seldom bumped into anything there, even when he was moving carelessly. Now, however, his movements became cautious and calculated, and he continued to step backwards, seeking with his hand for the dark mahogany edge of the screen and following it until he could grasp the round knob at the end. He held it.

'I preferred not to embarrass the schoolmistresses with an invitation,' he said.

'Oh, yes?'

'Unmarried women in a public restaurant, do you approve of such a thing?'

She smirked.

'Originally you intended to have your dinner party at the Lindh mansion,' she said, and he thought he heard the undertone of sarcasm in her designation.

'But I was forced to have it in a public restaurant.'

174

'Now you're confusing cause and effect, I'm afraid,' she replied, smiling even more openly.

He felt his neck go bright red, his flesh tightened, his heart pounded, and he seized the knob on the screen with all his might. He was tempted to reply, but recalled another occasion on which his wrath had misled him into a response that had become a blemish on his reputation and a standing joke in town. It was at the office, and he had howled:

'There's no need for logic here. I'm in charge!'

So he remained silent, and she went on:

'Anyway, everything's all right now. There is a party for the schoolmistresses, and it is being held in a private home.'

He knew her body so well that he would have seen any hostility that had been there. He would have heard it in her breathing and, if he had been standing closer to her, sensed it in the smell of her warm neck. She was simply amused. So he said:

'I would beg to differ as to the private nature of the home of the restaurant proprietress.'

For the first time during the conversation, he looked her straight in the eye. She was perfectly still, but breathing harder. The garnets rose and fell in their soft bed.

'Please go upstairs and see to your waitresses,' he said. 'It's more like a bar-room than a banquet room up there tonight.'

He thought to himself, 'That's all I should have said. That's all I should have said.' He headed out, suddenly afraid he might stumble over a carpet fringe, or a little ottoman.

Ebba rushed past Tora, her underarms pungent. She smelled like a hot stove someone had spilt paraffin on. Oh, this was great! 'I can just imagine how I must reek,' thought Tora in a panic. The girls were not allowed to smell sweaty here. Not even late at night, emerging through the haze of smoke with one last tray of drinks. You might have a headache, be seeing stars, have every ounce of your awareness trembling like the point of a pin at the small of your back. But you were not allowed to stink.

'Cleanliness! Cleanliness!' Mamsell Winlöf preached to them. This significant, substantial word should be written in every kitchen, great or small. Their only cash wages were the gratuities the guests left them, but they had free lodging, board, and uniforms. She had them sew round flannel patches to put into their black dresses, several sets for each dress. They folded them double and basted them in where sleeve met bodice, to protect the black fabric from the secretions of their armpits. They were supposed to wash their patches every evening, themselves. All their other underwear was sent out to Dahlgren's laundry with the other washing.

Tora's body had looked after itself, it had given her both pleasure and pain, but she had rarely given it a thought. That was until she was hired for the restaurant and had to think about it all the time so it would not tell tales on her: reveal that she was hot or ill or tired.

'The worst thing is when you've been with a man,' said Ebba. 'Not even holding your breath helps then.'

Mamsell would come up to their rooms at 'the Pigpen' and sort through their clothing herself, the girls shivering in their night-dresses, side by side in bed, clutching their knees.

'Cleanliness, cleanliness!' she preached, lifting up one soiled garment after the next. Still, she didn't make them wash their feet. Their boots effectively stifled anything their feet might have to say about their wretched condition.

So now Tora knew that a body was just a bother. It sweated and dripped and bled and swelled, but if you wanted to keep your job at the Railway Hotel, none of that must show. Mamsell had the girls crochet sanitary pads for themselves from candlewick. They were not allowed to use rags or newspapers. These pads, hanging by the dozens on the lines at Dahlgren's laundry, made a great hit, however, with the schoolboys, and so the girls refused to send them out. In the end, Mamsell Winlöf had to get the old woman from out at Tramphut to take in the embarrassing laundry. She lived so far out of town that the schoolboys would be hard pressed to find their way there.

'You'd best keep out of Mamsell's way,' Tora whispered to sweaty Ebba.

'Aw, she won't be up here tonight.'

She didn't appear to be coming. Merchant Lindh had been down to her place, so now people were letting on about her guests. Adolf was the first to let the cat out of the bag. Both Mandelstam and Finck asked Tora, but she kept quiet. Ebba couldn't, however, and told them, breathlessly, about the schoolmistresses. Mandelstam and Finck gave her seventy-five öre on their way out. The merchant gave Tora fifty. She curtsied extra deeply to both Cederfalk and Adolf Lindh, but it didn't produce a penny.

'Bugger them,' she said to Ebba as she unlaced her boots. 'Stingier than the parson.'

They shared a narrow room in the long, tall wooden building opposite the post office. It belonged to Mamsell

Winlöf, who rented out flats and office space there, and had had a couple of the flats made over into little rooms for her staff. Down in the yard, her pigs squealed. They were fed at irregular hours, often at night when the kitchen at the inn was being cleaned, and so they tended to squeal the moment they heard the gate open. The whole place, including the building where the girls lived, the pigsties and the mangling shed, was known as the Pigpen. There was almost never a quiet time there. The railway workers who rented the flats came home from the night shift, and the pigs squealed hopefully. There was the sound of sand clattering against the girls' window, and often, even before they could respond, other windows would open wide and women's voices would bark out curses.

'Just 'cause *they're* married, we don't get to have any fun,' said Ebba.

On this spring night, in a quiet moment the sound of gravel under thin shoe souls could be heard, followed by sprightly whistling, not unlike the first tentative trill of a canary. Ebba peeked behind the curtain.

'It's Mandelstam and that little turd Finck! The one with the girlie hands. Did you see them? But, oh deary me what a little nose that Fincky has! Shall I open, Tora? Let's see what they want.'

They wanted to drink a toast to Ebba, and had come around with a night-cap.

'Oh no, I don't take to that kind of stuff,' Ebba mouthed back.

'But Ebba, sweetie, it's nice sweet wine. Be a good girl now! Our toes are cold.'

'It must be freezing out there,' Ebba said in Tora's direction. 'Shall we have them up for a while?'

Tora didn't reply. Her dress was lying across the chair, her boots standing next to it, their necks flopping. She had crept down into her place by the wall, leaving Ebba's side of the bed free. She was already snoring.

'Are you having me on?' Ebba asked. The canary sounded again, but it didn't wake Tora.

'Aw,' said Ebba. 'You're just fooling.'

She shut the window with a huge yawn. Once she was in bed she listened to the gentle whistling for a while, and fell asleep smiling softly.

She was fifty-three years old and never daydreamed. For that matter she hadn't been much of a daydreamer in the bloom of her youth, either. She lived in the real world and did not fantasize about people. She very seldom talked about herself, and when she talked about others she was often quite critical. And she never talked to herself in the lame, vague, but fluid language of daydreams.

It was true: her movements were dignified and this dignity had originally taken shape in a dream she had had of herself. It was, however, a dream she was able to bring to fulfilment.

In Alma Winlöf's apartment there was only one single piece of furniture from the home of the late coffin-maker Eriksson, the only piece she had kept after her parents passed away. It was a roll-top desk of pale birch, made by a cabinet-maker at Great Kedevi. For many years this desk had housed some small yellow boxes that were the repository of her tools for living with people in the real world.

She had connections that reached down like a complex web of roots straight through strata upon strata of the community. There were dependencies that had originated in money lent and agreements made. There were also matters that were merely sensed, theoretical possibilities, smiles, concessions, and slight pressure that could be increased if necessary, but that might never have to be.

In the boxes with the yellow bone latches, she had stored promissory notes for many years. However, the most important ones to her had always been the unwritten debts of Alexander Lindh. He had borrowed wherever he could in the village during his early years, when he was short of money. Now the market had changed, was what Alexander Lindh said. Times were good. He had paid off his debts long ago.

That night she allowed herself the rare luxury of a nocturnal waking dream, sitting at the roll-top desk. For one moment, the whole Railway Hotel was silent. The smell of tobacco had penetrated all the way to her drawing room. She was usually able to keep it out, the stench of a public place. Then she remembered that Malvina Lindh and two of the schoolmistresses had smoked after dinner.

She had put out all the lights but the desk lamp. Now Alexander Lindh entered her dream. She heard his footsteps and his energetic breathing. Now he was standing in the dark over by the drapery. Her back sensed his presence. She had dimmed the lamp so low that the light only fell in a circle around her hand, resting on the birch desktop. She could never see her hands nowadays without noticing their dryness. Everywhere else on her body there was a layer of fat holding the skin taut, but the back of her hand was a grid of dry wrinkles 'Alligator skin,' she thought with disgust. A quick, dry hand with the skin of an ageing woman. She had kept him waiting beyond the drapery while she considered her hand. Now she brought him in. He crossed the rug in a few steps.

'Alma!'

His voice was low. He was pleading with her. She did not turn around, but she straightened her bowed back in the tight black satin.

181

'Alma, forgive me for what I said. You know my temper.'
She smiled down at her hand, resting on the grained, polished birch desktop. She knew his temper all right. It was his prime mover, the pistons of wrath, the hot steam driving him. She let her eyes rest on her hand, then turned slowly towards him. In her dream all her movements were slow and extremely deliberate.

'My dear Alex,' she said, in her dream both remaining at the desk, slightly stooped, and at the same time rising to move towards him, hands outstretched.

'So, for many years when you have come to see me, you have been visiting a public place. I do know, Alex. It was no surprise to me. I know that having a relationship with anyone but the restaurant proprietress would have done immeasurable damage to your status.'

She had to slow down, to swallow.

'But one thing must confuse your friends. If they scrutinize the taxation register they can see that I have the highest income, nearly eight thousand kronor. You come second, with just over five thousand annually. We are followed by Cederfalk, Wilhelmsson, Wärnström, and the others.'

She smiled gently.

'Your friends are thus forced to acknowledge that I have not been prompted by need.'

At that very moment she decides not to say a word about the taxation register and their incomes. Instead, she will just think it, just stay seated at her desk and think it. After which she will rise and move towards him; his face, a mere shadow.

'You need not beg my forgiveness, my dear Alex. I have known for ages what you told your friends. My friendship

182

with you has been big enough to survive that. In fact it has also encompassed your —

— cowardice,' she thinks. A greasy, slimy word. 'Your cowardice, Alex.' She feels nauseous. She leans over the desktop, spasms of queasiness seizing her. She breaks out in a cold sweat and opens the palm of her hand, sees its damp furrows and realizes that this is not part of the dream. She may be sick on the carpet.

Then she hears the clinking of the panes of glass in the outside door, hears the pantry door bang, rapid footsteps, knocking. 'Here he comes,' she thinks, irrationally, since she can hear very well that they are a woman's footsteps. 'He did come, after all.'

It was Tora Lans. She opened the door without waiting for a reply. She had a shawl around her shoulders, her dress was unbuttoned, her bodice showing.

'Tora!'

'Fire, Mamsell!'

Alma's nausea had passed. She folded her hands on the desktop and looked mildly at Tora.

'How dramatic, Tora dear.'

She was quite accustomed to these alarms. The grease in the ventilation system over the great cast iron stove often caught fire. Once a curtain in the guest apartment had been ignited.

'No,' Tora shouted. 'There really is a fire. The Pigpen is in flames! Don't you hear it, Mamsell?'

Not until that moment did the restaurant proprietress hear the switch engine outside, running up and down the track blowing its whistle, and she realized the sound had been going on for some time.

'Button your dress, Tora,' she said, rising. 'We'll go together.'

They say that when the Pigpen burned down you could smell the fried pork all the way to Backe and Vallmsta.

Yet not a single pig was burned alive. The first thing anyone did was to open the door to the pigsty, and fifteen fatting pigs rushed out through the fire line, consisting of boys who were supposed to keep people from coming too close. The pigs broke the boys' red and white rods, people shoved through from one direction and pigs from the other.

At Wilhelmsson's and Wärnström's, all the way on the other side of the railway, the factory whistles blew. Farmer Helmer Svensson, a member of the fire brigade, ran backwards and forwards between the buildings, shouting into a megaphone.

People stood about, commenting and staring at the Pigpen which had never looked so good as it did in flames. The fire roared, the window panes shattered from the heat. The hot air was filled with the sounds of breaking glass and sizzling. The locomotive went backwards and forwards, backwards and forwards, spouting white steam. Fifteen galloping pigs were herded with broomsticks, poked with broken walking sticks, squealing in anguish and fear of the crowd. The barrels of beer in the restaurant proprietress' storerooms exploded, and the barrels of oil and kerosene in the basement shop burst into flames.

Work shoes and heavy boots clattered on the stairs. *The men of the winged wheel fleeing from the red peril*, as the newspaper later reported. Truth be told, there were also thin-soled dress shoes fleeing down the stairs, and applause out in the yard when little Finck came running out with his braces flying, followed by a barmaid named Tekla, carrying his dinner jacket over her arm. Ebba sneered, standing there dizzy and icy cold with all her worldly goods in a bundle at her feet.

At the other end of the building people had to slide down ropes improvised from sheets, and came crashing to the ground in nothing but their night-dresses. Edvin Adolfsson, the engine stoker was applauded for his machine-made underwear. Yes, things had really changed since the days when a fire would have put every man, woman and child to work with a bucket, passing and pouring to douse the flames. Now lots of people just stood around with a cagey look in their eyes. The men stood there estimating what the place was worth, one sum more fantastic than the next. At last Mamsell Winlöf arrived, with a serving girl at her heels. She stood upright watching, and the heat hit her face but she did not move. The boldest of the spectators ventured:

"'It's got a case of the runs," like the farmer said when the privy burned down.'

In the end, the fire brigade did arrive, with the two huge hose cars. The chief fireman, Baron and stationmaster Gustav Adolf Cederfalk, was still in his evening trousers. The cold night air made him hiccough. The hoses were assembled, the horses unharnessed, and people tried to shoo the pigs and the crowd out of the way. The firemen aimed the flow of water, which was uneven and pulsating at first, until the sixteen pumpmen found their rhythm. But something wasn't quite right. One of the pumpmen spun around and shouted a question as the first straight stream of thick water hit Cederfalk in the back, and he danced away as if he had been seized tightly by the nape of the neck. The pumpman, frightened, lost his balance, and the stream of water arched over the crowd, showering them and spewing brown water into their open mouths, quenching their rude remarks and their cheers. Cederfalk turned around, regaining his balance, arms akimbo, and shouted the words that every source from brown ink in detailed diaries to newspaper clippings and letters that will soon crumble to shreds, have retained to the letter, unanimous even as to the spelling:

'Arrrre you daft, tin-smith???'

Yes, the hoses were rusty and the ladders rotten, that much is true. But it's a lie that carpenter Fredriksson who was supposed to signal the fire brigade to gather never arrived because he was lying dead drunk under a lamppost. He was cross-eyed, though, that part's right.

While people were still being hoisted down at the far end of the building, Valfrid Johansson and his brother Ebon went up to Tora and asked how she had got out. Well, there was nothing dramatic about how Tora and Ebba escaped, they had woken to the shouting and smelled the smoke immediately. 'Did you get everything out with you?' Valfrid asked, and Tora suddenly put her hand to her mouth as she was wont to do when she opened it involuntarily in surprise or laughter, since she was missing a tooth.

She felt shy around Valfrid. She had believed for a long time that he was her father, when she was young and foolish. In the end he had read her mind, and was upset.

'I couldn't have been more than twelve,' he had said. 'You mustn't think that. I don't even have an inkling who he was.' He also said he would never forget Edla.

'What's wrong, Tora?'

'I forgot the photograph,' she said. She took her hand from her mouth and swallowed. The fire wasn't funny any more and she was desperately cold.

'What photograph?'

'Of Edla.'

She never called the girl in the picture mother. He knew the picture she meant. Her grandmother had given it to her, and Edla was wearing a plaid dress in it. But her face was almost worn away. It was like ashes that would blow away with the first gust of wind.

'What a pity,' said Valfrid. 'I guess that was all you had of your mother.'

'You'd best go in and rescue it for her then,' said Ebon, and Tora was ignited with a mad hope, so she forgot to close her mouth to cover her faulty bite. Then she realized Ebon had been joking. He frightened her. He stood staring at the fire with his hands in his trouser pockets and his roll-brimmed hat down his neck. He was an instigator, those were factory owner Wärnström's words. He wasn't allowed to come anywhere near the workshop or Wilhelmsson's carpentry shop, and he was a brakeman now. When she served in the third-class dining room he tried to chat her up. But she was intimidated, he was nothing like his elder brother.

Then something strange and wondrous happened, although Tora didn't see it. She lost sight of the Johansson brothers, they got separated in the crowd of pigs, people and horses. Tora grabbed a pail and joined the bucket line running from Cats' End up to the mangling shed. The pigsties and the apartment building were beyond salvation, and the fire brigade commander shouted hopelessly to the hosemen and pumpmen, who were tripping over one another and over the rusty nozzles. Then an old woman said:

'It won't be long til the mangling shed's afire.'

And someone replied:

'I'd hate to see it go.'

There wasn't a better mangle to rent anywhere in the village than the one where the serving girls from the restaurant mangled the hotel tablecloths hard and shiny between two huge stone rollers. So two women from the village took command of the best hoses. This was reported in the record from the fire brigade command, a report which came to resemble the record of a disaster at sea. Every woman in sight then formed two long bucket lines running from Cats' End up to the mangling shed, passing the buckets fast as lightening. There were some spills in the fun and the heat and the eagerness and the anger, but most of the water reached the shed and soaked its scorched walls, rescuing the big mangle.

The Pigpen, though, went up in stately flames and thunderous heat. It burned all the way down to the foundations, and all the rats from inside scrambled between the feet of the screaming people and made the road furry for a moment as they crossed to Cats' End and turned hissing to hide in holes and houses and hedges.

When the strange and wondrous event took place, Tora was standing in the bucket line helping to pass pails of water and didn't get to see it. Later, though, she heard that Ebon Johansson had walked over to the as yet undamaged door on the north side and looked up. He had asked Ebba which room was theirs, and pulled his roll-brimmed hat down on his head, as far down his forehead as he could, buttoned his blazer and walked straight into the smoke-filled stairwell.

188

Women screamed and the fire chief shouted after him and the huge hose was aimed at the door he had disappeared through.

Twice he appeared in the windows along the stairwell. The flames were already threatening the window frames.

'He's done himself in!' shouted one woman, and it seemed to be true, because he never came back through the door. The window panes were already exploding and the fire was howling in the stairwell.

On the other side, people saw how he slid down a sheet that only reached halfway down, and how he jumped, landing on bended knees.

In the yard, however, lots of people took Ebon Johansson for dead and thought the fire at the Pigpen had cost one life. He found Tora in the crowd and gave her the photograph. It was uncharred, but blistered.

T here are dark rooms you might be wise to enter.

But many people are like Tora. She had quick feet and strong legs. Good at sums. The schoolmaster had never noticed, but it was reality now — all about pints of beer, bottles of wine, mineral water and arrack. She didn't go looking for dark rooms. What was past was past. Still, sometimes a cobweb brushes your face, and it becomes difficult to ward off the invisible. And the insults.

Mamsell Winlöf now rented the ground floor of the inn. The old bar-room had become a music café, the tavern a smoking lounge with potted palms. In the morning, before the cigar smoke permeated everything, you could still smell the paint. There was a new red shag rug and linoleum on the floors. Tora never found reasons to go into the inn. It was ancient history in there. It was frighteningly old and sombre, as if much more than twenty years had passed since Edla arrived there.

Tora was disgusted by the dirt and the sour smells of dried up beer and old wooden floors. The innkeeper's wife was dead now, but people still talked about her. She had been a hard woman. Tora didn't want to hear.

The first time she stood there she had been sent by Mamsell on an errand to Iskasson. She stated her business quickly. But something made her stop as she passed the staircase on her way back. Just this once.

190

The stairs led up to the club room. Up there, Edla had slept on the huge table. Tora walked up the stairs in the dark and into the room, and recognized everything from Valfrid's stories. There were the tile stoves, the stiff portraits, the big stained floor. The room was huge and freezing cold.

Who had it been?

She was standing there, at any rate, as if she believed that the darkening walls and the floor with its filthy cracks would tell her their secret.

Valfrid? No, he hadn't been more than a kid then. A traveller. Isaksson himself or a drunken farmer. The drivers ...

She felt a draught at her back because the door to the staircase was open. Downstairs doors were slamming and one of them led right out into the barroom. It would have been easy to open the wrong door on the way out to have a piss. In those days.

It was as if someone had forced her to listen for footsteps on the stairs. As if a face would soon appear and she would have to look into the eyes and be forced to feel things she didn't want to feel. Maybe hate. Contempt, aversion. Perhaps even compassion.

No! She didn't want to know the answers. Never in all her life did she want to know. She wanted to get out of there! She accepted the answer in the old walls and floors: it was darkness itself, there was no face. Edla might not even have seen a face herself. Why, anyone could open the wrong door and stumble up the stairs to the club room. Drunkenness and darkness. Was it cruelty?

If so, cruelty was blind and faceless. At once she knew that she had no other father than the harsh darkness that surrounded her.

191

There is compassion between people, deep down in dark rooms. But it's too much for us.

V alfrid Johansson came into the inn carrying a gilded
sword and some skulls. In his youth he had been
blacklisted and lost his job as stockboy for selling a
rag Isaksson would not have been caught dead using to wipe
— well, anything with. Valfrid was not partial to coarse
words, but he remembered bitterly when they were used
against him.

He hadn't exactly sold a lot of copies of *The People's
Voice*. He had, however, become an object of scorn in the
community and was overwhelmed with words that were
painful to him. Greasy, stinking, grubby — all kinds.

Ebon sold *The People's Voice*, too, but all he got was
beaten up. The world is a strange place. He didn't actually
get beaten up often, though, and he sold a lot of
newspapers. For several years he was one of the lame
activist's best salesmen. Valfrid had finally got a job with
shopkeeper Levander on the condition that he stopped
selling his papers. He did so without a qualm, having
realized that the fate of social democracy neither stood nor
fell with the few copies he was able to foist off on the most
inebriated of his victims.

Valfrid went on to become shop boy and later manager.
He became the right hand man of his employer in his
growing business. Levander was nearly a merchant by now.
The future was his.

But Valfrid had not abandoned the beliefs of his youth.
He would declare to anyone anytime that the social

democratic movement was dear to his heart. What actually distinguished one human being from another? Nothing.

The only problem was that as he matured, he had realized, to his dismay, that the fundamental idea of socialism was unrealistic. Something inherent to human nature made it impossible to transform the idea of socialism into reality. Still, he wished the best of luck to all those who tried to do so, yes, from the bottom of his heart he wished them success.

The world has always been a battlefield and man is his own worst enemy. History has always known injustice, and one man will always use another to climb on. That's the truth and, sadly, it cannot be disregarded no matter how badly one wishes to do so.

Still.

Contrary to what the most furious agitators proclaimed, things were getting brighter all along. 'Economic development, popular education, more humane conditions— those, you see, are concepts on the rise,' said Valfrid.

These were the two cornerstones of his philosophy of life.

He laid the gilded sword on its velvet pillow and placed the valise with the skulls in it in a closet. Isaksson greeted him with some respect, as the Order of Urdar paid a substantial sum to rent the old club room upstairs at the inn. The Urdar included a brewer and a veterinarian, the shopkeeper who was nearly a merchant and a watchmaker with a solid reputation. Neither the barber nor the photographer was voted in, while the furrier and Berg the foundryman had been initiated in a very moving ceremony. Naturally Valfrid did not even hold the lowest rank in the order, but his employer was the Grand Master and had assigned Valfrid the task of redecorating the old club room. He had it painted and wallpapered and had light brown linoleum with a Persian pattern laid on the floor. Now he hung the thirteen stars on the walls and the cracked shields behind the podium. He set a white plaster crucifix in the niche above one of the tiled stoves, and a reproduction of the Angel of Death in the other. He covered the new table with a black velvet cloth displaying gilded sets of digits. The rest — black hoods, sceptres, gilded chains, an eagle, an iron breast-plate, velvet pillows, paper clouds, balloting cups, Bibles, wigs and scythes — he placed in the closet with the skulls, and locked it. He waved the key under Isaksson's nose and instructed him that as landlord he was responsible for ensuring that nothing was disturbed.

'The Order of Urdar does good,' said Valfrid. 'How it does so is not our business. So no one touches this lock.'

Young gentlemen who frequented the music café on the ground floor found a crack to peek through in a papered-shut door to the club room, and carved a peephole with a pen-knife in the wallpaper. With Isaksson's blessing they then entertained themselves by peering at the mysteries of the Urdar. They tempted the waitresses to go upstairs with them and peek cheek to cheek. That room no longer held anything that frightened Tora. It had been papered over. Skulls didn't scare her, not even if they were silver-plated. Valfrid told her that just one year after it was founded, the Order of Urdar had allocated 478 kronor and 43 öre for needy children.

'Primarily for footwear.'

'My,' said Tora. 'Forty-three öre, too.'

'I keep their books,' Valfrid explained.

She didn't dare to tell him that she had actually watched the entire initiation rite when foundryman Berg had been made a member. She did tell Ebon and his friend Valentin. The foundryman had been deeply moved as he waited on bended knee in his black hood.

'What art thou lacking, oh brother?' asked Palmquist the watchmaker.

'Wisdom,' whimpered the foundryman.

'What dost thou seek, oh brother?' asked Valfrid's employer from deep inside his hood.

'The source of wisdom.'

Butt when he was supposed to respond to the other twin questions with 'goodness' and 'the source of goodness' he was so deeply moved that he wept on the pages of the Bible open before him and they began to disintegrate. That was a sight!

They were sitting by Mulle's grave, listening to the railway band, and Tora was telling her story. Valentin was doubled over with laughter and trying to imitate Berg's journey by knee towards the source of wisdom.

'Cut it out,' said Ebon. 'I've got a job at the foundry. I know the son of a bitch. And I know what kind of a bastard he is.'

'That's all we're saying,' said Tora, wiping tears of laughter.

'No!'

He stood up and stuck his fists in his trouser pockets. Tora shushed him. There were people sitting and reclining all around them in the grass, listening to the music.

'No!' said Ebon. 'He's not funny. He's dangerous.'

196

'I've seen him strike down apprentices. Do you know Deaf Lund? He worked at the foundry 'til last spring. Have you seen him?'

'Oh, yes. But the foundryman was still no more than foolish when he stood there huffing and weeping over the Bible.'

'You two would laugh at anything,' said Ebon in a soft, tense voice. He crouched down in front of them so they would hear him even if he didn't raise his voice. He was balancing on his heels, with his hands in his pockets.

'You laugh. But there is too little hate in this town.'

Tora turned away from him and listened attentively to the music. It was Kéler-Béla's 'Lustspiel-Overture.' She knew all their pieces from the music café. She had come out to sit in the grass and hear the music, and she wanted to listen.

'Come on, Tora,' said Ebon. 'Come with me and I'll show you how hate smells.'

She looked at his face, which never seemed to get really clean from the foundry dust but now was pale and sweaty, and she realized he was angry again and that it would only end in an argument if she insisted on staying. She got up and gathered her skirts and started to walk behind him on the familiar path up towards Louse Point, where a croft had stood. Behind the empty dancing pavilion Ebon sat down and started breaking branches. He snapped the little rowan saplings right off, so all that was left was a line of broken sticks.

'I'll show you how hate smells, Tora.'

She was angry because she felt she had had to go along with him. She didn't want to go off in her new skirt. She didn't want the back of it to get dirty, and she wanted to be seen in public while her skirt was still new.

197

Nowadays she went with Ebon. In the beginning, it just happened. Everybody knew what he had done for her when the Pigpen burned down. Of course she had known Ebon before that. She had felt his wolf eyes devouring her as she waited at table, and he had tried to speak with her. He was not the least bit like Valfrid. He was not easy-going.

'Ebon has always taken things to extremes,' Valfrid told her. 'As a child he was something of an idiot. Now he reads too much. And it's nothing but politics and heresy he reads.'

Wolf eyes was right; though admittedly lots of men had them. It was her term for the very hungriest eyes. But Ebon's could go yellow. Still, if you had a laugh and quick feet when you twirled away with your tray you could often avoid getting involved in peculiar conversations. Later she had no longer had to wait at table in the third-class dining room and had lost track of him. And then the Pigpen burned down and he did what he did for her. So she went with him after a dance up at Louse Point. They spoke of Edla and the photo. And it was the least he could expect from her.

He had hard hands. They walked the length of Lovers' Lane. It began on the birch-lined path and then turned off the real Promenade and wound all the damp, dark way down to where the point jutted out into Lake Vallmaren. She became accustomed to Ebon's hard hands, but she never laughed when she was with him.

He knew what he wanted. He didn't humiliate her. He never said a word about her kid out at Stegsjö, though everybody knew about him. He was a big boy now and she had never seen him. Ebon had not said a word, not once in all the weeks and months she refused and they just walked side by side, mostly silent. As soon as they left the village behind his hard hands were around her waist and she could

198

hardly turn her face towards him without his mouth being there, demanding and seeking. Constantly, constantly, he tried. It was as if he could think about nothing else.

Even now. They didn't talk any more about hate. He just made her smell the broken rowan branches. She didn't get the point and found his stories long-winded.

'Watch my skirt,' she said.

It was a long time now since Ebon had had his way. It just happened. But there was one thing she was sure about: not another kid! She wouldn't let that happen!

Sometimes she would expel him with all her might, shooting her hips and belly forward and pulling her legs up so fast that he landed next to her on his back. Because she did not want another kid, at least not without being married. There was no way she would let that happen! This particular fear was stronger than her fear of Ebon — which never really eased.

He lay beside her, faint with the shock, pounding with fury. He was panting.

'You're mad.'

'Could be.'

'I was nowhere near there.'

And he tried to lay her back down, held her forearms tightly and pressed them towards the ground, forced his knees between her legs and pried them slowly open. But the peculiar thing was that her other fear was even stronger than this one. It made her strong, too. She arched her whole body and sat up, free.

'You let me be.'

'I said I was nowhere near there.'

She didn't reply. But when he lay down, pale, with his eyes tightly shut, she sat watching his sexual organ, which was still erect. She took her index finger and touched its tip, capturing the drop that was hanging there. It smelled of earth.

'I think we'd best stop,' she said.

'I was nowhere near there,' he said again.

'You don't know what you're talking about.'

'Well, so what if I don't?' he asked. 'Would it be the end of the world? It's happened before.'

But he didn't mean what she thought at first. She had heard so much slander she was sensitive and felt contempt everywhere. All he meant was:

'We'd just get married.'

She didn't answer that, and nothing between them changed.

Louse Point wasn't always as dreary as when Tora and Ebon sat there by themselves and he broke off the young rowan saplings until there were nothing but sticks all around the pavilion. The Workers' Association made outings there, and then there were people behind every bush. Flags flapped in the wind and bicycles lay overturned in the grass. People spread out blankets and set out picnics.

Of course Ebon didn't want to go along, not really.

'So what's wrong with the Workers' Association now?' asked Tora. 'Isn't the Workers' Association at least something you can appreciate? Is there nothing in the whole world that's good enough in your opinion?'

He despised them: The Workers' Ring, The Workers' Society, the Labourers' Association. They were pointless.

200

Excursions and inauguration with a lot of fanfare. A big show. The hell with them all.

'But they provide sickness allowances for workingmen's families and pay for funerals. What's wrong with that?'

'The workers shouldn't be buying each other hearses,' said Ebon. 'There are more important things.'

'No, I'm sure you'll be satisfied with being pulled to the graveyard in a cart when your time comes.'

'The workers shouldn't be burying each other,' said Ebon. 'They've got to survive.'

In the end, though, he went along to Louse Point because he wanted to see the workers from Wärnström's and try once again to persuade them to unionize. Wilhelmsson's workers had been organized for twelve years, and the Manual Workers' Union had had a local office in the community for nearly ten. The Railway Workers' Union office had just opened up, and only the people at Wärnström's were still refusing to come around.

Tora sat on her blanket watching him walk from one to the other, watched him arouse distaste and annoyance on this lovely Sunday afternoon. Valentin came and sat next to her as always. She was annoyed at him. He was so hare-lipped and hopeless. His cleft lip slurred his speech, and he was so devoted. So there she sat with her arms around her knees and with no one but him to talk to while Ebon walked around riling people up.

'It's not gonna happen at Wärnström's,' said Valentin. 'They daren't.'

'No, right,' said Tora tiredly. 'I've heard that things are pretty good there, anyway. That they don't think they need a union. Wärnström personally pays their sickness allowances.'

'He *lends* them,' said Valentin despondently.

'Well, all right, but you can't expect him to *give* the money away.'

'No,' said Valentin. 'He lends them money. So then they can't go to work anywhere else. And they daren't start a union because he'll put the squeeze on them and demand repayment of his loans. That's slavery for you.'

'Well, not to my mind it isn't,' Tora said, standing up. She was furious. She inhaled to steady her voice and put her hands on her hips and stood above Valentin, who began to slide backwards on the blanket. She hadn't shouted like this since she waited at table in the third-class restaurant. Anger coursed through her body like waves, and it felt like the first time in months she could breathe properly.

'I don't want to hear another word about it! Slavery! I know people who work at Wärnström's, and I'm not an idiot. He doesn't force people to stay there like you say, that's one big lie! You can laugh at him when he's sitting there in chapel making eyes at Jesus if you like. But don't come around here claiming that he forces people to stay at his workshop if they want to go elsewhere. Because the truth of the matter is they don't want to leave! They're better off at Wärnström's than anywhere else around here. Ask anybody you like! Ask Ludde Eriksson, who's sitting right there. Ask him!'

Ludde saw her glaring and moved in the direction of the refreshment table, while everyone else stared at Tora, even Lundholm who was running the children's fishpond peeked over the curtain.

'Well for pity's sake,' Valentin slurred, looking more hare-lipped and hopeless than ever. People around them started to smirk. Tora turned away so fast that her skirt

202

brushed Valentin's nose as he tried to get up without overturning the picnic hamper and bottles. Tora gathered her skirts tightly and walked off.

'Tora,' Valentin cried. 'Wait! I'm coming!'

The road was full of people with dogs on leads, holding children by the hand and even pushing prams manufactured at Wärnström's. She realized that some people were staring vacantly at her and others were laughing hesitantly as she marched ahead blushing, with that miserable Valentin at her heels. She turned right off the road and into a grove, where her high heels got caught between roots and stones. Thankfully, she found a little path after a few minutes, but her wrath rose again when she realized she had ended up on Lovers' Lane and that Valentin was still following her. When she was nearly all the way down to the lake she turned back around and saw that there was now a regular little parade. First herself and Valentin. Then she spotted Ebon with his hands in his pockets, and last of all a black-and-white spotted dog.

'Get lost,' she screamed. 'I'm sick of you!'

Valentin stopped.

'Right, get on home. I don't want to see you.'

He turned around and started slowly back. But he looked at her over his shoulder several times and stood still with his arms hanging at his sides, as if he expected her to change her mind. Tora leaned against a boulder and tried to breathe more evenly. She had cramp. Ebon approached her coming slowly down the path and she shut her eyes until he was right up close.

'Get out of here.'

The dog was still there and started jumping up, pawing her skirt and licking her hand.

'Ugh,' said Tora. 'Get away.'

'It's only Lundholm's Muttie.'

Tora turned away towards the boulder, her head in her hands.

'I want to be left alone. I've had enough of you both. I want to have fun just for once without it ending like this.'

'But I think you're right,' said Ebon. 'They're not afraid of Wärnström and they are better off there than many other places. I think they quite like him.'

'Well then!'

'Slavery isn't just the lash, Tora. You can have it in your blood, too.'

'I don't know what you mean, and I don't care either.'

'Come on now.'

Muttie was jumping around them. Ebon took Tora by the arm and pulled her towards a bench by the lake. He set her down as if she had been a big rag doll.

'Stop it,' she said, but her energy had drained away. He drew the pins out of her hat, one by one, placing them on the bench. Then he took down her hair. She tried to ward him off but he set her hands back in her lap, speaking softly throughout.

'Wärnström and the pink Jesus he has had painted on the chapel ceiling are what people are laughing at,' he said. 'And Lindh and those French books he doesn't know how to read.'

'Don't touch my hairpiece.'

But he took it off and set it on the bench.

'I want to look at you like this. And Wärnström walks along the south side of the tracks, in the middle of the road with his silver-topped walking stick. The brewers' wagon has to stop and the hand carts have to move out of his way and people tip their hats. Lindh walks on the north side, in the middle of the street, with a long stick, too, but gold-tipped.'

'That's a lie!'

'Maybe so. But he does have a hand-carved walking stick. And people want it that way. They want to laugh at them and be cared for by them and they want to be well off. Tora! They can't hate them.'

She sat helplessly by, watching Lundholm's Muttie run off with her hairpiece. Ebon lifted her hands down when she tried to touch her hair. It was thin and fair. She was ashamed of it. It never got as long as she would have liked, because it split when it reached her shoulder, leaving nothing but thin, uneven ends.

'They can't hate.'

'You talk such — rubbish.'

'No.'

Muttie buried her hairpiece. He was eager. The moss flew.

'I hate them,' said Ebon. 'But that doesn't mean there's something wrong with me. Sometimes I think that it's the only strength I can count on.'

'Why? What did they ever do to you?'

He held her head in his hands and drew his fingers through her thin, disorderly hair. He was whispering.

'Because of the children in the workshops. The lads. They're just kids. Because of the dirt. Because of the machines that chop of fingers. Because of Deaf Lund.'

He slid off the bench and laid his head in her lap. Muttie came back hoping to get her hat, but she struck him on the muzzle with her free hand and then put her hat back on over her flowing hair.

'But you laugh at them, too,' she said. 'When they walk in the middle of the road.'

'No.'

'Oh, right. Tell me about it.'

'I'm disgusted and infuriated by it,' he said deep in her skirts, pressing his head hard against her belly. He had been breathing into the fabric for so long that her skin was sticky.

'Hush, now,' she said.

Lundholm's Muttie no longer dared to approach them. He barked a couple of times and then ran down the path. He flashed black-and white between the alderwoods and vanished. When Ebon quieted down she could hear the ducks quacking out on the water. The shore was dense with sprouting alders, but there was a clearing between the bench and the lake. Still, you could see almost nothing but reeds. They grew in a broad band and rattled when the wind picked up. Far, far out, a little water sparkled. She was cold. The only heat was in the indentation where he was breathing, otherwise she was cold.

Out at Appleton she had preferred not to mention Ebon, but gossip went everywhere. Lans was not pleased to hear that she was walking out with an agitator.

"Cause I've heard he's one of that kind,' said the soldier. 'And that kind don't keep a job.'

'Aw, keep a job,' said Tora. 'He works at the foundry.'

Still, he wasn't any more pleased with Rickard, and that made it a little easier for her. Rickard had stayed at the saddlemaker's in Ridgeview and completed his apprenticeship. Either of the two daughters was his for the asking, the one prettier than the other. At first it seemed understandable that he avoided making a choice; it was a bit awkward since they were both equally in love with him. They thought of Rickard as so special. Rickard had black hair and was tall and lithe. He moved easily and fast. He had a terrible temper when provoked, but was otherwise a cheerful fellow, with a quick answer to anything. Rickard Lans was the hero of both the attractive, plump, brunette Löfgren sisters.

Early in the summer of '87 he was out doing some saddlemaking for his employer. He was being put up on the big farm at Great Kedevi, to go through their whole stock of reins, harnesses, saddles and trap and carriage seats. When he left there he went straight to North America with Stella Johannesson, a housemaid and soldier's daughter from Vallmsta, and was not heard of again until they were married and wrote home that they had a son who was a citizen of North America by birth and christened Karl Abel.

For some time, the Löfgren sisters were miserable. The saddlemaker himself took it as a very hard blow, for he had had every confidence in Rickard, who had never uttered a word about wanting to leave them. He had been lodged and fed there since he was eight and had learned a trade. Actually, what he had done was beyond belief.

Stella Johannesson had been sixteen years old when she arrived at Great Kedevi. She had caught the eye of Emelie Högel, niece of the great painter Högel, who did some painting herself. Stella had modelled for a big oil canvas of Ophelia she was doing.

Every morning Stella had to sit for Fröken Högel. A servant would bring in flowers and reeds and a water lily or two to be reproduced with her. He sounded extremely annoyed — although not when Fröken Högel was in earshot — over the fact that he, who was far higher in rank than this housemaid, was forced to muck about the muddy lake shore each morning for cattails and lily pads. In the end he made a disparaging comment about the model, which triggered the first confrontation between himself and the saddlemaker's apprentice.

Stella was supposed to sit absolutely still with the flowers in her arms, leaning back and gazing at an urn. She was not allowed to see the portrait while Fröken Högel was working on it. By the time it was finished she'd gone off with Rickard Lans. But her parents were offered the opportunity to see it, and they arrived one Sunday after church, soldier Johannesson in his dress uniform with plume and sword. He knew that his daughter was beautiful, and he was not displeased with the likeness. He said as much. He went on to say (as he thought he should say a few words on such a ceremonious occasion):

'I suppose it will fetch quite a price?'

Fröken Högel, who was sitting on a chair beside her portrait, didn't deny it.

'It's already sold,' she said, speaking so softly the soldier could barely hear her. They also thought they heard her say something about the portrait being sent to England, but they didn't dare ask her to repeat it.

'To be boarded and clothed for all those years,' sighed Lans. 'And lodged. To be taught a trade. And not to have the common sense to realize one has incurred a debt of gratitude, but to run off to America. And marry a mad servant girl.'

'Stella wasn't the mad one,' said Tora. 'That was the girl in the play.'

'Well, there must've been some resemblance,' said Lans. 'Otherwise she wouldn't have wanted to paint her.'

Rickard never saw the painting of Ophelia, either. But he had met Stella the very first day he arrived at Great Kedevi. She was the most beautiful woman he had ever seen.

While Rickard's destiny was taking such a shocking, dramatic turn, Tora went on walking out with Ebon Johansson. However, she had less and less time to be out running around with the waitresses. Mamsell Winlöf had sold her entire enterprise and retired with her little dog Mimi to a newly-built house across the street from Petrus Wilhelmsson's.

The new owner was a head waiter from Stockholm by the name of Oscar Wilhelm Winther, and he arrived in September with two hounds and an overcoat with leather trim. Major changes were made. The music café in the former inn got various additional potted palms and was renamed the Winther Garden. He studied his staff for precisely four weeks after which he let six of the waitresses go. He told two of them they could stay on and wait table in the third class if they liked, but as that would have meant two others being sacked, of course they declined. 'À la bonne heure!' said Winther. 'Do as you please.'

He kept Tora and even gave her a new assignment. She was now responsible for the linens and for orders from the bakery. But three months later he called her into his office. 'My time has come,' she thought, changing her apron although she had a perfectly clean one on.

'Cross your fingers,' she said to Tekla.

'Aw, you've nothing to worry about. He'd have to be mad to ...'

'Hush. Think of me. Here goes.'

But she glimpsed Tekla's concerned face in the mirror as she pinned up a little hair that had fallen down onto her neck.

The big greyish dogs lifted their muzzles as she entered, and growled softly. Winther was writing something, and signalled to her to wait. His pen scratched on. He was always efficient.

'Tora!' he said without looking up. 'Smile!'

When he had finished writing and looked up at her face, she was just staring blankly at him, pale and taken aback.

'Give us a smile, then,' he said.

Wild guesses flew through her mind. She felt her mouth go dry. Did he think she was too solemn with the guests? Had she gone grave and dreary? Well, she had been more cautious not to fool around or behave like a barmaid since he let those other six go.

'I'm not going to eat you up,' he said. 'Just smile at me a little. Right. No, open your mouth. Not Mona Lisa!'

She opened her lips, facing him, her eyes not blinking. He sat there with his pen in the air above his stationary, looking at her. He looked very closely, and Tora's mouth began to feel tight.

'I see. Would you like to be my cashier, Tora?'

Now at least she pulled herself together, swallowed and said loud and clear:

'Yes.'

210

'That's good. So we know what our positions are. In that case, Tora, you must do something about that broken tooth of yours.'

'What?'

He showed his whole open mouth, tapping his pen against his front teeth.

'A cashier spends all day sitting facing the customers. She is the face of the restaurant, Tora! Get yourself some teeth!'

Her cheeks were burning, her face must be scarlet.

'I couldn't afford ... it's just impossible.'

'Borrow,' he said and went back to his writing.

She didn't know what to answer and started backing towards the door.

'Borrow from me if need be,' he said. 'You'll have a salary now, Tora. Think about it.'

'Thank you,' said Tora. 'Thank you very much. I will think about it.'

She didn't tell Ebon about the teeth, but she did tell him she might be made cashier.

'What about the others, then?'

'What others?'

'Your workmates! The ones you'll leave behind,' said Ebon.

'What on earth do you think? That the lot of us could all be made cashiers? That's just like you. This could change everything for me, you know. I'd have a salary.'

'And the others would go on as before, free uniforms and meals.'

'And what the guests tip them, you know that as well as I do.'

'You're the one who's said that the only generous guests are the whores when they're changing trains on their way back from the workers' barracks in Norrköping.'

That made Tora laugh.

'It's true.'

'Tora, Tora,' said Ebon. 'That Winther will be able to do what he likes with the girls. And there'll be no one left who'll speak her mind. Not if you move behind the cash register.'

'I'd be a fool not to.'

He sat there with his rowan stick, looking at her.

'Who are you to talk?' she burst out. 'Can you even hold on to a job? Answer me that! You preach till you're sacked. Nobody can stand you. You twist a person's words — now you have me saying *they're* the only ones who are kind to the girls. Women like them!'

'Whores,' he leered, 'tarts.'

'Shut up!'

'Lots of them have been waitresses themselves you see, Tora dear. They know what it's like.'

'But now I'm a cashier.'

'Aha. You'd made up your mind?'

'No, but now I have.'

No, she was no longer frightened of Ebon. She was nearly twenty-five years old and she was Winther's cashier. She didn't look bad, either. She had a black skirt with four panels that fit quite snugly over her hips. She wore an elastic belt at the waist with a shiny buckle, and she dreamed of having a watch to hang from it. Her blouse was white with an embroidered collar. At the throat she wore a round porcelain brooch with little roses painted on it. She had two more blouses in the cupboard. Now she was living alone.

Sometimes she let Ebon come up to see her. But she no longer lay on her back for him in the meadows and groves. She was first and foremost protective of her clothing. But she also said straight out: 'People may talk. I'm Winther's cashier now. You have to think twice.'

No, she had left the sweet peas and forget-me-nots.

March 1901 was the month of the big snowstorm. For a few days before it the sun had shone brightly, the ditches were full of water from melting snow, and the lumps of horse dung over which the sparrows battled had fermented and crumbled. The great tits were too busy singing to search for food.

The snow began on a Friday night with winds that reached storm strength and packed high drifts in the train yard. The snow was so heavy and wet no snowploughs could get through it. Day never really broke on Saturday; it was just one long shady dusk that eventually went dark. The storm howled through the chimneys. Towards evening the wind died down, but the snow didn't stop. It just got drier and denser.

On the train from Gothenburg, which had been unable to pass the switch into the station yard, sat a young man. Whispering and smiling to himself, he predicted that the snowfall would never end. His name was F.A. Otter. The pressure in the gas tubes had begun to fall; the harsh lamplight in the carriages was yellower and warmer, and shadows lengthened in the corners. The cold moved in slowly. For a little while longer the sounds of hissing gas taps and slamming doors could be heard. Then there was silence.

People began to feel chilled and to need to move around. Travelling salesmen were cold, as were preachers and timber buyers and her ladyship from Heavenside, who was on her way home from England. It's surely a good idea not to travel in the winter unless you have to.

The passengers were asked to disembark. Sinking and fumbling through the drifts they made their way to the town, where gates and fences were deeply buried.

'Perhaps the snow will never cease,' said F.A. Otter, and no one was sure whether or not he was joking. A long way ahead of them, the railmens' lanterns gleamed. They realized they had made it to town, that the streets might be right under their feet, when huge horses pulling snowploughs but unable to make any headway appeared in the darkness. The snow whirled in their eyes.

The court had been in session on Saturday, and the main courtroom was filled with farmers who had been unable to get home. They played whist and *marriage* and waited for the girls from the railway restaurant to bring them hampers of coffee, beef steak and sandwiches.

By the time the passengers from the Gothenburg train arrived there were no rooms left. Winther rented Tora's room out to a traveller whom railway clerk Finck had taken under his wing.

Her room was a peculiar one. Winther had redone Mamsell Winlöf's apartment to make an office and a storeroom, and at the very end of a hall that had come into being with this renovation was Tora's room. It was full of cupboards where the hotel linens were kept, and at the very back was the tiled stove that had been in Mamsell Winlöf's parlour, as well as one of the windows. It was the tiled stove that made Winther realize the space could be used as living quarters for one of his employees.

He was sitting on the bed when she returned to check that she had locked all the linen cabinets. It was late at night and the lamp was turned down. He was trying to remove one of his boots, but it was soaking wet and stuck to his stocking. He looked upset when his eyes met Tora's, and she apologized.

'I just wanted to check if I'd locked in the linens,' she said.

And was instantly embarrassed. It wasn't surprising that he looked even more annoyed. He was quite a gentleman. She looked at his coat that was hanging on her chair, and at his hands. He got the first boot off.

'Bring me some hot water,' he said.

He took her for one of the chambermaids, and she said, as gently as she could to dispel the foolish impression her comment about the linens must have made:

'I'll send one of the girls.'

He looked up. Now she could see that he was pale, his face white as chalk, and she felt a strange sense of concern. His bare foot was hanging over the edge of the bed, and she looked at it. His ankle was thin as a girl's, thinner than her own. He had lovely, high arches and straight toes in an even row. The skin of his heel was pink, but the rest of his foot was so white it must have been almost frost-bitten.

'Hurry up,' he said.

She brought the water back herself, after heating it. She didn't know why. There were still girls up and about. He was lying there just as before, but when she brought in the tin pan and a pail he sat up and began to remove his other boot. She took his coat to hang it up. Under the collar was

216

a label from a tailor's in Gothenburg, and under the label was his name: F.A. Otter.

'You'll soon be warm now,' said Tora.

He put his foot in the tin pan and she waited for a moment before she started to pour water from the pail. Both feet were equally beautiful.

'Of course they are! Aren't I the perfect fool?' she thought. 'If one foot is beautiful the other will be the same.' And yet it was precisely because she had found it difficult to imagine that anything could be so perfect that she had come back herself with the hot water.

'Good grief, what's this? Has the fire gone out?' she said, walking over to the stove and opening the doors. 'Why, no one ever lit it, no wonder it's cold in here!'

She unbuttoned her cuffs and turned up her blouse sleeves. He sat watching her.

'Are you going to light it yourself?' he asked.

She felt a surge of worry that he would think she was better than she was, so she said: 'I'm Winther's cashier. But that doesn't mean I don't know how to light this thing.'

She started to tell him it was her room, but changed her mind. Once she had the fire burning she shut the doors and felt the stove.

'It hasn't been out for all that long,' she said. 'There's still some heat. A little.'

She was in high spirits, despite the fact that he looked so solemn, sitting there staring at her with his feet in the pan. She threw her arms around the warm tiled stove.

'I usually call him my fiancé,' she said. 'This is my room.'

That made him laugh, but now she was embarrassed for having spoken just like the barmaid he took her for. She kept her arms around the stove because she was blushing, and waiting for him to reply: 'Oh you must have plenty of other boyfriends!' But when she finally turned around, hot and embarrassed, he was still just sitting there staring at her, smiling. He didn't even ask where she was going to sleep that night, just said:

'How kind of you to give up your room.'

'I'll get you some towels,' said Tora.

She unlocked one of the cupboards and lifted out heavy, twilled towels for his feet.

'Is it still snowing?' he asked, and now she could hear his Gothenburg dialect.

She peeked through the curtains.

'Just as much as before.'

'Open the stove doors,' he requested, sounding eager. She did as he said. The room was filled with playful shadows and the firelight made the copper pail she'd brought in gleam.

'Don't soak your feet for too long. It'll do you no good if the water gets cold.'

She spread a towel on the floor.

'If only it would go on snowing,' he said. 'If only the snow would just go on drifting.'

'I'll massage them dry,' said Tora. 'Take your feet out now. You mustn't get another chill.'

'If only the ploughs would get stuck and the horses couldn't go any further. And people were unable to open their doors and eventually the snow was above the chimney tops.'

'I don't think it'll get that bad,' said Tora, wrapping the towel around his absolutely perfect feet.

'If that happened the smoke would choke back down and everything would be dark and silent and very cold inside and the roofs and walls would creak from the enormous weight of the mass of snow. Because then it would be higher than the rooftops and the flagpoles and the last crown of the last tree on the last mountain in Sörmland would vanish and everything would be perfectly white and smooth in the moonlight when night fell and the moon came out.'

She folded the towel so his feet were wrapped like a little package and patted them lightly.

'Are there mountains here in Sörmland?' he asked.

'Well, I'm not sure, I suppose so.'

'I'll be living here now.'

He sighed and sounded as if he were speaking to someone else, so Tora didn't answer.

Now his feet were all dry and warm. She removed the towels and folded them. For a few more minutes she would be able to find things to do. She needed to stir the fire and add a couple of logs.

'Don't close the flue too soon,' she said.

'I won't,' he smiled.

'Good night.'

'Good night, Fröken.'

He went and lay down in the strange bed, listening. When he had closed the stove doors and turned down the lamp, the little room lined with cupboards was all dark. He was warm now, but when he tried to fall asleep he began to hear noises, and to see big, gentle horses growing up out of the darkness. In his dreams he battled with the snow as it just kept falling. He wondered if he had frightened the woman who had been in his room by talking about how the snow would cover everything. The buildings would be squeezed together and collapse under the pressure and the people would smother, entwined, and dogs and canaries would also be dead.

'Who's to say that the snow will actually stop falling?' he said to himself. 'Who's to say?'

But this was a game he was playing, and he knew it. He wasn't the least bit afraid of the snow. As he lay awake listening in the big building next to the station where ordinarily it was never quiet, he knew very well that the others would survive. No one would be smothered in the snow.

He lit a candle and got up, in a sudden panic about his life. The only thing he could do was to open the doors on the tiled stove and stir through the lukewarm ashes with a poker.

L ike others who are easily fatigued, he harboured dreams about long journeys. However, his first assignment was on the steam engine of a freight train to Hallsberg. Its huge tender held four tons of coal. F.A. Otter found the locomotive awesome. It was astonishing and somewhat frightening to see so much power bound in the gleaming black coal the train carried. His heart pounded as hard as the steam puffed from the locomotive when it climbed the hills, with him stoking in the coal. Although the shaft of his shovel was worn smooth, the skin of his hands still split and blistered. In spite of this, the forceful pillar of sparks, steam, and smoke rising out of the smokestack into the sky still gave him pleasure. 'This is power! This is power!' his body sang as the train, clattering along the tracks made him shake and, in the early days, threw him against the iron wall every time it braked.

'Never forget that all you're doing here is heating up hell for yourself,' the engineer joked. F.A. didn't understand, but regarded his statement as a general threat, a word of advice he gave to all the new stokers. F.A. didn't doubt that there would be difficulties. He noticed the tufts of hair in Malm's nose the first time they were near each other face to face, and lowered his gaze. It took very little to turn his stomach.

The previous stoker had been sacked because, in a moment of anger, he had addressed Malm too informally. That man, too, had been an apprentice aspiring to engineer's

221

school. Malm was out to get men like them, someone had pointed out to F.A.

He was to serve here for six months; this was a compulsory apprenticeship. Soaked with sweat from shovelling coal he would crawl along the carriage roofs to let down the brakes. Suddenly the weather turned cold, and the metal went icy. In the engine cab he would stare at Malm's back — in these first three weeks there had been one or two calm moments when he had actually had time to think. Six months here, and then engineer's school, after which he would be standing there himself, with his hand in a dead man's grip and his eye on the tracks, giving orders to a stoker behind his back. But after a short time all he could do was to stare straight ahead in empty exhaustion, too tired to think straight.

He had sent away for a cap from Stockholm, paying five kronor plus postage, COD. But the insignia was an ugly, clumsy copy of the original. He ordered a more elegant one from the Sporrong Company. F.A. had an idea — he wasn't the first to think it — that the men who ran the locomotives should be ranked officers. Malm was of the old school and wanted to be addressed as 'Master.' He wore a black top hat to the meetings of the Locomotive Workers' Confederation.

It took F.A. quite some time to figure him out. He had imagined that it would be easier to be subordinate to someone he despised, but he was wrong. Contempt and fear plagued him. His stomach ached.

His stomach ached in a serious way. He had never mentioned it to anyone. His mother in Gothenburg had said *en passant* that she suffered from something she called acid indigestion, but he didn't really know what she meant. Perhaps she belched slightly, had heartburn. He had alluded

222

to his stomach troubles in her presence. She assumed they were the same as hers, and gave him a bottle of bicarbonate of soda. If he looked uncomfortable she would bring him a spoonful of potato starch and recommend that he try to get it down. She said it eased the burning sensation. He would smile, rejecting the spoon and giving her a little hug.

Now he was stoking the engine in the blazing heat and crawling along the tops of the cars in the March wind. He was on duty for seventy-two hours straight, always on the same schedule as Malm. They were soldered together by their schedule, not to be parted for six months. The first night he was awakened at three to go to Hallsberg, where it was noon before they had switched the cars, filled the tender, emptied the ashes and filled the water hold. He did twelve hours on call there, after which he was given a room to sleep in that smelled of filth and stale tobacco smoke.

Odours were an unfortunate part of the job. He had always been queasy about the smell of oil on hot metal. Lots of things made him gag, especially oil on hot metal. Now he had two additional problems: the smells of the smoke from the coke and of tarred sleepers. He suffered from all this and from his stomach pains, and his mother wrote him anxious letters wondering whether his acid indigestion was troubling him. His reaction was exasperation.

The second day they woke him at four in the morning for immediate departure for Flen. There was a short dinner break when they got back home. He thought of it as home now, since his rented room was better than the rooms you were put up in when you were away on duty, and he had begun to make some acquaintances in the village. Railway clerk Finck was related to his mother. There was a Clarin at the post office he had met at the railway restaurant.

223

On his dinner break the second day he lay at home without eating. They went back to Hallsberg, where he did twelve hours on call and making repairs. At three in afternoon of the third day they returned home, but he wasn't let off until ten in the evening when he had emptied the ashes and filled the tender.

The fourth day was his day off, and he sat soaking his hands in soapy water. That evening he was going to the hotel. After a couple of weeks he had begun to sing with Clarin and his friends in the evenings, but he despaired of his grimy hands and neck. The smoke dust ate its way in. He tried to keep his hands out of sight as much as possible when he was with Clarin and the others. Their names were Kasparsson and Ahlquist, and they were not especially friendly at first. Not until they heard his voice singing Reissinger's 'North Sea':

The sea is grand when it peacefully rolls,
a shining shield over Viking graves!

Oh, it was lovely. They had noticed him conversing with Finck; they had stood in the station yard talking together for five minutes.

'See you on Sunday,' they had said. 'At the hotel!'

He waved with pleasure, then his stomach contracted and he had to hurry off. He blamed it on Malm. Somehow he had gotten the idea that Malm was operating the drill that was boring in his stomach. Now he really hoped that they wouldn't be called in extra the next time the fourth day, which was Sunday, rolled around. Or that Malm wouldn't come up with something he had to do. They travelled back and forth to Hallsberg in silence; they went in silence to

Flen. He still dreamt about long journeys, but he would first have to survive Malm, who was out to get him.

On the second working day of his third week, when he was on call in Hallsberg, he began to vomit. His stomach contracted in cramps and he shivered and shook. He was disgusted with himself. All his bodily excretions were anathema to him even when he was healthy, and this was sour and smelly and sickening. Not to mention the fact that he had to spend such a long time in the privy every morning. This was something he had never had any trouble with before, he was always finished in a minute or two. But now other workingmen tugged at the door with its diagonal slats and he sat there holding his breath. Soon they learned that F.A. Otter was the one in there who kept them waiting, and they would sling nasty comments through the door. They were disgusting and he despised them. In both Flen and Hallsberg he started going in through the door that said 'Ladies' instead. This worked if he looked carefully before going in or out. But one morning there was an enormous woman in a hat standing at the door waiting when he was done. His knees buckled under him as he walked away. He was frightened all day that she would report him, and he started imagining a look of triumph in Malm's eyes. Not until he had a full night off and got some sleep did he realize you wouldn't be sacked for going into the wrong privy. Still, he started going on the Men's side again, and he kept anxious track of his little turds as they fell. How had this happened? And how could he bear to look at them even if they were small and dry? In the past he would never even have turned around in one of those places. The next morning he had the runs. He thought of himself as undergoing a slow transformation into pure stomach. He was in great pain, and even greater embarrassment.

Twice Malm almost caught him vomiting on the job. He struggled through an endless three-day shift with Malm's suspicious stare and cramps that made him want to double over like a jack-knife. He was very happy when he thought it was finished and he returned home to rest on the fourth day. When it was time to get up at three in the morning to start the next shift, he was suddenly completely indifferent. It wasn't even that he was groggy with sleep. He just lay there staring past the lamplight into the grey dawn shadows. Then he got up and dressed and went down and reported sick to the station guard on duty without even having breakfast first.

Railway clerk Finck, who was related to his mother and familiar with some of his dreams, sent a message that he wanted to see him. F.A. dressed nicely and paid him a visit, telling him what the doctor had said when he examined him. Actually, he had been examined by two doctors, because the old doctor in the village had just accused him of malingering. 'So I suppose I have an ulcer,' said F.A. 'At least the doctor in Hallsberg seemed to think so.'

He felt provocative, optimistic. At least this was a way out of hell. He would probably never have to see Malm again. But what about his apprenticeship?

'Isn't there any other way of being apprenticed, any other job? I mean, I'd do anything.'

'Unfortunately, you have to do your six months. But you needn't do them now. Wait until you get better.'

'I'm twenty-six years old.'

This just made Finck impatient.

'It won't take more than a few weeks for that gastritis of yours to go away.'

Because F.A. did not have the wherewithal to be sick for long, Finck arranged for him to substitute as a ticket vendor. He sat there from seven in the morning until eight in the evening, and even got a dinner break. For the first time he dared to think about the fact that as a stoker he had worked nineteen or twenty hours per day.

At first, it felt like being on holiday. He just sat there. But even sitting turned out to be tiring. The ordinary ticket vendor would be coming back to work eventually, but Finck promised to try to arrange for him to do extra office work. He had seen his neat handwriting, and knew that he had four years of upper secondary education.

The late winter Sundays were long and lonesome. F.A. slept as late as he could, but as soon as he moved around and reached for the cupboard door to take out the chamber pot, he heard his landlady on the other side of the curtain. A few minutes later she was there with a breakfast tray and a smile so huge that it revealed the red rubber gums of her new dentures. She was a realist, and less concerned about the fact that he was in arrears with his rent than with the fact that he was related to Finck, the assistant clerk, whose mother was listed amongst the nobility.

He couldn't eat in the morning. The idea of food had to be given time, plenty of time, to take possession of him, if he were to be spared the nausea. By evening his cheeks were usually rosy and he could eat.

In the afternoons, the group of friends would meet in the Winther Garden, usually arriving so early that it was still empty. Carlin would sit at the piano playing 'The Sailor's Lyre,' Kasparsson and Ahlquist waltzing around with newly-

227

lit cigars in their mouths. Still, this was tiresome, too. Outside was the sound of the switch engines, and they pulled the curtains. Alongside the piano was a wooden Negro holding a brass tray of the necessities for smoking. F.A. used them to accompany Clarin, and for a while they sounded like cymbals and triangles. Afterwards, however, the silence was even heavier.

They spent a while shooting billiards in the empty billiards room, keeping score for themselves. The rest of the afternoon they sat in the music café with a bottle of Gothenburg arrack, grumbling cheerfully about its shortcomings to F.A., who defended his home town. Towards evening, they did some quick calculations to determine whether they had the means to move across the station yard to the railway restaurant. Other than that, they didn't speak of money, a tiresome subject. A month earlier, F.A. had borrowed against an IOU for the first time in his life, and it was no sooner said than done. His wages, however, were not much higher than a yardman's, and he was uncertain whether he would be offered a position at the station offices where he had temporarily been taken on as an extra thanks to Finck, his patron.

Twilight fell and then the wonderful darkness. When the candles and lamps were lit things warmed up, and Ahlquist's suit looked nearly black again. He would even his jacket cuffs with an embroidery scissors before they went to the hotel, but this was a rite intended to give the girls a laugh. The music café closed at seven, and the same girls then served supper at the hotel. The temperature rose, which did F.A. good. The music and the voices cheered him as well. Only the bursts of steam from the locomotives outside reminded him that tomorrow was another day, and that he would then be sitting scratching with his steel-tipped nib in the books — figures, figures.

Ahlquist started a song, singing softly in somewhat coarse but very warm baritone:

— 'The fragrance of ro-o-ses...'

and Clarin joined in

— 'In the garden bower ...'

— 'Pom-pom-pom-pom,' Kasparsson intoned slowly. Then F.A. raised his eyes as he sat leaning back in his chair. His gaze met Ahlquist's and he sang in his clear tenor that carried a tune so well and had such a delicate timbre (as the station engineer put it) that it had opened doors for him and taken him places he would never otherwise have seen. They sang in four parts, pretending they never rehearsed, just suddenly had the urge to sing together:

'Let's dream away the spring
forget the pain that winter brings.'

At the end, when not so much as a fork clinked against a plate and no one was clearing his throat, F.A. sang a solo, and the cashier at her desk clasped her hands on top of her pad of bills:

'Yes, let's!' his tenor voice with its mysterious tone celebrated, 'Let's forget the whole wide world!'

Ah, it was lovely. Winther himself tossed his head and initiated the applause. He might have been a bit worried the first time, but they never screeched. In fact, they had become an attraction, and he allowed them to have their way. They had become a tradition, one of many that had sprouted up in the town like toadstools in damp weather.

The yard master was the first one to treat them to a bottle of wine — a Niersteiner they had never forgotten. Now every evening someone asked for the honour of proposing a toast to the gentlemen, and it was plain sailing until the time Kasparsson made the mistake of hinting a little too forcefully when neither 'The scent of the rose' nor 'Over the glorious valleys' had exacted anything to speak of.

'I guess it's time to wring a tear out of Cederfalk himself,' he said. 'Time for 'Oh thou lovely evening,' fellows.'

It was public knowledge that the stationmaster felt so strongly about this lovely poem that he wished to have its first lines inscribed on his gravestone. When they got to 'every night the spirit flies in music towards the land of nod' he almost thought he had written the song himself, and by the time he silently signalled to Winther the restaurant owner to treat the singers to champagne, he was a broken man.

After Kasparsson's *faux pas*, however, it had become virtually impossible to get F.A. to sing again, because he had his pride and was sensitive about his lack of means. He never paid a great deal of attention to the bill, but one evening Kasparsson read a naughty poem he had written in a dull moment at the office, which embarrassed F.A. deeply, since he was easily offended in this respect as well. That time, he picked up the bill and pretended to be studying it. This improved his mood, and he showed it to the others:

HOTEL DE WINTHER

Bill

to: Postal clerk Clarin and his party
April 18   4 Soupees @ 2 kronor 8 Kr.
Signed: Tora Lans

This was no surprise to the others, who had seen it before and who said they assumed that it was Winther's unfortunate weakness for French that explained the spelling. Still, F.A. had to tease the cashier about it. After all, he had been to nearly four years of upper secondary school and was tipsy.

'I wonder, miss, if you would do me the honour of joining me for soupee some evening?' he said at the cash desk, with a slight bow that almost caused him to topple over, to the delight of Clarin and Kasparsson. Ahlquist took him by the arm.

'Thank you,' said the cashier. She sat up very straight, her eyes wide.

'I'm not allowed to visit the hotel when I'm off work, though,' she said. 'No one who works here is.'

To his horror he realized that she was pleased, and that she had raised her hand to her chest as if her heart were pounding. She still didn't blink.

'What a shame,' Clarin assisted, coming to his rescue, 'in that case there can be no soupee since ladies aren't allowed to go to the bars.'

'I'm sorry, miss.'

F.A. gave her an exaggerated bow, and at that moment he recognized her and was ashamed.

'Aha,' he said. 'Is it not the lovely Mary who bathed my feet and listened to my words that very first night?'

Now she had realized that he had only been pulling her leg about the supper. She hadn't moved so it was impossible to say how he knew. Perhaps her breathing changed. Anyway, he went on talking.

'Transformed to a Martha,' he said, 'a mistress of the house.'

'My name is Tora,' she said. 'I never bathed your feet, sir.'

She turned away and her pen scratched at the paper as she signed the next bill.

'You do make life difficult for yourself,' said Clarin, guiding him towards the door. Then it was all forgotten. By everyone but himself, he thought. When he committed a *faux pas* it plagued him terribly. So this one grew, he felt as if he had been rude to her, and every time he caught sight of her blond head behind the cash desk he was embarrassed. She had no doubt forgotten all about it; only he was bothered. He avoided the cash desk, and it took him completely by surprise one evening at the end of May when he found himself standing in front of it all alone, bowing like a schoolboy and asking:

'Fröken Lans, would you give me the pleasure of accompanying me on the outing to Gnesta?'

His association with Clarin, Kasparsson and Ahlquist had also won him a place in the Juno chorus, where the outing to Gnesta was the subject of the hour. Tora knew about it because the hotel was providing the picnic hampers.

'I would like to make it up to you,' he said stiffly, looking her right in the eye. When she didn't reply but just stared at him, he clarified:

'For the supper we were unable to have.'

Slowly her cheeks went pink, and finally she blinked.

She arrived for the outing to Gnesta in a new lilac wool walking suit. It had a corseted waistcoat and turned-up cuffs. She wore a hat of the same shade. When the choir was ready to sing, she spread a towel on a rock and sat down to listen. It was a lovely outing, and just as in the song, *the solemn evening hung gleaming in the air* above Gnesta.

232

It happened so fast. There was so little hesitation.

When she linked her arm in his, placing her hand on the carefully-brushed paletot sleeve, she did it as if she had done so many times before. But he still seemed to be hesitant, and she felt sorry for him.

When they were standing up by the pavilion at the rifle range, she realized that he was trying to decide whether to walk her along the Promenade or Lovers' Lane. He had been worrying about it for a long time. Decent couples walked up the tavern hill past the school and through the sparse woods to the pavilion. Then they walked down the road. However, practically invisible between the trunks of two birches, running steeply down into the hazel tree grove, was the turning to Lovers' Lane, which you only took if you wanted to be alone together.

She told him about the pavilion, that it used to be called Louse Point, and about Embankment Brita who had once lived there. She did so just to pass the time and give him time to sort things out.

'Let's move along,' he said, and they walked down the lane almost all the way to Gertrudsborg. She told him about the merchant's wife who lived out there without him, that she was a tippler. He said nothing. They crossed the meadows and saw Wärnström's big factory buildings and smelled the soot in the air. This was a walk for engaged couples. But he didn't want to walk down to the lake. The very smell of water made him shake his head and pull her the other way. And yet he said he could never live far from the sea.

They got to what once was Old Mothstead, now the cemetery, and they stopped to buy two mugs of fresh milk from some dairymaids in a field. Then he got cold, and they walked quickly back, like all the other times. He was a thin man easily chilled. Once he had been fine-limbed, had straight posture and filled out his vest, but he had been losing weight all spring. He blamed it on the cold he'd caught on his arrival. Naturally, if it rained they didn't go out. The least little bit of haze in the air could keep him inside. Then he would spend the whole afternoon in the music café, lost to her.

The next time they got to the pavilion he was just as uncertain as before, and often they walked down Lovers' Lane. She wished she could know which it would be in advance, because of her clothes. The hem of her skirt dragged and got wet on Lover's Lane, and moss would catch on her purple walking suit. In the Grotto there was a mossy stone that served as a bench. She sat down, despite her skirt. Her suit was too hot, too. The cowslips and lilies of the valley had flowered now. The air was sweeter. Between the alders there was a haze of blue-violet, where the cranes' bills were in full bloom.

'Well, it's almost time for the fern to blossom,' she said. F.A. grinned.

'Tora, don't you know the fern's a cryptogam?'

'Sounds like an underground tomb to me,' she replied.

'No, it's nothing but a plant without the capacity to reproduce through flowering and seeding.'

'Oh,' said Tora. 'Well, this is still the time of year when it blooms!'

234

'Tora, whatever do you mean?' he asked earnestly, since he had never noted much of a sense of humour in her. Moreover, fear and superstition seemed entirely alien to her.

'I hardly know myself,' she answered honestly, and they both burst out laughing.

She had never before considered bringing a man back to her room behind the linen cupboards; it wasn't worth the risk. But now she had to. The rain poured down the windowpanes. They were surrounded by the smell of laundry and freshly-mangled linens.

'Oh, what a sweet scent,' he said.

It was as if she had heard of someone long ago who had done what she was doing, and so she did not need to hesitate.

His landlady's sister was married to a man in Norrköping, so she sometimes visited them on Sundays. Then he would dare to take Tora home with him. To the right of the door there was a divan with big bolsters. The fabric was brown in a Persian pattern. He put her right there, and she could hardly suppress a smile. But he remained sitting for a long time on the edge of the bed, long after she was already lying there on her back, high up on the soft pillows. He had only removed his shoes, and they stood there next to one another, newly-polished that morning. Their tops were of black elastic. She didn't mind how long he sat there now that his stockings were off and she could look at him.

Everyone she knew had feet that had been squeezed into and deformed by shoes that had been too small and poorly made. She had chilblains on her heels, and her big toe bent inwards. Her bunions were so big that her shoes had shaped themselves around them. She had always thought toenails were naturally thick and yellow and ingrown.

He was the only person she had ever seen with uninjured feet. They were small. His toenails were thin and grew so straight that his stockings always got holes in the same place after just a couple of days. It was as if they had been sliced with a little razor blade.

He found himself unable to lie down beside her in the full daylight of the afternoon, at first.

'Come on,' she had said once. But she learned not to.

The divan was at an angle to the wall, and it was draughty at the foot end, near the door. Across the room, in front of the curtain, was his bed. They never dared to lie down there, because the curtain covered the door to his landlady's rooms. She might come home, and if she meant to spy on them she might tiptoe.

There was a high, narrow window with gauze curtains and a view of merchant Lindh's warehouse. On the drawstring was an extremely dusty plush rose.

She lay there familiarizing herself with the room. In front of the window was the desk, the top of which was covered in artificial leather. The chair came from the dining room set and had pine cones carved into the back. There was a pedestal between the desk and the divan, with a copper pot containing a leafy lily that never blossomed. There was a cowhair carpet, red and brown and worn right down to the weft. Under it the bleached floor was grey. He had a nightstand and a lamp with a green glass shade that he sometimes moved to the desk. There was a brown cabinet with a mirror on the door. The tiled stove was to the left of the door.

Every time she let her eyes wander she saw something she hadn't noticed before: on a shelf over the nightstand he had a little pillow to lay his watch on at night. The rope that regulated the stove damper was all knotted. The border of roses on the brown wallpaper with a pattern of golden lyres had faded to the colour of clotted blood.

She couldn't wash in his room because the commode was in an alcove outside the door. In any case she would never have dared.

Each time, she noticed something new. The ash tray of hammered copper. His black trunk under the bed. The folded copy of the Gothenburg Commercial and Seafarers' Daily. Gradually, she constructed the room by examining it. It had to be very real.

'What are you looking at?' he asked.

'At your room.'

'Mine?'

He let his eyes wander, too.

'In this whole room the only things I can see that are mine are a newspaper and a trunk.'

She still lay there looking at it.

He did not talk about his hesitation or how to throw it off. She just had to wait. Then he gently held her head and laid it on the pillow, so gently that he didn't disturb her hair. He wanted her to remain perfectly still throughout, she soon learned.

She learned not to touch his organ even if it didn't find the way in. It nuzzled its way in like the nose of a kind little animal and she had to wait patiently, smiling into his shoulder.

237

It wasn't especially wonderful, but it helped to draw them closer. They both needed the warmth. Still, she felt lonely and had no idea what he was feeling.

They decided to spend a night together. However, it would have to be when Tora had the day off so she could stay in bed until his landlady went to the coalyard in the morning to fill her copper coalbox.

'Give her these if you meet her crossing the yard,' said F.A., handing her a whole pile of Baptist tracts from the wood basket. 'Then she can't possibly get the wrong idea.'

But Tora looked as insulted as if he had seriously believed she was a holy roller. No, she could not appreciate a joke or any use of the imagination. He knew that about her. However, she was often happy, and then she could laugh at almost anything.

'What a big nose you have,' she said, pulling it. 'What good does such a big nose do you?'

Then she hid her head in his chest and laughed until her tears ran.

If his stomach ached and he tossed uneasily, she would wake up. But he might lie awake for other reasons and, strangely, that would wake her too. At such times she was almost exasperated. Now that they finally had all night together!

'What's wrong?'

He didn't answer. Was he lying in the half-light listening? She had to ask him again.

'Never mind,' he said. 'It's nothing.'

Now, however, she thought she could hear sounds too, although they were very, very soft.

'Did you hear that?'

'No.'

He shook his head and she felt it move with her hand. His watch on its pillow ticked ever so softly. They couldn't possibly hear it, could they?

'What on earth is it?'

'Maybe it's that little thing that's built into clocks and people,' he said. She didn't know what he meant, though.

'It's called worry.'

One night she said his name. She had been wanting to for a long time, but hadn't dared. His friends called him F.A., and from the beginning she didn't even know his given name. They had known one another for so long that she was embarrassed to ask. Then one evening she saw a piece of paper from the railway that said his name was Fredrik Adam. It took her a long time to dare to say it. It might sound a little put-on. Fredrik! But once she had said it it seemed perfectly natural to her. She was upset to see that he drew back as if someone had revealed something he would have preferred not to see, or asked him to do something unpleasant.

Much later on, there was a letter on the desk. It was from his mother and made sorry reading. The haulage company had been declared bankrupt after his father's death; the letter contained nothing but complaints, money problems, and my dear boy here, my dear boy there. Tora didn't like that woman. However, the letter began: My dear Adam. This made Tora blush bright red despite the fact that she was alone when she read it.

Clarin had been transferred to the post office at Eskilstuna. It was a promotion, so he could not turn it down, but it meant the end of the quartet. They tried to find a new second tenor, but, as Kasparsson said, it wasn't just a matter of the voice: we require an *homme de qualité* in every way and we must not make any hasty decisions.

One evening in early autumn Ahlquist and Kasparsson settled in at a table at the railway restaurant with a bottle of arrack on ice and requested paper and a pen, as it was necessary to write a letter to Clarin. They agreed that they would draft the letter on the paper and then write a clean copy on the back of the big menu from the Hotel de Winther, a souvenir of the good old days they expected Clarin would appreciate. They had finished the letter by the time F.A. joined them.

Tora had been keeping an eye on them from behind the cash desk, and she noted that F.A. read twice through what they had written on the back of the menu, quickly and attentively. Then he rose and tore the menu into pieces so small that it was impossible to rip the cardboard any smaller. He threw the pieces into the ashtray, and in the general clamour and the noise of china and cutlery, Tora could not hear a single word he said to them. Obviously, though, he was upset.

He left the dining room without looking round, and without a nod in her direction. Ahlquist and Kasparsson asked for the bill and returned the pen. Once they had left, Tora asked one of the waitresses to bring her the ash tray, and she secreted the fragments into her skirt pocket. When she got to her room behind the linen cupboards that night, she laid the puzzle pieces until she could read the letter. The beginning was gone.

'... that you send Ebba 50 kronor for the year, which is probably your best way out. There is, of course, an old woman here who takes in children. Her name is Strömgren and she rents rooms from Larsson the carpenter, across the road from the dairy. (If, in the end, you should find this a better solution in some way.) However, in addition to being more costly, this kind of arrangement is associated with certain risks. One does not know if the child will survive. Mind you, there are no evil rumours about Madame Strömgren in circulation, but we would still advise you to send the 50 kronor to Ebba. She will be glad for the money and the matter will be taken care of.'

After their signatures there was a PS and a little sketch of two pairs of eager feet extending from a trundle bed: 'We are not singing at all because we are having trouble in our search for a second tenor. Neither are we getting frigged as regularly as in your days. *Tempora Mutantur*!'

As soon as Tora was alone with F.A., she said:

'How gentlemanly of you to rip up that letter about Ebba!'

He just stared at her.

'So you read other people's letters?'

What was so terrible about that? Moreover, she could hardly have known it was a letter. On the menu!

'Disgusting,' he said. 'You put the pieces together.'

He looked at her as if she were unclean, but Tora was radiant. Suddenly he realized that she had not understood that what put him off was the post script of the letter. Crudeness didn't appear to bother her. No, she thought he meant that fifty kronor wouldn't make it up to Ebba.

'Well, Ebba's a human being, too, isn't she?' said Tora.

At first he was silent, then he said cautiously:

'Some day Clarin will be postmaster.'

'Yes,' said Tora, sighing loudly as a child, 'even I realize that he couldn't *marry* Ebba.'

'No, there would certainly have been practical ...'

Being totally immune to irony, she blurted out:

'But I still think it was gentlemanly of you to *think* about Ebba.'

Had he been thinking about Ebba? Perhaps somehow he had, after all. The more deeply he looked into those naive deep blue eyes, the more he seemed to learn about himself. But he was extremely upset at the thought that Tora might have seen the post script to that letter.

'Did you read the whole thing?' he asked.

'No, big chunks had gone missing.'

'Ah, well,' he said. 'Let's put it behind us.'

One month later, however, she placed her hand confidently over his and said:

'Now *we're* going to have a baby.'

He didn't seem to understand.

'I'm in the family way.'

She looked almost happy; she didn't blink. He leaned his head against the wall with the golden lyres and shut his eyes.

'How long have you known?' he asked.

That summer Tora had gone home just as often as before, but she had only stayed the night once.

The croft was unchanged, but every time she saw it it seemed to have shrunk under the birch tree. She stopped before going any closer, and had to smile. The sign on the gable had been taken down now that Lans was no longer a district soldier. But you could see where it had hung, as the rest of the timber of the cottage was dark brown, as if the tar had been brought out by the sunshine. 'Fear the Lord. Honour the King, Serve loyally.'

Since they could no longer produce enough to keep a cow, the cowshed was empty. The fragments of mirror in the cowshed window were so coated with dust and cobwebs that they did not reflect the sun. Sara Sabina had given over the patch outside the cottage door to vanity: mignonette was growing there. The vile lovage had been dug up, since the flies had left with the cow.

The butcher block by the well could be used for scrubbing a rug or other messy work. It had now been in the same spot for so long that there were clover and bottle-brush growing in profusion up the legs. There was still no iron stove in the cottage, but they pretended they didn't mind.

'Just think of the light coming through the hole in the old baking oven in the wall in the winter time,' said Lans.

'Just you wait,' said Tora. 'Times'll change.'

Inside the door was the chopping block Rickard had made a back for, where Johannes Lans spent his days, listening for hunting horns and clarinets in the woods, and the drumbeats marking the forward march of evolution.

'It's sure quiet all alone out here,' said Tora.

'Aw,' said Lans. 'Now and then we get a tramp who spends the night in front of the fire.'

Tora knew that was no longer true, though, because the symbols for both poor and stingy had been carved in the side of the barn down by the road. An uncommon combination.

She put a pile of old newspapers from the village on the table near their eyeglasses, and Lans put his on. He read about how many harvesters had been sold the previous week and about the Hercules traction engine, and said:

'"We're living in the age of invention," as the old woman said when she used a hoofing tong to pick off her lice.'

Sara Sabina ground coffee. Tora had also brought flour, butter and sugar so they could bake fresh rolls. She had mixed the dough and showed her grandmother a way of shaping them by cutting thin slices, twisting them and then turning them up like a braided hair bun.

'Isn't the egg teaching the chicken to hatch?' Sara Sabina asked, watching with her hands held under her apron.

'It's really easy,' said Tora. 'Watch.'

'Oh, yes, I see. The point is to try to make each one different from the next.'

And the old woman gurgled in one of her rare moments of amusement, while Tora, offended, kept silent.

'I don't bake much,' she said.

She slept in the main room that night. There was a mouse nest in her pillow, but she didn't have the heart to mention it. She laid the pillow on the floor next to the bed and rolled her shift up and put it under her head. In the kitchen, things never really quieted down. Lans muttered. She could hear their sheets rustling. Upstairs where the dried meat and grain and old linens were kept, the mice scurried about the floor.

The June night didn't sleep; the sky only shut its eyes for an hour or two.

She wanted to get up and drink a scoop of water, but when she opened the door a crack she could hear that both the old folks were awake, and she felt awkward, as if she were a little girl again.

'What time do you think it is?' Lans asked.

They didn't take down his old watch from its nail and carry it over to the window to look. Instead, Sara Sabina leaned out so she could see the edge of the forest in the east. The light was very pale. You couldn't see the difference between the crab-apples and the morello cherries out there. The dawn was as grey as the powdery ashes in the hearth. Lans had fallen back asleep on his pillow. He didn't hear Sara Sabina's answer.

In the silence, the grass stopped growing for a couple of hours. Soon the light would be back. There was some uneasy rustling deep in amongst the branches, where the dawn was greyest.

'Is it time now?'

'No, you just sleep.'

Tora went back to bed and she, too, slept for a while. She woke once again to their whispers.

'Is he coming?'

The floor was a bit cold under foot. Through the crack in the door she could see Sara Sabina wrap a shawl around the old man and carry him to the kitchen table. She sat on a chair opposite him, her hands on the table top. They were idle. She looked through the window and Lans, whose mobility was more restricted in his chair, asked eagerly:

'Do you see him? Is he coming?'

Tora walked over to the window in the room, looking out. She could see everything they could, but she didn't understand.

It was the time of day when the dew released the scent from leaf and grass. You might long to go outside, but you were also hesitant. It was the time of day when the Others came out. Now she remembered.

In the past, she had been frightened of grey shadows that rushed off under the timbered houses, and she had been afraid of night-time, even when the nights were lightest. She had been terrified of the witches' rings trampled deep into the grass, and not even during the daytime did she dare to go over to that side of the meadow. But her grandmother had told her that the rings weren't made by dancing witches. The roe buck and his mate made the rings and the symbols of infinity when they were in heat, and they made them every single year in the same place.

One summer morning coming home from a dance she had heard the hoarse coughs and piercing cries of the roe buck from over there, and instead of going inside to bed she had crept through the birch grove down towards the meadow. She stood stark still and freezing cold behind a birch and watched them rushing around in their rings, not understanding what she was seeing at all.

If his mate did not want to be mounted, then why didn't she run right away into the woods? And if she meant to let him have her in the end, why did she rush away? What was forcing her to keep running? The witches' rings had become even more frightening to Tora once she had seen them come into being.

The others were always out there, but they didn't always make themselves known.

There was a hare sitting in the clover by the well. He was there when the daylight arrived. His long ears twitched and listened in a new direction. Above the woods the sky was criss-crossed with thin strips in different shades of red, until the yellow gold came and overpowered them. A haze passed over the roof of the vegetable cellar and burned off. There was the blackbird. She had been hearing him for a while, singing in the shadows. Now here he was, hopping around in the garden patch and silently pulling up worms.

'Has he come?' asked Lans.

'Not yet.'

'He does know how to keep you waiting,' he said, but not impatiently. Tora tramped her feet for a little while, trying to pull the rag rug towards her. Her feet were now ice cold.

Outside, everything had come alive. The wheatear was stalking up and down the low wall by the cellar, his white tail sparkling. The hare left a long trail of tracks in the clover dew, vanishing around the corner of the cowshed. Now the sunshine reached the front steps. It warmed Sara Sabina's hands on the table top. Then he appeared.

He moved along the cowshed wall, then quickly crossed the grass, so fast they almost couldn't keep track of him. He seemed to be running up the edge of the well. It was surrounded by the lilac shoots that were growing up all over the place; no sun got in there. Now with a gentle leap he was up on the butcher's block. The greyish wood was

247

warmed now; he was flooded with sunlight and sat upright. He was small and beautiful and cruel, and they sat watching him. He was playful. If he felt like it and the sun was warm and rosy enough he would do tricks on the block. He had no idea there were spectators. His coat was so fine and brown it sparked in the sunlight. At the tip of his tail was a black tuft, his eye was a little pearl. When he sat upright and was on his guard you could see the white spot on his chest. He looked as if he were sitting there tanning it. You couldn't help but smile at him.

'He's such a mischievous chap,' Lans whispered. 'Full of tricks.'

'He can be stubborn as can be, too.'

'Right. You wouldn't want to have to grapple with him when he's in that mood.'

Tora took off her pink flannel knickers and wrapped her feet in them when she crawled back into bed. Her eyes were burning, as if she had got fine-grained sand in them. She would have liked to go out and get a scoop of water because she had a sour taste in her mouth, but she didn't want to disturb them. They were still sitting there although he'd gone. She didn't know whether they were waiting for something else; she was too sleepy.

Yes, the Others were always out there. They probably had laws and regulations of their own, too, but you didn't know. They appeared to be strict and perhaps also beautiful. They were also playful and cruel and capricious. You knew nothing about them and their unrelenting compulsion. You didn't know the rings they ran in any better than you knew your own. What did you think you would discover? An order that was beyond mankind? Still, it was beyond your reach, always. You could only look for it, your eyes dull from the yearning.

She fell asleep although the sun was in her eyes. Then she dreamt it all again. It was still night and there was the peculiar summer light, grey as hearth ash. Then the sun rose. An ermine arrived. He played and strutted, a white spot on his chest. The idle hands resting on the table top were also warmed by the sun.

I believe in public opinion,' said Winther. 'Public opinion is power. It's the new age!'

He had oranges distributed to all the schoolchildren, and cigars to their teachers.

Their chorus performed for him, and he was considering giving each child a toothbrush with instructions on how to use it, in honour of his fiftieth birthday.

'That's a damned good idea,' he said. 'I'll give them fifty toothbrushes with Winther engraved on the handles. That's advertising! I believe in advertising.'

He put this idea into effect even sooner, in commemoration of King Oscar's nameday. He owned three railway station restaurants and was the majority shareholder of the new spa at Ridgeview springs. However, he was considering putting his money into a renowned Stockholm restaurant instead.

'I may be moving along,' said the loyalist and friend of the children. 'The Winther Palace may soon be down-graded to a general store.'

The twelve-room wooden mansion was next door to Levander, the merchant's, which was expanding. The street with the court house and the larger homes was now called King's Road all the way up to Tavern Hill. The large white mansion was lit up late into the night, and singing could be heard: 'Chirri, chirri, bim...'

For his sake, travelling players stopped there and performed even though the spectators made fools of themselves by laughing when there was nothing for an educated person to laugh at. 'There is a dearth of cultivated taste here,' said Winther. He had to comfort them, the divine Helens of Troy, the women of the world, the little countesses, the Ninichkas, saints and Cossack peasant girls, he consoled them all with his candlelit meals. Eventually, he had enough champagne bottles to pave the dirt floor of his gazebo, and their high heels got caught between them. The huge grey dogs growled softly when they entered the house, but they didn't mind. And they sang: 'Chirri, chirri, bim, Chirri, chirri, bim...' .

Poets spent the night on their way home from readings, drunk as skunks but always with their country's name on the tips of their tongues. Sometimes they had to be persuaded to stay. Was the chamber maid any good? They all were! No one wanted for anything at Winther's! Fresh brioches in the morning, coffee as strong as in Paris. One morning Ebba left the mansion with a volume of poetry in her hand. She walked through the railway park where the large dogs did their business. They lifted their long legs and peed against the iron lampposts. Ebba went in and showed Tora the book. There were flowering chrysanthemums on the binding.

'Look what I've been given,' she said.

They read some of it. This bard's work was not philosophically inclined, but the words were difficult.

'You can have it if you like,' said Ebba.

In honour of his fiftieth birthday Winther chartered a train and invited two hundred of his friends to Norrköping for the best dinner Kneipp's could serve.

'I want to stay on at the hotel to see that celebration,' said Tora. 'After that I'll quit.'

Still, she hadn't spoken to Winther yet. After the party the whole North Side was hung over for a week. Then there was Christmas, and the inventory. She moved the buttons on her skirt, couldn't quit in the middle of the heaviest work load of the year. Her job entailed more than just sitting behind the cash desk. She was responsible for some of the storerooms, and had to keep them stocked. She would never have been able to wait at table and carry trays in her condition, she was much larger than the first time. As things were she was exhausted, and made her way out to the kitchen where the sound of the coffee grinder could perk you up even when you were ready to drop. She drank her coffee standing up, in the hustle and bustle between the hot stoves, pouring it into the saucer to cool faster because she was in a hurry. She should tell him, she should quit, but it was also a matter of money. Otter said everything would work out, that she just shouldn't worry. And she didn't as long as she was working. But she had found out what he was earning as a replacement office worker, and she couldn't imagine how it was going to work out — afterwards.

'You quit in good time,' Ebba warned her. 'You remember what happened to me.'

Oh no, she was not going to have a miscarriage. In the evenings she would lie on her back with both hands on her belly.

'You just stay right there,' she whispered, her eyes filling up with tears of pent up laughter, all alone. 'We'll find a way. You just stay. Stay in there, please.' She rolled onto her side and curled around her belly. She felt gentle movements, and as she was falling asleep her last conscious reflection was: 'Don't you sleep when I do? How funny.'

One morning just after the first of the year, Winther called her into his office. He shifted through papers, made telephone calls. But she was used to that, she waited.

'Damnation, young lady, haven't you anything to say for yourself?'

Astonished, Tora stared at his red face, at the whirlwind of papers in the air.

'Not a word? How so?'

'Well, I don't know...'

'Do you think people are blind?'

Then she understood. She had to stop her hands in mid-air from flying to her belly. This was humiliating and awful and she regretted her behaviour deeply. She had intended to come in of her own free will and tell him calmly: 'I'm handing in my resignation now, as I'm getting married.' She had intended to say just that, even at the risk that it would reach F.A.'s ears.

'I'm getting married,' she stammered, but now she didn't even sound convincing to herself. 'I should have come and told you...'

'Getting married! To whom?'

Of course she didn't dare to answer that question, since he hadn't exactly given her his word about it.

'Has the entire quartet proposed?'

That hurt. Wide-eyed with shock, Tora stared at him, astonished that the pain that shot through her whole body was a real, physical sensation, not the least bit metaphysical. Her knees buckled.

Just fifteen minutes later she was sitting, hands icy cold, packing her belongings in the room behind the linen closet.

'What will you do?' asked Ebba.

She shook her head. All she could think of was Otter, that she would go straight to him when he got off work and tell him what Winther had said. However, only for the first hour did she say to herself over and over again that she was going to tell Otter about it. Then her head cleared. It might provide momentary solace. But if she had any sense she wouldn't tell Otter everything Winther had said.

'I've got to get back,' said Ebba. 'Will you go home?'

'Home?'

'I can't stay any longer,' said Ebba. 'I've got to go. I'll see you later. Oh, Lord, I think it might've been best for you if it had gone the way it did for me.'

No, she had no intention of going to Appleton. Certainly not. She tried to think, but without much success. Out of habit she went and laid her icy cold hands on the tiled stove, but there was no heat in it at this time of day, she'd forgotten. Well, she'd have to think something out, even if she wasn't very good at that.

When F.A. Otter got off work and walked out of the station building, one of the newspaper boys approached.

'Someone's waiting for you round the other side.'

He walked around the building in the slush, stepping high since he only had his galoshes on.

254

Tora was sitting on a bench with her bundles and a case, as if she were waiting for the train. For a moment he felt an utterly irrational sense of relief, until she raised her head and looked at him.

'I've had to quit.'

She didn't bother with the more cultivated pronunciation he preferred. She stared at him, her eyes unblinking. She was as usual, but different.

'But Tora, my dear,' he said, sitting down on the bench but finding it so cold he was on his feet again instantly, pulling her up with him. 'Where will you go now?'

She said nothing. He took her by the elbow, carefully leading her past the window, trying to warn her by silently mouthing: 'The stationmasters!'

'There's no harm in talking,' said Tora.

'What do you expect me to do?' he asked once they were around the corner. 'I'm at a total loss.'

He was carrying her case, she had her bundles.

'Don't ask me. But I'm not going home.'

He was touchy and cheerful and sickly. Somewhat debonair he was — well, at least he dressed nicely for everyday. He was irreproachably polite, but vulnerable. He was afraid of something. In the end, she managed to track down his secret, but that was much later. Now, at any rate, he was sufficiently soft-hearted not to abandon her in the slush, slink away into the restaurant, run off to America. What could she know about what was going through his head? Tora stayed tight-lipped and learned a few things.

255

Three nights in a private room at the widow of the constable's. After which he was desperate. He simply could not afford to pay the rent at two places.

'One place for the two of us will be fine,' said Tora. 'The widow's starting to give me funny looks. You know, I could ask around. I'm sure Valfrid Johansson at Levander's would know a place.'

'No, no, no.'

He was gone for a whole evening. She guessed he was at the hotel, which proved to be correct. The next evening he was out again, and she gathered her forces. However, on the third afternoon he arrived, saying:

'Lundholm the master painter has a one-room flat to rent.'

'So did you take it?'

They went together, but he told her not to come up with him. Even when he came down and had arranged things he didn't want her to go up.

'There's the window of the main room,' he said, pointing. It was dark. 'And the kitchen window looks out on the courtyard.'

The building was painted a greying yellow. It was diagonally across the road from Wärnström's factory, and the foundry was visible at the bottom of the hill. On the right was the chapel Wärnström had had built for the parish.

'I don't believe I know a single soul around here,' said Tora.

In the early days she learned a bitter lesson about what it is like to have forced yourself on someone. He fell ill again and she boiled him the milk gruel he could stomach. If she hadn't been nursing him there would have been total silence between them. He lay facing the wall on the bed in their one room. He explained that he was lying on his good side, and it was the only position he could stand. Shouldn't they put the bed somewhere else, then? He couldn't just lie there staring at the brown wallpaper! But the door was in the other wall, and there was no space long enough for the bed. He couldn't lie under the window, and opposite the window was the tiled stove. So he lay staring at the wallpaper until, one day, Tora pulled the bed out into the middle of the room.

He had had to borrow a little money again so they could buy kitchen utensils and a little used furniture. A few things also arrived from his mother by freight train from Gothenburg. There was a footstool and a dresser, a little nightstand with a chamber pot, and a shaving stand with a mirror that had cracked in transit. The whole shipment was wrapped in burlap and rag rugs. Tora kept the worn rugs, redid the fringes and laid them on the floor. He looked at the arrangement without saying anything, but she could see that he found it pathetic.

They had bought a used kitchen settee and table, and an iron trundle bed. Tora was terrified the bed would collapse in the middle, as they often did, and close him up like a jack-knife, his bottom on the floor and his arms and legs sticking out of the iron trap. If anything like that happened, he might take off. It might have been ridiculous and pitiful, but she was frightened and unable to see the funny side of it. Nothing was funny. Every time he lay down, she hoped he was being extremely careful.

To the left of the bed she put the nightstand. It was marble-topped, and she put the footstool, upholstered in black with embroidered roses, underneath. She squeezed the dresser into the corner so he would be able to see it from the bed. She set the shaving stand on it. It had a drawer with a bone knob, and he kept his mother's letters there. She put *Chrysanthemum*, which Ebba had given her, on the dresser. The poet had signed it inside, a looping signature, and she wished F.A. would open it.

Yet as she tried to please him and arrange things around him as nicely as possible she might suddenly feel furious and barely give him the time of day if he asked her for his razor strap or the newspaper. She couldn't understand herself. She didn't remember very much about the other time she had been pregnant, which was at least six or seven years back. She must have been more even-tempered then, though. She had been so ignorant. Now at least she knew what it was like to force yourself on someone.

She became touchy, and started to react to the way things were said, although she had never been the kind of person who thought words really were decisive. When he lay there talking about the sea, his cursed and beloved ocean whose moist fogs he apparently couldn't live without, she thought he meant her.

'The sea pulls back from the rocky beach,' he said. 'The sea falls at ebb tide.'

'Well, the sea must have somewhere to go then,' she said, surprising him, because he didn't expect any deep comments from her.

'When the kitty ebbs out,' she added, thus completely ruining the spirit of the conversation.

After two weeks he went back to work. At first she was relieved. She had been worried about how they would pay the rent, buy their food and kerosene and wood, and pay the doctor's fee. She knew he had to make payments on one of his loans, too.

Now she was alone all day, and it was as if she had just begun to discover what kind of neighbourhood she was living in. It felt far away from the station. She was unaccustomed to not hearing the trains. Sometimes she woke up at night from not hearing them any more.

In the evening you could see the electric lights at Wärnström's. There were two street lights down at the corner that shone on the parishioners when they came out of his chapel. She had been in there once with Ebba. They had gone along to have a good giggle at the outpourings of the congregation, but it hadn't been funny. Their religion turned out to be almost as dull as that of the official church, and she hadn't given it a thought since then. Now, however, she began to realize that religious people were many and powerful.

Once at the shop she heard them talk of her as Otter's housekeeper. This was on one of her hot-headed, angry days, and she held him accountable.

'But Tora, please,' he said.

'Well, it was news to me! Yes, indeed, news to me. You always learn things by going out amongst people.'

She could annoy him most of all by allowing her Sörmland dialect to shine through unashamedly.

She could feel her mouth preparing to really lay into him.

'I'm sure you understand I had to say that,' he said stiffly. 'This is such a free church neighbourhood. I'm sure our landlord is a free-churchgoer.'

'If Lundholm's religious I'll eat my hat. That's news to me, too.'

'At any rate, I did say you were my housekeeper, and I consider it the best possible explanation for the time being.'

His 'for the time being' cut the discussion short. Tora regretted her outburst deeply. Why could she never learn to manage this business sensibly? She didn't dare ask him anything outright. He was sick and irritated and she had forced herself on him quite enough already. But when she was feeling calmer she realized there was a way to approach the subject obliquely without having to mention the word marriage. She asked him whether he wasn't eligible for a railway worker's flat.

'An extra office worker?' he asked. 'You can't be serious.'

'Well, what about later on?'

He was sitting with the newspaper held to his face and it seemed as if he did not intend to answer until he finally folded it and began explaining with a long-suffering air.

'I can't stay here, Tora. You know I cannot conceive of living my whole life here.'

'I see.'

'I could never live so far from the sea.'

She looked mean when she gazed past him out the window, because she was thinking about the damnable sea that she had only seen in pictures.

'Not to mention the fact that I haven't completed my training,' he said.

She had no idea he had begun any training. But she knew she was getting bigger and bigger.

She was stared at. She would have preferred not to go out, but there was no choice since she had to fetch water down in the yard. So the women had a close look at her. She had not yet spoken with any of them, but they already knew how many sets of sheets she had in her cupboard. Or rather, they knew that she had two sets and could not save up and do all her laundry once in the autumn and once in the spring, but had to boil her sheets in a big jam pot on the stove and hang them out to dry so she could use them the same night. She bought a few more linen towels and another two sets of sheets, and she had plenty to keep her busy.

She was supposed to do the cooking. She owned one cast iron frying pan and two aluminium pots. There were a grater and wooden spoons and one big kitchen knife on the bottom shelf in the kitchen cupboard. There was a divided wooden box with a carrier handle for the metal cutlery. She took the greatest of care with their six plates, although she hated them just as much as she hated every single one of the used wooden kitchen utensils that were dark brown and worn down from long prior use, and from being kept with blackened, spotted metal ones. She had come to this from the hotel, where the linens were stored in huge aromatic piles, where she had used silver-plated ladles to serve with and set the tables with durable, attractive bone china.

Actually, there was very little for her to do. Make the meals. Wait. The flat was so empty. She found stitching dull, as she had never been taught how to do it and hers did not come out well. She just had to smile at the idea that Sara Sabina Lans would ever have sat bent over a sheet to monogram it.

The worst part, though, was the neighbours. She would have liked to sweep past them on her way out, going to the station or the hotel, dressed in her lilac walking suit with its flared skirt. But she couldn't button it at the waist. She had to go down to the yard to fetch water dressed in a big striped pinafore. After some time, they began to speak with

261

her. However, she would just as soon they hadn't, because they were so cutting. They gossiped and chewed things over and spat them out. She sensed that there was one way to avoid being the object of their tattling, and that would have been to sacrifice F.A. Otter at their altar. That was exactly what those old hens wanted, she would think, standing stiffly at the pump, looking her neighbour women unabashedly in the eyes.

She would sit in the window of their room watching the people leave the chapel, lifting their faces to feel whether it was drizzling. They did up their coats and bundled themselves in. She had never heard a single word emerge from that chapel, not even singing. She remembered the Jesus inside, on the pink and blue ceiling. His big clean feet were resting on a cloud.

In the mornings, she watched the workers on their way to Wärnström's and the foundry. It got light early at this time of year, she could see them wending their way down the hill to Berg's, their lunch boxes in hand. In the evenings they would return, and if Otter hadn't come home she would stand in the dark looking at their dirty faces under the streetlight as they passed Wärnström's office. Ebon was among them. So they hadn't sacked him.

Never once did he look up at her window. Still, she was almost sure he knew by now that she lived there. Sometimes, when she thought about him or when she saw his face under the street lamp, she was afraid. It would have been better if they had ended things properly. But all that had happened, about a year ago, was that they saw less and less of one another. When Winther had given her the room behind the linen closets, she had refused to let him come to her there.

'It would cost me my job,' she had said. Then she had purposely put him out of her mind, since thinking about him was both troublesome and disagreeable. He had disappeared. But she had no idea what he thought. And he had always been out there, somewhere. Now she could see him from the window of her room every morning and evening. If she wanted to and if Otter wasn't home.

From the kitchen window she saw nothing but the women hanging out their striped washing. They did their white wash at Dahlgren's laundry, which was now a roofed building by Trash Moat. The kids played by the woodshed and around the privies. They would shout up towards the windows:

'Ma! Toss me down the privy key and a treacle sandwich!'

F.A. Otter blanched with disgust. This kind of thing went on all the time and he couldn't help but hear it. She felt sorry for him because she knew his stomach troubled him and he had to spend a lot of time in the draughty privy every day. She did not believe it made his stomach any better that he was upset and disgusted by what he heard from the connecting privies, or that he could never tell her what bothered him. Once, out of compassion, when he had come up from spending a long time there she had asked him:

'Is it loose or hard?'

He blanched and did not speak a single word to her as he changed his clothes. Then he went out and didn't return until late.

She didn't like the kids who played in the yard, either. It was inconceivable to her that the one who was growing inside her bore any similarity to children like them. She asked Otter to have his mother send a photograph of himself as a child the next time he wrote to her.

'How do you know I write to her?'

She was silent, since she could not tell him that she always read the long, dull letters in the shaving stand drawer. They were full of complaints. She also knew from those letters that his mother apparently knew nothing of her existence, but she supposed there was no hurry. And when it came right down to it, there were things about which she was more immediately bitter.

'What do you want that for? A photograph of me as a child?'

She looked down and suddenly he put his hand over hers.

'Dearest Tora, would you really like that?'

'Yes,' she nodded.

He embraced her, his lips tracing her brow along the hairline, and mumbled softly. She could not hear what he was saying, and she was close to tears. At moments like this, she was afraid it would all too soon be over.

'I'll write Mother and tell her that we are going to have a little one,' he mumbled softly. 'And I'll tell her you'd like a photo. Will that please you?'

She nodded. But deep inside she was suddenly afraid he might think she was conniving. This made her angry, and so she went on to spoil what had just made her so happy. Nothing was simple any more. Nothing. Sometimes she even thought it was nice that he was out singing until late in the evening so she could be alone. But the days were lonely and boring and she gazed down at the yard until her eyes burned, staring without seeing.

Lundholm's Muttie was the only being down there she liked. He was dirty, black and white spotted with longish bow-legs, a curly tail and a pointed muzzle. He was her friend in the yard, despite the fact that he had never gotten a crumb of food from her. She didn't even want to touch his filthy coat. But she would talk softly with him.

'Are you laughing, Mutt?' she asked. She remembered when he had buried her hairpiece, thinking she might just as well give him the ones she kept in the dresser drawer, too. She certainly couldn't wear them here. Otter's housekeeper.

Muttie was in his element now that there were so many dogs in the community, not least the dogs belonging to the gentry, real pedigreed bitches. Agile despite his bow-legs, he ran around sniffing for bitches in heat in every courtyard, mating with them at every opportunity, dragging them down into the ditches if their legs were so long he couldn't reach up. They would come home or be found in the fields near Wärnström's. And they were dirty, panting and ravaged. Muttie was huffing from all his energetic running. His lips were pulled back to expose his yellowed incisors.

'Yes, you are laughing, Mutt,' said Tora, since it almost looked that way.

The photograph arrived in the post from Gothenburg, and she also knew that the envelope had contained a letter and that it was in the shaving stand drawer. 'Now she knows I exist,' Tora thought. But she never read the letter. She had held the dull violet stationary in her hand, thinking: 'What you don't know can't hurt you.' That wasn't, however, strictly true.

She set the photograph on the dresser, but when he went out in the evenings to choir or quartet rehearsals she would take it into the kitchen with her. She would also put it in the window of their room when she sat there sewing after she had finished the washing up. The boy who was F.A. bore no resemblance to the kids in the yard. He was a clean child in a smocked garment with a huge lace collar that had gone a little crooked. He had surely been crying and struggling against being placed on the chair before a big black camera. He had long, fair curls. That was odd, since F.A.'s hair was completely straight. But perhaps that was because it was so short now. His big round eyes were readily recognisable, and the little boy's nose was already aquiline, so she was sure it was he. Otherwise she might have suspected that scatterbrained woman in Gothenburg of having mixed him up with a brother.

She looked at his feet in the little boots with a whole row of little bone buttons down one side. She wondered whether his mother had enclosed these tiny feet in her hands.

He would not be like the kids in the yard, she was entirely certain of that. She believed it was a boy, he kicked so hard. He would not be one of those filthy skinny brats with cold sores round his mouth. He would not get worms in his behind and be constantly itching, and he would not develop rickets. When he was fully five years old he would still have perfect teeth, like tiny shiny grains of rice, and not stained brown stumps.

'And he's never going to say dirty words, either,' she said to F.A. one Sunday morning, looking at the photo. He burst out laughing.

'That's me, you know Tora. And look what became of me.'

She was astonished. She stared at him with wide eyes. 'You, why you're the handsomest, you're ...' She realized she was gaping, and he was getting annoyed.

'What is it?' he asked.

'It's so strange,' she answered.

His mother had also sent a long, embroidered band to hang from the damper of the tiled stove. It might have arrived with the photo, but she didn't get to see it until the next Saturday. She was speechless, and spread it carefully out on the kitchen table after she had wiped the table clean.

'She sent it for our home,' said F.A.

'Is that what she wrote?'

'Yes.'

She was almost happy when he went out to sing (as he said, although she was quite convinced he had gone to meet Ahlqvist and Kasparsson at the hotel). Now she had the whole evening to herself with the linen band.

It was about six inches wide and nearly as long as she was tall. It was lined with thin Japanese silk. His mother had embroidered one long tendril of pink and white flowers with pale green leaves from top to bottom. She thought it was meant to look like honeysuckle. It was beautiful handiwork, and must have taken forever. It was embroidered with satin stitches and tiny little fishbone stitches as well.

She could never have made the whole thing in the short time that had passed since he wrote and told her. Or could she? So many hours of work, and such fine linen, such thin silk.

'What a cow he must think me!'

She went and tied the band to the damper by its silk tassels. But after a while she removed it and took it over to the window to inspect the stitching again.

267

So what had she accomplished? Hemmed a couple of dozen nappies, and made three infant shirts. If only she had had some rags she would have woven a rug. She didn't have many weeks left. Now she was seized by a restless desire to be productive. 'I could have taken in sewing and done shirts from home if I had only learned to sew properly,' she thought. 'I would have. I'll speak with Mamsell. She might have some ideas.'

But when she approached Mamsell Winlöf's huge home with the wooden turret, she lost heart. Although she came close enough to see the housemaid walking the little dog out on the soggy lawn, she did not dare to enter. She was getting so large. She was wrapped in a grey shawl, and the ends were tied across her big belly. No, she did not go in.

T here were handsome tail-coats and low, black patent leather shoes on the platform of the village railway station as early as eleven o'clock in the morning. There was an air of preoccupation, singing and preoccupation and large bouquets of flowers.

Fru Lagerlöf, the widow of the former postmaster, always got flowers and full-pound bags of chocolates from friends who saw her off when she went away. She would hand the bags to the conductor in annoyance before the contents started to melt on the hot velvet seat, and by the time they reached Sparreholm the flowers had wilted. But that was the way things were done, she had to be attended to. Still, the bitter old woman was less important now than she had once been in the community, as her salons were no longer its hub.

She would truly have been astonished if a men's chorus or a quartet had been waiting on the platform to welcome her back from her visits to her grandchildren in Stockholm with *Come away, my sweet love*. The young wives of the up-and-comers who worked for Alexander Lindh, and of the new civil servants in town, however, had to feign astonishment, since this kind of musical tribute was now *comme il faut* in the charming new order that had been introduced in opposition to the gravity and dreadful tristesse of society, as Mandelstam called it. For the last ten years, the Railwaymen's wind band had routinely been there to play when Alexander Lindh returned from his travels, and the merchant listened with the composure of a general. The younger generation of professionals who comprised his welcoming committee, though, smirked behind their hectographed programmes, despite the fact that they had arranged for the entertainment. A barbershop quartet was considerably more chic. A quartet could be ironic and playful, and was always beautiful enough to melt the hardest heart. A quartet possessed everything the tooting of a brass band lacked.

Kasparsson's quartet was the most coveted. They had found a satisfactory replacement for Clarin, and were now engaged to sing at the nameday parties held in honour of the pharmacist and Winther, and on the King's nameday in December. They performed time and again throughout the spring season, hired by one young man after the next to enthral what they all called their lovely young ladies, as in fact one or two were.

Shareholders' meetings had previously been occasions on which the grey tristesse of society made itself most triumphantly known. Young career-climbers with nasty hangovers had created something of a scandal by falling asleep during the vote on the allocation of funding to the clerks' pension fund. When the dividends were being voted they tended to keep their eyes open. Now, however, the new spirit of the times had even penetrated to the annual shareholders' meetings, which were always rounded off with dinner. The quartet would perform over coffee, and was appreciated even by the older generation. There was no telling whether the shareholders themselves were able to interpret the feelings that seized them as the percentage of dividend for the year was settled, but the quartet could do it for them.

There were also feelings that threatened to darken the spirit of community and temporarily bring the erection of the social structure to a halt. But song gives rise to pure emotion, or at least causes murky ones to settle to the bottom, from which point they would not arise until the next time the rights of free men to shape, run, distribute, put a price tag on, and own were threatened by destructive forces. Song muffles bitterness and suffering. It can easily drown our earthly pain, still the storm in the human heart. It can even suspend the battle of life.

In fact sharper and sharper voices were clamouring chaotically for an upheaval, and were threatening to turn the community into a battlefield.

'Still,' said former stationmaster and Baron Gustaf Adolf Cederfalk, 'there will always be the refrain of *hill and dale, and home sweet home.*'

He had a heart attack. It was the most bizarre and terrifying event of his life. With aching arms and gagging with fear, he lay listening for his chambermaid's steps on the stair. She looked stern.

Doctor Hubendick had said that he must lie perfectly still and be nursed. She washed him. He watched helplessly as she pulled up his night-shirt and exposed his wrinkled organ. He did not dare to struggle against her for he believed it would be his death.

People arrived with freshly cut narcissi from their gardens, telling him he would soon be on his feet and that on his birthday on June the sixth there would be a great musical celebration.

'*We wrap ourselves in Sweden's flag, our bridal shroud in death,*' Cederfalk reminded himself, his gooseflesh rising at the scent of narcissi. He wasn't nearly as grateful as he

271

should have been, his mouth was dry as a desert. If it could be done, he thought, and if he lived, he would rather celebrate the annual anniversary of his heart attack. Not until that day did he realize what a human life actually was.

It was odd that he had never before asked himself what he had accomplished, what he had done with his life. He thought about Wärnström and about Alexander Lindh. Surely they would die without anguish. In fact, he was completely unable to associate the thought of angst with Alexander. He would close the last page of the great book of his life with two neat solid lines and blot them dry before giving up the ghost. He was a wealthy man. He had made his own position in society.

Wärnström, he supposed, would go to Jesus. When he arrived his sins, if any, would be accounted for, accepted as both necessary and forgivable for a person of his status. 'He, too, is a wealthy man,' Cederfalk thought. 'He started out as my blacksmith.'

'But what am I?'

When Kasparsson's quartet was engaged to sing as a token of respect for someone or to celebrate a social occasion, they wore full evening dress. F.A. had to hire himself a white tie and tails each time, but one day at the very end of April Tora found a letter in his overcoat pocket from a tailor's in Eskilstuna. She read it, and it was an appointment to come at the end of the week for a fitting for the tail-coat he had ordered. In response to his inquiry in his letter of the twentieth, the price had not yet been finalized, but they were prepared to say that the one hundred and forty kronor that had initially been discussed as a rough estimate would not have to be substantially exceeded if the final fitting proved satisfactory to both parties.

Tora read it again. At last she was sure it was about one hundred and forty kronor. One hundred and forty.

She folded the letter and placed it on the kitchen table. When he got home she was sitting there with her hands in her lap and a far-away look in her eyes. He was in a hurry. Wasn't his dinner ready? Well, in that case he couldn't be bothered. In fact, he wasn't hungry. It didn't matter. He enjoyed the quartet's many engagements so much that spring that he was able to forget his stomach, or almost forget it, anyway.

'Are you going to Eskilstuna?'

He stopped short on his way out of the kitchen. Then he noticed the letter on the kitchen table. He did not even blink once during the entire time he looked her straight in the eye, and slowly he paled with fury. He tried to keep his voice under control, and spoke softly.

'I know you read my post,' he said. 'Is there anything else you want to say?'

'Yes, indeed,' she retorted. 'That you make nine hundred kronor per year.'

'How on earth do you know that?' he blurted out.

'I just know.'

He went into the other room and slammed the door behind him. However, he had to come back out to get the shaving water she had heated for him and to strap his knife, at which time he made the mistake of beginning to argue.

'My dear Tora,' he said. 'You must understand that in the long run hiring evening dress is not less expensive. Moreover, it is extremely unpleasant to wear clothing that

273

has been worn by others. You don't suppose they clean them each time?' But Tora put her hands on her hips like a fishmonger and reminded him that they were expecting a baby at the beginning of June, and that they still did not have most of the things that child would need.

'But I'm going up to see Mamsell Winlöf! I am. I'll ask her for some worn out napkins from the hotel, because those make the best nappies in the world. And they're cheap, too!'

'Tora!'

'What's wrong with that? We're poor. You're soon going to perform at the Society ball — isn't that held for the benefit of a poor family? Ask for the proceeds for us!'

'Do you even know what proceeds means?'

'I know a few things. I've worked at Winther's. I know quite a lot about promissory notes and borrowing, too. And I know what happens!'

'For God's sake keep your voice down!'

He turned his back to her and started sharpening his knife on the strap. A few moments later he said, so softly she had to strain to hear him: 'Just remember, Tora dear, when you use that tone of voice, that something is forever broken between you and me. Moreover, I hardly know what I could do about the matter at this point.'

'You don't have to pick up that tail-coat. It's that simple.'

'No, it's not at all that simple. A tail-coat isn't sewn. It's constructed. It is not just stitched together like any old dress or blazer. It is constructed around one single human being, and cannot be sold to any other at the price commanded. These things are beyond your ken, and I beg you to stop.'

She was still furious and had no intention of stopping just because his voice was cold and superior. It no longer frightened her, she was beyond that. But as he approached her with the shaving bowl and the towel, all she could see in his face was anxiety. Then she realized with surprise at herself that she would have been able to force him, but she did not dare, for the fear she could see in him.

He sang in the spring in his new tail-coat. She only saw him as he was leaving, because she was so heavy now that she did not want to go along to their public performances in the railway park or up by the pavilion at the shooting range. He didn't want her there, either. Tora had been nearly pretty last year in her pale lilac walking suit. At least she had been statuesque, he thought, decorative from a distance. But now it would be impossible to invite his friends home. Embarrassing for everyone, not least for Tora, he believed. Still, he felt sorry for her because she was so isolated in the neighbourhood, and he made no objections when Valfrid Johansson, who worked for Levander, came to see her.

'You know, you should be more careful, though,' he said when he heard that Valfrid had come around when she was home alone.

'Aw,' said Tora. 'If I were trying to please the old biddies around here, I'd have to take up being God-fearing.'

But when Valfrid was there she did something she deeply regretted afterwards, and that surprised her. She complained about Otter. She didn't tell about the tail-coat, but she went on about his being out all the time and sitting around the hotel, and said that it was expensive in the long run despite the fact that he wasn't a drinker. Valfrid, however, completely misunderstood her concern, and tried to placate her by saying that she should pay no mind to his running around.

'Every young man has to sow his wild oats. It's just the flirting instinct.'

'Gosh,' said Tora, who had never even thought in those terms. After which she went cold as ice, her heart seizing up with fear, and told herself she had been a fool. Now she couldn't fall asleep until he was home at night. When she brushed his tail-coat and picked up his underwear in the mornings she was rigid with worry that she would smell the scent of another woman.

She asked Valfrid only to come up when Otter was home. Hare-lipped Valentin would also stop in occasionally, but she now just told him not to come around. So there she sat, all alone with her sewing in her lap untouched, thinking that FA begrudged her even the chance to see people.

Sometimes she would start to weep as she sat idle at the window. There were a few tears, and the occasional small sob. But she could turn it off at will, and felt cold inside and oddly alien to herself.

Now her belly was round as a ball, and she carried it high, her back slightly swayed. She was much bigger than last time. The skin over her belly was taut and ivory, stretched so tightly it shimmered.

One evening at dusk, her grandmother was standing in the kitchen. She had come in so quietly Tora didn't notice her until she came out of the other room to get some wood from the wood basket. There she stood in her grey shawl, with her headscarf so far down her forehead her face looked little and shadowy. Tora thought everything about the old woman looked small in these unaccustomed surroundings. She was carrying a rug rolled up under her arm.

'Well, I suppose you've come to see how I'm living,' said Tora, inviting her to come in and see the other room. But she didn't, just stood on the threshold looking.

'The dresser's Otter's. So's the nightstand.'

They turned back into the kitchen.

'I'll make us some coffee now,' said Tora. 'Not chicory. It's real nice here, don't you think?'

She looked around herself. She had new curtains, and there were two potted balsams in the window.

'Ah, yes,' said Sara Sabina. 'That it is.'

She padded around the kitchen, touching the curtains and feeling the towels that hung alongside the tin tub.

'But it's damned draughty,' she added.

'Right, the wind comes straight through the crack by the larder door.'

'So can't Otter just nail something across the crack?'

'Maybe so,' said Tora. 'I'll get that coffee pot going.'

She saw her grandmother looking at the rag rugs on the kitchen floor, and hastened to explain that they were only temporary.

'These are some old rugs the furniture was wrapped in when Otter got it from Gothenburg.'

'So he's from Gothenburg?'

'Yes.'

The old woman sat down and watched as Tora lit the stove with a little kindling so it would warm up quickly. It was always difficult to set the flue right, so not too much smoke came in.

'Isn't your stove any good?' Sara Sabina asked

'I suppose it's worn out,' Tora confessed. 'So in a way the extra bit of draught in the kitchen is a good thing.'

That made the old woman laugh, and she chuckled just as she always had. They drank their coffee steaming hot, pouring it into their saucers. The second cup went down more slowly, drunk from the cup with a rusk to dip. After that, Sara Sabina brought out the rolled-up rug and gave it to Tora. Tora spread it out. Where had her grandmother got the rags from? It was almost as if Sara Sabina had heard her question, for she said:

'Oh yes, I've been saving up rags for ages now. So there you are.'

It was a rug in dark colours. There were ash and earth, with blue and a shade of brownish purple.

'Well, it's just the simplest kind. I've never been much for patterns.'

True, she had never woven anything that wasn't perfectly plain, and her loom was also of the most primitive kind, where the shaft was tied right to the pedals with heavy knotted twine. Tora thought Lans must have made the loom himself, long ago.

'Do you think it's too dark?'

Tora shook her head.

'It'll wear well and stand the dirt, anyway,' said Sara Sabina.

She never got hold of any white rags. In the stripes of the rug, all you could make out were dark checked and striped frocks and blue work shirts. There was probably a black skirt in there, or Tora's confirmation dress. Even Tora now wore red-striped flannel slips for everyday, but she had a white one for special occasions. Her grandmother's rags didn't even contain one bright-coloured, inexpensive piece of heavy Swedish cotton.

'My, when you start to look at one of these, it brings back memories,' said Tora. 'I remember sitting under the morello cherry tree back home cutting up rags for you to weave. You were making something for the parson's wife over at Vallmsta. What a lot of fine things we cut into rags that time.'

She thought she recognized the striped apron fabric, but it was so long ago. She remembered how when she buried her head below her grandmother's belly it would smell dank from dirty dishwater or sooty from the stove. And how lovely it smelled when she had on a clean apron for baking.

'Isn't that Grandfather's shirt?'

'It may just be.'

'Looking at the rags really brings back memories,' said Tora. 'So does cutting them up.'

'I'd say there are more exciting things to do than to sit rifling through old rags. But the weft is strong. New string. And the rags will wear well, too.'

Tora now spread out the rug on the floor between the kitchen table and the window, and poured them a third cup of coffee. She waddled, her stomach protruding, feeling awkward because her grandmother hadn't asked when the baby was due. And anxious. What if the old woman didn't come for her delivery? Maybe she was thinking that Tora didn't want anybody but the midwife there, now that she was living in town. What if she didn't want to leave the old man on his own?

'It'll be the first week in June,' she said abruptly.

'Yes, I can see that you're almost there. It's dropped.'

'Has it?' Tora said worriedly.

Her grandmother dunked her rusk and held it so long in the last swallow of coffee that it fell apart. Tora sat there staring, but her grandmother just finished her rusk with the spoon, silent.

'Mother, will you be there, please?' she finally asked.

'Oh, yes, I do suppose I will,' said Sara Sabina. 'I surely will.'

But she asked no more questions, and Tora began to suspect that the old woman felt sorry for her. She knew that during this pregnancy she had been touchy and quick to jump to conclusions, and that she might just as easily burst into tears as be angry. Still, it was difficult for her to get the idea out of her head that her grandmother was sitting there feeling sorry for her. Perhaps she didn't believe Otter would do right by her.

'Otter's going to marry me,' she said curtly.

Sara Sabina was silent. Tora interpreted this as disbelief, and went at it even harder. At that, the old woman said it didn't matter. She stood up, having finished her coffee.

'Better to have no ox at all, than one that won't keep to the road,' she said.

Did she mean this to be comforting? The old woman swept the rusk crumbs off the kitchen table into her cupped hand and went over and threw them away in the stove. Her face provided no clues. Maybe she had meant it as a piece of advice, counsel or warning. What did she know about Otter? Tora felt the same cold anxiety she'd had to face for some time now, but she did not want to ask.

'What do you mean by that?' she just asked, the tears rising in her eye so she had to blink and blink to hold them back.

'All I said was that it's better to have no ox at all, than one that won't keep to the road.'

'I heard you!'

How could she sit there and say something like that, when she knew how impossible it would be?

'You've got to have someone to pull the load,' said Tora. 'You can't do it alone.'

'Well, I don't think that's all it's about for you,' said Sara Sabina, looking Tora straight in the eye. Tora lowered her eyes then, staring at her hands on her lap, but she bent her head and the old woman, who was carefully examining her face, also nodded slowly once.

'I'll be off now. Lans will be waiting.'

'Is he all alone?'

'I put him to bed, and he's got the chamber pot and the watch. But I'd best be getting home.'

'I'll send one of the fellows when my time comes.'

'You do that. But don't wait until your waters break.'

'Thank you for the rug,' said Tora, taking her hand.

When the old woman had gone she was sad, and burst into the kind of tears she had almost learned to turn on at will during this long, dull pregnancy. She sat at the window sobbing. But after a while she felt embarrassed, and blew her nose loudly.

The rug looked really dark until she lit the lamp, and in its dusky light the colours gained depth in the kitchen. There were five different stripes repeated six times along it. It must have taken a lot of planning to be sure that there would be enough of each colour to repeat the whole pattern over and over. The first strip was grey as stove ash, the next brown. It reminded her of the acidic boggy soil from which Johannes Lans had found it so difficult to extract anything edible. The black stripe was tinged with different shades, like church dresses outside in the sun. Next was the dark blue one from the work shirts and big aprons. The final one ran to purplish brown and Tora didn't recall what it had been, but it reminded her of the birches on the slope below Appleton in late winter. She noticed that the weft really was new, and knew that Sara Sabina would also have cut away every worn or torn spot from the clothing. These rags were strong.

In the hallway downstairs, F.A. met an old woman as he came in. She was grey as the earth. When they came face to face, she did not turn aside, but stopped right in front of him. She was wearing a kerchief and it was difficult to see her expression.

'Are you Otter?'

She inspected him openly. He was not wearing his uniform cap but a black bowler hat, and was carrying his coat over his arm. She looked him straight in the eye, and he could not get to the stairs although he tried to squeeze past.

'Yes,' she said at last, nodding firmly and not unkindly. 'Tora is a good, solid worker.'

He was too astonished to respond, and when she received no confirmation she added:

'You'll be finding that out.'

It sounded sharp, and she left him through the hall door, moving quickly off along the side of the building.

When he got upstairs Tora was standing in the middle of the kitchen floor in her big, striped apron. She had not yet lit the table lamp.

'You know what?' he said, and then he noticed that she had her foot on a little rug and was pushing it towards him.

'Mama's been,' she said. 'With a rug.'

He didn't usually like it when she spoke like a country girl, but now he just laughed, and walked over and put his arms around her, trying to lift her a couple of inches off the floor.

'Are you a good, solid worker, Tora?' he asked.

'I most certainly hope so,' she said, very sharply.

'Well, I wouldn't call you modest!' F.A. laughed. 'I really wouldn't call you modest!'

When he had looked at the rug Sara Sabina brought, she thought for a little while and then said: 'She's not really my mama. She's my grandma.'

She had the urge to get the photograph of Edla and show it to him. She even went into the main room fumbling in the gloom until she found the picture in the second dresser drawer, and unfolded the tissue paper. She couldn't see anything, the lamp wasn't lit in here, either. But she was so familiar with the face that was being eradicated from the piece of cardboard and with the solemn expression that was always there that she thought she was looking at the picture just by holding it.

She regretted her impulse, and refolded the tissue paper around the child who had been Edla, replacing the photograph where it belonged, under her two white blouses.

One evening when he was going out, he stood whistling a Widerström waltz as he tied his tie and straightened his collar. She knew it so well she could have joined him in whistling. He was happy. She couldn't imagine he was feeling anything but better than he had in a long time. The last she heard of him was the clicking of his heels on the stairs, and the waltz from 'The Sailor's Lyre'.

He returned around ten and Kasparsson was with him. He was so ill that he couldn't make it up the stairs himself and was too ill even to show embarrassment in front of his friend. Tora asked Kasparsson to fetch Doctor Hubendick on his way home. She began to undress F.A., but he was suddenly sick, and vomited down the front of his shirt. Afterwards, he was quite rigid with disgust and fear, and it was almost impossible for her to get his shirt off him without ripping it. Doctor Hubendick asked whether he'd been drinking heavily.

'He doesn't!' Tora answered.

The doctor asked to see his vomit, and F.A. turned his head away. Tora showed the old doctor the shirt out in the kitchen, with the thick, black vomit. He shook his head, but said nothing to calm her. Now her heart, too, began to beat faster; it was pounding so loud and hard she could feel it. She sat with him all night, and Doctor Hubendick's medication soon put him to sleep, but his pulse fluttered unsteadily and his breathing was noisy and uneven. In the morning he was somewhat better, but she didn't dare to leave him, so she sent someone round to the pharmacy and the shop.

Doctor Hubendick said that he would have to spend at least two weeks in bed. After the first few days he improved quickly and began to find his helplessness embarrassing. He would no longer allow her to wash him or to bring him the chamber pot. She had to start emptying it while he was asleep and pretending she hadn't.

'Poor Tora,' he said. 'You'll need somebody to carry water up for you now that you're so big. Be a little kind to yourself.'

But even his concern about her sounded distant and odd. He had changed so fast that she couldn't imagine how it had happened. She had always known he was delicate. But she had mainly sensed it, some ultimate fragility, a constantly accentuated state of irritation. She could not imagine him any different, not even long ago when he must have been perfectly healthy. She didn't really believe there had been such a time.

Now, however, he was extremely frightened. She could hear it in his voice, and even in his way of joking when he began to improve again. She had been aware of his fear, too, it was also an integral part of his being. But now it was contagious. Only once did he express it, his voice sounding almost nonchalant.

'I believe there's something growing in my stomach.'

'Nonsense!'

She brought it up with Doctor Hubendick the next time he came, closing the door to the room carefully and asking in a soft voice while he was washing his hands in the bowl of warm water she had readied on the kitchen table.

'Otter has an ulcer,' said Hubendick.

'But he thinks it's something else. He's afraid.'

'Just as well, in my opinion. Then he'll go on taking care of himself. And if he does, he has nothing to fear.'

She didn't dare to ask any more questions. The word both she and F.A. were thinking she would never have dared to pronounce, anyway.

'He's only twenty-seven!'

'Right,' said the doctor. 'Some people develop ulcers early. It's a matter of his constitution. He'll have to watch himself.'

He was back on his feet again by the end of May and returned to work. As soon as he had left, the same hopeless world surrounded her again. People streamed into and out of the chapel. The workers came up from the foundry and from Wärnström's. To her they seemed to be dragging their feet, and she recalled the excitement of the station, heels clicking rapidly on the floor of the main dining room. She couldn't go in there now, and the world over there became more and more unreal to her. She could hardly believe any longer that she had seen Cléo de Merode, had risen from her seat at the cash desk to greet her as she passed so close by that her huge plumes nearly brushed Tora's cheek. The King of Portugal, Holger Drachmann, and the Countess Casa di Miranda! She could no longer believe they existed.

When F.A. returned home in the evenings, Tora was often sitting staring out the window. She had prepared his dinner in such good time that it had gone cold and had to be reheated. It was twilight and he didn't like the fact that he always had to light the lamp himself.

'What's wrong?' he asked.

'Nothing.'

287

Wasn't she satisfied? Goodness, was she still upset about the tail-coat?

'Tora!'

'I'm just sitting here mulling.'

He wasn't sure exactly what she meant. He lit the lamp himself, dirtying his fingers on the wick, and smelling them after he had washed his hands.

'Well, the fun's over now,' said Tora.

'Ah. So what was so much fun, then? Running around with trays at Winther's?'

'I didn't run around with trays. I was the cashier.'

'All right.'

She was silent for a few minutes, still staring out at the courtyard in the dusk. But now she was smiling to herself.

'Do you know what I thought Fun was when I was little?'

'No ...'

Good grief. She couldn't tell him about the man who beat his old woman. He wouldn't think that was funny. And it wasn't. Every now and then she would recall the three figures her childish thoughts had conjured up, and her heart would ache. There was the old man who wanted to dance and whose stick ruled his missus. There was the bowed would-be gentleman, smiling knowingly. He was Shame, an old acquaintance of Tora's. And Want, well Want was just a baby.

'Adam!'

She had never said it before. Suddenly it was just poised in her throat, and she didn't mind him staring at her, either.

'Adam, what are we going to do?'

'What do you mean?'

'If you get worse?'

But he was silent and she realized, of course, that she had hurt him.

'I really only meant until you get well,' she added. 'I don't know what comes over me sometimes. It happens to women in the family way. And all this sitting around with idle hands. Not to mention this place!'

'I don't like it here, either,' he said. 'But it's only for the interim. I can't live here.'

'But where *will* we live?'

Had she dared to say 'we'? He shouted:

'I cannot live without the sea!'

But the truth was: he could not live. She rose and started getting the stove and pots and pans ready to heat his cold dinner.

'You sit down,' she said. 'This kind of talk will do us no good.'

To their misfortune, he fell ill again just when the baby was born. The midwife arrived and put on a huge white coat that buttoned down the back. She gave authoritative orders to Sara Sabina who did her bidding but without looking particularly accommodating. Nor was it much easier than the first time for Tora, despite the presence of the midwife. She was both trained and experienced but required a great deal of assistance and a lot of coffee, and she spread her instruments all over the room and never tidied after herself. On the other side of the closed door to the main room, F.A. lay in his bed and could hear every sound. Tora tried to take him into consideration, but it was a difficult, long delivery. She didn't scream until the very end, but she heard herself

289

moan long and loud time after time as she was bearing down, to ease the pressure and the pain. She would look at the door, and even at the very end she was aware of it and afraid it was going to open and that F.A. would come right into the terrible mess around her of half-empty water glasses and dirty sheets and half-full coffee cups.

She was quite conscious throughout, even after the last excruciating contraction and during the moment of relief and emptiness. The midwife had put a big towel across her knees, but she had let it fall down, and Tora could see the woman with the white coat lift up the child, oily, wet and bloody.

'It's a boy. A big one!'

'Give him to me!'

But the midwife laughed and carried him over to the kitchen table, where the water was.

'Give him to me,' said Tora. Sara Sabina stood beside her the whole time as she washed the child and tied the umbilical cord and before she could begin the whole business of dressing him, plastering his navel, putting on his nappy and shirt and wrapping him in a blanket, the old woman took his bare body in her hands, which looked very thin and dark alongside the midwife's. She lifted the naked boy over to Tora in the bed, despite the protests of the midwife.

'He's big,' said Tora indistinctly, through her very dry, cracked lips. 'He's got a big head, I felt that.'

He lay in her arms and his mouth was moving although he wasn't crying. She felt the crown of his head carefully with one hand, it was still damp. He had no hair, and there was a pounding under the thin skin that covered his fontanel. There was still a little white oil in his ears and in the folds on his neck. She wondered what it was. It had covered his whole body. She touched his little hands, trying to open them and feel his palms. His toes were all curled up, too. It looked as if they were sound asleep, while the rest of his body was moving and searching. His thighs were thin and red, and between them rested his testicles and his penis, which looked almost unnaturally large. He twitched and drew up his legs.

'There's nothing wrong with 'im,' said Tora.

She thought his stomach looked big, and she could feel his ribs under his skin. They were fragile, as if they were still more cartilage than bone. She hurt now, and it was very difficult for her to move down far enough in the bed so that she could lower her face to his. His eyebrows were puffy and spotted, but he could open his eyes, and she saw that they were very dark and a strange murky violet colour she had never seen before, not on anyone.

'He'd better not get a chill,' she said, and her grandmother took him and gave him to the midwife, who began to dress him.

'I s'pose you're tuckered out now,' said Sara Sabina.

The boy began to cry loudly and the midwife assured them he sounded like a two-week old infant already.

'He's a strong one, there's no mistaking it.'

They gave Tora a little coffee and she drank it as hot as she could and then she no longer cared what they did with her. She was having some afterpains, and although they were much easier she felt absolutely exhausted and sick of everything that pulled at her and hurt her, and just wanted to be left in peace to sleep. They laid clean cloths under her bottom, and she wondered why they bothered since the placenta would be coming soon. But what did she care, let them do it their way. All she wanted was sleep.

Through the window she saw the evening June sky, and for one moment she wished she could walk over and lean out to see more of it. All that was stopping her was exhaustion, and the fact that the other two women would raise their voices in fussy concern. It felt good to wish for something, when there was very little preventing you from getting it.

They put the baby beside her and now he was a big bundle with a little face that was quite bright red from the unfamiliar exertion. She had to turn down his collar with its crocheted edge to be able to see his mouth. She wiped away a little spittle with her index finger.

Something seemed to be happening inside him. He was struggling hard, but she had no idea what brought it on. His face wore an expression at once self-absorbed and worried. He snorted as he breathed, and occasionally he hiccoughed. She laid a hand under his back so the little dark red face with its puffy eyebrows was raised a little, and his saliva ran clear and thin along his chin. His difficult, inexplicable struggle continued. But she could hear that he was breathing steadily and if she inserted her fingers beneath the cotton blanket and his thin pyjama top she could feel his heart beating.

The bones of the man who was found dead with a communion wafer in his mouth long ago on the rubbish slope below Old Man's Alley rested in the churchyard at Backe. Who he was and where he had come from was never explained, but the Backe parish organist was fascinated by his fate and asked Pastor Borgström if it would be all right for him to make a simple wooden cross to mark the grave. The pastor acquiesced. But he never asked what the organist intended to engrave on the cross and fill in with black paint. So it read:

A RAILWAY PASSENGER
D. 1877

For another twenty years, too, Backe churchyard had to receive people who were not born in the parish, and some who had not even lived there but had come travelling by rail. Later, the dead no longer had to rattle along the rutted road to Backe to be buried. A cemetery was established in the town, and it was lucky Old Mothstead was gone when that happened, as the owner of the estate allowed the very best farming land on the whole leasehold to be set aside for this purpose. It was an area above the boggy fields that were usually flooded when Lake Vallmaren filled to the brim and then overflowed each spring. Some of the people from Vallmsta also bought burial plots in town, to feel safer, since Vallmsta church yard was rumoured to be full of underground streams and currents that carried the dead away or disintegrated them.

The minister sent to inaugurate the cemetery might have known Old Mothstead had harvested his best wheat there when he said:

'And now this site shall be a field of the Lord.'

Probably no one thought this land would bear a crop again until the Day of Judgement, but they were mistaken. One still, cold Saturday afternoon in September 1902, some relatives of former stationmaster and Baron Gustaf Adolf Cederfalk were tidying up around his grave when they made a discovery. His niece Gerda was going to plant some narcissus bulbs when her spade suddenly pierced something soft, frightening her. She started to cover the hole as fast as she could, but her husband bent down and looked, and quickly took the pointed spade and started exploring.

Truffles were growing on Cederfalk's grave. Soon they had dug up a fungus the size of an infant's head. They held it in their hands and it was tender and had that wonderful aroma only truffle has. Where the spade had run through it the flesh was exposed, firm and lovely. This was both embarrassing and exciting. Although it was as exquisite as the very best truffle from Périgord, piety compelled them to refrain from sampling what smelled so indescribably good — they could hardly eat something that had grown where their old uncle, the former stationmaster, was slowly decomposing. They even agreed to say nothing of their find, but that was easier said than done, and the cat was soon out of the bag. There were people so lacking in respect that they asked Gerda what she'd done with it.

The story gradually reached postmistress Lagerlöf's ears and she, who had been so renowned for her gift of irony, was expected to comment. But now she was old and crocodile-skinned and so blunt that most of the time all she could get out was the truth.

'When I think of all the good dinners our dear Gustaf Adolf ate during his lifetime, I'm not at all surprised that there are truffles growing out of his corpse.' This was her summary, delivered as always with little puffs of breath through her nose.

The minister had said, with a pointed reference to the class struggle in which the community was engaged, that this spot, that is the cemetery, was where all battles ceased. Even the man who had little or nothing of his own in this world won a place here of which no one could deprive him.

One bright red October day in 1902, the Workers' Association hearse was also inaugurated. It had taken four years to collect the funds to buy it, and the inauguration had been postponed several times. First both the carpentry work and the upholstery were delayed, then a meeting voted that the association should acquire a new banner for the occasion. John Lundell, foundryman and standard bearer, better known as Big John, travelled to Norrköping on behalf of the Association to order the new banner at a special studio. He fulfilled his commission in every detail.

'We want a red one,' he said. 'But not too red, and made of silk.'

This was in early spring. A strike threatened, new factions developed, and a local branch of the Swedish Social Democratic Party was founded. Big John resigned from the Workers' Association and bore the standard of the Social Democrats, instead, when Branting held a speech at Starvation Meadows. It was autumn again before the Workers' Association, which had been shaken to its very foundation, was able once again to begin preparations for inauguration of the hearse. Now, however, new and previously unanticipated difficulties appeared on the horizon. They needed an appropriate inaugural corpse.

True, the whole idea was for this elegant black carriage to bring the insignificant to their final resting place — the burned-out, the unsung, the ignorant and powerless. Still, there was some hesitation when the first person to die after the hearse was ready was a painter's apprentice who went and did himself in. The newspaper reported on this occurrence, as usual, in some detail, so there was no way of keeping it secret. They decided to wait, but did so with rising unease, since suicide was second only to emigrating to America as a way out. And they had bad luck the next time, too, when a half-grown youth known as Deaf Lund died in a fire. It was said that he had been unable to hear the firemen's alarms, which led to three weeks of exchanges in the newspaper as to whether there had actually been any alarm, and whether the fire brigade had been well prepared and had done their utmost.

The fire chief stated that he had had the confidence of the people until a couple of individuals had moved to the village and begun to sow the seeds of unrest and slander, mocking all that was eternal and wanting to see it torn down without themselves being able to offer anything better to replace it with. His main opponent, a fireman in the brigade, had the final word, however, because he was also editor of the paper and took his manuscripts personally to Eskilstuna twice a week to have them set and printed.

At any rate this death, too, was controversial. Instead, Hjalmar Eriksson, who had spent the last ten years of his life grinding ash at Wärnström's Workshops for 30 öre an hour, inaugurated the hearse. Admittedly he was both too light and too young (at 41 kilos and 35 years of age) but they couldn't start weighing corpses and their dignity, so it was he.

And thus his light body rocked down the road wrapped in a black funeral pall with a silver fringe. The journey began on the north side at the building behind the pharmacy where he had lived with his old mother. They drove past Alexander Lindh Sales Co., Inc., where the merchant himself and all his office staff were waiting outside on the pavement, and Lindh had his black top hat in his hand. At the Railway Hotel and the post office, too, the procession was acknowledged as all the staff went outside and stood in the street to watch. At the railway crossing young lads sat on the booms, and at the bottom of the hill, Mamsell Winlöf's little bitch barked hysterically as the large procession rolled by.

They crossed Adolf Street and Caroline Street, the last of the streets named after the merchant's family, and moved along to the south side, where things were named after the Wärnströms, passing his red brick residence on the hillside. Wärnström's eldest son could be seen reining in his horse on the lawn among the arbour vitae bushes, and sitting stiffly at attention as the procession passed.

The final part of the journey was on the rough, rutted road to Vanstorp, which led to the cemetery, where Big John's successor entered first, carrying the salmon-coloured banner which was puffed out like a canvas sail in the wind.

Thus ash-grinder Eriksson arrived at his final destination, where his light, dry body, which had inaugurated the hearse, would never turn into topsoil conducive to rare mushrooms.

It was a Sunday afternoon in June 1903 and it was Tora's wedding day. She stood in the kitchen pressing her black dress and wishing Fredrik wouldn't insist on crawling around the floor messing up her rugs as she walked back and forth exchanging the cool iron for the hot one on the stove. There was an odour of steaming wool and damp pressing rags.

She hadn't worn this dress since just after Fredrik's birth a year ago, when her old grandfather had died. The first thing Tora did after eating Sara Sabina's confinement gruel and getting out of bed was to attend his funeral. That bothered her.

She had not needed to worry about buying something to wear, since she still had her black waitress dress from her days at Mamsell Winlöf's. She hadn't had time to alter it then, but now she had bought a piece of black duchess silk from Elfvenberg's Textiles and Fabrics, and made big new puffs at the shoulders, putting the bottoms of the old woollen sleeves back on below. She had also made two black silk insets at the waist, and let out the side seams.

For many months after Fredrik's birth, she had not bothered to mention marriage because, just as she had expected, everything improved once the baby was born. Otter did not leave her. For a while she had been extremely worried because she knew people in the neighbourhood were gossiping about her first child and she thought it would reach his ears.

She also knew that one of the things that made life easier was the fact that she no longer wept, either out of hate or self-pity, she just let people talk. She had realized that pride was a gem that could be polished in many different ways, and she often thought of Sara Sabina's words about it being better to have no ox at all. In April, however, she discovered that she was pregnant again.

She had nursed the baby for a long time, and therefore thought she was completely protected. When she finally had to tell F.A. about her condition she was so frightened that she first spent hours thinking out different ways of putting it and then just burst out bluntly with the news over dinner. He did as she instinctively had anticipated, dropped his spoon into his bowl and went into the room and lay down with his back towards the kitchen door.

Tora walked around in the kitchen, washing up and putting things away, feeling hateful. This only lasted until she entered the room and walked around to the other side of the bed, where she could see his face. He must have been crying.

'What am I to do?' he asked.

He had been on sick leave almost the entire spring. She thought he must be paying the rent with money borrowed from his friends. The idea that he might be writing IOUs terrified her. Her contribution had been to take in paying guests for dinner in spite of the inconvenience to F.A., who was spending so much time at home.

Four foundrymen shared a room at Lundholm's. They had previously eaten out of tin lunch pails they got from the widow of a carpenter in the next building, who didn't have room for them in her kitchen. Tora knew the woman kept a filthy house, and she also felt sorry for the foundrymen when she watched them eat out of their pails after warming them in the tiled stove. They were all good friends of Valentin's. All four of them were obsessive savers, however, as they intended to buy tickets to America and emigrate together.

When they started having dinner at Tora's, F.A. refused to eat at the same table with them. She served him in the main room, but pointed out that the foundrymen were paying for his dinner. She had become sarcastic, and often found herself regretting things she said impulsively. Afterwards, she actually understood him, because the foundrymen had disgusting table manners. They ate with their jack-knives, almost never touching the cutlery she set out. They often stayed on at the table and lit their pipes after eating, which made her nervous at first. But she enjoyed talking with them and when they had left, she aired out the kitchen and put the chairs back in place, removing with some regret the cover she'd put over the kitchen settee, as the evenings were long and silent that winter.

At the end of April, F.A. was somewhat better and she persuaded him to take a walk on the north side. They met railway clerk Finck, and F.A. had to stop, because Finck started asking about his health. He introduced Tora as his fiancée. She had never said more than 'good morning' to Finck, and now she was absolutely dumbstruck and stood there looking down, knowing her cheeks were so hot they must be bright red. This made her angry with herself, but the pride she'd lived on all winter seemed to have vanished without a trace.

Finck asked about F.A.'s mother's health, and inquired about some relatives she had never heard of. Not until afterwards did she realize that no one had mentioned

Fredrik, but that was quite natural. What could he have said? 'So by the way, how is your fiancée's baby, Otter?'

He asked if they would like to have a drink in the Winther garden, and they went in together, although none of them really felt like braving it. Finck talked non-stop. They attracted some attention, and rumours circulated afterwards along long, winding paths until they reached back to Tora via master painter Lundholm's wife, whose name was Emma. At first she didn't want to give anything away, waiting to be begged. Although Tora never stooped so low, Emma finally admitted, as if under duress, that Finck had said Otter had gone and gotten engaged to a very simple girl, who obviously didn't even know how to drink a glass of wine.

'Drink a glass of wine?' Tora asked dumbly.

'Yes, properly, you know.'

It had never occurred to Tora that there was more than one way of drinking a glass of wine. She doubted Fru Lundholm's words. Finck was a very kind man. But they had clearly had other eyes on them as well.

The bans had been read. Perhaps F.A. felt compelled; she didn't know and didn't want to know. He had spoken lightly of it. Made it sound like an unfortunate mishap, as if he were convinced that if they put their heads together they could surely come up with a better solution before the three weeks were up. He spoke almost comfortingly to her as they walked home from the registry, and that was the last it was mentioned.

Now it was Sunday afternoon, and she wondered if he had forgotten that they were supposed to be back at the registry at five o'clock. She didn't really think so. But perhaps he did not intend to say anything about it until she

301

reminded him. She was determined to say nothing. When she had pressed her dress she sat on the kitchen settee stitching a little white lace collar into the neckline. In a box in the second dresser drawer she had a piece of tulle she still hadn't decided whether or not to use. She had also bought a rather long white silk ribbon.

Fredrik was playing with empty spools on the floor. He was not like the boy in the photograph. When he looked at you he appeared to be keeping his eyes open without blinking. But Tora knew this was an optical illusion. She often walked over to the shaving stand mirror and looked at herself, and she would encounter the same unabashed wide-eyed look. Her own eyes had become darker, almost grey, during this third pregnancy. She reminded herself of old bitches who had had a lot of litters, with their light-yellow eyes, and this horrified her.

She was going to give the boy something to eat and then take him down to Emma Lundholm.

'Would you like a little gruel when Fredrik has his?' she asked into the room.

He said yes, but added nothing about dinner being late. She felt a dim bitterness. Well, there was one thing she could be sure of, and that was his punctuality and his thoroughness in dressing. Sooner or later he would ask her if she had brushed his tail-coat and if his collar and cuffs were starched. She could wait.

When she had washed up the gruel bowls, she took Fredrik down to Emma Lundholm's although there were more than three hours left. She sat down on the kitchen settee and began to edge the seams of the black dress in tiny little stitches to pass the time. In the larder she had some food ready. There were jellied veal and some small minced beef patties. On Saturday evening she had marinated some herring. She had bought a full bottle of sherry at Levander's, a brand they said was quite nice. If nothing else, he must have seen the bottle, as it was on the dresser alongside his shaving mirror and a tightly tied bouquet of little daisies.

She felt as if they were playing cat and mouse on either side of the wall. This upset her but she could not make herself say anything. She heard him turning the pages of his magazines, and sometimes snorting, as if laughing to himself. He was reading the Locomotive Engineer and Machinists' Journal, which he had borrowed whole volumes of the last time he was sick.

'Tora,' he shouted. His voice was cheerful and bright and his off-handed tone shot through her. 'What are you doing out there?'

'I'm sewing.'

'Why don't you come in here?'

She hesitated, but took the dress into the room with her and sat down on the bed. She lined up her thread, scissors and thimble on the top of the nightstand, trying not to look up. She threaded the needle again, holding the eye up against his pillowcase, to see it better. They didn't use a bedspread. He often needed to lie down in the middle of the day, and it had long ago been folded and stored in the bottom dresser drawer.

'Listen to this,' he said, and she realized he meant to read something out loud to her again.

'However old an engineer may be, however well he has familiarized himself with the practical and theoretical sides of his discipline...'

He was sitting in the rocking chair by the window, and every time he looked up from his magazine to check whether she was following he rocked, suddenly and violently.

'... it is still impossible for him to see a fast train without a sense of respect and admiration. In one single moment, from a dark silent point afar, you see a phenomenon moving at the speed of a cyclone and screaming like a banshee, making the earth shake under your feet and the trees along the tracks bend as if to a sudden storm.'

Tora nodded to show that she was still listening.

'After which there is an instant of pure noise and din, and then within just a few seconds it is once again nothing but a dark spot in the distance!'

He shut the magazine and patted it on his lap.

'Tora!'

'Yes?'

'How long will it be until Fredrik is big enough to understand that?'

'Never,' said Tora.

'What?'

'He'll never understand that.'

As usual, at first he thought she was serious, because her face was. Then he burst out laughing.

'And did his mother understand what I was reading, then?'

'Yes, pretty well,' she said, warming up inside and regretting her bitterness and the morning spent dully on her guard.

'I've brushed your tail-coat and aired it out for you,' she said.

'I'd better have a look at my shirt and collar, then.'

He rose and crossed the floor with steps that seemed light and bouncy from the good cheer he still felt inside. When he was ill, Tora was always dry-eyed and practical. However, it was becoming more and more difficult for her to see him so lively and quick as he was at intervals. He moved as if he had never known illness.

She laid his tail-coat on the bed, and he went and got the stiff shirt and a loose collar from the drawer himself. He was not the kind who looked for his collar and cufflinks at the last moment. He kept everything he needed in a little cut glass bowl on the dresser. She started to ask him if he thought she should try to arrange the piece of tulle like a little veil. Then she felt embarrassed and changed her mind.

'My shoes,' he said.

She thought she had remembered everything, down to the very last detail, until now. She recalled she had lent his shoes to Valentin, and thought they were wrapped up in the hall closet somewhere. The whole of the past winter and spring came back to her. Her despair when F.A. was sick in bed again. She had felt hostile, at first towards him and then towards the signals coming from her own body. She just *couldn't* be pregnant again. But she was. At the same time she began to be increasingly convinced that he was never again going to be on his feet.

Valentin had come to visit. His mother had recently died. He said bitterly that not many people would turn out for Embankment Brita's funeral, and that he couldn't even go himself because he didn't own a decent pair of shoes. She thought he could wear his everyday shoes until he stretched out his legs and showed her his feet. Then she had to agree.

So she lent him F.A.'s black dress shoes. It was unthinkable that he would ever sing in the quartet again.

305

Neither of them had missed the shoes although it took Valentin over a month to return them. F.A. never knew they were gone.

'I'll polish them for you,' said Tora, moving towards the hall closet. Valentin had wrapped them in two newspapers and tied them with the string from a rock sugar package. When she had unwrapped them she thought Valentin must have been trying to trick her, but he wasn't like that. The shoes were completely ruined. He must have worn then every day for a month's time. His pointed heels and chilblains had stretched them out and deformed them. There was no point in polishing them. They were completely stained and worn. He had ruined them.

'F.A. will never get married in these shoes,' she thought, feeling the nausea overcome her in the narrow closet, where she had closed the door behind her the moment she opened the package.

'He won't. He's too fussy.'

She thought about Valentin, hare-lipped and well-meaning, sloppy and unwitting. But it was useless.

'There's a spot on my tailcoat,' he said, when she came back in. 'Could you remove it?'

'I didn't see it.'

He showed her the sleeve. When she scraped it with the nail of her index finger it turned white.

'Arrack,' she said.

She took it away with hot water.

'If you want shaving water, it's ready.'

She glanced at the alarm clock on the shelf over the stove. Just past three. She quickly removed her shift and pulled on the black dress. She had intended to heat a kettle of water and have a serious wash first, but she would have to skip that. There wouldn't be time.

'I've got an errand to run,' she said in the direction of the room and left, her grey shawl over her arm. She shut the kitchen door before she could hear his answer.

It was natural for her to go across the tracks to the north side when she needed help. She went to Levander's and knocked, asking whether Valfrid was in. He was still a bachelor and had a two-room flat on the second floor of the house. Levander's maid said he was out, and Tora's mouth went dry.

'That's all right,' she said. 'I've just come for a pair of shoes.'

He would understand. It didn't matter if things were a little muddled for now. There was no time to lose.

'Which shoes?' asked the maid.

'I'll show you,' said Tora, walking up the stairs with the maid. She had been there before and knew he kept his key under the mat in front of the door. But she didn't want the maid to know she knew, because people will talk. So they stood there, eyeing one another pointedly.

'Oh, it's locked of course.'

'Maybe he's left the key above the door,' said Tora. But the girl knew where it was, she could see it in her eyes.

'How about under the mat?' said Tora, at least getting the maid to do the bending and lifting. Tora unlocked the door herself. The girl crossed her arms and stood staring at her while she ripped through Valfrid's closet. When she had pulled the shoes out she could immediately see that they wouldn't do. How could Valfrid have such absurdly big feet? Why had she never realized? Well, he was tall, perhaps you didn't notice.

307

'These are the wrong shoes,' she said vaguely.

'I don't think he has any but those and the ones he has on,' the maid said.

Tora rushed out trying to think of anybody else who would have a pair of black dress shoes. F.A.'s own friends, the other members of the quartet? No, she just couldn't do that. Halfway back to the tracks, she turned once again and ran in the direction of Lindh's house and tavern hill. Her shoemaker lived up there.

They let her in to the kitchen where they were at dinner. She wondered why they ate so early, and whether his wife was sick as she just sat there and let him get his own food from the stove. There was a sour smell. He wouldn't let her into the workshop. His wife made him wary.

'What's she wanting shoes for?'

'She wants to borrow a pair 'cause they're getting married, she says.'

She had to tell them about Valentin. Still, they went on looking at her suspiciously, blinking furiously.

'Well, I just can't do that, you know. They're not my shoes. I couldn't take the responsibility.'

'He wouldn't even have to walk in them,' said Tora. 'Just wear them for the ceremony.' But they were both silent. They'd made up their minds.

As she ran on she realized that there would be talk about this. It would become a story. Have you heard the one about Tora Lans on her wedding day running all over town trying to borrow a pair of shoes for the groom? But she didn't care, at least not at that moment as she rushed through the short village streets looking for a door to knock on. It was a hot Sunday afternoon. The yards smelled of rubbish and lilacs. A few people had moved out their kitchen chairs and

308

sat on their front steps, looking. Tora started to sweat in her black dress. She had asked at a couple more places whether anyone had a nice looking pair of men's shoes to lend her. But it wasn't easy. They were so big. F.A. had such small, beautiful feet. It was difficult to explain this to one helpful person who offered her a pair of Sunday boots in wrapping paper. And the ones that weren't too big were worn out or worn down or had crooked heels or big holes in the soles that would be clearly visible when he knelt for the ceremony. It was even more difficult to explain how fussy he was.

Time was flying, she knew it but didn't dare ask anyone for the time. She thought hatefully of the shoemaker, and that he was probably religious. And the time, the time. She would soon have to get home with a pair of shoes if they were going to make it at all.

It was so cruel it could hardly be happening. She was doomed to run up and down the streets of the silent Sunday town looking for shoes that were good enough for him. She thought of the auctioneer and hurried there. He didn't understand what she wanted, but let her into the storeroom.

'Shoes,' she said. 'For a man. Black dress shoes.'

He had piles of them. She tore through the belongings of dead men, but now the whole task had taken on impossible proportions, despite the fact that she had tons of shoes to choose from. Impossible shoes, unthinkable shoes, with toes long as elephants' trunks, wide hopeless shoes.

'I can't do it,' she said.

He simply stared at her, and was still standing in his storeroom door when she left. When she got to the tracks she had to wait for a train coming from Stockholm to pass. 'If that's the 4:58 it's already too late,' she thought, but she didn't turn around to look at the station clock. She had given up and walked more calmly across the square on her way back. He would probably not have found his shoes himself, as she had stuffed them into the wood box. But she would show them to him. It was just as well to get it over with.

He would probably be furious and have a thing or two to say to her. She knew one of his lines, at least it was easy to imagine:

'Have you been wearing them yourself?'

But no matter how angry he was and no matter what he came up with to hurt and humiliate her, none of this would be able to keep the truth from him in the long run. And the truth was too cruel. She had not believed he would ever be on his feet again when she lent out his shoes.

She walked slowly up the stairs and heard Fredrik gurgling and giggling at the Lundholms' through the thin walls. She would go down and pick him up, but not until she got it over with F.A. He was probably sitting reading his magazines and waiting, fully dressed in his white tie and tails and starched shirt but with nothing on his feet but black stockings.

The clock was ticking loudly on the shelf as she entered. She forced herself not to look at it. The afternoon sun was shining into the room. Rays fell across the bed in a wide band that always bothered him when he was sick, so she had to pull down the shade. The blinding sun across the bed prevented her from seeing him at first.

He was lying on his side and his shirt front was creased. She could see no traces of vomit, but his face was grey and damp. 'What is it?' she asked. 'Have you been sick?'

He nodded with closed eyes. She went and pulled down the shade and a blue dusk fell across the room. She no longer knew whether she was frightened or frantic.

'We can't go,' he mumbled, searching for her hand. But she didn't want him to touch her just now.

'Did you throw up?'

'No.'

'Does it hurt?'

'Yes, dreadfully. I'm exhausted.'

She began gently to remove his tail-coat, one arm behind his back.

'We may not make it,' he mumbled.

'We wouldn't have anyway.'

When she had got him in bed she went down to Lundholm's and asked them to send their eldest boy for Doctor Hubendick. She almost expected him to be making a house call and to have to wait, since everything was going so irrevocably wrong that day. But he was there within a quarter of an hour and examined F.A., touching his frail body carefully. Tora folded up his clothes and hung up his tail-coat. The doctor glared at her, but she couldn't stop herself, she had to busy herself with something.

'Is it serious?'

'It's been serious all along. He's probably bleeding again. Save his vomit.'

She nodded.

'Save his stool as well.'

Tora was about to hush him but he had closed the door well before starting to talk with her.

'How serious is it?' Tora asked. He didn't reply.

'We were supposed to be getting married.'

'Yes, yes,' the doctor said.

311

'We were getting married today.'

'He can't get out of bed now, I'm sure you see,' Doctor Hubendick mumbled, looking distraught. This surprised her. She felt absolutely cool and clear-headed for the first time in hours. What had she been wasting her time on? Looking for shoes. Posing new obstacles. She wondered whether the F.A. she had been imagining really existed. Would he have sat there in his stocking feet with a magazine in front of his face and refused to have anything to do with the ruined shoes? Possibly. But she hadn't tested him, hadn't dared to try.

Now there was no longer time for such things. Now she had to be clear-headed and make a decision.

'I'm going to get the parson,' she said. She didn't care that the doctor was staring at her as she went into the room. She sat down gingerly on the edge of the bed and took F.A. by the hand.

'I'm going to get the parson,' she said softly. 'We'll have to do it here at home.'

His eyes were closed, his eyelids shimmered as if the blue of his eyes was shining through. When he looked up he seemed pensive and solemn, but neither surprised nor upset like the doctor.

'You know why,' she whispered. 'It's not for my sake, but for Fredrik's. And for the second child's.'

'Yes,' he said. 'I know.'

'But you don't want it?' was on the tip of her tongue but she pulled herself together because she couldn't afford that kind of thing right now. She let go of his hand and tucked it under the covers.

'I'm going to get him,' she said to Hubendick. 'Don't leave Otter.'

312

As she put her shawl on and left it struck her that this was the first and surely the only time in her life she would be ordering a doctor about. It was half past five as she crossed the tracks again.

The pastor sat working on the register and was outraged by the delay. He was somewhat placated when she told him that Otter had been taken seriously ill. The witnesses sat there waiting in silence. There were Kasparsson and a ticket vendor called Engquist. She told them they could go home. They looked at her, unable to utter a word of sympathy. She had an idea they were frightened, but didn't realize it had anything to do with her own voice or her quick, nervous movements.

Old Pastor Hörlin was an unkind man, she knew. He had shown his contempt for her the very first time they had come about the bans, when he asked whether F.A. was the father of Fredrik.

'Of course.'

'Of both children?'

To which Tora had been very quick to reply: 'It's in the parish register. Just look it up.'

F.A. hadn't understood.

'How could he see you were pregnant again?' he had asked.

Now Hörlin wanted to postpone the wedding.

'No,' said Tora. She looked him straight in the eye. Her ears were buzzing, she felt herself go pale. 'Don't let me faint now,' she thought.

'This is his final request,' she said.

'I'll come,' Hörlin replied. 'I'll ask him myself.'

'You do that.'

313

She walked three steps behind him all the way back. 'I'm doing what I don't want to do,' she thought. 'Because I have to. Most things happen that way. There's no choice.'

'It's like running in witches' rings,' she thought, despising the pastor in front of her. She hated him because she had begged him to come, because she had lied to him, and because she was rushing across the square to come up alongside him and get him to walk even faster.

She asked Emma Lundholm to come upstairs and be their witness. Doctor Hubendick stayed. He was bewildered and perturbed, but grumbled obediently, and he never took his eyes off his patient. F.A. was weak and Tora wondered whether he would go through with it. He seemed indifferent.

'Is this your wish?' asked Hörlin.

F.A. nodded. He looked almost impatient. It only took a few moments to marry them.

He remembered that it had been evening and that the light went grey and dull in the room. She hadn't even lit a lamp. She had been in a great hurry, he thought. But she could have lit a candle. It would have made things a little prettier.

He remembered nothing of the early morning hours. Suddenly he was lying there looking at the daisies and the shiny black bottle of sherry on the dresser. Tora was still dressed in black, and the carts had begun rattling down the street. 'She's going to be a widow with one child who's just learned to walk,' he thought, 'and another on the way. She was in a rush, but people will understand.'

By Monday morning his breathing was much easier. Doctor Hubendick was there again, and his voice was different. Tora was pale as a corpse now. He had never seen her like that.

'Get out of that dress,' he entreated her. 'Please put on something light-coloured.'

He slept a great deal. Fredrik must be somewhere else, because the kitchen was absolutely silent. She said it was Tuesday and that he was much better. Outdoors, it slowly turned into a cold, rainy early summer. He wished he had had something to look at other than the rain-streaked window.

'I'm not going to die,' he thought, feeling more astonished than anything else. 'Not this time.' It was as if he were sitting beside his own bed, looking on.

315

It took many days for him to move back into himself. His old irritation began to return. Tora did not say much. He would take her hand and try to lay it on his stomach. Lightly and gently he wanted it to rest on the thin cloth of his nightshirt, but she was frightened, and her hand awkward.

'Don't be afraid,' he said. 'There's nothing scary in there. I thought there was, but it's just a big sore.'

She drew back her rigid, heavy hand as if she were terrified.

'It's not on the outside. And deep inside, Tora, there is health — in here. It's just so deep down in me. And at the same time I can taste death in my mouth. Isn't that peculiar?'

He lay still, forgetting all about her, feeling quite absent-minded.

'You mustn't talk like that,' was all she could say.

He had forgotten, completely forgotten, that there was a time when he had been unable to talk about things like that.

Tora was different than before. Her mouth was a thin line as she did her chores, her eyes staring without seeing. He thought he could probably wave his hand before her eyes without her noticing. It took a long time for him to realize that she was ashamed.

This was confusing, and stood everything on its head in his mind. He knew what Tora was like, with all her shortcomings and with her faithful eyes and — he had thought — her absolute lack of pride. He had often felt bitter when he thought about her, finding her earthbound and materialistic. Even simple. There was something fundamentally unspiritual about Tora and her view of life. He did not believe that, deep down, it could be changed. She was not merely uneducated. Something must simply be missing, he had often thought.

Now he had to adjust to a new Tora, unfamiliar to him. She was ashamed about that Sunday afternoon, about having rushed him into marriage. But everyone would understand! Even he understood!

He didn't think it would do any good to talk to her about it. He wasn't even sure he would have dared. Tora was ashamed of herself, and it was strange to think of her as really being like that. 'It would have been better for me to die,' he thought. 'It would have been easier for her to forgive herself.' He remembered that long, difficult night, and Tora in her black dress with the poorly hand-altered shiny sleeves. His old impatience began to come back, itching inside him.

'Don't cry over me!'

She picked up the wood basket and started piling up kindling sticks.

'What did you say?' she mumbled, her head turned away.

'I said: "Don't cry over me."'

She picked up Fredrik and took him out into the kitchen, closed the door and straightened out the rugs. Her mouth was pulled tight in distaste.

'But I don't mean it,' he said. 'By the way, do you ever cry at all, Tora?'

She didn't answer, but at least she looked up at him, and her eyes were no longer blind and glazed.

'Let me tell you something,' she said softly. 'Once and for all. You don't talk like that when Fredrik is listening!'

'The lad's too small to understand. But no harsh words now, Tora. I'm almost done in.'

She dropped to her knees on the hard sheet metal in front of the tiled stove and started sweeping up wood shavings that had fallen out of the basket, making a little pile of them and sweeping it dully back and forth. He kept his eyes fixed on her.

'Don't you talk like that,' she mumbled.

'Well, at least I'm not lying to myself!'

'Oh yes you are,' she said, rising and stumbling off in the direction of the kitchen door. 'Somehow you are, anyhow.'

The moment she had shut the door he had forgotten the whole conversation, and lay there feeling absent-minded and a bit tired.

The mist had cleared. The sea gleamed as if through polished glass, the cold making the air tangible, as if it had substance. Far out, the water was different and darker, and the sound of the distant waves could be heard. On the shore, however, the most audible things were voices and laughter, the restless gulls, heels clattering on wooden stairs, and the clinking of the big picnic hampers. A little boat rounded the point. Most people expected it to pass, and a few people waved excitedly, as you do to people you'll never see again. It was a small white boat with a covered deck, and the sun glimmered off each pane of glass. The engine puttered and the aroma of fried steak rose from it, not in reality but in memory, making everyone smile. It was called the Hebe II, and everyone was now aware that it was drawing close to the dock and blowing its horn loudly. Most people were surprised, and expected it to run aground or up onto the land and be stuck there like a slanted veranda with the sun glittering in the windows.

'It's all right,' said their host. 'The water's three fathoms deep by the dock.'

With those words, everyone realized that this was a surprise, that they were being taken for a boat outing. Quickly, the conductor gathered the entire chorus in front of the building. Then roughly but cheerfully he dragged the host up onto the veranda under the hollyhocks that had already begun to turn, this first week in October.

'We sing our greeting, sing!' they sang. *'Receive our thanks in sooong! Hurrah, hurrah, hurrah, hurrah!'*

Tora stood alongside, holding F.A. by the arm. It was this sort of thing she had been worried about when he had insisted on going along. But she didn't feel him tugging at her at all. He stood absolutely still and was as pale as ever. He looked amused and slightly stern. Like a little old man, she thought with a stab of grief.

She had come, too, to protect him from his own excitement and enthusiasm, but so far he was having no feelings that could do him any harm. He walked slowly and with a slight stoop, sometimes moving uncertainly, as if he wasn't really sure where to tread next. His friends found it awkward, probably it upset them to see how pale his face was, how easily his forehead perspired, to see his thin hands tremble slightly when he held a cup or glass. He only drank hot water with lemon, or sparkling water, and this was awkward for them, too. They didn't know how to behave or what to offer him. Their smooth young faces reminded her of sad-eyed dogs, Tora thought. They gave themselves away. She was glad she had come along.

She wondered for a moment if she embarrassed him, as she was hugely pregnant now. She couldn't have more than a couple of weeks left. She couldn't button a coat, and her belly was like a barrel. She laughed bitterly to herself when she thought about how she and F.A. must look together. They walked down to the boat last of all, he placing one foot cautiously in front of the next like an elderly gentleman and she waddling like a duck.

'So, now at least you'll see the sea,' she whispered, pressing his hand. He smiled as if he, too, were embarrassed.

320

They had travelled to Flen by train, changed there for the local, arriving at Oxelösund late in the morning. Generally, the chorus only made day trips during the summer, but it was a lovely autumn and the board of Juno had made a last-minute decision to arrange an outing to the seaside. Wives and fiancees had brought their summer hats back out. Tora was wearing a black varnished straw hat with a red velvet flower in front. She knew that the flower was old and droopy, but it made no difference since she had to wear a shawl instead of a coat and her face had that blotchy mask of pregnancy.

'I look like hell,' she had said to her reflection that morning. 'But better days are ahead! And at least we're going along to Oxelösund. I just hope I can hold out until we get back!'

It was only possible to pull up to the little dock in very fine weather. Even now there was a slight swell that slowly pulled the boat sideways. The captain was concerned, both about the swell and the sharp rocks that jutted out around the dock. He hurried them, wanting to get going. Kasparsson and a couple of the others waved eagerly from the stern. They were saving a seat for F.A. Tora thought it would't hurt if they were a little less willing and eager to please. F.A. was extremely pale again by the time he was seated.

'How are you?' she asked softly.

He shook his head.

'Not well?'

'No.'

He sat leaning slightly forward for a few minutes and she could see the others looking at one another over his head. Her skin prickled with fear and irritation. Then F.A. suddenly rose and laid his hand on her arm.

321

'I think we'd better give this a miss, Tora.'

They began walking slowly toward the fore and the gangway. Kasparsson asked uneasily how he was.

'I'm sure I'll be all right,' he said. 'But I think it would be wise of me to have a rest now.'

Their host offered them the key to the house, and F.A. let Tora take it, staring straight ahead as if it had nothing to do with him. She hadn't seen his face so ashen since early last summer.

She figured they would make their way as quickly as possible up to the house, but he turned around on the dock and watched the boat pull out. Kasparsson could be seen talking with the captain and gesticulating towards the shore. The boat headed straight out for a little while, and then turned and stood still against the swell, the engine thumping steadily. Kasparsson ran down and joined the second basses, for the entire chorus had now assembled on the side facing the dock.

'*Captain, full steam ahead,*' they sang. '*Full steam ahead!*'

Tora looked at F.A.. He was smiling, a sudden smile that seemed to have taken him by surprise, and his colour was starting to improve.

'*Full steam ahead!*'

'*Captain!*' roared the basses.

Now she could see that his eyes were full of tears, and she felt her own throat constrict.

'*Our friends on the shore, our tune drowns the sea's roar,*' the playful melody continued after its commanding beginning, '*to hail you in song from our sails.*'

'Good fellows,' F.A. mumbled, and both he and Tora waved. Actually, she thought it a very good thing they had had to go ashore. It was as if they had been intended to stand right here. He sang along softly to the very last refrain, when the boat had headed out to sea again and the pounding of the engine finally drowned out the chorus. They could see Liljeström, who had replaced F.A. Otter, amongst the first tenors. He exerted himself tremendously when he sang, his whole body trembled. He reminded Tora of a bird puffing up his chest, a chaffinch singing for all he was worth in the ecstasy of springtime.

Like the embrace of the waves and the shore
So is my love of thee faithful
So faith.....ful my love
Of thee.

'Oh, that was grand!' said Tora, waving her handkerchief for as long as she could see the Hebe II. He nodded.

'Good fellows,' he repeated, and they began to walk away from the sea. Tora thought he would want to go into the house and lie down, but he turned off along the cliffs.

He now raised his face, and didn't seem to be walking so cautiously. A gentle breeze came in off the sea over their faces, and Tora felt like having a walk, too. At the same time, she was worried.

'We'd better not overdo it,' she warned him softly. She tried not to read his expression, she knew he didn't appreciate it. But it would be scary to be too far away if something happened.

The men who had driven them out to this summer place were gone, and had taken the horses with them. The carts with all the benches were just standing there. They were decorated with autumn foliage, and the red and yellow October leaves had blown around them throughout the drive. Now that no one was there, it was evident that the summer house had actually been closed up for the season already. A heavy stone lay on the well cover. The garden furniture had been put away and the walkways raked, although the birches hadn't lost all their leaves and some were still falling on the paths. Tora didn't like the sound of the weather vane as it creaked and turned.

'Brrr,' she said.

She had not been this far from other people for years, and she wondered what she would do if anything happened to F.A. The thought crossed her mind that Kasparsson could have arranged something more useful than a chorus performance. They were all alone now.

'Shouldn't we go in?' she asked.

'No, we're going for a walk. After all, we're here now and can have a look at the sea.'

'So you feel better?'

'Yes.'

She was still dubious and fell behind. He turned around and helped her up to a flat place on the rocks.

'How come it passed over so fast?' she asked.

'I wasn't ill,' he said in an almost jolly tone, but she didn't like the way it sounded.

'Come on, Tora, let's walk.'

The stones were smooth and it wasn't difficult to walk there except when they had to get across a crevice. Now he was the one helping her, and she waddled carefully, bow-legged.

'Take off your shoes,' he said.

'What? Are you mad?'

'No, the rocks are nice and warm. You'll walk more easily barefoot because it won't be slippery.'

He had already sat down and begun unlacing his own. He stuffed his stockings in his pocket. Tora sat looking at his lovely feet. They were white, and the sinews and blue veins were clearly visible. The skin covering his ankles was tight and smooth, without the slightest crease or wrinkle.

'Are you sure you're not going to get a chill?' she asked, leaning forward to cover them with her hands, but her belly got in the way and she couldn't reach.

He began to unlace her boots. At first she tried to pull away, because she was ashamed of her own deformed ugly feet. 'But he already knows what I look like,' she thought, and stayed. It was warm on the rocks. She could even feel the heat through her stockings. Now he turned away when she lifted her skirt and petticoat to pull down her garters. Then she unrolled her stockings until they were short enough to pull off, and put them in her boots. The smooth cliff warmed as if it were flesh, but the air was chilly. After a little while he stood up and helped her to rise, and they began to walk slowly along the shore, watching out for the crevices and hollows, where driftwood, pieces of broken rafts and the bodies of dead birds had collected.

Far out to sea they heard the muffled rumble of the boat, and from further inland the wind in the treetops. But it was all very distant. The wind chilled their skin but the sun was as clear as before. She wondered how far they dared to walk like this, and she must have looked at him quickly out of the corner of her eye, for he asked:

'Are you tired? Would you like to sit down?'

Tora nodded and they sat down on another rock. She felt the baby kick just as she sat down and smiled softly. She imagined that it was tired of lying for so long on the same side and had decided to turn over to the other. 'I wonder if

325

they listen,' she thought to herself. There was no more than a thin wall between the baby and the rest of the world, a wall of skin. It didn't seem unreasonable to imagine that the child could hear the rumbling of the sea and the wind in the treetops. Perhaps it could hear their voices the way you can hear things under water, stifled harmonious sounds far away.

'This is how we would have sat if he had been healthy,' she thought. Then she got confused. He was still worried about her and put his arm around her shoulders.

'Would you like to turn back?'

'Not yet,' she said, not letting on that she had been about to ask him the same question.

'Do you know why I didn't want to go along on the boat?' he asked. She thought he had an almost caustic look in his eye.

'You didn't feel well.'

'No.'

She really didn't want to know now, but that didn't help.

'I get seasick,' he said. 'The moment I came aboard I felt the swell. Even in that little boat. The slightest little roll is all it takes.'

She nodded that she had heard him, without looking at him. Now, however, he appeared to be driven by a strange desire to make himself suffer, and he told her that he had always had a tendency to seasickness. He had once been an apprentice in the merchant marines, and had tried to get used to it. He had always dreamt of going to sea. That was why he quit school, he was restless and wanted to get away. He was aware that he didn't have sea legs exactly, but he intended to fight it and beat it. He had tried to ignore the nausea and the terrible pain inside that he felt even when the wind was still. But he couldn't vanquish his seasickness. It

took hold of him and wracked his whole body. He had been
ready to do himself in. It threw him into a dreadful state of
despair and changed him both inside and out. He had
struggled. Did she believe him?

'Why yes, of course.'

Then he had to give up. He wanted to become an
engineer after that. He had already got a certificate in
navigation. He got a job at the shipyards in Gothenburg. He
needed six months practical experience in the yard. Then he
would have to work six months as a stoker before he could
be eligible for the school for locomotive engineers.

Tora couldn't imagine it.

'You mean you were working as a stoker?'

'Yes.'

They sat quietly looking at the cliffs and the worn down
pieces of grey wood at their feet. The sun gleamed off the
sea, making their eyes smart. 'So I would have been an
engineer's wife,' Tora thought. But that felt inconceivable.
She squinted at him.

'Don't you believe I struggled?'

'Oh yes,' said Tora. 'I don't doubt that.'

'But, you know, my illness. I thought I was in hell. But I
was only in Hallsberg sitting there and ... oh Tora, Tora!'

She embraced his head and moved closer so he could lean
on her. She tried to manoeuvre his head between her breasts
and her huge barrel-like belly that was always in the way,
and she threw her arms around his back that was now so
sharp and thin, trying to hold him close. He didn't weep.
She thought he felt rigid with fear, and he probably was
frightened. 'But it'd be better if he could cry over his
misery,' she thought. In the old days her grandmother used
to advise her to save her tears until she needed them more.

327

But when could anyone possibly need them more than now? After a while he broke away roughly and sat beside her, his face in profile.

'Now I suppose you have nothing but contempt for me,' he said, looking down at his bare feet.

'Oh, no!'

'You, who are the most beautiful...' she thought, amazed. But how could she ever tell him?

'You, who are the most beautiful thing in this awful world. In this shameful — oh my goodness! You are my world. So lovely I can hardly bring myself to touch you.' She bent as far forward as her belly allowed and hid her face in her arms. The sunlight and the water kept getting to her eyes. 'I'm so ashamed, so ashamed. I'm no one but me. But if I were only able to share my warmth with you perhaps it would be some small help. If I could only say it. If only I knew how.'

From a great distance, she heard the wind blowing through the treetops. It was a worried murmur. 'Worried, always worried,' Tora thought, trying to see the face he had turned away. These were words he had said and she had not understood, and now they came back to her. That's all we have to give one another. Warmth and worry. She leaned forward again with her arms on her knees, running her cold fingertips along her bright cheeks and silent mouth.

'We'd better be heading home now,' he said.

She thought of what a long way from home they were. First the cart to the station. It would be rough and shaky and she would have to sit there holding her belly. Then the local train with the velvet seats that had been baking in the sun all day. Then they would change in Flen and have nearly an

hour's wait for their train. Home was terribly far away, but
she didn't correct him.

I nside the iron oven door, the fire burned so it sang. Tora peeked through the light hole and closed the flue when she thought the heat was too white. The birch logs were going fast. She had to start early to get the baking oven thoroughly heated up by dawn, but perhaps she had started too early, after all. You couldn't know the first time. She cast an eye towards the pile of logs, thinking that it had shrunk terribly fast. Fuel cost money.

The cellar smelled like a cobbler's shop. The cobbler had his workshop in the room facing the street, with a little set of stone steps leading down at the corner of the building. It had once been a milk and bread shop, but people said they hadn't done a very good business. They were too far from everything.

The building was at number 60 on the street Wärnström had named Carl Fredrik Street after his son, although no-one ever called it anything but Hovlunda Road, which had been the name of the old stump of road that had led up to the croft on the hillside. Now, however, both Hovlund and the Agricultural Guild barn had been torn down, and Wärnström had built Carlsborg up there for himself. He had had a park put in around the mansion, and planted yew trees and arbour vitae.

At first number 60 had been pretty much alone on the block, but now that the brewery was in operation one building after the next was built. The cobbler was doing a booming business.

330

Tora had moved in just after the new year in 1904, taking one room with an iron stove on the second floor. She remembered that the shopkeeper used to sell home-baked bread, and so she went looking in the cellar for the bakery. All she found was one room with a baking oven. She asked the custodian to let her see if it still worked.

The room was full of the cobbler's piles of soling leather, but when Tora asked it turned out that he was only renting the front room. She asked whether she could rent the room with the oven. The cobbler had to clear it out for her, which had made for some hostility between them since there wasn't room for his soling leather in his shop. She thought it a shame that they weren't going to get on, but he was a very odd type.

'One man's bread is another man's poison,' he said, in a voice of resignation, as he removed his things. This shocked and offended her at first, until she realized that she had misunderstood him. She had taken him to mean her loaves of bread and F.A.'s death.

Still, he was a grouchy man. He hardly raised his eyes when she brought in a pair of shoes for new half-soles, although she had only done it to appease him. The holes weren't all that big — she could have used the shoes for a while longer.

It was unfortunate not to be on good terms with her closest neighbour, but there was nothing to be done about it. Otherwise, people had been decent to her. She had bought flour from merchant Levander's and Valfrid had arranged a good price for her. His brother Wilhelm was foreman at the carpentry shop now, and he had gotten his hands on some waste lumber to make her sawhorses. She had bought her baking board at an auction.

However, when she counted up all her expenses, it had been dreadfully costly. And the wood was worst — she was literally burning up her money, and burning it so the chimney roared. Still, this was no time to be miserly or anxious. Mamsell Winlöf had told her that.

Tora had still been in mourning when she went to see her, but she had waited until the younger boy was born so she could get her coat on. She had felt solemn and formal in her long black tulle veil edged with silk ribbon, and she had not been afraid to knock at Mamsell's door. Mamsell had recognized her dress and said that she'd done a very good job of altering it.

'Well done, Tora.'

Then she had asked if Tora would like a cup of cocoa in her parlour. She had said it in so many words: 'Tora, I would like you to join me ...'

'Put on the kettle,' she called into the kitchen to her housemaid, and Tora had to smile, it sounded so familiar. She sat there feeling envious of the long-legged unwitting thing who was Mamsell's housemaid.

Mamsell inquired about Tora's plans in great detail and approved of them. An excellent old recipe was actually a little nest egg, she had said. The only problem with the rye and potato breads Tora was planning to bake and sell was that she called them potato loaves. Mamsell thought the name would remind people of the lean years, when in reality they were better than ordinary rye loaves, and the name should reflect this.

She did not want to lend Tora one hundred and fifty kronor, but three hundred instead.

'Now, Tora, you mustn't be too worried and start cutting corners. There's no guarantee that that is the most economical policy in the long run.'

Tora was relieved. She had been terrified of taking on too heavy a debt, but a hundred and fifty kronor would have been too little, and she knew it.

Yes, Mamsell Winlöf was wealthy and no, she wasn't stingy. You could tell she was rich when you were in her home. You had to walk carefully to your chair so as not to knock over any of the fine things the former restaurant owner had everywhere. Tora wished she could touch the thick apricot silk curtain fabric and to lay the palms of her hands against the walnut of the table, but she held herself still and erect. Just recently, Mamsell had donated an older building, completely furnished, to serve as a home for the mentally disturbed. You couldn't help but wonder if it would be possible to keep the inhabitants indoors, since the prospective inhabitants were a little group of feeble-minded lunatics — mostly elderly people with Fia Fifteen as their ringleader — who hung about the streets and squares of the town.

In Tora's experience, it was unusual for the wealthy to make a loan without wanting complete control of how the money would be spent. But here she was, being lent three hundred interest free and no strings attached. When their discussion about the money was over, Mamsell Winlöf folded her chubby white hands in her lap and said:

'Yes, Tora, you and your boys have suffered a terribly great loss. I have heard that Otter was a very kind and excellent man.'

Tora knew she could now cry if she chose. Mamsell Winlöf's face was illuminated by the light coming in through the window. It was grey and dull. She was very much her old self, except that she seemed to gradually grow fatter. On her left hand, resting on the black moiré of her dress, was her big garnet ring. It was lustreless and reddish brown, like rock candy.

Tora was on the sofa, with the light coming from behind her. Her face was shielded, and she knew Mamsell was sympathetic. But she could not cry.

'Did Otter live to see the little one's birth?' Mamsell asked, and Tora shook her head.

'He was born in November,' she said, and could hear the roughness in her own voice. No, she couldn't cry, and after a short silence Mamsell bowed her head. She changed the subject back to Tora's plans about baking and selling potato bread.

Something may sound sensible and practical, it may even sound simple, as long as you are only talking about it. But when Tora stood there all alone in the basement with the roaring oven, the sack of flour and the wooden bowl of cold boiled potatoes, she was nearly seized with panic. She had sat peeling potatoes almost all morning. Now she began to mash them with a wooden mallet. It certainly wasn't the same thing when there were so many. They mustn't be lumpy, but she couldn't spend all night at it either. She felt the grey mush with her fingertips. 'If some old biddy chomps down on a piece of potato, I've sold my last loaf,' she thought. 'I know what they're like.'

She added the water and the first scoop of rye flour. The flour was rather coarsely ground. She was worried that it might be too coarse, that it might be difficult to get the dough to rise. It grew heavy and sticky. She had to work it in batches to make it manageable, beating the dough in the

334

bowl with the wooden spoon and feeling the muscles in her forearm begin to tire. She remembered Sara Sabina's voice: 'Put your arm into it, girl,' and she thought she could probably put her whole self into such a large batch of dough, now that she was grown up. 'Put your arm into it, girl.' She would be twenty-seven in March. She had retained a lot of weight after the second baby, but her face was less full and smooth than before. Her hair was darker, too, and didn't seem to be changing back after this pregnancy. 'But just wait til the summer,' she thought, kneading the grey dough with a firm, steady hand.

Now she was maintaining the heat in the oven with as little wood as possible, to be economical. She could tell it was going to be plenty hot, was sure she had lit it too early. Every now and then she would glare at the peep hole and her enemy inside that was wolfing down the wood.

It took her two full hours to mix the dough. 'You go mix it up while I do the milking,' she recalled. But that hadn't been twenty-five litres' worth of dough. The sweat dripped down her back and her feet were freezing cold. This basement wasn't a nice place to be, she said to herself. Maybe the cobbler should have insisted. She laid a cloth over the dough, intending to go up to her room and make a cup of coffee and check that the children and the girl who was looking after them were asleep. Suddenly, however, she was overcome with worry that when she came back down to activate the sour-dough culture it wasn't going to work. It was her regular culture that she had dried in a bowl from the last time she'd baked, and now she poured a little water over it to soften it, worrying that she was starting too late and that it wouldn't work, but reminding herself at the same time that it was easy to get all worked up about nothing. 'Freshen up the culture the evening before the morning you're planning to bake,' she remembered, and of course that was right.

As she walked up the stairs she realized that her feet were swollen in her felt slippers. What if she couldn't get her shoes on when it was time to go to the square? Actually, it was silly to sell the bread just after it was baked, it was better the next day. But there was no telling if people would buy bread if they couldn't feel that it was warm and straight from the oven.

Of course the girl had fallen asleep and let the fire go out. The room was cold. She couldn't find a single spark in the ashes. 'Ah well, she's no more than a child herself,' Tora thought as she took some kindling and a little newspaper to light. She was sound asleep in Tora's bed and had let her hair down. Fredrik had spread buttons and spools all around her on the cover. Ingeborg was small for her thirteen years, her chest almost concave. Tora thought she had probably had rickets, and didn't really like her very much. All she had to do was look at her to start worrying about Fredrik and Adam. But at least she was kind, and patient with Fredrik who was at an age where children are everywhere and won't stay still.

She heard the peaceful breathing from the kitchen settee. She had divided it down the middle with a board, so each child had his own sleeping area. She thought the two small heads, one at each end, looked sweet. Adam was dark-haired, and she thought he would stay that way since he still had his dark hair at three months. Even as a baby he had an aquiline nose and heavy eyelids. He looked like a little gentleman.

It was really cold in the flat, and she touched the top of Adam's head gently to see if he was cold. Some dough from her floury hands stuck in his thin hair. She picked it out gingerly, blowing a little to make it go away. His sucking reflex started right up, and though she did not want to wake him, she couldn't remove her hand from his warm, downy, floury head. 'How can anything in the world be so beautiful?' she thought. 'Don't let him wake up. But if he does, I'll feed him. There'll be no screaming at all here tonight.'

She tucked the quilt in around Fredrik. It was folded double and felt much too heavy. His fists were tight in his sleep, and spittle bubbled from the corner of his mouth. He was such an eager child. Eager even in his sleep.

Tora shoved Ingeborg over a little towards the wall and settled down on the iron bedstead with her shawl over her. She rested for a few minutes. She mustn't be more than half an hour, though. She found she was so tense and anxious about how the sourdough was doing downstairs that she couldn't lie still. She was soon on her feet again, heading downstairs yawning and stiff-armed to finish the sour dough culture and work it into the bread.

She slept for a couple of hours around midnight, and then went back down to check whether the bread was rising. When she pounded down the dough it was loose and difficult to work and she was up to her forearms in dough. She worked in more flour with the wooden spoon, thinking irately that the dough was so sticky you'd have thought she'd never baked bread before. But she wasn't so worried any more. There was something ceremonious about setting the dough on the board and kneading the extra flour in. It was warm and strong beneath her hands. 'We're finally getting somewhere,' she thought, covering over both bowl and board.

She went upstairs and re-heated her coffee while the dough rose on the board. She held a sugar cube between her teeth and swallowed the hot coffee through it, her feet on a footstool. Darkness and silence surrounded her. There was a window high up in the basement wall, but she could see nothing through it. She had the feeling she was the only person awake in all the world. 'But, heavens, there must be millions of people in the world,' she thought, 'though this whole town is asleep.' Then she remembered the area around the station, the trains she could hear all night when she had been living at the Railway Hotel. Even earlier, when she'd lived at the Pigpen, doors had slammed and stairs creaked all night long. 'I'd like to live over that way,' she thought. 'On the north side. This place is really far away, and behind this building the fields take over.' She yawned and her head felt heavy despite the coffee, but she knew that these were the worst hours of the night. She'd feel better later.

She took some more flour and started working the dough, separating it into loaves. She weighed them in at exactly one and a half kilos apiece, just as she'd been taught, but they felt very heavy and unworkable. When she started to shape them, she couldn't get the bottom seams right. The tops looked all right, smooth and rounded, but the bottoms were coming out all creased and furrowed, no matter how hard she tried. When they rose there would be big holes and bubbles inside. It would be impossible to cut a single decent slice from these loaves that didn't crumble.

Her hands grew nervous and she suddenly couldn't remember how to do it. It wasn't exactly something you usually thought about, your hands worked on their own. In

338

the end, she put aside the loaf she was working on; it was never going to come out right. She wiped her floury hands on her apron and had a little warmed-over coffee. She remembered the miller's wife in Vallmsta, who was so angry by nature and who baked such wonderful bread. When it wasn't coming along well even the miller was afraid of her. He used to peek cautiously into the room to see what kind of a mood she was in before he entered.

'Are they risin' for you Fia?' he would shout.

Tora remembered her grandfather's voice imitating the anxious miller. She smiled and her hands started working on their own. Her right hand did the turning and her left hand held the dough. The bottom came out right. She made one high, round loaf after the next, and quickly, too. She set them to rise on feather pillows, and the sight of them delighted her. Now she would have time to go up and nurse Adam while the loaves rose. It had gone well, but she wished she hadn't thought that thought yet, because she still had to bake them. She touched wood lightly with the knuckle of her index finger against the baking board, to be on the safe side.

Adam was still asleep, but she lifted him up and put him quickly to her breast so he wouldn't cry and wake Fredrik. He was so sleepy that he only took a couple of gulps before her nipple slid out of his mouth and he was lying there with little bubbles of spittle mixed with milk at the corners of his mouth. It took a while for Tora to notice, she was so preoccupied trying to figure out how many loaves she would have to sell to pay for the flour.

She thumped him lightly on the bottom when she noticed he had given up, and he started over. After a while, he was nursing fast and hungrily. Tora had lit the lamp now and sat looking around the room. Fredrik had pulled out all kinds of things she didn't let him play with. Ingeborg was obviously too soft, but that was better than the other extreme. On the dresser she saw the death announcement. Tora had saved two copies to give the boys when they grew up. Fredrik must have climbed up onto the dresser and pulled out the shaving stand drawer. She looked angrily at Ingeborg who was sniffling in her sleep, her mouth wide open.

When Adam was finished and she had changed him, she laid him back in the settee-bed and went over and picked up the letter and some buttons that had ended up on the dresser. A vase was on its side but not broken. It was lucky he hadn't ripped the death announcement. He had strong, chubby fingers. 'It wouldn't have mattered anyway,' she found herself thinking, because in retrospect she was embarrassed to have spent so much on the fine paper with a three centimetre wide black edge bright as silk with silhouettes of grieving angels with their brows resting in the palms of their hands, surrounded by greenery, a crucifix and beams of light. That splendour had cost a pretty penny.

Afterwards she realized that she had ordered such expensive announcements for the sake of the single one that would be sent to his old mother down in Gothenburg. When you thought about it afterwards it was madness. But at the time it felt both necessary and appropriate. The same went for all the expenses associated with that time. Afterwards they were madness.

Valfrid had helped her with the text. He was really in his element. He had wanted her to have this printed: 'My darling, my dearest husband.' But Tora had made him sober up and they had settled on: 'This is to announce the death

340

of my beloved, faithful husband Fredrik Adam Otter.' Valfrid
had composed the poem as well. He had been extremely
eager. 'Well, I know nothing at all about poetry,' Tora had
said. 'But Otter did!' Valfrid retorted, and so she included
the poem. Now that she had read it over and over again, she
had begun to understand it. She thought it was very
beautiful.

Slowly she smoothed out the stiff paper that had wrinkled
under Fredrik's fingers. She put the announcement in the
dresser drawer instead, under her blouses. He would never
get that drawer open, it was too heavy and unyielding. After
closing the drawer, she stood looking at it for a moment.
She knew that grieving was a difficult task. But it was still
ahead of her. Right now she didn't have the time. Right now
she didn't have the strength.

She felt a little solemn as she went back down to the
basement. It was a lot of bread, the biggest batch of baking
she had ever seen. The loaves must have risen by now. They
rested heavy and round in the indentations they had made in
the pillows. The tops had just begun to crack. This was
exactly the right moment to put them in the oven. She fired
it up a little, swept it out, and closed the oven door. Then
she got the bread-stick. 'I should have had a girl to help me
now,' she thought. 'You prick them loaves while I sweep out
the oven,' Sara Sabina used to instruct her.

The loaves baked for an hour, and then she put them on
a rack and brushed each one with a rag dipped in hot water.
It was starting to get hot around the oven, but the floor was
still cold and it was draughty by the walls. She was glad she
had used those pillows. 'Otherwise they would never have
risen properly in this draught,' she thought.

Her feet ached as she moved back and forth in the room. 'When this day is over,' she thought, then decided not to finish that sentence yet. She hoped she would develop a circle of customers, regulars she could depend on. Then she could explain to them that this particular bread was even better if it aged for a day. Then she could bake a day ahead of time, and not have to be up all night. People should be able to understand that. Not to mention that it was the truth.

Outside the window it had begun to get light, and the cobbler was hammering on the other side of the wall. 'If he weren't such a fool I'd take him a cup of coffee,' thought Tora. She had made a pot of good, strong coffee, and now she brushed the first finished loaves, this time with coffee, both on the rounded tops and on the bottoms. They were shiny and brown.

She sat down and drank hot coffee from a saucer while she waited for the next round to bake. The sun was up. From her basement window she could see nothing but the snow that went half way up the window and a strip of sky, pale and cold. Her back and shoulders were stiff and painful. She touched her forearms, following the tender muscle all the way up to her elbow. Her skin was rough with dough all the way up. She mustn't forget to wash before she changed to go to the market.

The coffee warmed her right down to the pit of her stomach. She felt her head clear, too. She wasn't going to get a headache. It had gone well, she thought, gazing at her shiny loaves of bread. Now she actually dared to think it had gone really well.

When Sara Sabina was going to die, she sent to town for Tora to be with her. It was the second week in May, the week the cuckoos start calling in the woods, when the leaves only stop growing for a couple of hours during the cool, humid nights.

Tora knew at once this was serious because Sara Sabina had never asked for help before. She didn't know exactly what was wrong with her grandmother because she had never revealed that she was ill. Sometimes, however, she had said she was tired and needed to lie down, and the last year she had grown much thinner. Tora knew that she was in pain, because she couldn't button her skirt without looking tense and uncomfortable. A strange grey shadow would cross her face, and she would sit down gingerly and unbutton a couple of buttons at the waist to loosen it.

Once that spring when Tora had come to Appleton, she saw her grandmother's face at the window. It was grey and insubstantial and did not look welcoming. Although the old woman had never tended to display emotion, it was entirely unlike her to be rejecting or indifferent. Tora was embarrassed and looked away. When she raised her eyes again the face was gone, but she recalled the expression as clearly as if it had still been there, reflected in the thin glass of the window that was full of rainbow-coloured blisters.

When she walked into the croft, her grandmother hadn't been there. She came in a little while later with a small bag of pine cones she had been to collect for kindling. Tora then

343

realized that she had seen a sign. She interpreted it as auguring that Sara Sabina didn't have long to live.

Tora decided to take off from her baking and her market stand when her grandmother sent for her, and asked Emma Lundholm to look after the boys. Adam was six months old now, and already weaned because her milk had run dry. At first she was sad about this, and disappointed in herself, but now that she needed to leave him it undeniably made things easier. She turned him over to Emma, thinking as she left that he looked tiny and thin. Stable, chubby Fredrik who was nearly two did not even watch her leave. He was used to Emma looking after them on market days.

She arrived at Appleton on Sunday afternoon, and spent almost the whole walk there thinking about the children and the fact that she would be missing a week at the square. Towards the end she had a sudden feeling she'd better hurry, and she felt her anxiety rise as she rushed across the birch grove below the croft. There were still blue anemones blooming in the damp area to the north, but they were almost past, and petals dropped onto her shoes.

Everything looked to be in good order at the croft. Tora's worried eyes took in the yard, and she saw that the steps were swept and the milk pail had been washed and was drying upside-down on the bench. But then she saw a bucket in the grass. Sara Sabina must have put it down on her way in from the well, unable to carry it any further. Yet there was very little water in it. Tora ran the last steps across the grass and to the cottage door in extreme agitation.

She was in bed. Her little body rested deep down in the trundle bed of the settee, covered with a stiff, soiled quilt. She was fully clothed underneath. Tora could see instantaneously that her face was grey and stern with pain

and her eyes were dark as she looked up. But they grew
lively when she caught sight of Tora, and there was a tug at
her thin lips, as if she wanted to smile.

The first thing Tora did was to run out for some water to
give her. She thought her grandmother looked dry around
the mouth, and that her tongue was stiff when she tried to
greet her. But the well water was so icy cold she had to light
the stove to bring it up to lukewarm. Nowadays the stove
was simple to light. Rickard had sent the money to buy a
new one, and for nearly a year now there had been a little
Norrahammar built into the wall under the big hood.

Tora moistened her grandmother's lips, which were
difficult to find. Her mouth had caved in over her gums and
her skin was dry and hard. But there was life in her eyes,
and they were dark. Tora had never thought about it before,
her having such dark eyes.

'Are you in pain, Mother?'

The old woman shook her head. She already looked
much better. Then Tora took out the clean linen sheets she
had brought along, and made up the bed with them. They
were her best sheets. F.A.'s mother had sent four sets when
she had been told that he had married. They were
embroidered with hemstitching, and monogrammed with an
intertwined *FAO*.

She removed her grandmother's sweater and skirt and her
grey woollen slip. She was probably cold, and gave Tora a
dark look, although she said nothing, and Tora began to
wash her gently with a cloth she had dipped in the lukewarm
water and wrung out thoroughly.

'You tell me if you get cold,' she said.

She had withered. The skin over her stomach and breasts
was all wrinkled. The trunk of her body and the tops of her

hands were covered with brown warts and spots. You could see the sinews in her arms and legs through the skin, and her joints appeared to be enlarged. It was difficult for Tora to handle her fragile body. She did so with no distaste, but with an anxiety that made her movements awkward. She dressed her and helped her into the bed. There, she looked even smaller, and she shivered at first from the cold sheets. Tora had dressed her in one of her own night-gowns. It was made of pale yellow flannel and hung in huge folds around her body. Tora took a comb and pulled it gently through the thin greyish brown hair so as not to scrape her scalp. She gathered her grandmother's long hair at the back and plaited it into a braid as thin as a twist of grass. She twisted it into a bun and tied it up with a ribbon. She didn't dare use hairpins, which might be uncomfortable for her grandmother to lie on.

Finally, Tora lifted off the heavy patchwork quilt and took a crocheted blanket out the chest. It had been made from yarn remnants in many colours. She laid her own grey shawl over the top, knowing it would be both light and warm.

'That's my best cover,' her grandmother scolded, but Tora didn't answer and just tucked her in.

She was not sure how bad the old woman's pain was. Sometimes a grey shadow appeared to cross her face, but Tora didn't know where it came from. Now she was dozing, her fingers plucking absently at the edge of the sheet. She had long ago lost the ability to sleep deeply. There were constant uneasy flutterings of the eyelids, and she woke up at the least sound, only to doze off again when she was unable to do anything about whatever it was that had troubled her.

Tora had sweet rolls in her hamper and she now cut off the crusts and soaked them in hot fresh milk, adding a little sugar. Her grandmother opened her mouth when Tora fed her, but couldn't really swallow. Milk trickled from the corner of her mouth.

'Try to get it down,' Tora said, lifting her higher up onto the pillow. She felt panicky, as if she were handling her too roughly.

'Please swallow,' she begged. 'Just this one spoonful.'

Her thin body was labouring. After some time she was more restful, breathing more peacefully. She opened her eyes and looked at Tora, who could not remember her grandmother's gaze being so dark and so clear. 'We see so little of one another,' she thought. 'We seldom get close enough to anyone to really see them.'

Sara Sabina slept. Now she was breathing easily. Tora took her wrist carefully and felt her pulse under her dry skin. It felt like a bird's heartbeat.

The Sunday evening was warm when Tora walked to the earth cellar, and she had to stop and listen to the blackbird who was perched on the birch. He sang with confidence, appealingly, as if he were asking her for something. Pensively, extremely thoughtfully he spun his trills into melodies, as if there were no unrest or hurry in the world. She could just barely see him at the top of the croft's birch which had got its leaves early that year; they were already fully out. It was a weeping birch, and when summer came the branches would move as heavily as seaweed when the wind blew. It would remain green late into the autumn, because it was an unusual birch. But it had been years since anyone mentioned the white serpent that lived under its root.

Returning from the earth cellar, she saw that it was getting dark already, and a hedgehog ran out from under the cottage. Bats rustled under the roof gables, but didn't dare to come out among the trees. The May evening was still too light. The hedgehog was fussing and crunching at something near the rock over by the door, and appeared unafraid. Tora understood that her grandmother probably put out milk for it in the evenings, and was on her way back to the cellar when she realized that the cottage would soon be empty and it was just as well for the hedgehog to get used to not being fed. She went inside and shut the door on the long, pensive notes of the blackbird's trilling.

Now Tora was tired. She sat beside Sara Sabina for a while, but when she was sure her grandmother was asleep and breathing easily Tora decided to lie down on the settee so she could sleep off and on while still keeping an eye on her grandmother. She slept for longer and longer periods, until at dawn she fell soundly asleep, awakening with the sun on her face. The old woman appeared to be rested, and looked at her from her bed, her eyes dark and very clear.

'Are you feeling better?' Tora asked.

'I'm all right,' Sara Sabina answered.

Tora whipped her up a wheat flour gruel, trying to get it really fluffy and light. She added a dab of butter. But her grandmother couldn't get it down.

'It turns my stomach,' she said, and just drank a little water. While Tora was making the trundle bed where she had slept, Sara Sabina lay watching her for a while, and then said:

'This may take some time, you know.'

'Don't you give that a thought,' said Tora. 'You just try to rest, nobody's in any hurry.'

'I'm thinking about your market bread.'

'It can wait.'

Her grandmother was silent for a while, breathing heavily. Then she asked where the boys were.

'They're at Emma's,' said Tora. 'She'll look after them as long as is needed. And now I'm going to straighten things up here.'

'Well, if you have time, that would be fine,' said Sara Sabina. 'A person wants things to be in order at the end, but lacks the strength to do it.'

Tora started by going out to the barn to see if it needed cleaning up. It was a low building dug out under a big rock, so the one or two cows Lans had kept there had basically been living under ground, with huge boulders alongside their stalls. The floor was nothing but trampled-down earth, but there had been wooden planks for the cows to stand on, and hay spread out when they calved. Their stalls had been made of the dark brown worn wood Tora stood holding onto now, recalling early mornings long ago when she and Rickard had carried little piles of hay to put in front of each cow, being careful not to drop any.

Now the barn was cold and there was an odd, strong, ancient odour. A long long time ago there had been the scent of fresh manure and warm animals. The cobwebs hung in clumps in the windows. Tora wanted to get out.

In the loft were a few rakes and a little wooden harrow, the plough with which he had turned the thin brown soil. There was a tin bucket with a hole in the bottom she could have thrown away, but there wasn't much else that needed to be done there. It was all over and done with long ago.

Sara Sabina had had help to lay in wood for the winter, but now the woodshed was empty expect for some crooked

sticks she had collected in the woods and a sack of pine
cones. Tora brought in a basketful of these odds and ends,
but decided that she'd better go out in the woods and collect
some wood in the afternoon.

She thought her grandmother perked up a little when she
came inside and started to take stock of what needed to be
cleaned and straightened in the cottage. Tora was normally
a fast worker, but now she wanted to take plenty of time, to
make sure there would always be something to keep busy
with. That didn't work for long, though. Before she knew it
her cheeks were rosy and she felt herself growing cheerful
from the bustle of accomplishment. Although Sara Sabina
was in bed and only following her with her eyes, it was still
almost like the old days when they did things together. They
discussed what to throw away and what to save.

She looked through the clothing in the chest. All that was
left at home after Lans was his everyday uniform. His parade
uniform had always been kept in a chest at Skebo farm.
There were also a black skirt, a black silk headscarf, thin
with wear, and a grey knitted sweater Tora recognized. It
had wound knitted balls instead of buttons that were pulled
through crocheted loops. She laid out the clothing on the
butcher block by the door. The morning sun was no longer
there.

'Well, at least they'll have an airing,' she said to Sara
Sabina.

'I'll keep an eye on the window in case it starts to look
like rain,' the old woman promised, but she was tired and
kept falling asleep, waking up worried that she had neglected
her duty.

On Tuesday morning Tora got up to a silver-grey dawn,
and the cobwebs were heavy with dew. The flycatcher who

was building a nest in the birdhouse on the side of the woodshed lost his impulse in the grey weather, and went silent and puffy.

Tora scrubbed the floor of the main room. The door was open and Sara Sabina's dark eyes watched her. She said nothing, but Tora still went and got a nail to clean between the boards. The kitchen floor was uneven with wear, and the wood in front of the stove was worn all the way down to the dowels.

'Do you want me to do the windows next?'

'No, I think it's going to rain.'

Both Wednesday and Thursday were hazy and drizzly, and outside the summer seemed to be standing still, the land breathing restfully through the damp grass, and the blackbird was silent. The greenfinches, though, who had nested in the little fir trees outside the woodshed, chattered and trilled and weren't bothered by the misty weather.

Tora had put a sack on the kitchen floor to collect things that were to be thrown away. Although Sara Sabina owned very little, there were still things that were too far gone or worn out that she wanted Tora to get rid of. There were a couple of iron forks with bent tines, a cracked tin mug, an old quilt that had been up in the attic and served as a nesting place for the mice for so long it had nearly disintegrated. There were some worn out boots, and empty bottles from Lans's time.

'You don't want things like that around after you're gone,' said the old woman.

The sack filled up and Tora took it to the bog to toss it away. She walked the path slowly, finding a couple of morels in a spot where she remembered they grew. The wood anemones were still in bloom but they were past their prime and going pink. New ferns were heading through the network of withered leaves from last year, their fronds covered with brown fuzz. The forest was acidic with all the new growth, but there was also a murky, spicy smell from the evergreens, the mosses and the lingonberry plants. When she got back to the croft with the morels in her hand, she could see that the first barn swallow had arrived.

Sara Sabina lay still, her hands resting on the embroidered edge of the sheet. Time had slowed down for her. They were alone now and it seemed a long way to the rest of the world. 'Though it wouldn't actually take long to fetch a pail of milk,' Tora thought. But her grandmother didn't want any and Tora ate sandwiches and drank coffee she re-heated time and again.

She had brought along a piece of smoked ham, and she cut pieces for the sandwiches she made on her bread. Still, even when she cut some of the very first chives that had shot up a stand near the stone and sprinkled them over her sandwich, it didn't taste good to her. She felt herself growing more and more melancholy the less there was left to do, and sometimes she just sat looking at the tiny grey face on the pillow. Sara Sabina's features were beginning to cave in and dissolve.

Early Friday morning Tora woke to hear a window rattling loudly, and then she lay there listening to the wind that had picked up at dawn. Sara Sabina was awake, and lay staring at her. Now the kitchen and main room were tidy, and there wasn't much left to do. Outside, she had moved the butcher's block and taken away the cracked pail that had been lying by the well. Everything was orderly as far as the eye could see, but Sara Sabina's eyes were dark and upset as she looked around.

'It's all neat and tidy,' she said.

'Yes, I'm just going to do the windows. I think the weather's clearing.'

'You've always been a hard worker, I'll say that.'

The shadows of pain around her mouth had come back. Her fingers pinched and pinched at the sheet.

'I guess you'll have to let the others know. Afterwards.'

Tora was silent, trying to figure this out, and then she realized that her grandmother was speaking about her other children, who were much older than Tora and whom she seldom saw. They were really her aunts and uncles.

'They've got work,' said Sara Sabina. 'Every one of them. They'll get by. That's all I can say. Every one of them.'

Tora just nodded.

'Well, Frans died, of course,' her grandmother went on, 'and Edla.'

'Yes,' said Tora.

'Rickard can fend for himself, he's been apprenticed. He'll be all right. Though you can't tell about America. Don't know if things are the same there.'

'He'll be all right.'

'I don't know a thing about the woman he got hold of, either.'

'Why don't you lie back down?' said Tora. 'Sitting up like that's tiring.'

'I was thinking about your boy,' she said, her eyes restless, not staying on Tora's face. Tora tried to help her lie back down, but it was more difficult for her to breathe that way. And right now she wanted to sit up and finish what she was saying.

'Your lad,' she said. 'I was thinking about 'im yesterday. He's all right too. He's fed and has a roof over his head. And they're good folks.'

Tora wanted to ask her about him, but she froze up. Couldn't get a word out.

'He's nine now,' said Sara Sabina.

'What do they call him,' Tora finally managed to say, but her throat was so dry that she had to say it twice to be heard.

'His name's Erik. And theirs is Johansson, you know. But his name is Erik Lans. The pastor registered it.'

She was silent for a little while, and her restless eyelids were closed for so long Tora almost thought she had fallen asleep. But then she started talking again, and Tora had to lean forward to hear her.

'It will be heavy going for you with two boys. Heavy going. All by yourself.'

'I'll have to cope.'

'A person has to cope,' Sara Sabina mumbled. 'A person always does.'

Now she did seem to be sleeping. Tora felt her hand and it was so cold she put it under the cover. She felt her misery growing inside as she looked at the dry, furrowed face now resting expressionless and motionless. Only her eyeballs behind her thin, creased eyelids couldn't keep still. 'She may never wake up again,' Tora thought, heavy with grief and pain. She had to exert herself to get out of her chair and not just sit there with idle hands.

The wind blew all day on Friday, but it was a warm southerly breeze, and the sun came out from behind the clouds. The bird-cherry over by the edge of the woods burst into bloom, and the butterflies, yellow brimstones and quick

354

little blues, whirled through the grass as if the blue anemone and pilewort leaves had been ripped loose by the wind. A huge mourning cloak perched trembling on the well-turner. Tora didn't want to frighten it off, just stood there with her pail until it rose and flew away.

When she came in from the bright light, Sara Sabina looked grey and thin in the bed. She was like ash, the sun could shine right through her. Tora felt to see whether the quilt and shawl were too heavy. She had lost interest in Tora's cleaning and turned inwards towards her pain. She breathed heavily and quickly with a sound that followed Tora wherever she went in the kitchen and the other room.

In the evening the wind fell still and the air felt warm and aromatic with so many things just starting to bloom, but mostly from the huge bird-cherry at the edge of the woods. The wood warbler sat at the very top, singing with his head thrown back, the little yellow spot on his chin quivering. But in the kitchen Sara Sabina had to work harder and harder to breathe, and Tora moved her cautiously up on the pillow to no avail. She hardly slept that night, sitting next to her, and once had to change both her night-gown and the sheets.

It was warm and quiet on Saturday morning, and Tora went out to inspect her clean windows, pleased with her work. Sara Sabina was breathing a little more easily and responded when Tora clasped her hand, but she didn't look up. Tora decided she dared to leave her for a few minutes while she was resting, to get some fresh pine branches to lay on the front steps. But she went no further than to the woodshed, where little pines had begun to spring up now that no one was clearing the yard around the croft.

The last thing she did that afternoon was to whitewash the stove hood. Now Sara Sabina had been lying there for so long without moving or looking up that Tora suddenly wanted to stop where she was. She had to force herself to finish whitewashing, and then she sat down, the tears stinging under her eyelids. When she had sat still for a while she felt calmer, and able to bear her grandmother's heavy breathing now that she was sitting beside her looking at her face. She no longer looked up at all, but Tora thought she was listening, because her facial expression seemed to change with the sound of Tora's voice.

The door was open, and Tora heard Vallmsta church ring in the Sabbath. A full working week had passed, and the croft was all clean for the weekend. No matter where she looked, there was nothing she could busy her hands with. She hadn't brought any sewing with her. Through the open door to the main room she noticed Lans's Bible on the dresser. Neither of them had mentioned it earlier in the week, but she remembered that her grandmother had described sitting reading out of the Bible to Lans when he lay ill and dying.

Tora didn't suppose that Sara Sabina would want to be read to, and it was too late in any case. Now each breath was a major exertion to contend with. Tora took her hand and sat still until it got too cold with the door open at dusk. She got up and closed it, but that was the last time she got out of her chair until the long, arduous breathing had ceased. By that time it was night, and dark.

She held Sara Sabina's hand in hers as long as it contained any warmth at all. Now it was too late to go down to Vallmsta and make the necessary arrangements. There was no point in waking people up. She was tired. She knew that she should make up a bed for her grandmother in the main room and carry her in there, and sit a night vigil in the kitchen herself. But they had spent the whole week in the kitchen together so Tora would be close at hand, and she didn't think it made much difference now. Her tiredness nearly overcame here, and she decided just to sleep where she had all week. She was not afraid. She simply felt a little lonelier with the silence coming from the other bed. After a while, though, Tora was able to sleep.

She woke at dawn feeling that she had done wrong. There was no sun yet and the kitchen had gone cold. When she touched Sara Sabina's hands they were hard as horn and icy cold. Tora shivered and dressed quickly. Now she regretted not having done as she should have. She felt strange about having slept in such close proximity to her grandmother's rigid corpse. She sat down at the table and waited for it to be a decent hour when people down at Vallmsta would be up and about. Now the sun rose and stretched across the grass to the spot where the butcher block had always stood. The sunshine came in through the window and warmed Tora's hands on the kitchen table. She felt the tears rise and sting behind her eyelids, and finally begin running down her cheeks. They were warm and the pain and the icy cold slowly loosened their grip on her. She rose and opened the door to the morning, and as she stood there with her hand on the doorknob, the wind blew in from the west, carrying a completely new aroma. It was lovely and almondy, just the barest cool touch on her cheek, vanishing even as she tried to capture it. She knew instantly that the morello cherry had begun to flower.

She turned around. Everything was washed up and in order. She didn't want coffee. Sara Sabina's body was under the sheet and there was nothing more she could do. Just as well she got going.

357

She saw that the swifts had come. They cut through the air like thin black scythes, and now it was full summer. Before she left the croft, she stopped under the morello cherry. The treetop was as messy and wild as a magpie's nest, but in a couple of hours, early that morning, it had been transformed. On branch after branch clusters of white flowers had opened. There were still thousands of round buds, and as the morning sun reached them each one opened into five petals, thinner than flakes of ash, whiter than the first snow that would pile up in light drifts six months later, making a poor, icy imitation of their glory. When Tora saw this galaxy against the grey timber of the barn wall, she remembered looking up at it as a little girl, and how the white petals snowed down in the wind. She wished she could just stand there for the very few hours she knew it would last, because the morello cherry blooms so briefly. But that was quite impossible.

She walked quickly, looking at the dandelions and marsh marigolds alongside the road, dark yellow as new spring egg yolks. Wild violets edged the meadows, and puffs of white bitter cress had grown tall, past their prime on the stony hillsides. Now summer rolled in like a broad, green river, and the woods were in bloom. The water in Lake Vallmaren was shiny as oil and topped with the yellow pollen from the fir trees, making rings and islands on the surface and drifts along the shore. Rosy red and chubby, new pine cones swelled, and the wood warbler, invisible amongst the dark branches, sang along. When she left the woods to cross the meadow to Vallmsta, she heard the drumming of the woodpecker. It was the sober sound of the return to everyday life, and a new work week was about to begin.